P9-CQP-708

A Panicked Premonition

TITLES BY VICTORIA LAURIE

Psychic Eye Mysteries

Ghost Hunter Mysteries

A Panicked Premonition

A Psychic Eye Mystery

Victoria Laurie

BERKLEY PRIME CRIME
NEW YORK

BERKLEY PRIME CRIME
Published by Berkley
An imprint of Penguin Random House LLC
375 Hudson Street, New York, New York 10014

Library of Congress Cataloging-in-Publication Data

Names: Laurie, Victoria, author.
Title: A panicked premonition / Victoria Laurie.
Description: First edition. | New York : Berkley Prime Crime, 2017.
Identifiers: LCCN 2017000368 (print) | LCCN 2017005629 (ebook) | ISBN
9780451473905 (hardback) | ISBN 9780698186620 (eBook)
Subjects: LCSH: Cooper, Abby (Fictitious character)—Fiction. | Paranormal
fiction. | Women psychics—Fiction. | Women detectives—Fiction. | BISAC:
FICTION / Mystery & Detective / Women Sleuths. | FICTION / Occult &
Supernatural. | GSAFD: Mystery fiction
Classification: LCC PS3612.A94423 P36 2017 (print) | LCC PS3612.A94423
(ebook) | DDC 813/.6—dc23
LC record available at https://lccn.loc.gov/2017000368

First Edition: July 2017

Printed in the United States of America
1 3 5 7 9 10 8 6 4 2

Cover design by Adam Auerbach
Cover art by Monika Roe

For my favorite detective, amazing inspiration,
fellow bird lover, and wonderful friend,
Nicole Gray.
Surprise! This one's for you, kiddo. ☺

Acknowledgments

Special thanks go to: Jim McCarthy, Jessica Wade, Brian Gorzynski, Sandy Upham, Steve McGrory, Leanne Tierney, Katie Coppedge, Anne Kimbol, Bonnie Manzolini, Cindy Martin, Dean James, Drue Rowean, Hillary Laurie, John Kwaitkowski, Matt McDougal, Juliet Blackwell, Lisa Peterson Haser, Martha Bushko, Maryelizabeth Yturralde, McKenna Jordan, Meg Guzman, Molly Boyle, Nicole Gray, Nora and Bob Brosseau, Mike Brosseau, Pam Whitehead, Shannon Anderson, Sheila Doherty, Sally Woods, Terry Gilman, and Thomas Robinson.

Love to each and every one of you. xoxo

A Panicked Premonition

Chapter One

· · ·

Hovering over the counter, I tried to explain. "You see," I began, "I've been working out really, really hard. My best friend is, like, a serious fitness badass. She's crazy in shape, and she sort of insisted that I get in shape too, and since she's also seriously scary, I had to say yes. So now it's been six months and my whole body has changed. I'm broad where I used to be narrow, and narrow where I used to have a little junk in the trunk. But I'm not complaining. I mean, my husband loves the new bod. He, like, *loves* it, if you get my drift . . . ha-ha! *Any*way, because of the workouts, my body fat percentage has gone way down while the muscle mass has gone way up, and I've been eating superclean. I mean, I haven't had a piece of chocolate or a cup of coffee in *ages*. And I don't even crave them anymore! Yesterday, do you know what I ate? I had a whole plate of jicama. *Jicama!* And the craziest part? I *liked* it! Can you believe that? Okay, so it was slathered in hummus, but I swear to God it tasted good. And I'm totally off gluten. Also caffeine, dairy, sugar, and anything processed. I'm, like, the Paleo *queen*, and I don't have that layer of blubber around my middle anymore. Like, you should see my abs. Do you want to see my abs? Because you can *actually* see my abs!"

I paused for a moment with my hand on the hem of my shirt, waiting for the gentleman behind the counter to give me any indication that he was interested in seeing my six-pack.

When he simply stared levelly at me with a mixture of annoyance and boredom, I felt my cheeks heat. "Uh . . . I'm sorry. What was the question?" I asked.

"Your height and weight?" he said drolly.

"Ah! Yes, well, as I was trying to explain, I don't look like I weigh as much as I actually do, so maybe I should shave off a few pounds so that nobody gets confused—"

"You look about five foot four and a buck fifteen."

I blinked. "Uh . . . that's actually exactly right."

He clicked a few keys on his computer and pointed toward a white screen. "Step over there to have your photo taken."

Feeling a tad deflated, I stood in front of the screen and began to ask if I was centered okay when the Department of Public Safety clerk snapped my photo. I was positive my mouth was open and my eyes were closed when the flash went off. "Can we take that over?" I asked.

"Nope," he said, stamping some paperwork before handing it to me and indicating the small strip of white in the corner. "That's your receipt and this is your temporary license. Your new ID will be delivered in the mail within the next ten days."

"But—," I tried. I really wanted a retake.

The clerk ignored me, turned to glance at the digital counter behind him, and shouted, "Number ninety-seven!"

"Awesome," I grumbled, shuffling out of the area and over to the exit.

I found Candice—said badass BFF—leaning up against her Porsche, looking like someone straight out of a fashion magazine. She's taller than me by a few inches, broader in the shoulders, and narrower in the hips, and owns the most gorgeous set of gams. She looks like I want to, but probably never will. Still, thanks to her, I was looking and feeling mighty fine these days. "Sundance," she said warmly as I approached. "You were chatting up the guy at the counter pretty well."

I sniffed. "Yeah. He's not that into me."

She wrinkled her nose, a glint of humor in her eyes. "He wasn't up for a peek at your abs of steel?"

"Not so much."

"Poor man. Doesn't know what he's missing."

I scowled. "Clearly, you're making fun of me."

"Clearly," she agreed. "Now hop in."

I scowled again and trudged over to the passenger side. I thought about a mean little retort, but I couldn't really afford to be too contrarian; Candice was my ride home. Since I'd lost my driver's license two days earlier somewhere between the running trail and the farmers' market, she'd been my ride everywhere. "Lunch?" I asked as we set off.

"Can't. We have a client."

Candice and I are not only best friends but also business partners at a private investigation office in downtown Austin, Texas. We work lots of different cases together—some domestic, some corporate, and some we work for the FBI. It helps that both our hubbies are federal agents and they send us some work when they can. Every little bit helps to pay the light bill. Or, in my case, for a new barbell and set of weights I was saving for.

What? You're surprised? After years and years of me living on my ass, eating a diet of not much else besides nachos, pizza, chili cheese fries, and Coney dogs, you're shocked that I'm now a fitness and nutrition freak?

Join the club, ladies and gents. I'm as surprised as you are.

It happened during a case that Candice and I worked out in California. She pointed out something key: namely, that there was definitely some extra junk hanging out in my trunk.

Now, I've always been the slim chick with the fast metabolism, and over the years I have absolutely taken advantage of that metabolic miracle like you would not believe! But somewhere in my late thirties my inner engine likely became more "fuel efficient" and it started storing up the excess calories and depositing them in the bank of Big Butt & Muffin Top.

After Candice made an effort to point out the physical changes that everyone else—including me—had been ignoring, I got on board with the whole "Eat well and exercise!" plan. And I let Candice be my guide.

At first, allowing her to be my diet and fitness coach seemed like a bad idea. I mean, in those early days, thanks to a few misplaced wall balls, there was more of my DNA on the floor than at some of the crime scenes I've been to. But I got better fairly quickly and here's what happened: I started to *like* working out. (I'll pause here for dramatic effect. . . . Pause . . . pause . . .) I know, crazy, right? But the emotional and physical lift I kept getting after pushing myself to my physical limits wasn't easily denied. And then I noticed something else seriously weird; my intuition became sharper, more focused, and even more specific.

Oh, maybe I should also mention, I'm psychic. Like, I'm *actually* psychic—and not like your one weird aunt who insists she's "sensitive." I am legitimately able to predict the future. It's well documented, actually.

Anyway, my point is that all that cleaning up of my diet and regular exercise had a significant effect on my abilities, and I will confess here that it totally took me by surprise, because who would've thought that the two were even connected . . . but then, *everything's* connected, so, like, duh.

Still, as Candice had so "sweetly" pointed out, the better care I took of myself, the better care I could take of our cases, which in no way means she's more concerned with our bottom line than my well-being. She's equally concerned about both. (Smirk.)

"So, who's the client?" I asked.

"Someone you won't like."

My brow furrowed. "Now, why would you say that?"

"Because you don't like most people."

The furrow deepened. "That's not true!"

She chuckled merrily. "Abby, I love you, but you do not like most people. You complain about everyone all the time and you can be a cranky beast when it comes to interacting with the world at large."

"I like people!" I shouted. "In fact, I like *lots* of people!"

"Okay," she said, clearly humoring me. "Name someone you like. Anyone."

I was about to say her, but at the moment, I didn't much. "I like that guy at that café we go to for lunch," I said. Dammit, what was his name?

"Really? Tell me his name and I'll believe you."

"David," I said quickly.

"Tyler," she corrected.

"Crap. I knew it was one or the other."

She considered me demurely over the brim of her sunglasses. "I think my point is made."

I sighed wearily. It wasn't really that I didn't like people; it's more that I'm an introvert at heart, and as I'm a professional psychic, it can be hard having all that need piled into my lap day after day. It's draining and it makes me cranky, and, well, yes, sometimes it makes me not like people so much.

Reflecting back on the previous week, I had to admit that perhaps Candice had a point. I'd read for more than my usual quota of clients, due to a mix-up in scheduling, and I'd perhaps voiced a few (many) complaints about all that interaction to Candice. "Fine, who is this client that I definitely will not like?"

"Murielle McKenna," Candice said. "And, I gotta warn you, Sundance, she's not gonna like you much either."

I pulled my chin back to consider Candice. "Why not?"

"Because you two are more alike than you are different. Except for the fact that she's loaded. Like, seriously loaded, with a heavy dose of entitled. And as you've no respect for rich, snobby people, I think it'll be about ten seconds after you two meet that you'll take offense and say something rude."

I wanted to argue—really I did—but the truth is that I actually *don't* have any tolerance for rich and entitled. "So why're we meeting with her if you know it's not going to end well?"

"Because we have to take her on as a client," Candice said.

"Why?"

"Because your husband referred us and asked me directly if I could possibly get you to play nicey-nice."

I held up my hand in a stopping motion. "Wait a second. . . . Hold on here. You're telling me that you and Dutch had some sort of secret conversation about me interacting with this client?"

"Yep."

"That's not fair, Candice! You're supposed to be *my* best friend. And if he wants to do an end run around me, you're not supposed to let him!"

"I am your best friend," she said simply. "Which is why I granted him the favor. She's commissioned *three* panic rooms, one for each one of her homes, Sundance—with all the bells and whistles, I might add."

"You mean, she bought the *premium* package?"

Candice held up three fingers. "Thrice. And, according to Brice, she's also already paid for them in full."

I sighed heavily and frowned in frustration. Six months earlier, Dutch and his business partner, Milo, had decided to end their partnership. Nothing bad happened between them—it was more that Milo was given a chance for early retirement with the police force he worked for up in Michigan, and he decided to retire from all his jobs and spend a lot more time with his family. He'd flown down here to Texas to have a long talk with us about his reasoning and his plans, and Dutch had offered to buy out his end of the business. Milo had jumped at the chance and the transfer had been smooth and easy, and their friendship remained as strong as ever.

And then Dutch and Dave—our former handyman/carpenter/ really good friend—had gotten to talking about how all new construction blueprints for homes in the seven figures were now including panic rooms as a standard feature.

Dave had said that there was a good business in retrofitting large homes in the area that'd been built prior to the panic room craze, and Dutch agreed. Dutch had offered to trade Dave some shares in his security business if Dave agreed to come on board, help start up a new division of the business, and run the crew. And then Dutch had approached Candice's husband, Brice, about also becoming a partner.

Within a few months the three had launched the new division of the business, and things quickly took off.

In fact, they took off so fast that Dutch, Dave, and Brice were caught completely by surprise, and none of them had any time to interview for an administrative support team. So Candice and I had been helping where we could, taking and making phone calls, helping with schedules and appointments, mailing out brochures, etc. Anything for the cause.

Even with our help, however, things were so busy that we barely saw our men anymore.

Between their two now-full-time jobs, Dutch and Brice were rarely home and Candice and I were starting to really miss our husbands. Brice and Dutch were working so much that the only days we could count on seeing them were Sunday afternoons, and the poor men were usually so tired by then that they weren't much fun.

Still, Dutch and Brice seemed to like the idea of all that work, and it was nice to know that Brice was quickly catching up to Candice in the moola department. I'd long suspected that it'd been a bit of a thorn in his side that Candice was worth so much more than he was. She'd been the sole beneficiary of a sizable fortune that had made her portfolio a whole lot thicker than his, and although I knew she didn't care, I'd always thought he did.

"If my husband thinks I'm such a problem," I said, getting back to my hurt feelings, "then why are you guys risking having me meet this woman at all?"

Candice shifted in her seat. "It's complicated."

"What does that mean?"

"She's heard of you and wants to meet you."

"Ah," I said, but I could see that there was more to the story, and I could also see by the way that Candice was avoiding looking over at me that she was hoping very much that I didn't ask about it. "What else aren't you telling me?" (I like to ignore subtle and not-so-subtle social cues. It's all part of my considerable charm.)

"You're not going to like it."

"I already don't like it."

"You're *really* not going to like it."

I rolled my eyes. "Out with it, Cassidy," I demanded, using my favorite nickname for her.

Candice took a big breath. "Well," she said, "it's like this: Apparently, Murielle has a big crush on your husband and she wants to meet the competition."

"Wait . . . what, now?"

Candice stopped at a red light and turned to look at me directly. "Murielle McKenna has been hitting on your husband for weeks, Abs."

I blinked and then I pointed right at her. "I *knew* it!"

I'd told Dutch about a month before that some woman at work was going to develop a major crush on him. At the time, I'd thought it was probably going to be a witness on one of his FBI cases, and I'd warned him that she seemed very aggressive and there was a legal issue he'd need to step carefully around. It didn't bother me too much when she'd cropped up in the ether, because my hubby is a serious hottie, and women flirt with him all the time. He always handles it with polite but firm disinterest. Plus, if he were ever going to cheat, I'd probably know about it before he would.

"You knew Murielle was going to hit on your husband?" Candice repeated.

"Well, not Murielle per se," I admitted. "But I saw someone crop up in Dutch's energy who was going to vie for his attention and present a difficult challenge to him."

"Ah," Candice said. "I should've known you would've seen it coming. Still, I want to assure you that according to Brice, Dutch has been ignoring all of it, and he's also been avoiding her at every turn, sending in Dave whenever she wants a meeting to discuss the panic room renovations, or Brice when she has an issue with one of her bodyguards. But she's being persistent, and she keeps forking over more money while threatening to sue if Dutch and the boys decide to drop her as a client. So, until construction is finished on all three panic rooms, the guys feel like they're trapped."

"Wait, how long have you been in on this?" I asked tersely. It irked me that Candice had been told about Murielle, but I hadn't.

Candice avoided looking at me again. "About a week."

I glared at her. "Thanks for the heads-up."

"I was hoping Dutch would tell you."

I turned to shake my head at the window. I knew exactly why he hadn't mentioned it. I'm a *tiiiiiiny* bit hotheaded, and . . . rarely . . . sometimes . . . occasionally . . . I can be known to fly off the handle when situations that are upsetting to me present themselves. (I know, I know. . . . You're *reeling* in shock right now.)

"He should've told me," I muttered.

"I think he was trying to spare you—"

"Oh, he wasn't trying to spare *me* anything!" I snapped. "Please don't go making excuses for him. He was trying to spare all of *you* the embarrassment of me confronting her."

"True," Candice said. "But did I mention that Murielle McKenna is particularly litigious?"

I waved a hand in dismissal. "Yeah, yeah, whatever. It's not like I'd hit her or anything."

The corner of Candice's mouth lifted with the hint of a smirk. "As much of a relief as hearing that is, I looked into Murielle, and she's got a number of lawsuits ongoing. Along with suing several contractors whose work she found unsatisfactory, she's sued plenty of other professionals for the slightest infraction, like a dry cleaner who couldn't get out a spot on one of her gowns; a hairstylist who cut Murielle's hair too short; an area dog walker who let his charge get too close to her, and the dog nipped at her hand; and she even sued the artist who painted her portrait."

"You're kidding," I said.

"Nope."

"What was wrong with the portrait?"

"Don't know."

"Maybe he painted her riding a broom," I said.

Candice laughed. "Anyway, Abs, the important thing here is that Murielle wouldn't hesitate to throw some legal shade our husbands' way if she felt insulted. We definitely need to meet and play nice with her."

With that, Candice pulled into a gas station and got out to pump some fuel, leaving me to think about the situation.

As I sat there, I had to reflect that Dutch had always been a little flinchy when it came to the possibility of getting sued, which was why he was always so careful in his business practices. He'd told me once that when he was eleven, his parents had been involved in a bad legal battle that had cost his dad his business, and for a few years afterward the family had struggled to make ends meet. I wondered if my hubby's inability to confront Murielle had much to do with old childhood wounds.

"So, what's the plan?" I asked, opening the door to talk to Candice.

She pressed a button on the gas pump to receive a receipt and said, "We meet with Murielle, allow her to size you up, let her know that you're neither naive nor timid, and if she's going to continue to make your husband feel uncomfortable, then she'll have both of us to contend with. And we're going to do all of that by being courteous, polite, and avoiding any opportunity to insult her."

"Doesn't sound like nearly as much fun as my going in there, grabbing her by the throat, and telling her to back off, bitch!"

Candice grinned. "We'll call that plan B."

We arrived at Murielle's home about ten minutes later. And I use the word "home" rather loosely. The size of a hotel, the place probably had more rooms than the local Hilton, and was definitely twice as grand.

"Wow," Candice said as we eased past the guard at the gated entrance, and made our way down the long drive to the ginormous, three-story mansion with two one-story wings flanking the central section, and a series of fountains and exotic flora dotting the landscape.

"It's a little showy, if you ask me," I said.

"Of course it's a little showy," Candice replied, parking her Porsche next to a golf cart. "I doubt this woman does anything subtly."

We walked to the front door, which opened before we could even ring the bell. A slight gentleman with wispy silver hair, thin mustache, and black-rimmed glasses greeted us wearing a butler's uniform. "Ms. Fusco. Ms. Cooper. Welcome. Ms. McKenna has been expecting you. This way, please."

We followed the butler into the cool interior and I tried not to ogle all the expensive artwork lining the walls, and lost that battle thirty seconds in. In my defense, there was a freaking Picasso, a Warhol, and, I suspect, a Lichtenstein on the wall, and if you can't make googly eyes at a private collection that contains the likes of them, then you don't appreciate art. Or money.

What else struck me about the interior of Murielle's home was that, other than the sculptures and the paintings, the entire place was white. Like a brilliant, blinding, whiter-than-white shade of white. The walls were white, the tile floor was white, the area rugs were white, and what little furniture we saw was also white.

It made walking through the halls feel a bit surreal, almost otherworldly. At last we were shown to a room with a glass desk and two high-backed wing chairs, upholstered in white suede. Turning to us, the butler said, "Might I prepare you both a cup of tea?"

"That would be lovely," Candice said. I wasn't really in the mood for tea, but I nodded agreeably all the same.

The butler waved to the wing chairs. "Please make yourselves comfortable. Ms. McKenna will be with you shortly."

Candice and I each took a seat in the wing chairs and I happened to catch a small camera above the desk aimed in our direction. After Jeeves left, I caught Candice's attention, and motioned to it with my chin. She nodded and we waited without speaking. The butler returned with our tea, and we sipped at it while we waited some more. Then some more. Then a whole lot more.

After forty minutes, Candice very obviously lifted her wrist to check her watch, rose to set her teacup on the desk, and said, "Let's go."

I grinned, got up, put my cup next to hers, and began to follow her out of the room when behind us there was an audible click. We both paused and turned around to discover that a hidden door had opened in the far wall, and out from it stepped a tall, leggy brunette, wearing a chic black silk suit, cut wide at the shoulders, narrow at the hips, and low at the front to expose a great deal of skin. It was perhaps the most perfectly tailored piece of clothing I'd ever seen.

The woman herself was exquisite, with a flawless olive-tanned complexion, and long dark hair, pulled back in a severe ponytail, which helped to accentuate her high cheekbones and almond-shaped eyes. She had the kind of lips that all women crave, perhaps only a touch shy of Angelina Jolie's perfect plumpness, and a delicate nose, which allowed all the focus to go to her light brown eyes and seductively shaped mouth.

I hated her on sight.

"Good afternoon, ladies," she said in a rich, husky voice as she entered the room. She walked toward us with the practiced step of a runway model, her décolletage bouncing in rhythm to her steps. I suddenly wondered how the hell Dutch had ever resisted the urge to strip off his clothes and have a mad fling with her. I mean, to a married man, she must be like walking, talking kryptonite.

Meanwhile, Candice stood up taller and edged a little closer to me, obviously sensing that I was ready to admit defeat and hand over my wedding ring. "Hello," she said coolly. "We were just leaving."

Murielle cocked one perfectly shaped eyebrow. "Leaving? But we have an appointment."

"Had an appointment," Candice replied sweetly, as she eyed her watch again. "And now we have another one. Perhaps we can reschedule?"

Murielle laughed lightly. "Oh, come, now," she said, without a hint of apology. "I couldn't have kept you waiting that long, could I?"

"Forty-five minutes," I said, barely able to keep the irritation out of my voice.

Murielle made a dismissive hand-waving motion. "I blame my team of lawyers," she said. "They're notorious for distracting me with legal papers to sign and settlements to collect. You two must know how that is."

"Not really," I told her, and smiled wide.

"Well, it's endless," she said, matching my smile. "But I'm here now, and certainly you can spare me a few minutes to chat. I insist on it, in fact."

I glanced at Candice and she made a tiny shrugging motion. She'd let it be my call. "I believe we only have about ten minutes and then we'll have to leave," I said.

Murielle motioned with one long, elegant finger to the wing chairs and we settled back into our seats. Once we were comfortable, our host glided over to the front of the desk, propping her rear against it to peer down at us with a smug smile.

I held my own expression in check, because the move on her part to hover over us was clearly a power play and we'd fallen for it. She was in the position to *literally* look down on us, and we were stuck staring up into all that gorgeousness. Jesus, no wonder Dutch wouldn't meet with her anymore. It was a miracle Brice had survived their encounters.

Glancing sideways at Candice, I could tell she thought as much too. I mean, Candice is *beeeeautiful*, and, on a good day, I'm no slouch either, but this woman was like something right out of a Greek tragedy, and by that, I mean that she was like something lifted off the top of Mount Olympus and planted down here in front of us tragically, aesthetically flawed mortals.

Candice smiled tightly and said, "Ms. McKenna, as I stated before, Abby and I are pressed for time, so perhaps you can fill us in on why you require our services?"

Murielle's big brown eyes locked on me. I realized in that moment that she hadn't been quite sure which of us was Dutch's wife until Candice made it clear. Still keeping her gaze on me, she said, "I need to run a background check on someone."

"Who?" Candice asked.

"An associate of mine I'm thinking of hiring for a specific job, not related to my businesses."

"We can take care of that by late this afternoon," Candice said. "Just give us a name and a Social Security number if you have it, and we can run a thorough check of all public records."

"I want more than that," she said.

In all the time she'd been speaking, never once had she turned her eyes away from me. I wanted to laugh. Did this woman really think it would be so hard to intimidate me? I mean, she had me at "Hello." I wasn't competition. Maybe Gisele Bündchen was her competition, but only if Mrs. Tom Brady was having a really, *really* good hair day. So it was weird that Murielle was going to all this effort to make me feel inadequate in her presence. And maybe that's why, after thinking about it for a few seconds, I didn't.

I mean, Dutch and I are super-duper in love. Maybe even more in love now than we were on the day of our wedding. And trust me, we were *beyond* crazy about each other back then. I love Dutch like I love to breathe, finding both necessary to even exist. And if I ever had one of those moments where I doubted his love or loyalty to me, all I had to do was check in with my intuition. My third eye is incapable of being deceived in that way. If I look at someone's motives with my radar, I will see one thing clearly: The Truth. You can't hide what you feel from a psychic. It's the ultimate in X-ray vision.

And Dutch doesn't hide how he feels about me. He's totally open about it. Which I find incredibly endearing, because I have a harder time expressing my feelings, even to him. No, there'd been no change in his feelings; of that I was sure. So, I realized, if Murielle made a full-court press effort to garner my husband's attention and failed to do so, that must mean that *she* was actually intimidated by *me*.

I allowed my own smug smile to spread across my face, and in my most pleasant, professional voice asked, "What other services besides a background check did you need, Ms. McKenna?"

Her eyes narrowed. She probably couldn't figure out why I wasn't a simpering mess by now. Waving a perfectly manicured nail at me, she said, "You're the psychic, right?"

"I am."

Murielle crossed her arms and tapped her shoulder with that same finger. "I'd like your opinion of the man," she said.

"My opinion?"

"Yes. I'd like to know everything I can about him. What his strengths and weaknesses are, if he can be trusted, that sort of thing. I'm especially interested in his personal life. He's very mum about it, which makes me wonder if he's trying to keep secrets."

I shifted in my seat. "I'm not really comfortable with that kind of request."

"Why not?" she said.

"Because you're basically inquiring about him in ways that no employer is allowed to. The types of things you want to know would be personally invasive to this man, and for ethical reasons, I'm not willing to snoop into his life like that without his express permission."

She looked at me like I had to be kidding. "You're kidding me, right?"

"I never kid when it comes to protecting my ethics."

Murielle rolled her eyes. "Listen," she said. "What I'm asking you to do is as legal as conducting a background check. If I'm not asking you to break the law, you should be okay with my request."

"It's only legal because lawmakers haven't thought to make it illegal," I said. "You don't really have the law on your side here so much as you have ignorance on your side. It's ethically wrong, and I won't do it."

"Won't or can't?" she said, a flash of anger in her eyes.

I smiled tightly. "Can. Won't."

"I still don't understand why," she complained. "What is it that you think you'll discover about him that would be so invasive?"

"Don't know," I said. "Which is the point. I wouldn't say yes to breaking into his home and going through his journal, his e-mail, or eavesdropping in on his personal phone conversations, and I won't say yes to this. There's not a lot of difference between the two."

"Oh, please," she said, getting up from her stance in front of us to move to the other side of the desk and take a seat. "I've been to a few psychics before. They never told me anything that wasn't ridiculously generic and obvious."

I gave a small shrug. "I can't speak to their capabilities. I can only speak to mine. And I'm good enough to know that peeking into a stranger's life for a potential employer is way over the line."

Murielle placed her elbows on the table and laced her fingers together. "What if you're not as good as you say you are?"

"It's not her who's saying it," Candice said in a smooth but authoritative tone. "It's *thousands* of her clients, well over two hundred and fifty closed-case files between the FBI, CIA, and local PD, and a string of requests for demonstrations and instruction from various law-enforcement organizations across the country."

If I'd had a microphone, I would've dropped it at that moment, grabbed Candice by the arm, and walked out of Murielle's presence. As it was, our host's eyes widened, which I found super satisfying. "I see," she said. And then she cocked her head slightly, her focus back on me, and asked, "What can you tell me about me?"

I heard Candice take a breath as if she was going to answer for me again, so I quickly said, "If you'd like an appointment for a reading, please log on to my Web site and reference the scheduling calendar. I believe my first available appointment is in February.

But if it's a very quick peek into something simple, like if a particular guy you're interested in like likes you back, I can answer that, no problem." I flashed Murielle my toothiest smile just for kicks.

Her eyes widened again before narrowing to slits, and then she pursed her lips, clearly irritated. "Actually, on second thought, I'd prefer to know your thoughts about a contractor I'm thinking of suing. They're taking too long to complete the job I hired them to do."

It wasn't lost on me that Murielle was making a casual reference to her contract with my husband and the boys, just like I'd made casual reference to Dutch with my statement.

She wanted to play? Okay . . . let's play. "Oh," I said sweetly. "Is that all? Well, that I can answer, no problem. If you bring that suit, you'll lose. And more than just legal fees, if you get my drift."

"I don't," she said, still squinting meanly at me. "What does that mean?"

"It means that things will get leaked to the press which maybe you were hoping to keep quiet. Things like how you have a close relative, probably a sibling, who's a drug addict and a gambler. Your brother, I believe. He's been burning through the family money like a gasoline salesman at a bonfire. And your father's mental condition continues to deteriorate. I wonder what people would think if they knew the head of Milonas Enterprises had dementia? Oh, *and* there's a pretty big scandal involving you and a girlfriend that could come out. It's something you've been working hard to keep hushed up, but I suspect that, should you continue to throw your litigious weight around, it'll be revealed. And that scandal, Ms. McKenna, well . . . that's not one your image will ever recover from."

Murielle's face flushed and for the first time I saw her beauty marred. The flush didn't spread evenly, but formed a series of red blotches on her face and neck. She seemed to know that her appearance had been compromised, because her hand flew to her neck to cover her throat. "Stop it!" she hissed.

I got up and collected my bag. Candice rose too, her expression unreadable. "Like I said, suing that contractor would be unwise, Ms. McKenna. I think you should find a way to work it out with your contractor, and I'm sorry, but we really do have to go."

I began to exit and I saw Candice pull out her business card and lay it on the glass desk. She then said, "If you'd like me to run that background check for you, just send me his info to that e-mail address and I'll take care of it."

We then made like Elvis and left the building.

Chapter Two

· · ·

"I'm not gonna sugarcoat it, Sundance," Candice said after we'd gotten to the car and hopped in. "But that was epic."

I grinned. "Did you see her *face*?" I asked, mimicking the way Murielle had clutched her throat and looked stricken.

Candice laughed all the way down the long drive. "I can't believe you pulled all that stuff out of the ether! I mean, I did a thorough check on her, and except for the brother's drug problem, there wasn't even a hint of any of those other scandals!"

"Child's play," I said smugly, wiping my hands together for emphasis.

Our cool satisfaction lasted exactly ten more seconds until my phone rang. "*What* did you say to Murielle McKenna?!" Dutch demanded.

Uh-oh, I thought. "Why? What did she say?"

"She said that we're fired!" Dutch yelled.

"Oh, crap," I whispered.

"What?" Candice asked, nudging me with her elbow.

"Abigail," Dutch said, using my full name, which meant he was really, really, reeeeeeally mad. "Do you *know* how much money we've got on the line with those three rooms? Do you *understand* that we'd have to refund her most of what she's paid us even though the special order materials for her remodels have all been ordered *and* they'd be nonrefundable on our end, which means that we'd have to eat the cost, which would then mean we're sunk unless we can complete the project?"

"Wait!" I said. "Don't you have a contract? I mean, don't you have any legal redress in case she fired you to help cover your capital outlay?" (When I'm freaked-out, I use big words like "legal redress" and "capital outlay.")

"Of course we have a contract! But she had her lawyers tweak it so that she didn't have to cover the cost of materials unless the job passes code! If she fires us before we finish the job, then the job doesn't meet code and we're *out the money!*"

Gulp.

By now Candice had pulled the car over to the side of the road and I was holding my phone so that we could both hear him. (Of course, Dutch was yelling loud enough so that most of *you* could probably hear him . . . but I digress.)

Candice looked at me and winced. I decided then that my best defense might be a good offense. "Well, *maybe* I would've been more cooperative with her if *my husband* had told me about how his client has been making the moves on him!"

Dutch made a low, guttural sound of irritation. "I didn't *tell* you, Abby, because I didn't want you to call her up or head over there and confront her when I was handling the situation. She's not the first woman to come on to me, you know."

Candice and I both sucked in a breath. Did he really just say that to me? Narrowing my eyes, and speaking through clenched teeth, I said, "Handling it just fine, eh? Is *that* why you asked Candice to take me over there and play nice with her? Oh, and maybe I should also ask if this is going to be the regular routine from now on for the *hordes of women who come on to you?*"

Dutch sighed heavily and we heard some muffled knocking. I had a pretty good idea he was hitting his forehead with the phone. "I'm sorry," he finally said. "That was out of line."

"You'll get no argument on that from me!" I snapped.

"Edgar," he said gently, using his favorite nickname for me. "I am sorry. But this is serious. If she fires us, we're screwed."

"Well, it's not my fault!" I shouted, all worked up and unwilling to be mollified. "You *know* I'm not good with people! Why'd you send me in there to play with a tigress when you *know* I pack a Taser for those times when the cats get all mean and snarly?"

Candice reached for the phone and plucked it out of my hand. Putting it to her ear, she said, "We'll fix this, Rivers." She then hung up, tossed the phone back into my lap, and pulled a U-turn.

"How are we going to fix this?" I asked her, my voice pitchy with panic.

"By going back there and making nice, Abby," Candice said. "And agreeing to her terms."

"What terms?"

"She wanted you to look into that guy she wants to hire, right? Do it."

My jaw fell open. "Are you *serious*? Candice, I *can't*! It's ethically wrong!"

"I'm not telling you to reveal his secrets," Candice said. "I'm telling you to look up a few tidbits that can't possibly be used against him—a few personal but actually impersonal things about him, like that he cheats on his golf game or something silly like that—and we'll feed them to the tigress to show her that she wins this round and there's no reason to bankrupt our husbands."

I made a face at her. "This sucks."

"Yes," she agreed. "So let's get in, apologize, and get out as fast as possible. Oh, and one more thing, Sundance. This time, maybe let *me* do the talking."

An hour and a half later we'd made peace with the tigress. Or, more accurately, my partner and best friend had made peace. I'd sat quietly and nodded a lot while Candice oozed charm and solicitude and heartfelt apologies for our rush to exit earlier. And then Candice nudged me with her elbow as she said, "And of course Abby can look into the energy of this associate of yours. Right, Abby?"

I took a deep breath and ate a big bite of crow. "Sure. Of course, Ms. McKenna."

"Perfect," she purred. Then she looked at me expectantly.

"Oh . . . uh . . . you mean now?" I asked.

Murielle bounced one eyebrow in reply.

"Okay, so now." I averted my gaze to the floor while I gathered my intuition. "So, this man in question—I don't need to know his name, but think about him real hard so that he shows up in your energy. . . ."

It took a few moments, but soon, through Murielle's energy, I felt a connection to the man in question, and I did *not* like what I was picking up for him. The guy was a scuzzball.

I'd also already decided that I'd share nothing too personal about him with Murielle; instead, I'd simply focus on how he related to her, which I doubted she'd find fault with—if she even noticed. It was the only way to hold on to my ethics and still appear to be cooperative.

"He's someone who's quite cunning—even creatively so—and he's careful about money, and details. He likes to win, and he'll do anything to make sure he comes out on top. Still, to your earlier point about the way he keeps his personal life close to the chest, I think the reason he reveals so little about himself is that he's learned to be protective of his private information so that it can't be used against him. But I also want to warn you, there's a trace of the pathological in him. It's what drives him. He'll do or say almost anything to come out the winner, no matter the consequences."

"What about personal relationships?" she asked, interrupting my train of thought.

"You mean his romantic connections?"

"Yes."

I wanted to laugh. From what I could pick up, this guy used

people to get exactly what he wanted; then he threw them away like garbage. He was someone who thought romance was for morons. I also had to tread very carefully here, because we were dipping into waters about this man's personal life that I didn't feel comfortable sharing with Murielle. So, again I approached her question as it related to her directly. "He's not attached to anyone that I can see," I said, which was true. Interestingly, however, I saw the strong possibility that Murielle and the scuzzball would end up having a brief but very physically passionate connection. That part I also kept to myself. Let Murielle play with fire and get burned, which was what she deserved after going after my husband so aggressively.

"Can I trust him?" she asked me next.

I sighed. I couldn't lie. "No. Truthfully, you'll have to keep your eye on him, because he'd double-cross his own mother. He's not someone who recognizes loyalty or love, but he does recognize opportunity. As long as he works for you, he'll do whatever he needs to do in order to get the job done quickly and efficiently, but at the first hint of a better deal somewhere else, he'll be gone."

Murielle smiled. "He's perfect."

"Great," I said. She'd get no argument from me. I hoped Murielle and her scuzzball associate double-crossed each other into oblivion. "Anyway, that's all I'm picking up for him."

Murielle sniffed, like she didn't think I'd said enough. Candice nudged me again with her elbow. I badly wanted to roll my eyes, but made an effort to tune into Murielle's energy once more to find something she might like to hear. "If you're thinking of having a cosmetic procedure sometime soon, you'll really like the results," I said.

Almost instantly her frown turned upside down and she practically purred. "Really?"

"Yep. It'll look very natural too. No one will be able to tell you had the work done."

Murielle sat up in her chair and arched her back slightly, the way a cat might react when you petted it just the right way. "Do tell," she said, her eyes sparkling with interest.

Inwardly I smiled. I'd found the key to making nicey-nice with her. All I had to do was focus my intuition on the superficial and Murielle was bound to be happy. "I see a whole series of clothes with your name on them," I said.

Murielle sucked in a breath. "My new clothing line!" she said. "Tell me everything!"

Fifteen minutes later, we were once again driving away from Murielle's. She'd seemed quite happy with all the wonderful things I'd told her about the success of her new clothing line. It'd been an effort to keep coming up with new ways to say, "The clothes will be very pretty, everyone will love your designs, and you'll make lots of money from the venture."

"Are we heading back to the office?" I asked, rubbing my temples.

"We are," she said. "I know that you've got clients tonight, but we've got a ton of calls to make on behalf of the boys."

I groaned. An article in *Texas Monthly* from four months earlier had featured a spread on the popularity of panic rooms among the wealthy set, and it had devoted a whole five pages to Safe Chambers—the name of our panic room building company. The article had even shown a nice photo of Dave, standing next to his truck, parked in front of a large mansion where we'd installed a hidden room under the stairs. Ever since that article came out, we'd been getting busier and busier, and I think we all had expected for there to be an influx of interest, but nobody expected for the level of interest to continue to rise month after month. I knew it was mostly because Dutch, Dave, and Brice had a great crew who got right to work and completed the job quickly and without a lot of hassle. Dave was excellent at the retrofitting of the rooms in the existing space, and he didn't skimp on materials or cut corners, and our customers had been really pleased. One thing about the one-percent crowd—they don't hesitate to recommend and talk up a contractor they love.

As a result, we'd been flooded with more and more referrals every week, which was nice, but it was starting to get a little hairy for the five of us. "They need to hire somebody to do their secretarial stuff," I said.

"I think the hard part is finding the time to interview people."

"We could do it."

"Oh, no," Candice said with a laugh. "No way am I hiring my husband's admin."

"Why would that be so bad?"

"The second the new employee makes a mistake, or calls in sick, or doesn't work out—we're to blame."

"Ah," I said. "Yeah, you've got a point. But this extra workload is starting to dig into our schedules, Candice."

"Which is why we'll put the boys on a deadline. We'll agree to pinch-hit for them until the end of the month, and if they haven't found someone to run the office by then, one of them will have to do it."

"I like it," I said.

"Don't cave, though, when they miss the deadline and ask you to give them more time."

"Why do you think I'd cave?"

"You'll do anything for Dutch when he gives you that look."

I laughed. "What look?"

Candice tried to mimic a sad-puppy-dog face. I laughed harder. "That's a seriously good impression."

"I've been practicing."

"Okay, I won't cave. They have three weeks to get it together and hire somebody."

"And don't cave," Candice pressed.

"I won't!"

We both knew I'd totally cave.

*   *   *

Back at our office, which overlooked Congress Avenue and was composed of a series of rooms connected by a tiny lobby, I followed Candice into her immaculately kept office, and waited for her to print off my list of calls. "You can start on these clients," she said. "They're all within close geographic proximity to each other. Since my sweet husband totally lowballed the estimate on the Broadwell house, and Dutch is too busy with the accounting side, Dave is going to be doing all the estimates this month until he can figure out who he wants to train from his crew to take over that duty."

I worked hard to hide a smirk. Poor Brice. He didn't have any kind of construction background to draw from—unlike Dutch, who'd worked construction in college—and Brice had done his best to give a fair price on a panic room that had turned out to be short about ten grand. Luckily, Dave and Dutch were able to make it work without losing too much, but Brice was no longer giving estimates to build anything bigger than a doghouse.

"This Saturday, I've loaded in two stops on the roster where we've completed the work, but there's an issue that Dave will need to address and fix." Candice paused to point to my spreadsheet at the fourth and last names on my list. "At both Mrs. Schultz's house and Andy Roswell's residence, the panic room door isn't closing."

My eyes widened. "That's not good," I said.

"True," Candice agreed. "But it's easily fixed. These two locations have one of our pocket door models, which requires a motor to slide the door sideways. The manufacturer sent us a notification last month about some of the motors dying due to a bad wire. In turn, we sent out an e-mail to everyone with this model door, letting them know that we'd be replacing the motor as soon as the kits arrived from the manufacturer, and the Roswells and Mrs. Schultz are the last two on the list. They're also the only two that've recently reported an issue."

"It's always in the last place you look," I said with a smirk.

"Right?" Candice said. "Anyway, when you speak to Mrs. Schultz, you'll have to talk nice and loud, and repeat the appointment details a few times. Ask her to write it down."

"Is she forgetful?" I asked.

"Definitely. She's sweet, but she's elderly and she can't hear and her memory seems to be fading. Last week Dave arranged with her to send one of his crew out to fix the door, but when he got there, she claimed not to know anything about the appointment and wouldn't let him in. Then, just yesterday she left a message on the company voice mail that her door wasn't working and she wanted it fixed right away."

"Poor thing," I said with a small *tsk*. Getting on in years isn't always a picnic.

"Give Dave the same thirty minutes at Mrs. Schultz's before setting the next appointment," Candice continued. "You don't have to worry about his time once he reaches the Roswells' place; that'll be his last stop of the afternoon."

"Will do," I said.

Candice moved on to the other names on the list. "The rest of these are all requests for an estimate. Dave will need a half hour at each location to assess the property, take photos, and make a few notes. Allow another fifteen minutes for travel and he should be able to knock out a whole ton of those in the next couple of weeks—remember, you're working between the hours of eight and two. I'll take all the clients who requested Sunday appointments so that we don't get our wires crossed."

I skimmed the names on the spreadsheet, and stopped halfway down the list to let out a squeak. "Holy freakballs!" Pointing to the celebrity name, I said, "*He* wants a panic room?"

Candice grinned. "He does."

I used the spreadsheet to fan myself. "Ohmigod. I had no idea he was still in Austin! I mean, I thought he moved to New Orleans, or back to L.A. God, if I call, do you think he'll answer? Should I make small talk? What if I crack a little joke, like, 'All right, all right, all right, let's get you a panic room, sir!'?"

Candice threatened to snatch the sheet out of my sweaty fingers. "No small talk and no jokes, Sundance. Got it?"

I made a face at her. "Killjoy."

An hour and a half later I set the phone down and happily crossed another name off the list. I was a brilliant saleswoman. I'd talked three people who were on the fence about going with another builder into letting Dave come out and give them an estimate. He was fully booked for every Saturday of the month, and I was smug with satisfaction that I'd helped my husband and his business partners secure even more business.

Trotting into Candice's office, I waited until she was off the phone with a prospective client, who appeared to be passing on Candice's offer to have Dave give them an estimate (not everyone can have my amazing sales skills), and showed her my spreadsheet.

"Whoa!" she said, after scanning it. "All of these are booked?"

"Yep."

"Way to go, Abby!" She pointed to the celebrity name that had made me break out in a sweat. There was an *X* by his name. "No answer?"

I frowned. "No. The number rings to his business manager, and she said he's finally decided to sell the home."

"Awww," Candice said in mock sympathy. "And you were *so* close to leaving your husband for him."

"His loss," I sniffed.

Candice set the spreadsheet in a file and glanced at her watch. "Can I take you out to dinner after your last client?"

"You can," I said, sitting down in the chair across from her desk. I still had a little time before my first of three appointments for the evening. "Do Dutch and the boys have enough crew to handle all this work?"

Candice tucked the file away and leaned back in her own chair. "Brice said he and Dave have hired three more crews for a total of seven. They've gotten each room down to three weeks to complete if it's just a retrofit, six if it's a complete build-out."

"What are they retrofitting?" I asked. Dutch never talked

about the details of his business, which I honestly appreciated, because blueprints and construction . . . ? Hello, boring.

"Usually a walk-in closet. To retrofit it, they have to tear out most of the Sheetrock, insert a separate ventilation system, electrical, and plumbing, encase the exposed walls in two-inch steel, put the Sheetrock back in, and install a bulletproof door with a security lock."

"Wowsa. I had no idea it was that involved."

"A lot of them are even more complicated. The highest-security rooms aren't in the closets, but a separate room located somewhere else in the house."

"Why?" I asked. Man, Candice knew *way* more about this stuff than I did.

"Because closets are the obvious panic room choice, and someone intent on kidnapping or harming one of these superwealthy people would start there. Dave came up with a schematic to have a false panic room made out of the closet, so that any intruders would be stalled there, while the residents snuck out the back of the closet through a secret door that would lead them directly to the real panic room somewhere else."

My jaw dropped. "You're telling me that there are people who live *here* that are so concerned with their safety that they essentially have *two* panic rooms?"

Candice cocked her head slightly, as if she couldn't believe I'd asked the question. "Abby, have you ever seen Dutch's security business client list? He's got at least six billionaires on it."

I sat forward. "There're *six* billionaires living here in Austin?"

"Oh, I'm sure there're quite a few more. But I don't think they live here—I think they just have a home here. One of many. Austin is a seriously cool place to live now, in case you hadn't noticed."

"I notice it every day on my drive home. The traffic here sucks."

"True, but it's also a place that's been attracting tech giants and people with major money for the past few years now. We've got some big wealth pouring into the city, and your husband keyed in on a phenomenal niche at exactly the right time."

"Go, Dutch!" I said, waving my fist in the air.

"Go, Safe Chambers Inc.," Candice corrected. "It's now a group effort." And then Candice said, "Abs?"

"Yeah?"

"Has Dutch talked to you about quitting his day job?"

I blinked. "Quitting the bureau? No way. He loves that job."

"Oh."

"Hold on," I said. "Has Brice talked to you about it?"

"A little," she admitted.

I sat forward. "Brice is thinking about quitting the FBI? But he's got, what? At least several more years before he could retire with full benefits, right?"

Agents could retire with full benefits if they had at least twenty-five years of service.

Candice sighed. "Yeah, he's already got seventeen under his belt, so it'd be another eight for him, but lately he's been wondering if that's the right move for him. I mean, you know how grueling that job can be. How hard on the soul it is to look at so much murder, crime, and corruption. It eats at your humanity to work that grind day after day. Right now both Brice and Dutch are making more than enough to live on, and with what they'll continue to pull in, it makes their regular salary look like a joke."

I sat back in my seat again and tapped the arm of the chair. Dutch had been making serious coin with his security business for quite a few years now, and in all that time I'd never heard him mention that he wanted to quit because he was making a better living arranging for bodyguards and home security systems for the superrich. It was my understanding that my hubby worked at his true calling during the day, and made a comfy extra living during his off-hours.

"Does Dutch know Brice is thinking about quitting?"

"I doubt it," Candice said, before eyeing me keenly. "Don't tell him, okay?"

"Okay," I agreed. But it'd be hard to keep that confidence.

"Candice," I said, after thinking about it for a few seconds. "This whole panic room surge probably isn't sustainable."

"Agreed," she said. "At least, not here. But I know the boys have talked about branching out into other cities. Dallas, San Antonio, and Houston are ripe for the picking for starters. Lots of money in those three places, and I heard Dave suggest Nashville as another location to scout."

I was a bit less optimistic. "Yeah, but what makes Dutch, Brice, and Dave think that there won't be tons of competition for them to contend with? I mean, just tonight I talked to three people who were thinking of going with another builder."

"Oh, I'm sure the competition will be fierce," she said. "But Dave is a magician when it comes to schematics. Some of his designs are exceptional, Abs. Have you really not seen any of the photos?"

"I haven't," I said, feeling a slight blush touch my cheeks. I definitely should've taken a bigger interest in my husband's entrepreneurial endeavors.

"Well, they're incredible. Dave thinks of everything, even in instances of a breach. I saw one plan that had a false panel where the residents could go if the main door to the panic room was breached, which would make the room look empty to intruders. There're also hidden places for gas masks, antidotes to several toxins, extra food rations, emergency medical supplies, even a landline phone if you want one installed, but that's a big extra, so most people don't opt for it."

"A landline? What use is a landline when everybody's got a cell these days?"

"It's not very hard to block a cell phone signal," Candice said. "All you need is a simple call jammer aimed at a specific location and presto, no service. But with a landline installed with a cable that goes underground all the way out to the junction box, no one would guess that you've got a very secure way of communicating with the outside world, and a way to call for help. But it's superexpensive, because the junction box could be a quarter or even a half mile away."

"Huh," I said. "Leave it to older technology."

"Truth," Candice said. "Anyway, the point is that Dave's thought of a million details like that."

"Wouldn't it be easier to simply arm these people and suggest that if anybody tries to kidnap them, they should shoot them?" I was being only slightly sarcastic when I said this to Candice.

She laughed. "It would be easier, but the reality is that a lot of these people have families and keep their guns locked up. It's sometimes faster to get to the panic room than it is to get the gun out, and then what if you have multiple intruders with multiple weapons? You could end up in a shootout with lots of collateral damage. Dutch's clients are trying to avoid that kind of scenario. To them, a panic room with all the bells and whistles is the way to make themselves feel safe."

I sighed and got up from the chair. "Well, if it makes them feel secure, then okay, we'll deck out their mansions with a bulletproof room full of fancy gas masks and landline telephones. In the meantime, I'm going to go try and solve real-world problems, but after my last client, I will take you up on that offer of dinner, okay?"

"Sounds good," she said. "And, Abby, remember, don't tell Dutch I said Brice was thinking about retiring from the bureau."

"Lips zipped. Got it," I assured her.

Later that night I sat in bed reading and waiting for Dutch. He came in just before ten and looked weary to the bone. "Hey, beautiful," he said, leaning down to give me a kiss.

"Brice is going to quit the bureau!" I yelled, even before his lips touched mine.

My hubby paused, still hovering over me, probably regretting not stopping for a stiff drink before coming home. Finally, he leaned in again, kissed me, then moved around to the closet to begin shrugging out of his work clothes.

"Did you hear what I said?"

"The neighbors heard what you said."

"You have to talk him out of it, Dutch."

"Out of what?"

"Quitting! He's too good. He can't leave."

My husband pulled off his T-shirt, exposing his broad shoulders, rippling biceps, and perfect pecs. (I threw that description in for you, ladies. You're welcome.) "If Brice wants to quit the bureau, then he's earned the right to leave without being talked out of it," he said.

"How can you say that?" I demanded. "Seriously, honey, you guys are a team. There's no way that bureau would operate nearly as efficiently without him. Plus, he's your friend! You guys work great together. You're the best team out there!"

Dutch came over to sit down next to me and take up my hand. "All of that's true. But if he wants to quit, Edgar, then the best thing I can do for him, as his teammate and his friend, is support his decision."

I tried pulling my hand away, but Dutch held it tight. "Some friend," I snapped. "He'd be making a stupid decision. He's only eight years away from retiring with full benefits."

"I think it's a little less than that, actually. Brice served in the military for three years, so it's more like five."

I slapped his arm with my free hand. "See? He'd be so dumb to throw that away!"

"You know what we worked on today?" he asked me.

My brow furrowed. "What you worked on? I don't know. Some cold-case files?" The bureau branch that Dutch and Brice worked at was one strictly devoted to cold-case files. It was arduous work without a lot of results and depended as much on luck as on the superior investigative skills of the agents.

Dutch's expression was patient, but his eyes were serious. "We worked the case of a human trafficking ring from El Paso. And these girls aren't women. They're young. Illegally young, and these scumbags specialize in providing young girls and virgins to men who prefer children to women."

I put a hand on Dutch's chest and turned away. "Don't tell me any more," I whispered. Those kinds of cases were some of the worst I'd ever worked on. I was still haunted by a series of videos I'd seen in a child-pornography case I'd consulted for Dutch on. I'd never forget the fear and pain in the young girls' eyes.

Dutch squeezed my hand. "Now you know why even five more years might feel like an eternity to Brice."

I sighed and nodded. "Okay. I get it." And then I had another thought. "Do you ever think about quitting? With the side business, I'm assuming we could afford it."

"On days like today, I think about it every single minute. But then I come home to you, and I think about all the good you and I have done over the years and about all the pond scum we've put behind bars, and I wonder how I could think such selfish thoughts. I have more to give, Abs."

"Don't you think Brice has a little more to give too?"

"Why are you pushing this?"

I lowered my gaze to my lap. My miniature dachshund Tuttle was curled up there, fast asleep. "Brice has your back," I said, unable to look at my husband because I was the one now thinking selfish thoughts. "If he weren't there, who would protect you? Who would keep you safe? Who would look out for you both politically and in the field?"

Dutch stroked my cheek and lifted my chin. "Maybe it's time I did that for the guy reporting to me," he said. "Maybe I can be the guy at the top who looks out for everybody else."

"You'd take Brice's job?"

"If it was offered, sure."

I sighed. I loved my husband with all of my heart—I truly did—but I also knew that Brice was the far savvier politician, and in the role of special agent in charge, a keen understanding of politics—and the ability to play them—were an absolute must. "Maybe he won't quit," I whispered.

Dutch chuckled. "We'll hope that, whatever his decision, it's the right one for him." And then he got up and went to the dresser for his pajama bottoms. "Thanks for smoothing it over with Murielle," he said, changing the subject and reminding me about our encounter with her, which, shockingly, I'd completely forgotten.

"You should've warned me about her, babe," I said.

"I warned Candice. It seemed safer."

"I don't mean about what a bitch she is. I mean about what a freaking goddess she is."

Dutch turned to face me with raised (innocent) eyebrows. "You think she's pretty?"

I rolled my eyes and waved my hand dismissively. "Pfft!" I said. "No, she's hideous. I can totally see how you'd be repulsed by her."

"I am repulsed by her."

"Oh, come on!"

"Check the ether," Dutch challenged. "See if I'm lying."

I was about to argue more with him, but then I did as he'd asked and checked the ether after realizing that I hadn't heard that familiar singsong *Liar, liar, pants on fire* . . . in my head when he'd said that he was repulsed by her. "But . . . ," I tried, totally at a loss. "*How* can you not be attracted to her? The woman is like . . . liquid sex!"

"Not to me," he said simply. "To me she's overly confident, self-absorbed, narcissistic, materialistic, and a royal pain in my ass."

"Huh," I said, honestly shocked that Dutch could've looked past all the gorgeous trappings to see the real person underneath. But then, my husband is pretty great that way. In fact, he's pretty great in general. "I wouldn't have blamed you if you'd said you found her attractive."

Dutch leaned forward to cup the back of my head and lay his forehead against mine. "In case you hadn't noticed, I'm kind of blind to anyone but you, Edgar. You're all I want. End of story."

Reaching down, I began to lift off my nightshirt.

"What're you doing?" he asked.

"Getting naked."

"Really?" he said in that way that suggested he was totally for it.

"Yeah, really. Now, get your gorgeous self under these covers and make mad love to me."

"Yes, ma'am," he said, saluting. (And not just with his hand . . . wink!)

Several days later Dutch and I were spending a lazy Sunday morning out on our back patio, sipping coffee (him) and a caffeine-free tea (me) while talking about going somewhere for breakfast, when he suddenly looked up toward the door to the kitchen. "Is that your phone?" he asked.

I sat up and listened. Sighing, I said, "Yeah. I think it's Candice. She was talking about going for a long run this morning and I might've said I was interested in joining her."

"And now you're not interested?"

"Not after the workout she put me through yesterday. That woman is obsessed with the kettlebell."

Dutch leaned over and squeezed my bicep. "You're looking really fit, Edgar."

I reached up and squeezed his arm in turn. "Want to arm-wrestle?"

Dutch bounced his eyebrows. "I'd rather just wrestle."

I laughed. "I'm game."

He surprised me by leaning both arms out to scoop me up and plunk me down in his lap. "You don't have to ask me twice," he said, nuzzling my neck.

I laughed some more and pushed my hands into his robe to lay my palms against his chest and touch his skin.

God, I love the feel of my husband. His skin is smooth and soft, and his chest is as perfect a thing as you can imagine. Even as busy as he'd been, he always took forty-five minutes of his lunch hour to work out at the gym across the street from the bureau. Years of that dedicated regime had molded a body fit to be sculpted into marble.

Dutch is lean at the waist, broad in the shoulders, solid in the pecs, and has the biceps of a god. And, for those of you wondering, he never skips leg day either. . . . I mean, his ass could make you cry—it's so beautiful.

I love to look at him and drink him in, but I also love the feel of him. Running my hands over his skin, tracing every taut muscle, is one of the greatest pleasures I've ever known. And when he sucks in a breath in reaction to the way I touch him, well . . . there are no words to fully describe how powerful and close to him that makes me feel. We've always had this amazing chemistry, but I've come to realize that it's more than that, much more. It'd be better described as a tightly controlled volcanic eruption that happens in slow motion. It's transformative.

"Hey," Dutch said, lifting his lips away from my neck.

"What's the matter?" I asked, my mind already a little hazy.

"Is that my phone?" he said, tilting his head again toward the back door.

"Isn't it out here?"

"No. Remember? It's no-pants Sunday. No pants means no phone to shove in a pocket. I left it on the counter next to yours."

"Well, it's definitely ringing. Should I get it?"

Dutch looked undecided, which meant that if he didn't answer his phone, he'd be preoccupied with thoughts about who was trying to reach him at eight thirty on a Sunday morning.

For the record, no one with good news ever tried to reach him at eight thirty on a Sunday morning.

As I was putting all those thoughts together, my phone started ringing again. "Well, shit," I said. "That's gotta be trouble."

"Maybe it's just a coincidence," Dutch said. "Candice calling you and some idiot calling me."

Sighing again, I got up to head to the back door. "It's never a coincidence, babe."

I reached Dutch's cell on the last ring. "Dutch's phone, hold, please," I said before answering my own cell—which was displaying a number I didn't recognize across the top. "This is Abby."

"Abby?" said a woman's voice. "This is Gwen. Have you seen or heard from my husband?"

Now, I know my brain had been a little fuzzy just moments before, but nothing about what the woman said to me rang a bell. "Come again?" I said.

"Can you hear me?" she asked.

"Yes . . . I can. I'm sorry, but who is this?"

"Gwen," she repeated. "Gwen McKenzie."

Okay, so that still meant nothing to me. "Uh . . . ," I said, furiously sorting through the list of acquaintances I had, and the name still wasn't registering. Was it one of our neighbors? Was she a client? And if she was, was she one of my clients from my psychic practice or the PI business?

"I'm Dave's wife," she tried again.

I actually slapped my forehead. "Ohmigod! You're Dave's old lady!"

Now, Dave had been referring to his common-law wife as his "old lady" for *years*. It was an ongoing joke between us that I'd actually never been able to tweeze her name out of him. He always just called her "my old lady."

But saying that to her on a Sunday morning probably wasn't polite. "I'm sorry," I said quickly. "He always refers to you as that. I hope I didn't offend you."

"No, you're fine," she said, her voice taut with tension. "I know he does. Have you seen or heard from him?"

"Have I seen or heard from him?" I repeated, still relishing the boon of *finally* learning her name. "Um, no, Gwen. I haven't. Should I have?" I almost never saw Dave anymore—he was so busy. Quite a change from a few years ago, when I couldn't get the man out of my house. Especially if it was mealtime.

A voice sounded from Dutch's phone and I said to Gwen, "Sorry, can you hold on just a second?"

Lifting Dutch's phone, I said, "Hi, sorry, who's this?"

"It's me, Abs," Brice said. "Have you or Dutch heard from Dave? We were supposed to meet this morning at eight, and I can't reach him on his cell."

A small shiver of cold crept along my backbone. Uh-oh. "Brice, lemme call you back." Returning to Gwen, I said, "How long has it been since you last saw him, Gwen?"

"Yesterday morning," she said, and now I could hear the hoarseness in her voice. She sounded like she'd been crying. "He didn't come home last night. I was out late with some girlfriends, and when I came home at midnight, he wasn't here. There was a poker game last night, and I thought he was just out, still playing, so I went to bed. But when I woke up this morning, he hadn't come home, and Brice Harrison called, looking for him. He's never stayed out all night before without texting me to let me know where he is. I've called his cell a dozen times, and I've called all of his friends, and no one's seen him since Friday. He never showed up to the game last night and he never answered any of their texts either. I'm worried sick!"

My heart began to beat a little faster in my chest. Not being able to raise Dave on a cell was bad. He practically had that thing glued to his hand. And although he looked a bit irresponsible, with his long hair, thick mustache, full beard, and arms covered in tattoos, Dave McKenzie was a solid human being who could absolutely be counted on to show up when he said he would.

That Dave hadn't arrived at a poker game with his friends was worrisome enough, but the fact that he missed a business meeting with Brice was totally unlike him and a cause for real concern. In the pit of my stomach, a very bad feeling was beginning to settle in. Still, as calmly and gently as I could, I asked, "Gwen, have you tried any of the local hospitals?"

There was a small sob on the other end of the call. "N-n-no," she stammered. "I . . . I don't know if I can do that. Oh, God, what if he's been in an accident?"

"Sit tight," I said as the back door opened and Dutch peered in curiously. "I'll reach out to local law enforcement to see if anybody's got any information and get back to you, okay?"

"Oh my God, Abby!" she cried. "What if something bad happened to him?"

"Nothing bad happened to him," I said. My inner lie detector went off quietly. *Oh, shit!* I thought. *Oh, shit!*

Chapter Three

. . .

"Talk to me," Dutch said the moment I hung up with Gwen.

Before I could answer him, his cell rang. He reached for it and answered it swiftly. "Brice, what's going on?"

While Dutch listened, I called Candice. Her cell went to voice mail, because, of course, she was out on some twenty-mile running excursion and she'd have her music on and her ringer off. "Dammit," I muttered, clicking off to send her an urgent text. By the time I was done tapping it out, Dutch was telling Brice to hold on.

"Dave's missing?" he said to me. Even though I was sure Brice had filled him in, I knew what he was asking. He wanted my intuitive input to confirm whether we should be worried.

"Yes," I said, that dreadful feeling in the pit of my stomach increasing with each passing second. Then I thought of something. "Do you have any pictures of Dave?"

Dutch grimaced, because he knew what I was asking. One of the truly quirky talents that I have is being able to tell from a photograph if someone is alive or dead. The best way to explain it is that when I see a photo of someone who's alive, to my mind's eye everything about it is normal and probably exactly matches how it appears to the average person. But show me a photo of someone who's passed away, and something changes. It's as if their image becomes flatter somehow, as if their visage goes from being three-dimensional to two. And it doesn't matter if the person has been dead for a hundred years or five minutes; if I look at a photo of someone who's deceased, I can tell very quickly that they've passed on.

"I think so," Dutch said. Lifting the phone to his ear, he said, "Brice, let me call you back." After hanging up with Brice, Dutch sifted through the photos on his phone until he found one with Dave in it. "Here," he said, making the image larger. "I took this last week at Murielle's house. Dave's in the background next to a section of wall that we were going to have to remove to meet the dimensions."

I squinted at the screen, bracing myself for what I might see. With a huge sigh of relief, I said, "He's alive."

Dutch leaned against the counter, obviously relieved too. "So where is he?"

I went to the kitchen table and sat down. Even though I was convinced that Dave was still alive, I wasn't at all certain he was well. In fact, that dreadful feeling in the pit of my stomach confirmed that something was very, very wrong with my longtime friend. "I think he's been in an accident," I said, trying to piece together the images and feelings I was getting intuitively.

Dutch tapped at his phone before raising it to his ear. A moment later he said, "Hey, Abby thinks Dave could've been in an accident. Can you call your source at APD dispatch and see if there was anything reported in last night?"

I felt something cool on my leg and looked down to see Eggy, my other beloved mini dachshund, nosing my shin. He'd obviously sensed my concern. Lifting him into my lap, I went back to focusing on Dutch, who was just getting off the phone. "Brice has a contact," he said. "We'll find out if something happened. In the meantime, we should reach out to all the local hospitals."

Dutch and I divided and conquered the list of four main hospitals within short driving distance of where Dave would have been on Saturday morning. None had a patient admitted within the last twenty-four hours by the name of Dave McKenzie or a John Doe that fit his description.

Just as Dutch hung up with the last hospital, shaking his head to indicate he'd had no luck tracking Dave down, Brice called us back. Dutch put the call on speaker so that we both could hear. "I think I've got something," Brice said, and I could tell by his voice that it was bad. "There was a report of an accident involving a truck fitting the description of Dave's F-one-fifty, but when APD rolled up on scene, the only thing they found were some skid marks and some broken plastic they think came off one of the headlights. A report was written and a search for both the truck and the witness vetted nothing."

"How did they learn there was an accident in the first place?" Dutch asked.

"Got an anonymous nine-one-one call," Brice told him. "The caller didn't stay on long enough to be identified."

"Doesn't APD have caller ID?" I asked.

"They do, and I asked about it. My source says the call was blocked."

"That's fishy," I said while Dutch nodded.

"Yep," Brice agreed. "But it may not have been Dave's truck. I haven't heard the call, so I don't know what else the witness may have seen or said. There's still a way for them to trace the call, though, but it'll take some time because they have to go through all the carriers and triangulate the signal. If the phone was a burner, we'll never know who made the call."

"What time did the call come in?" Dutch asked.

"A little after ten in the morning," Brice told him.

"So, Dave's been missing for almost twenty-four hours?" I said. "How does that track?"

"He could've hit his head and become disoriented," Dutch said.

"So where is he?" I pressed. I had this terrible, foreboding feeling.

"That's the sixty-four-thousand-dollar question, Cooper," Brice said. "My best guess is that if it was Dave who was in the accident, he suffered a concussion or head injury, and maybe he tried to make it to the hospital but couldn't, and now he and his vehicle are off the road, somewhere no one's seen him yet."

"We have to find him," I said. "Soon, you guys. We have to find him very, very soon."

"Meet me at APD," Brice said. "We'll ask to hear the call and see the photos of the scene, if any were taken. And then we'll go to the site of the accident and try to find Dave from there."

"We'll be there in twenty," Dutch promised, clicking off the call. He then looked at me and even though his expression was reserved, I could see the worry in his eyes. "How fast can you change?"

"Fast," I said, setting Eggy back on the floor to hurry to the bedroom. Just seven minutes later Dutch and I were out the door.

We didn't speak on the way to the APD station. I think we were both too worried to talk. On the drive, I did notice that Dutch glanced over at me a time or two, and I knew that he was hoping I'd say something like, "Don't worry, honey, my radar says we'll find Dave and he'll be fine!" but nothing in the ether was giving me a warm and fuzzy feeling about Dave's future, and that greatly troubled me.

We walked into the station and Brice was already there at the front door. "This way, guys," he said, waving us forward to follow him. He led us through a maze of corridors to what felt like the back of the station, and there he paused at a door and knocked. After hearing someone say, "Come in," we did.

Through the door we found a woman in uniform, sitting behind a desk with a laptop. She nodded to Brice. "Special Agent Harrison."

"Thanks for meeting with us, Officer Seabright. These are my colleagues Special Agent Rivers and our consultant Abigail Cooper."

Officer Seabright's eyes showed interest when he said my name. "Abigail Cooper. I've heard a *lot* about you."

"If it's good stuff, then it's all true. If it's bad stuff, then it's still probably all true," I told her.

She chuckled, but then Brice cleared his throat and I immediately regretted making the joke. He was right; we weren't here on a social call. Our friend was quite possibly in serious trouble. "Sorry," I said. "I make jokes when I'm nervous."

"Don't worry about it," she told me. "I do the same thing. Now, you wanted me to queue up the call about the accident on Lost Creek Boulevard, correct?"

At the mention of the street name, Dutch lifted his phone to tap at it. Over his shoulder I could see he'd pulled up a map of the street, which was over on the wealthy side of town, where I'd set up most of Dave's appointments for the day before. Lots of money ran through the surrounding bluffs over that way.

Meanwhile, Brice had answered Seabright in the affirmative, and with a click we began to hear the call.

"Nine-one-one, what is your emergency?"

"There's an accident," a man's voice replied. "On Lost Creek. I think a truck went off the road. Y'all should send somebody over there."

"Sir, what is the exact location of the accident?"

"Uh . . . I'm not for sure on this, but I think it's right off Lost Creek, just past Quaker Ridge Drive. Maybe a little further."

"East or west of Quaker Ridge, sir?" she asked.

"Um . . . hold on. . . . I guess it'd be east."

"Can you describe the vehicle?"

"I don't know," he said. "It was a truck. A big one. Maybe . . . an F-one-fifty?"

"What color?"

"Silver."

"Was there anyone in the vehicle?"

"I think there was a guy in it."

"Just one person?" she asked.

"Yeah. He's all I saw at least."

"Did he appear to be moving?"

"I don't know. Maybe?"

"And what is your location?" the dispatcher asked.

There was a pause, then, "Wh-wh-why do you need to know that?"

"We'd like to send an officer out to get your statement, sir," she said.

"Uh, no, I don't think that's a good idea."

"Sir, may I have your name, please?"

"Yeah, I gotta go. Just send somebody out there. I think the guy might be hurt."

"Was anyone else involved in the accident, sir?"

There was an audible click as the caller disconnected.

"Sir? Are you there, sir?"

Shortly after that the call stopped and Officer Seabright looked up at us. "That's all there is."

Brice, Dutch, and I traded a series of concerned looks; then Brice said, "The number was blocked?"

"Yes. If you need me to send in a trace on it, I can, but it'll be at least a few days before we'd get anything back."

"Do it," I said, feeling that sense of urgency in my gut.

Seabright looked to Brice for confirmation and he nodded.

"Is it just me or did the caller sound like he was under the influence?" Dutch asked.

"Yes," I said, "I noticed it too. Some of his words were slurred and his cadence was slow."

"Ten a.m. is pretty early to be driving around under the influence," Brice said.

"He sounded young too," I said. "He could've been at a party and passed out, then woke up still buzzed but thinking he could make it home."

"He could've also been the reason Dave's truck went off the road," Brice said.

I hadn't thought of that. "Shit," I muttered.

Brice then directed his next question to Seabright. "Did the responding unit take photos?"

"They did," she said. "Would you like me to e-mail them to you?"

"Please, Patricia," he said. "And if you could include the exact location of the accident, I'd appreciate it."

"Yes, sir," she said with a smile.

We all thanked Officer Seabright for her time and assistance, then headed out to talk about what to do next.

"We need to go to the scene," Dutch said, stating the obvious.

Brice reached for his phone and took a look at the display. "Patricia sent me the location and the photos. You guys follow me and we'll go over the photos once we get there."

It took about twenty minutes to wind our way over to the west side of town, and again, neither Dutch nor I spoke during the ride. When we got to Lost Creek, Brice's car—in front of us—slowed down and I could tell he was trying to find the exact location of the accident by comparing the road with the photos Officer Seabright had sent him. At last he seemed to find the spot and he put on his turn signal to cross the road and park on the shoulder. Dutch had to move up the road a bit to maneuver in ahead of him, but by the time we got out of our vehicles, I knew we were in exactly the right spot.

The section of road where the truck had gone off the street was absent of houses or pedestrian traffic, and there was very little vehicle traffic to speak of. The shoulder was narrow, and on the other side of it, the ground sloped downward dramatically, ending in a rocky gully just in front of a series of huge bluffs.

If Dave's truck truly had been the vehicle that'd gone off the side of the road here, he probably would've hit either the bluff or some of the rock, and the jolt from the shoulder down into the gully would've been jarring to say the least.

"Skid marks," Dutch said, pointing to a distinctive series of black tread marks that formed a large S, which began on the south side of the road, crossed the double yellow line, and ended at the very edge of the road.

Brice pulled up his phone and showed us the display. "The responding officer took a photo," he said.

I shielded the screen to see the photo better in the daylight, and little had changed about the skid marks in the past twenty-four hours.

When I looked up from the screen, it was to see my husband stepping out onto the road, and looking right and left as he moved to where the skid marks began. He ended up moving down the road quite a ways, before he waved at us and shouted, "They start here."

Brice frowned. "That's got to be two hundred yards," he said.

Dutch moved forward along the tread marks while I watched the road anxiously for oncoming cars. "Car!" I yelled as one approached.

My hubby got out of the way, then resumed his careful assessment of the skid marks. At one point he went back a few feet and knelt down, and it looked like he picked something up off the ground.

"Car!" I yelled at him again.

He shuffled out of the way, allowing the car to pass before trotting over to us. "What'd you find?" I asked.

"A piece of black plastic," he said.

"What's it go to?"

Dutch looked back toward the road. "If I had to guess, I'd say it's a piece from a bumper."

"Dave's?" I asked.

Dutch shook his head. "Not sure. The other curious thing is that right at the spot where I picked it up, the skid marks pivot a little."

"What do you mean they pivot?" Brice asked.

"There's a wiggle in the middle of them, almost like the driver was trying to adjust for an overcorrection."

"So he lost control of the car and skidded off the road," I said.

Both Brice and Dutch nodded, turning their attention as one toward the north side of the road. Without a word the pair started to navigate the steep decline off the shoulder, and I followed them.

It wasn't until I was making my way down the grassy embankment that I realized just how steep it was. If Dave had gone off road here, it would've been terrifying, and it was a wonder his truck didn't flip in the process.

We reached the bottom of the embankment and Dutch and Brice began to survey the ground. "There," I said, pointing to a patch of smashed and torn-up grass, which was obvious only once you were down the embankment and could see it up close.

"Did the responding officer take any photos from down here?" Dutch asked as he picked his way over the rocks to the patch of ruined grass.

Brice paused to flip through the images on his phone. "Doesn't look like it," he said. "He took the shots of the road and two from the shoulder pointed in this direction, but it doesn't look like he came down here to have a look."

"Lazy bastard," Dutch groused.

But Brice merely shrugged. "The truck wasn't here when he arrived on scene. It's no wonder he wasn't as thorough as he should've been."

I stared back up the embankment and shook my head. "If Dave really did go off road here, how the *hell* did he make it back up there?"

"Easy," Dutch said. "His truck has a hemi engine and four big wheels. He could've gotten himself out of here without a lot of effort."

On that note I walked back over to the embankment and moved along it until I found a patch of grass that appeared to be flatter than the surrounding scrub, and which was also torn in places. "Here," I said.

The men came over to have a look and Dutch nodded. "Yep," he said. "This is where the driver went back up to the road." He then turned to look back at the patch of grass that appeared to be where the driver had landed after heading off the embankment. "If he came to a stop there, then it doesn't look like he hit anything."

"Probably safe to assume that his air bag didn't deploy," Brice said.

"Yep," Dutch agreed. "Maybe he got his cage a little rattled, but it doesn't look like he would've been injured, and if he drove himself out of here, then he didn't suffer anything too traumatic."

And yet, my gut said different. Standing on that rough patch of torn-up ground, I could feel the violence of it in the ether, and sensing that made me very worried for Dave's well-being. "So where is he?" I asked.

Brice and Dutch shook their heads. None of us had any clue.

"Maybe Gwen had it wrong," Brice offered. "Maybe Dave did make it home last night and left again early this morning before she woke up."

"But what about the meeting with you?" I countered. "No way would he miss that. And the poker game with his buddies? He didn't show up for that either. I've never known Dave to miss a poker game."

"Did he show up for his appointments?" Dutch asked, and Brice and I looked at him in surprise.

"No clue," Brice said.

"Did anybody call you to complain that he didn't show up?" I asked.

Brice shrugged. "I haven't heard from anybody. You?" he asked Dutch.

"No," Dutch said, scrolling through his phone, probably looking for e-mails or texts from disgruntled clients.

"So he made the rest of his appointments," I said. "Probably."

"Only one way to check," Dutch said. "Abs, you worked on the list for yesterday, right?"

"I did, but I gave it to Candice and I think she's still got it locked up in her filing cabinet at the office."

Brice grunted and glanced at his watch. "She's out on a twenty-miler, and I don't think she'll be home for another hour or two. And I have no idea which trail she took."

"I do," I said, my shoulders sagging. It looked like I was going running after all.

"You can find her?" Dutch said.

"Yep," I told him, pointing to my feet. "Wouldn't you know I'd grab the first set of shoes I reached for this morning and they just happened to be my running shoes?"

"Edgar, you're seriously going to run twenty miles to find Candice?" he pressed.

"No, honey," I said, already moving back up the embankment. "I'm going to run five. Candice runs a five-mile loop on her long-run days so that she has access to water and her glucose supply. All I have to do is run the loop in the opposite direction to find her."

"Or you could just wait by her car," Brice pointed out.

"She parks in different lots all the time," I said, knowing that from experience. "While we're searching for her car, she could have come and gone on the loop. Plus, sometimes she skips the stop if she's feeling good," I told him. "She has to step off the trail to get to her car."

"Man," he said. "I feel bad for not volunteering to run with you, but I wouldn't make it past mile two."

"It must be nice to feel no shame that your wife is in such better shape than you," I said with a smirk. Of course, Candice was in better shape than just about everyone—including me.

"She's been after me to sign up for a ten K," Brice admitted.

"You should do it," I told him.

"No way, Cooper," he said.

"Why not?"

"Because it's a slippery slope. The second I sign up, she'll be after me to run with her, and have you seen how fast my wife runs?"

"She is crazy fast," I said.

"Yeah. If it's all the same to you, I'll continue to make work an excuse for not being able to train, and hold on to what's left of my manhood."

"Good plan," I told him, and knew that that way of thinking was probably why Candice and Brice were still happily married.

*　　*　　*

About thirty minutes later I found Candice. She was indeed running her five-mile loop and it took only three miles for me to find her. "Abby?" she said when she spotted me. "Why are you out here without water?"

I came to a stop and pinched my side. I'd gotten a small cramp ten minutes in and it was killing me. "Dave's . . . missing," I said as I panted for breath.

She pulled her earbuds out of her ears and said, "What?"

"Dave. He's missing."

"What do you mean he's missing?"

"I mean that yesterday morning he appears to have had a small accident, then later on he skipped his poker game, checking in with his wife, and a meeting he had with your husband this morning."

Candice offered me her water bottle. "Drink," she ordered. "Then tell me everything."

We ran back to the car at a blistering pace. I'd taken a moment to text Dutch and Brice the location of Candice's car and they met us there. "I have a copy of the spreadsheet in my office," she told them, not even pausing to greet them formally. "Follow me there and we'll see if we can get a better handle on when Dave might've gone missing."

I rode with Candice back to the office, which was a serious mistake, because when she's on a mission, she drives like she runs—crazy fast and somewhat recklessly.

Still, we managed to arrive in one piece and after parking, we didn't wait for our husbands, but headed straight inside.

Candice took the stairs up to our floor, and I regretted my decision to ride with her yet again. That girl can *move* when she's feeling inclined, and I lost sight of her on the second-floor landing.

I found her again in our office suite, hovering over her computer and looking very concerned. "Here," she said when she'd printed off several copies of the previous day's schedule.

I took it and noted that I'd lined Dave up with eight appointments. "He would've kept very busy with this many in one day, but I think we only need to worry about the appointments after the accident, so that'd be these five clients," I said, pointing to the block of names, addresses, and phone numbers.

"Yes," she agreed. "The houses in that group are all fairly close together, though, so his drive to them wouldn't have been long. His fifth and six appointments are even right next door to each other."

"It's so crazy that all these people want panic rooms. I mean, there'd have to be a serious spree to think that thieves would hit up everyone in one neighborhood."

"Intruders don't have to hit up every home, Sundance. They just have to hit up your home. It's that thought that makes all of these people lose sleep at night."

"Ah," I said. "Good point."

"Hey," we heard from the doorway, and we both turned to see Brice and Dutch coming into the room. "Is that the list?"

"It is," Candice said.

"You sent him to eight clients?" Dutch asked, peering over my shoulder. "How was he supposed to make all eight?"

"Candice figured it out geographically and we allotted Dave a full half hour to get in, take pictures, assess the property, and get back on his way, which also gave him fifteen minutes to get to the next appointment."

"He would've needed to hustle, but it was mathematically doable," Candice said.

"Still," Dutch said. "You know Dave. He likes to gab. If he stopped to chat, he would've thrown the whole schedule off."

"Which is actually great," Candice said. "If he stopped to talk to any of these clients, then they might have a good insight into what could've happened to him. Maybe the drive off the road shook up his brain and he was suffering a concussion and didn't realize it. If he seemed at all off to these people, then we might be able to tell if he's gone missing due to some medical issue."

"Okay," Dutch said, folding his sheet. "Abby, you take the first two, I'll take the second two, Brice can have the last one, and, Candice, can I ask you to call the clients on tap for today and tell them that we'll need to reschedule?"

"Already on it," she said, waving the sheet with that day's schedule. "He'd already be late for this first one, so I'll have to schmooze a little."

As I sat down in my office to make the first call, I groaned out loud. "Why?" I muttered. Taking a deep breath, I dialed and Mrs. Schultz connected after only one ring. "This is Barbara," she said.

"Mrs. Schultz?"

"Yes?"

"Hello, ma'am, this is Abigail Cooper calling from Safe Chambers."

"Who?" she said loudly.

"Abby Cooper," I repeated. "We spoke a few days ago. I'm calling from Safe Chambers, the company that installed your safe room."

"Oh, yes!" she said.

I relaxed a little. She'd remembered. "I'm sorry to disturb you on a Sunday morning, ma'am, but I'm following up with you about the door to your safe room and the gentleman who came out to fix it yester—"

"I'm so glad you called!" she interrupted. "That door won't close and I need someone to come fix it."

Tension set in my shoulders. Had Dave not shown up after his accident? "Someone should have been there yesterday, Mrs. Schultz. Did he not stop by?"

"A man came here yesterday," she said. "He was a scruffy-looking thing," she added.

I blew out a breath of relief. Dave had been there. "Oh, that's great!" I said.

Mrs. Schultz continued as if I hadn't spoken. "He played around with the door for a little while and said he'd need more tools to fix it. Is he coming back out?"

I bit my lower lip. I didn't know. "Dave is unavailable at this time, but we could get someone else over there very soon. Can you give me a good day and time to have someone come by?"

"Well, I'm going away later today, so it'll have to be when I get back."

"When are you due to come back, Mrs. Schultz?"

"Next month. I'm going to Germany to visit my daughter. Her husband works at a big company over there. He's a very important man. He's even met the German chancellor!"

I'd heard about Mrs. Schultz's son-in-law on my first call (and about her grandson, and her daughter, and her daughter's two dogs, and all about her glaucoma, which was getting worse, and about a weird rash on her back that her doctor—who didn't know anything—had said was a bacterial infection, and he'd prescribed antibiotics for her, but she was already on antibiotics for a bad tooth, and since she didn't like to take too many pills, she was skipping the one and doubling up on the other . . . and on and on). With all that she'd told me on that first call, I was surprised that she hadn't mentioned that she was headed overseas to visit her family.

"How about we give you a call next month and arrange something?" I said, jotting a note to myself.

"That would be good," she said. "I really must go now. I have to finish packing. Send someone out to fix my door next month, all right?"

Before I could even answer, she hung up.

After getting off the line with Mrs. Schultz, I tried the next client. "This is Roger," said the client.

"Hi, Mr. Mulligan, it's Abby Cooper from Safe Chambers calling. I'm just following up on your appointment with Dave McKenzie from yesterday—"

"I haven't made up my mind about the installation yet, Abby," Mulligan interrupted. "I told your guy that yesterday."

I let go another relieved sigh. Dave had made his next two appointments after the accident just fine. "Yes, sir, I'm sorry, I haven't had a chance to catch up with Dave yet, but I did want to call and check that he met with you and that everything went well."

"I met with him," he said. "He's kind of a rough character."

I smiled. "Only on the outside, sir. On the inside he's actually a very kind and gentle man."

"If you say so. Like I told your guy, though, I'm on the fence about all this. We already have a safe room upstairs, but my wife's best friend has one on the ground floor, so now she thinks we should have one off the family room." At that moment, in the background I heard a child scream and another one start yelling, and then what sounded like two big dogs began barking. Above the fray a woman shouted, "*Roger!* Get off the phone and come help me!"

Mulligan groaned and said, "Listen, Abby, I'll talk it over with my wife again and get back to you in a week or two, okay?"

"Sounds great, sir. Thank you for your time."

Once I got off the line with Mulligan, I went back to Candice's office and found that I was the last person to get off the line with my assigned clients. "Any luck?" Candice asked me.

"Yes. He made Mrs. Schultz's and Roger Mulligan's appointments just fine."

"Nobody picked up at the Roswells'," Brice said.

"I got through to Sylvia Ramirez and Chris Wixom," Dutch said. "Both said Dave made his appointments on time, took some photos, and left. They didn't report anything unusual about the visit, or Dave's behavior."

"There wasn't anything unusual about his behavior according to Roger Mulligan or Barbara Schultz either," I said. "Although he wasn't able to fix the motor on the door at Mrs. Schultz's house."

"He couldn't fix it?" Dutch said, his mind momentarily drifting into business mode.

"No. She said he mentioned something about needing more tools or something."

"I'll get Hector to go out tomorrow and replace the motor," Dutch said.

I shook my head. "You'll have to wait until next month. Mrs. Schultz is headed out of town to visit her daughter and son-in-law."

Dutch smirked. "He's a very important man, you know," he mocked. "He's met the chancellor!"

I laughed. "So you've had the pleasure of meeting Mrs. Schultz?"

"Longest appointment of my life," Dutch said with a roll of his eyes. "She's sweet, but she's a nut."

"Well, at least we know that Dave was there and tried to fix the door. That suggests he was feeling okay even right after he went off the road."

"Who was the last person we've reached so far to have seen him?" Candice asked.

Dutch looked to Brice, who shook his head, reminding us he hadn't reached Dave's final appointment. "I guess that would've been Chris Wixom. He left his place just before one."

"Who's the last person on the list, again?" I asked.

"Andy and Robin Roswell," Brice said. "He would've arrived at their place around one fifteen or so."

"We'll need to follow up with them and see how he was when he left their place and if he mentioned where he was heading," Candice said, inching over to ease the sheet away from Brice's fingers. I smirked, because it was clear that Candice was taking charge of that. My best friend was all about the details, and doubtless Brice would've followed up with the clients, but this way, Candice would make sure it got done.

"Dutch and I called a couple of the hospitals in that area this morning. Nobody had a patient come in under his name or a John Doe fitting his description, but maybe we should call a few more north of the area in the direction of his house just to cover our bases."

Dutch pointed at me. "Good thinking," he said.

Candice glanced at the piece of paper she'd claimed and walked over to her desk to type a search into her laptop. "What're the hospitals you guys called this morning?" she asked. Dutch rattled off the list, Candice typed, and a minute later she was scribbling on a couple of sticky notes; she handed us each one and said, "Call. See if he's been admitted."

"On it," I said, and headed off to my office to start making the calls.

Chapter Four

. . .

A few minutes later I walked back into Candice's office. I shook my head at her, then at Brice and Dutch when they came in again too. "No luck?" Candice asked.

"No," the boys said together.

"So what do we do?" I asked.

"Wait," Candice said with a hint of excitement. "Does Dave's truck come with LoJack? If he's got an antitheft device on his truck, I might be able to trace it."

"If it cost extra," I said, "you can pretty much lay money down that Dave didn't buy it." He'd driven his old pickup into the ground, and only after it was towed away and his "old lady" refused to loan him her car did he finally break down and get himself a proper construction site vehicle. The F-150 had been a huge splurge for my frugal friend. No way did he say yes to anything aftermarket unless it was absolutely necessary.

"I told him to get the security package," Dutch said with a sigh. "He refused."

"Can we track his cell?" I asked.

Dutch, Brice, and Candice all traded looks with one another. We were on dicey ground here. The FBI has *very* strict rules about whose phone they'll try to track through its GPS, and if we conducted that kind of a search without a warrant, we'd be very clearly stepping outside the boundaries of the law.

"We should call Dave's wife," Candice said. "Maybe she has the same phone plan as Dave, and she'll be able to track it using a tracking app."

"Oh, that's a good plan!" I said.

Candice made the call after I gave her Gwen's number, and put the call on speaker. The poor woman was nearly beside herself with worry. "He was in an accident?" she cried when she heard the news.

"At this point, we don't think he suffered an injury," Dutch said, trying to reassure her. I felt conflicted about telling her that Dave was probably fine, since something in my gut was telling me that Dave wasn't okay, despite what every one of our clients had said to us. There was something about Dave's condition that was bothering me. Regardless, I let it go, because I didn't see the need to further upset her.

"Gwen," Candice said, pulling the conversation back. "Are you and Dave on the same phone plan?"

"Yes," she said. "Why?"

"If you call your carrier, they should be able to assist you in tracking Dave's cell. If we find his phone, we'll find Dave."

"I'll do it right now. Call you back," she said, and hung up. We waited anxiously for Gwen to call back, and it took a little while, but she finally did. "I found him!" she said when we answered her call.

"Where is he?" Dutch asked.

"Is he okay?" I asked.

"Is he hurt?" Candice asked.

"Why didn't he show up this morning?" Brice asked.

There was a pause on the other end of the line before Gwen said, "You guys all asked that at the same time, so let me just say that I found his phone, which he's still not answering, on Lost Creek Boulevard, not far from Quaker Ridge Drive."

It was our turn to be silent while we processed that. "We were just there," I whispered to Dutch. He nodded at me but said to Gwen, "We'll head out there right now, Gwen. Try not to worry."

"Thanks, you guys. But I am going to worry until I hear from him. I can't imagine why he hasn't come home, or called!"

After clicking off the line with Gwen, Candice looked at me and said, "Was Lost Creek the site where Dave's truck went off the road?"

"Yeah," I said. "There was no sign of Dave when we were there."

"Maybe he went back," Brice said. "Maybe something fell out of his truck, or came loose when he went off road, and he's there right now looking for it."

"What if he leaves again before we get there?"

Candice waved to us to go and said, "You three go check it out. I need a quick shower and a change, and on the way to the condo, I'll call Gwen and ask her to let me know if Dave's phone looks like it's moved from that location. I'll meet up with you in a half hour or so."

Brice, Dutch, and I hurried to Dutch's car, and he drove much like Candice does when she's on a mission, which meant that I was white-knuckling it all the way back to Lost Creek. Candice never called to tell us that Dave was on the move, so I was hopeful that we'd find him there, sifting through the grass looking for a missing part of his truck. But when we finally did arrive, there was no sign of Dave, or his truck. "Shit," Dutch said when he pulled over to the shoulder again.

I called Candice. "Hi, honey, have you heard from Gwen? Is Dave on the move?"

"No," she said. "I literally just hung up with her. She said she can see that his phone is still there."

"Well, he's not," I said.

"Dammit," Candice swore. "Do you see his phone?"

"Dutch," I said, getting out of the car and motioning for him to follow me. Brice followed too. We crossed the road and I said to Dutch, "Call Dave's phone."

He did and the three of us listened, but we didn't hear anything. Fanning out a little, we all cocked our heads and strained to hear, and that's when Brice went sprinting off to the left. Dutch and I hurried after him and as we caught up, we could hear the faint sounds of a cell phone on its last ring.

"Call it again," I said to Dutch. He did, and Brice moved quickly but carefully down the side of the embankment before thrusting a hand toward the grass. He came up with Dave's cell and walked it back to us.

"Did you guys find it?" Candice asked, and I realized she was still on the line.

"We did," I said.

"The battery is just about dead," Brice said, holding up the dust-covered phone.

"I have a charger in my car," Dutch said.

After plugging the phone into the charger, Dutch hit the home button and said, "Anybody know what Dave's code is?"

We all looked at each other blankly. "I'll call Gwen," Candice said. "Back in a sec."

She clicked off and we waited. And waited. Finally my cell rang again with her number. "Everything okay?" I asked.

"I had to let Gwen know that we'd only found Dave's phone, not him. She's pretty upset and I had to calm her down. I'm on my way to you guys right now."

"Did she know the code?" I asked.

"She said to try his birthday and if that didn't work, then we should try her birthday. I have both sets of digits."

Her birthday worked and we were able to access Dave's phone, which yielded nothing useful. Dave had about thirty unanswered calls and texts, most of them from either us or his wife. There were no searches in his phone that seemed suspicious, and, what was even more odd, his maps app hadn't been used to help him navigate to any of his appointments.

While we sorted through Dave's phone, Candice arrived and came over to hop into Dutch's car.

"Did he have a nav system in that truck?" Dutch asked, as

Candice—freshly showered and changed—settled into the seat next to me.

I shrugged. "It would've been extra, but Dave might've found the added expense worth it."

"He had it," Brice said. "I remember driving with him to a site to look at a finished room and he used it."

"So he might not have noticed that his phone was missing when he got back onto the road," I said. "And that's why he hasn't been in touch."

"It still doesn't explain why he missed his poker game and hasn't been home yet," Candice pointed out.

"No," I said with a frown. "It doesn't."

"So where the hell is he and what the hell happened to him?" Dutch grumbled.

My husband appeared irritated, but I knew better. I knew that he was just as worried about Dave as I was, if not more so. Dutch had a soft spot for the contractor, especially when it came to allowing Dave extra time to finish projects or the fact that for almost a solid year Dave had dinner with us every night. I should also point out that Dutch is the cook in the family, and a very good one at that.

"What about surveillance footage?" Candice suddenly said.

We all looked curiously at her, so she explained, "I'd like to see if we can find Dave in his truck on one of the tollway cams or traffic light cameras. If we can find out where he was geographically after the last client meeting, we might be able to narrow down where he is."

Dutch and Brice traded uncomfortable looks. "We'd need either a warrant or a really good reason to ask APD for that kind of access," Brice said.

"You have a really good reason," I said. "One of your workers has gone missing."

Dutch looked at his watch. "Has Gwen filed a missing persons report?"

I pulled out my phone and called her. She answered with a, "Have you found him?"

My heart sank. She sounded so frantic, and we really had nothing more to tell her. "Not yet," I admitted. "But we're trying to narrow down a few leads. Quick question for you, though—have you filed a missing persons report on Dave yet?"

There was a pause, then, "No. When he didn't come home, I just called around to all of you. Should I file one?"

"I think you should, Gwen. The more eyes on the lookout for Dave, the better. Plus, it might give us access to traffic cams to help us figure out what direction he went in."

Gwen's voice was shaking with emotion when she said, "What if he went off the road, Abby? What if that first accident he had yesterday gave him a head injury, and maybe after his last appointment he was driving home and blacked out or something, and his truck went off the road?"

I pressed my lips together anxiously. I'll admit that a very similar thought had gone through my own mind. We were in an area of town with lots of massive hills and great big limestone bluffs. If Dave had gone off the road somewhere around here, he could very well be in real trouble. And it was the real-trouble part that was eating away at me, because my radar was humming with that kind of vibration. Still, it wouldn't help things to make Dave's wife any more upset or worried than she already was. "Gwen," I said gently, "we have no reason to believe that anything bad has happened to Dave. And until we either find him or find a definitive reason to be worried, let's you and me stay positive, okay?"

I heard her inhale a big breath and blow it out. "Okay," she said. "Yeah, okay."

"Great. Now, if you could call in a missing persons report to APD, that might help move things along."

"Don't I have to go to the station?"

"No," I said. "You can file that over the phone, and there's no waiting period, so make the call and text me after you've done it, okay?"

"I will," she said.

After she hung up, I tucked my phone back into my pocket and looked at my companions. With a shrug I said, "I'm out of ideas about what else we can do."

"What if we drove Dave's route home from the accident through the rest of what would have been his workday and then the route he likely drove home?" Candice suggested. "I know it sounds weird, but it might give us some insight into where he could be."

"It doesn't sound weird to me," I said. As soon as Candice suggested it, I wished I'd thought of it, because as we retraced his steps, I'd have my radar on and reaching for anything about Dave that I could get.

Dutch nodded while looking thoughtfully at us. "How about you two retrace the route he would've taken from Lost Creek Boulevard to the rest of the clients on the list, and Brice and I can take the route he would've taken home?"

Candice consulted her spreadsheet. "His last appointment was on River Run Lane," she said.

"Oh, yeah," he said. "The Roswells'. Nice house. I gave the estimate on that one. That street ends at Wilshire, which has an exit onto MoPac. Dave would've taken that north to One Eighty-three and then home. We'll start at Wilshire and head to his place."

"What if he stopped to get something to eat?" Brice said. We all looked at him. "If he finished with the Roswells sometime after one, he could've been hungry."

"He loves In-N-Out Burger," I suggested.

"No In-N-Outs on MoPac, but there're a couple on One Eighty-three," Dutch said.

"Okay," Candice said as she opened the passenger side door. "You two take Dave's route home, and Abby and I will retrace his route to all the clients. We'll text if we find anything; otherwise let's all meet back at your place, Dutch."

Candice and I headed to her car and got under way. About ten minutes into the drive, my phone pinged with an incoming text from Gwen. "Dave's missing persons report has been filed," I told Candice as I forwarded the text to Dutch.

"Good," she said. "The more eyes out there, the better."

Candice followed the directions from her phone for the first house on Dave's list after he'd seemingly run off the road, and we immediately found ourselves in a very wealthy part of town, where the homes weren't measured in feet so much as in number of garage bays. I saw one mansion with a six-bay-door garage, and another that looked like it might have a helipad to the side of the house. Every single home, of course, stood majestically behind a very tall security gate, and most had privacy walls. The glimpses of opulence that I'd snagged were all from the vantage point of the driveway as we hummed past.

We moved steadily until we came up over a steep hill to look down a row of mansions, each with its own majestic view of the Colorado River. As we crested the hill, I thought to myself that if it was true that money didn't buy happiness, buying some of those views might be a pretty swell consolation prize.

Sure enough, Candice's first stop was in front of a white eight-foot privacy wall, bisected by a big black iron gate, which was the home of Mrs. Schultz. Candice parked on the side of the road opposite the house, and we got out and wordlessly looked around.

I moved across the street, stepping onto the driveway, which allowed a view of the front of Mrs. Schultz's mansion. It was an impressive structure, perhaps not quite as big and audacious as Murielle's place, but still *way* above my pay grade.

Through the gate I could see a Town Car parked near the front door, and a man in a black suit was loading luggage into the trunk. I eased back from the driveway, not wanting to appear like a Peeping Tom.

"Anything?" Candice asked me. She knew I was trying to feel Dave's imprint in the ether.

I shrugged my shoulders. "Not much here," I said.

"Okay, let's keep going."

We arrived at Roger Mulligan's place just over ten minutes

later. His home was stately and tasteful, and there was a large modern sculpture on the front lawn. The backyard was partially visible from the road, and when I got out of the car to get a feel of the place, I could see three youngsters running around the backyard boisterously with two enormous Great Danes trotting along beside them.

Candice took off her sunglasses and peered at the yard next to me. "There's a couple that have their hands full," she said.

"I think what you meant to say was, 'Yikes.'"

"Definitely," Candice said, donning her sunglasses again and motioning with her shoulder for us to head back to the car.

We hopped in and she said, "Anything?"

"Not really," I said again. "I can feel him, but it's subtle."

"Well, let's hope it gets more clear as we go along," she said.

I admired her optimism.

We stopped next at Sylvia Ramirez's home, which was smaller than most of the other mansions around, but maybe only by two thousand feet or so. Still, the estate was on a large plot of land with a sizable stable and a large garden. There were people all over the property, coming and going, and several cars parked in the driveway. Candice and I didn't get out of the car here, because we didn't want to spook anybody by standing at the foot of the entrance and looking around. "Should we keep going?" Candice asked after a minute or two of sitting off on the shoulder.

"Yeah," I said. "There's nothing here."

Ten minutes after that, we arrived at Chris Wixom's place. There were no visible cars parked in the driveway, and all the blinds were closed. "Is he traveling?" I asked. The house had that shuttered feeling.

"Don't know," Candice said. "Dutch talked to him, I think."

I frowned, feeling uneasy. Something was bothering me, but I couldn't put my finger on it other than a sense of urgency had just settled into the pit of my stomach. "Let's keep going," I said.

Finally we arrived at the last stop on Dave's list. It was only about three miles away from his previous stop, and we pulled up to the front gate, which was formed out of solid metal and offered no view of the home or the surrounding grounds. "These guys really like their privacy," I said.

Candice surprised me by ignoring the shoulder and pulling forward into the driveway right up to the call box.

As she rolled her window down to get to the button on the box, I said, "We're going to talk to them?" We hadn't bothered any of the other clients.

"Brice never got ahold of them, remember? And they would've been the last people to have seen Dave. He might've mentioned where he was going after he left them."

"Right," I said. "Good point."

While we waited for someone inside to pick up, I leaned back in my seat and sighed. I'd used a lot of effort to keep my intuition up and running all morning. It was draining stuff and I needed a break soon or I'd get a nasty headache. In fact, I had one already starting. Thinking I might need some Excedrin, I opened my eyes to reach for my purse, where I had a bottle of the painkiller, when my breath caught. My gaze had landed on something that made me forget all about my headache.

"Candice?" I whispered.

She was busy craning herself out the window to press the call button again. "Yeah?"

"I don't think anyone's going to answer."

She pulled her head back inside the car and looked over at me. "Your radar telling you they're not home?"

"Oh, I think they're home. Or they were when *that* went down." Raising a shaking hand, I pointed through the windshield to the front gate.

Candice's gaze shifted accordingly. "Holy shit!" she exclaimed. "Is that . . . ?"

"A bloody handprint? Yeah. I think it is."

For a moment we sat there frozen and mute. And then Candice reached under her seat, withdrew her gun, and was out of the car and moving toward the gate faster than you could say, "Annie Oakley." I followed right on her heels.

"Call nine-one-one," she said over her shoulder as we trotted forward.

My hands were trembling and I fumbled the effort of pulling my phone out of my pocket, but managed it just as Candice pushed the butt of her gun against the metal panel of the gate. It swung inward a few inches.

"Shit!" I said just as the 911 operator came on the line.

"What's your emergency?" a woman's voice asked.

I stared at that bloody handprint, which was already a rusty brown in places, and my mind went blank. For several seconds, I couldn't seem to articulate in my mind what the emergency actually was. "We're . . . we're . . . at this house, and something bad has happened."

"What is your location, ma'am?" the operator asked.

Candice waved at me to get behind her while she pushed the security gate open a little more to reveal the concrete driveway leading to the house. On the pavement were small droplets of dried blood. "Oh, sweet Jesus!" I whispered. "Candice, that's bad!"

She looked back at me and motioned with her free hand for me to continue on with the call. "Ma'am?" the operator said again. "I need your location, please."

"I'm at . . . ," I began, only to realize that I didn't have a clue where the hell we were. "Hold on," I told her, then pulled up my own maps feature and focused on the blue blinking dot on the screen. "We're at seven-five-six-three River Run Lane."

"What seems to be wrong there, ma'am?"

"There's blood," I told her, inching closer to Candice, who was now tiptoeing forward through the gate. "There's a lot of blood."

"Where are you?" she asked.

"I'm in the driveway."

"Can you see if anyone is hurt?"

I looked around the front yard with tense anticipation, expecting to lay my eyes on a dead body or two at any moment. "Uh . . . not that I can see."

"Can you see inside the house?" she asked next.

Candice was still moving forward, and I was right behind her. We were edging close to the home, which was a beautiful modern structure of stucco, wood, and glass. "Not quite yet," I said. I was trembling now in earnest. The energy all around the house was radiating violence—as if all the blood hadn't already spoken to that.

"Okay, ma'am, I'm going to ask that you stay where you are and wait for the police. I've already dispatched them, and they're on their way to you."

"O-o-okay," I stuttered. I was scared shitless.

Candice had now reached the front walk, which led to an over-sized wood door with a big metal handle. The door had more blood smeared on it and it was partially open.

That's when the acrid scent hit me. Blood has a very distinctive smell. It's part metallic, part organic, part stomach turning. For it to have reached my nose from out on the front porch, there must have been a lot of it inside, and I shuddered anew.

Candice must've picked up on the scent too, because she turned to look back at me, her lips pressed tightly together and her eyes narrowed. "I think we're too late."

"We should wait out here," I whispered.

She shook her head. "If there's even a chance that someone's still alive in there, I gotta go see," she said softly.

And then, there was a question in her eyes, and I knew what she was asking. She wanted to know if I was coming with her, or staying out on the porch.

I *badly* wanted to run back to the car and stay there with my fingers in my ears and my eyes tightly closed, because I knew there was no unseeing whatever horror lay past that front foyer.

But Candice would never have let me go inside alone. That is the sole reason why I nodded to her that I'd have her back.

We proceeded cautiously, but not exactly slowly; stepping very carefully over the droplets of blood, we kept to the edges of the entryway and then the front hall. In front of us was a large spiral staircase, and the droplets appeared to have originated up the steps.

I bit back the bile forming in the back of my throat as we climbed them one stair at a time, me wondering why I hadn't heard the sound of sirens yet.

At the top of the stairs, lying on the threshold to the hallway, we found the first dead body.

I clamped my hand over my mouth when I took in the petite woman with silver hair, dressed in a gray smock with a white apron. She was slumped against the wall and there was a large bloody smear mark directly behind her. She was pale and stiff, and clearly dead, but Candice paused to put her fingers against the woman's neck anyway, feeling for a pulse.

She rose only a second or two later, turned to me, and shook her head.

Tears stung my eyes and my knees were shaking so hard I didn't know if they'd hold me up. I felt a wave of sadness for this poor woman who'd been here innocently working her job when she'd been gunned down. She looked like someone's mother. Or grandmother. I wondered, who at home was worried for her well-being? Who would soon learn that today would forever be the worst day of their life?

Candice reached out and squeezed my arm, calling my attention back to her. "You okay?" she mouthed.

I shook my head, the tears spilling out onto my cheeks. "Yes," I whispered, because I knew I had to be.

Her expression turned sympathetic, but she motioned over her shoulder with her gun. We had to continue to check for victims who might be alive, and clear the house if we could.

I nodded and we continued forward while I sent out a small prayer to the deceased woman behind us. I didn't know her name, but I hoped very much that she'd managed to cross over to the other side and was free from the horror of this home.

Candice led the way to the the open door of what I thought might be the master bedroom. We entered and I was so tense that

I couldn't seem to take more than a shallow breath. The room was dim, but not dark, made so by the cocoa-colored paint on the walls and the partially drawn drapes.

It was a big room with thick wool carpeting and an enormous headboard that rose from floor to ceiling. At first, no one appeared to be in the room, but then I saw that the door to the closet was wide open, the interior lit.

Candice advanced and very faintly I heard the first sound of approaching sirens. It seemed like forever ago that I'd called for help, but realistically it'd probably been closer to three or four minutes. I almost turned back then, because help was almost here, but Candice continued to advance like she had to know what was in that closet, and I didn't think I could abandon her now.

We came to the doorway together and as we took in the sight, a small, horrified gasp escaped my lips.

A couple, quite probably Mr. and Mrs. Roswell, had died in each other's embrace. They were riddled with bullets, rendering their faces all but unrecognizable, but they'd gone down holding on to each other to rest in a heap of tangled limbs and so much crimson.

There was so much blood, in fact, that I couldn't escape the smell, and I turned away from the scene and fled. I didn't stop until I was outside, close to the car, and that's when I lost my cookies.

For an hour or so after that, I wasn't able to take anything else in.

Chapter Five

. . .

Dutch squatted down in front of me. "How you doin', dollface?"

I wiped my eyes and sniffled. "Shitty. You?"

"Not quite as bad as that, but getting there," he admitted.

"Did you see the crime scene?"

His gaze fell to the ground and he nodded. "Yeah. Grim stuff."

I worked to swallow past the lump in my throat. "They were butchered. I've never seen anyone cut to ribbons like that."

"Assault rifles will do that," he said. "Which means that whoever did it was playing for keeps."

I looked over my shoulder at the half-dozen police vehicles and all the responders currently gathering evidence. There was a crime tech carefully photographing the bloody handprint on the security gate, which I hoped would yield the perfect set of fingerprints to nail the son of a bitch who'd committed such carnage.

"Have they confirmed that it was the Roswells?" I asked next. The murdered couple upstairs in the house were unrecognizable, and while I strongly suspected it'd been the homeowners, I wasn't certain.

"It looks like it," Dutch said. "Their fingerprints match those found most consistently all over the house on several personal articles. The coroner will have the final say, but nobody here thinks it's anyone different."

"What about the woman on the stairs?"

"That was Rosa Torrez," Dutch said with a sad sigh. "She was the Roswells' live-in housekeeper. I met her when I first came out here to do the estimate. Really nice woman. APD found her green card in a purse located in one of the back bedrooms that appears to be hers. APD is working to locate her next of kin."

"Anybody know what the motive was, yet?" I asked.

Dutch rubbed the back of his neck and adjusted the lanyard that held his FBI badge. "Definitely a robbery, but we're not sure yet if the murders were premeditated," he said. "There's cash and a laptop missing. The safe in the panic room was also breached, but I think that Andy Roswell might've opened it himself."

I studied the house with my intuitive senses in silence for a moment. The energy surrounding the home was thick with violence and tragedy. I hate lingering at crime scenes for that very reason. "The scene is all wrong," I said to him. "Why weren't any of the alarms triggered?"

"I can't say for sure, but it looks like they'd been disabled. There's a panic button in the security room, but it was never triggered. My guess is that the Roswells turned off the alarm during the day, and only set it at night, so the home would've been vulnerable if the home invasion happened after about nine a.m. And it looks like the motor to the panic room door still wasn't working, which means they were even more vulnerable to an attack."

There was a pause between us and I wondered if Dutch was feeling as infuriated as I was about the replacement kits for the motor to the panic room doors not working. If Dave had been able to fix the door when he was here, maybe the Roswells would still be alive.

"Was there any security footage?" I asked.

Dutch stood up from his squatted position to kick at a pebble. He didn't answer me right away and there was a tense set to his shoulders, and a look on his face I didn't at all like. He seemed riddled with guilt. And even though the malfunction with the door wasn't in any way his fault, I suspected he was blaming himself for it regardless.

"Babe?" I asked.

Rubbing his neck again, he said, "The cameras were disabled. There's no footage."

My brow furrowed. "Wait, if the cameras were disabled, wouldn't you still have access to the feed right beforehand? Doesn't that get routed to some security center somewhere?" I could've sworn I remembered Dutch talking about how, during a home invasion scenario when a client was sealed inside one of the panic rooms, a video camera would automatically route the feed directly to a monitored hub, and police would be alerted while someone in a remote location kept in communication with the homeowners.

"I've checked, Abs. The surveillance cameras were taken offline sometime within the past couple of days."

"So, whoever breached the house knew about the cameras and somehow took them off-line right before the house was breached?"

Dutch cleared his throat. "Yeah."

An unsettling feeling planted itself in the center of my chest. "How could someone do that?"

He shook his head. "It would've required some extensive casing of the house. Which means that a lot of thought and effort went into this home invasion, and it wouldn't have been random. Someone targeted them, learned their habits, took out the security cameras, might've even known about the malfunctioning door to the panic room, and waited to hit them at exactly the right time when they'd be the most vulnerable."

Again I looked toward the house and this time I shuddered. I felt so strongly that what we'd discovered inside was only a piece of a larger puzzle. There was more information to come that would have an even bigger significance in some way.

Brice walked up to us with Candice at his side. "Hey," he said by way of greeting before focusing on me. "Cooper, are you okay?"

"I'm fine, Brice, thanks," I said, standing up from my seat on the curb. While I was grateful for his inquiry, I seriously wished people would stop asking me that. The truth was, I wasn't fine, but the more attention that was called to me, the less focus went to what was important—namely, the murders of the Roswells and their housekeeper. "Did you guys learn anything?"

I knew that Dutch, Brice, and Candice had been busy talking to different law-enforcement individuals at the crime scene, hoping to gain as much information as possible from all the sources available. The murders weren't FBI jurisdiction, but because Candice and I had been first on the scene, and Dutch and Brice were head of the company that provided a security room for the couple, and all four of us were connected to the FBI, there was information to share and to glean.

"There's a fourth victim," Brice said with a grimace. "They just found another of the Roswells' staff in the backyard."

I sucked in some air. "Who was it?"

"Looks like a groundskeeper," he said. "A man with a set of pruning shears still in his hands was shot in the back of the head at point-blank range. He was wearing earbuds and his music was turned up, so I doubt he ever knew what was happening inside the house before he was killed. There was ID in his pocket, and APD is working to notify his next of kin along with everyone else murdered here."

I muttered an expletive and turned my head away for a moment. I hated getting emotional in front of people, but that rarely stopped me from having all sorts of meltdowns on a regular basis. Dutch laid a supportive hand on my shoulder, and swallowing past the lump in my throat, I was able to focus on my companions again.

"Candice?" Dutch asked when he saw that I was okay.

"APD is going door-to-door asking neighbors for any surveillance footage of the road. Two doors in that direction," she said, pointing to her right, "they hit pay dirt. There's a camera pointed directly at the street. With any luck it'll give us a glimpse of the killer or killers and what kind of vehicle they may have been driving."

"APD thinks the whole thing went down sometime before six p.m. yesterday," Brice said.

"So, after Dave had come and gone," Candice said. I knew why she made that declaration. If Dave had been here, he would've been one of the bodies found inside. I wanted to feel relief that he'd escaped such a close call, but I could only feel an anxious sadness and worry in the pit of my stomach. We still didn't know where Dave was, and that alone was troubling enough without the added note that he'd been in a home that'd later seen such unspeakable violence.

"That's some relief at least," Dutch said.

"Maybe that's why the alarm had been disabled," Brice said. "Maybe they turned it off to let Dave in and forgot to turn it back on again after he left."

"That'd be tragic," Candice said sadly.

We all nodded without comment and for a long moment the four of us were silent.

I glanced again at the security gate, which blocked off the driveway from the street. "How did they get past that gate? I mean, there's a call box, right? If the Roswells were home, why would they let strangers through the gate without first being sure who they were?"

"Don't know," Brice said. I suddenly realized he looked pale and very troubled. Brice's temperament was a lot like my husband's: cool and collected, especially at crime scenes. But this scene had clearly rattled him. I thought it must be because the Roswells were clients and all the security measures Safe Chambers had put into place had so clearly failed.

"What about fingerprints?" I asked, still watching that same tech work carefully and methodically to document the bloody handprint before he'd attempt to remove it.

Brice glanced behind him toward the tech. "So far, that one handprint seems to be the only one we can link directly to the murders. It doesn't already belong to anyone dead in there," he said. "They're taking their time pulling it before they do a search on IAFIS."

IAFIS stood for Integrated Automated Fingerprint Identification System, which was a national fingerprint database kept by the FBI but used by local law enforcement everywhere. It held something like a hundred million fingerprints, and once a new set of prints was uploaded, the system could search through all those records to find a match. Sometimes it found a match fairly quickly. Sometimes it took a while. Everything usually depended on the quality of the print recovered from a crime scene, which was why removing the prints from the Roswells' security gate was so critical and needed to be done as perfectly as possible.

"Has anyone commented on known enemies of the Roswells?" Dutch asked Brice and Candice.

They both shook their heads. "Not yet," Candice said. "I was going to work on that after we leave here."

Brice glanced sideways at his wife. I knew that even though APD was willing to dole out a little information to us about the case, they sure weren't going to feel warmly about sharing the actual investigation should Brice and Dutch decide to join the team in any official capacity.

"You're going to investigate?" Brice asked Candice.

"I am," she said, squaring her shoulders, as if she was anticipating an argument from her husband.

"Good," he said. "Keep Dutch and me in the loop, okay?"

Candice offered him a soft smile. "Of course."

"I'm in too, Candice," I said.

It was Dutch's turn to eye me sideways, his concern for my well-being after the trauma of witnessing the crime scene evident in his expression. "You sure that's a good idea, babe?"

"No," I confessed. "But I'm going to do it anyway. We can work this case and look for Dave, since one led to the other and I almost never think that's a coincidence."

Just then a man in a black dress shirt and tan slacks approached us. He was waving an electronic tablet as if he'd discovered a piece of evidence he wanted to share. "Harrison," he said.

"Detective Vargas," Brice said. "You find something?"

Vargas—a stout man I'd put in his midforties—turned to position his tablet directly in front of Brice. Dutch, Candice, and I moved to stand behind the two men and look over their shoulders. "I just pulled this off the security cam of the house down the street. The guy who owns it said he heard someone setting off a firecracker sometime in the early afternoon—he thinks it was sometime after noon but before three. He said it bothered him that one of his neighbors was ignoring the fireworks ban, and after stewing about it for a while, he sent an e-mail to the neighborhood association about it. The time stamp on the e-mail was three ten p.m."

"You think he heard a gunshot, not a firework," Dutch said.

Vargas nodded. "I just talked to the ME inside and asked him if it was possible that the murders went down earlier than between four and six. He's a new guy and this is only his fourth scene on his own. He said that it was definitely possible, especially accounting for the different liver temps of all four vics and the varying temps of the areas where they were found.

"Anyway, after reviewing every car on the surveillance video that came down the road here between noon and three, the only one that stands out is this one of a truck taken at one oh six p.m."

A jolt of alarm went through me, and judging by the expressions on Candice's and Dutch's faces, they were equally worried about the new revelation.

Unaware of our reaction, Vargas tapped the screen with one fat finger, and a short clip of video began to play. The time-stamped video was grainy and in black and white, but a truck could be seen moving slowly down the street, quite obviously under the speed limit, as if the driver was searching for an address. It made one slow pass by the camera, then reappeared, moving on the opposite side of the street before making a U-turn and heading back again toward the Roswells' home. It reminded me of a shark circling its prey, but really appeared to be someone casing the street, looking for any signs of trouble before striking.

The truck was a light-colored—probably silver—Ford F-150 with an extended cab. No other truck is as plentiful on Texas roads as the F-150. It's everywhere, and easy to identify. But this particular truck was distinctive for another reason even beyond the extended cab. There was a black truck box at the front of the bed that was usually a common aftermarket purchase for those folks who worked in the construction industry. There was too little detail to make out the driver, but the truck looked a *lot* like the one Dave drove. Still, the last time I'd seen Dave's truck, it'd been absent the dent in the right front bumper, but maybe that'd been the result of an unexpected off-road slip down a steep embankment.

And although the video showed no clear image of the driver, it was obvious to me that it was Dave's truck. Especially since he'd been set to arrive at the Roswells' home right around one p.m. And if I was right and it was Dave's truck, then the path he drove on that video was even more suspicious, because Dave had been out to this house many, many times, and there was no way he would've needed to make two passes to find the house. He would've gone straight there, so that pattern of easing up and down the street slowly had another, perhaps sinister purpose.

I took my gaze off the video to glance at my companions and judging by the set to everyone else's shoulders, they were thinking the same thing I was. Only Detective Vargas was clueless to our worries. "There's no view of the license plate," he said, "but that damage to the front bumper might help us find this truck on some traffic cams and maybe even one of the tollways."

We'd been planning on using that very tactic to track down Dave, and although I still very much wanted to find my friend, I wasn't so sure that I wanted to find out what he'd been involved in.

At that moment, Candice moved away from us, and my gaze followed her as she walked over to the tech working on the bloody handprint on the gate. It appeared he was getting ready to lift the print.

Candice sidled up quietly next to him and used her phone to take several close-up photos of the handprint. The tech didn't look thrilled to have her crowd his space, but she carried herself with such authority that he didn't verbally protest.

She then rejoined us a moment later, sliding her phone into her purse and offering us a serious look.

I knew what she was thinking. I was thinking the same thing. And I hated both of us for it.

I glanced back at that bloody handprint. To my knowledge, Dave had never committed a crime, but he had been fingerprinted about seven years earlier when he'd saved me from a guy who'd tried to kill me. He'd tossed that asshole down a set of basement stairs, killing the man but saving my life.

It'd been a routine thing when the local Michigan police had shown up to take our statements and fingerprint Dave, placing him into temporary custody until he was cleared of all charges just a few days later.

The probability that his fingerprints had then been uploaded into IAFIS was around a hundred percent; it was simply protocol for the Royal Oak PD, and I knew that because Dutch had been a detective there before he got a job with the FBI.

In other words, Dave was in the system. And if that was his bloody handprint on the security gate, then APD would also know it before too long.

Candice would want our team to know it first, though, so it was time to get the hell out of there and hurry to analyze some loops and whorls.

A glance at Dutch and Brice told us they were each thinking what I was, and they'd also both seen Candice slide over to the handprint and snap the pic.

Behind Vargas's back, I motioned to Candice and myself, then pointed to the bloody handprint on the gate. Dutch nodded, but Brice seemed reluctant to give his assent.

Candice reached over and squeezed his hand and he finally shrugged his okay.

"Do you need Candice and me for anything else, Detective?" I asked Vargas. Another detective had taken my statement a few hours earlier, but I remembered that Vargas had taken Candice's statement and had talked to her at length about what she'd seen when we first entered the home.

He looked over his shoulder at me as if he was having trouble placing me at first, but then he seemed to remember. "No, you can go," he said. "I'll call if I have any follow-up questions."

"Thanks," Candice and I said before we each turned to our husbands for a quick kiss on the cheek and ducked away back to Candice's car, which was now parked well down the street.

Neither of us spoke until we'd driven about a half mile away from the Roswells' home. "Maybe it's not his bloody hand on that gate," Candice said.

I didn't reply. That terrible, worried knot in the pit of my stomach felt heavier and harder to bear.

"We'll get back to the office, upload the photo of the handprint, and compare it to Dave's, and then we'll see. It wasn't him. It *couldn't* be him, Abs. Not our Dave. He couldn't be mixed up in something like this. Right?"

I turned my head toward the window and closed my eyes.

"Hey," Candice said after a moment, reaching for my hand to squeeze it.

I turned back to her. There were tears in my eyes that I couldn't hold back.

She took one look at my anguished face and her expression fell. "Fuck."

I went back to staring out the window.

It wasn't until we got back to the office that we realized we didn't have anything handy that might have Dave's fingerprints on it. He hadn't done any work at my house in quite some time, and to my knowledge he'd never been to my office. So the only way to get something with his prints on it was to call Gwen and nonchalantly ask her about it.

Candice made the call. "Hi, Gwen," she said while I listened. "We haven't found Dave yet, but we're not giving up until we do.

I think what might help is to have a set of his fingerprints to keep on file here, just in case we suspect he's been somewhere and we can compare any prints we find to his." There was a pause, then, "Yeah, it's a new thing we do in investigations. I know it sounds weird, but when there's no surveillance footage, it can be the next best thing for finding out where someone's actually been. What I need is for a clear set of Dave's prints."

There was another pause, then, "Well, anything that he uses a lot. Like his hairbrush might be perfect if he has one."

Dave had very long hair, which he kept in a braid while he worked. He looked like an aging hippie, and in fact, he was. There was no way he used a comb given the amount and length of his hair. I had to give Candice props for thinking of his hairbrush.

"Awesome," Candice said as she gave me a thumbs-up. "No, you stay put. Abby and I can come over and pick it up. Just shoot me your address via text and we'll see you in about half an hour."

Once she'd hung up, Candice said, "Let me upload the photo from the crime scene to my computer. Then we'll head over to get Dave's hairbrush."

"Okay," I said softly, before I followed with, "How long do you think it'll take APD to run those prints?"

"Not long. But the techs are going to be at that crime scene for several more hours at least. There's a lot to catalog and process. With any luck we'll be finished with our comparison well before they start theirs."

My phone pinged with an incoming text as Candice and I made our way back down to her car. "It's Dutch," I said. "He wants to know if we have anything yet."

"Tell him it'll be at least two hours or so from now."

I sent Dutch the note and Candice and I didn't really talk again until we pulled into Gwen and Dave's driveway twenty minutes later. I'd never been to Dave's house before. It was surprising in some ways, not surprising in others.

He and Gwen lived in a single-level ranch with an attached garage, a brown brick facade, and chocolate-colored shutters.

His front door was like a piece of art, carved wood with intricate relief and a small glass window at eye level. Candice rang the bell and we heard the clicking of heels on a wood floor approaching.

When Gwen pulled the door open, I was struck by how pretty and petite she was.

Much like her husband, Gwen had long blond hair with streaks of white, pulled back away from her face and braided down her back. Her eyes were a gorgeous ice blue, and her nose was delicate. She was thin, and shorter than me by a few inches, making her appear almost doll-like. But there was something about the set to her eyes that embodied strength.

Dressed in torn jeans and what looked like one of Dave's white T-shirts (given the fit on her), she sighed with either fatigue or relief when she saw us. "I've got it right here," she said, waving us forward into the home.

Candice and I stepped over the threshold and looked around. The place was neat as a pin, and the fresh scent of lemon and pine wafted up to us. Down the hall I could see that a vacuum was still plugged into the wall socket, and I thought that Gwen had probably been trying to deal with her frayed nerves by cleaning.

We followed her down the hall to a room just off the central hallway. It appeared to be a den, containing shelves and shelves of books and a big leather chair that had seen a lot of use, given the rounded dent in the cushion. Dave's hairbrush was resting on the side table next to the chair. I was relieved to see it was an older brush with a big round back and a large handle. There'd be plenty of prints on it.

Candice pulled a Baggie out of her pocket. "Did you handle the brush much?" she asked. I hoped that Gwen hadn't smeared any of Dave's prints.

"No," Gwen said. "I was very careful. I used my rubber gloves to bring it in here."

"Perfect," Candice said, picking up the brush only after placing her hand inside the bag and then turning it inside out. "We'll get this back to either you or Dave in the next day or two."

"Don't lose it," Gwen said as she wrung her hands together. "That brush was a present from Dave's mom. She left us last year, and I'd hate for anything to happen to it."

I remembered hearing about Dave's mom passing away the previous December. Dutch and I had sent flowers and a card. "We'll be extra careful, then," Candice assured her.

Gwen attempted to offer us a smile, but she really couldn't get one to form. Her eyes misted and she wrung her hands some more. "I'm just so worried about him," she said.

"Us too," I told her.

"I can't understand why he doesn't call or come home," she said next.

Us either, I thought but didn't say.

Gwen sighed and stared around as if she were lost in her own home. "I have an early meeting tomorrow with several staff members that I normally would never miss, but right now I can't imagine going in and being able to focus."

"What do you do?" Candice asked.

"I work for a health insurance company. I'm a registered nurse and I oversee compliance protocols for our entire company. Tomorrow I'm supposed to lecture my staff about several key changes in the health-care code, but I can't even think about what I want for dinner or even if I *want* dinner, much less speak coherently to a dozen staff members about the recent changes."

"Take the day off," I told her. I felt like she needed to give herself permission to take care of herself. "Work will still be there when you're ready to get back to it. Your staff will carry on without you for a day or two and everyone will understand, given the situation."

A tear leaked down Gwen's cheek as I spoke. She wiped it away and said, "Maybe you're right."

"I am," I assured her. "Anyway, we should get back to work finding him." I was uncomfortable in her presence. Maybe it was just the fact that we knew things that she didn't, and suspected things that even we were too nervous to say out loud. It all felt icky to me.

"Sorry," she said, her face flushing. "I didn't mean to keep you."

"No worries," I said, and Candice and I turned toward the door.

Gwen caught my arm just as we were about to leave and she said, "Please find him, Abby. Please. I love him. I love him so much."

I took a deep steadying breath. It was hard to look Gwen in the eye, and even harder to work past the giant lump in my throat. "We love Dave too, Gwen," I said to her. "Candice and I won't stop until we find him. I promise you."

Gwen looked at me earnestly for a moment before she launched herself at me in a big hug. She held on so tight it was hard to breathe. I hugged her back just as firmly, and thought it was so strange that she and I had never met before, even though we cared about the same person so very much.

At last she let me go, and Candice stepped forward to hug her too, and then we were off to find out what the hell had happened to Dave McKenzie.

Chapter Six

. . .

Once we were back at the office, Candice wasted no time pulling prints from the hairbrush. She had several within an hour, and just a few minutes after that, we were each comparing them with the enlarged image of the bloody handprint on her laptop.

It took only moments to discover several similarities. A little longer to determine that two of the prints from the handle on the hairbrush perfectly matched the index and middle fingers of the handprint found at the Roswells' house.

"Son of a bitch," Candice whispered as she traced with her pencil the distinctive loop and whorl pattern between the prints. Turning to me, she said, "It's him. He was there."

I shook my head. "It's not what we think. It can't be. I mean, Dave essentially built that panic room. His prints would be all over the place, right?"

Candice's lips pressed down in a frown. "Abs . . . the finger-prints I'm comparing here weren't in the panic room. They were on the security gate, which he shouldn't have needed to touch. Not to mention the fact that this handprint is covered in blood. That can only mean that Dave's whole palm was bloody when he transferred his prints to the gate."

I shook my head again and started pacing back and forth behind her chair. "There's got to be some logical explanation!"

"The only one that comes to mind is the obvious, which is that he murdered the Roswells and their staff," she said.

That stopped me in my tracks. "Candice . . . he didn't, okay? Not Dave McKenzie. No way. He couldn't!"

"How do you know, honey?"

I balled my hands into fists. I was scared, and upset, and so furious with Dave. What the hell had he gotten himself into? "Because I know Dave. Hell, *you* know Dave! He couldn't kill any—"

And then I remembered. Dave *had* killed someone. He'd killed for me, even.

I went back to pacing.

Candice perhaps took pity on me because she also knew that Dave had killed someone to save me; she said, "I think it might be a good idea to come up with a scenario where Dave left this handprint but didn't actually commit the crime."

I snapped my fingers and pointed at her. "Yes! Yes, okay, so . . . he cut himself when he was building the panic room and left his handprint behind."

Candice squinted skeptically at me. "Do you remember Dave cutting himself badly enough on a job to leave behind a full bloody impression of his hand?"

I scowled. "No. But that doesn't mean that he didn't. Maybe he just cut himself and took care of it with a few stitches and didn't tell any of us about it."

Candice drummed her fingers on the desk. "So, you're saying that *Dave McKenzie* wouldn't tell *us* about a severe cut to his hand that he got while on the job?"

I balled my fists in frustration again. A month previously Dave had smashed his thumb with a hammer and it was all we heard about for the next three days. His nail had turned purple and we seemed to get a daily update on the saga of Dave's poor swollen thumb. "Okay, so how about this? Dave checked in on the Roswells, found them dead, then fled the scene because it was so traumatic for him."

Candice tapped her chin. "Why didn't he call nine-one-one?"

"Like I said, he was too traumatized."

"Why didn't he go home to his wife and tell her? Or call Dutch or Brice, or even one of us?"

I held up three fingers and ticked them down. "Traumatized, traumatized, traumatized. Oh, *and* he lost his phone, remember? Maybe he *couldn't* call any one of us!"

"Seriously?" she asked me. "You're going with, he lost his phone and didn't ask anyone to borrow their phone because he couldn't remember any of our numbers?"

"Oh, please, Candice! That's not so weird. I mean, all I ever do to call you is swipe across your name on my favorites list. Nobody remembers anybody's phone number anymore."

"I do."

I lowered my lids. "Really? What's my number?"

"Five-one-two, five-five-five, seven-six-one-eight."

"Fine, so *you* remember my number. Maybe Dave didn't."

"Even if he didn't remember any of our numbers, he'd probably remember Gwen's. And he was in his truck, Abs. He could've just driven home."

"Maybe he was too freaked-out and he left his truck behind."

"Then where's the truck?"

"Maybe it got towed."

Candice's brows knit together. "It got towed from the driveway of a dead couple? Without anyone alerting police?"

"Why are you poking so many holes in my theories?" I yelled, so frustrated because I couldn't come up with a plausible scenario to explain why Dave's bloody handprint was found at a murder scene he'd left in haste and hadn't been heard from since.

Candice laced her fingers together and sat back in her chair to look up at me over her shoulder. "Because," she said gently, "I'm as desperate as you are to come up with a reason why Dave is in the clear on this. An hour or two from now, APD is going to get their own analysis of the handprint back and realize that Dave McKenzie was there. And they're also going to see that he drives a silver F-one-fifty of the same type that was in the video, seen driving down the street toward the Roswells', and just like that, they're going to peg Dave as the killer. And then they're going to figure out that Dave hasn't been seen or heard from in over twenty-four hours, and his wife just filed a missing persons report. And then they're going to begin a citywide search, and they're going to find him, charge him with murder, and stop looking for any other suspects, because that bloody handprint is as good as a smoking gun. In other words, in an hour or two, APD is *literally* going to catch him red-handed."

I moved away from my position behind Candice and over to one of her visitor chairs. Sinking down onto the cushion, I bent over and put my head in my hands, closing my eyes in dismay. This was so bad. This was so very, very bad. "We need to call the boys," I said when no other theories came to mind.

"Yeah," she said with a sad sigh. "I know, but I don't want to do it. I'm sure that after the video Vargas played for us, they already suspect it's Dave's print, but I'm not looking forward to confirming it, given that this is their business partner and friend we're talking about."

"Maybe they'll have a scenario that makes sense?" I suggested, lifting my head to look at her.

"The only person that has that scenario is Dave. And right now, we don't know where the hell he is."

I sat up tall again as a thought hit me. "One thing we haven't even considered here is motive, or lack thereof."

She blinked. "Motive? You mean, Dave's possible motive for murdering the Roswells and their staff?"

"Yes. I mean, other than the obvious money thing, which doesn't really make sense to me, because Dave's been doing well lately. Business is booming, right?"

"It is."

"And Dave gets an equal cut of the profits just like Brice and Dutch. While I don't know figures, I do know that Dutch has been extra happy every Sunday night when he's finished balancing the books. We've been making a good profit, and there's more work coming. I think it's even safe to suggest that Dave's doing better financially than he's ever done in his life."

"The Roswells were still worth far more than Dave could even hope to make over the course of a lifetime, Abs."

"But if they're dead, what value would they be to him?"

"Maybe they had a lot of money hidden in that panic room," she theorized.

"Really? How much money could they have on hand?"

I tried to recall the size of the Roswells' safe, where I could only guess they'd stashed some emergency funds. It'd been a decent-sized safe, about three feet tall by two feet wide by another two feet deep.

Candice shrugged. "I don't know, maybe at most a couple million, but probably a lot less than that."

"So, what? Dave just throws away everything he's ever built— his life with his wife, his booming business—and all of his morals for a couple million dollars?"

Candice closed her laptop and rubbed her temples. "It doesn't sound at all like Dave, does it?"

"No," I said. "And you know what else is bothering me?"

"Besides absolutely everything about this case so far?"

"Yes, besides all of that. What else is bothering me is that the Roswells were killed with a semiautomatic, right?"

Candice grimaced. "From what I saw at the crime scene, I'd guess that the killer used an AR-fifteen."

"Dave does own a gun," I said. "He's got a hunting rifle for when he heads back up north to go deer hunting with his brother. And I know that because every year in November he's gone for the week before Thanksgiving to go do his bonding-in-the-woods thing. But I remember a talk we had once when he got back about how he'd camped next to some guys who were shooting up the woods with an AR-fifteen, and he was sickened by it. He specifically told me that nobody should be able to own one of those, because they're too dangerous in the hands of drunken amateurs."

"Okay," she said. "So what's your point?"

"My point is that if Dave McKenzie were going to suddenly lose all common sense, and every one of his morals, to murder the Roswells in cold blood for this supposed cash they may or may not have had in their panic room safe, then he sure as hell wouldn't bring an assault rifle to do the job. He'd bring his regular rifle. Or a handgun. He wouldn't make it messy."

Candice slowly nodded. Murdering anyone in cold blood was certainly out of character for the Dave that we all knew and loved, but even beyond that, the method used to commit the murders wasn't a choice Dave would ever even think to make. He just wouldn't, and I knew by the expression on Candice's face that she could see that as well as I could.

"And the other thing that's bugging me is the landscaper in the backyard," I added. Candice tilted her head curiously. I got up and started to pace again. "What possible reason would Dave have to kill a random man who had his earbuds in and probably never even knew that anything was going on, or had gone on, inside the house? It just doesn't make sense why Dave would be inside killing Rosa and the Roswells, and then go outside to murder this landscaper by sneaking up on him from behind and shooting him in the back of the head."

"Maybe he didn't want to leave any witnesses behind," Candice said, playing devil's advocate.

I shook my head. "So he shoots the gardener but leaves his bloody handprint on the gate for everyone to see when he knows his fingerprints are in the system? No way, Candice. Dave might be a little naive about a lot of things, but he's not stupid. Even he'd know that his fingerprints could be traced back to him."

"Maybe the gardener saw something and Dave panicked."

I shook my head again. "If he saw something, he wouldn't go on pruning the damn hedges. Plus, there's just something so cold-blooded about the way that guy was killed. I know that the crime scene in the house was unspeakably awful, but it takes an extra dose of evil to walk up to someone from behind and shoot them in the back of the head.

"My point is that even if Dave had had a psychotic break, he'd still retain an essence of himself and his experiences. Shooting that man in the back of the head is probably the most compelling reason I'm one hundred percent convinced Dave did not do this."

"Okay, so you're right. None of it fits with a Dave-going-cuckoo-for-Cocoa-Puffs theory."

"None of it fits *Dave*," I corrected. "He's not the killer. He just isn't."

"Fine," she said, putting her elbows on the desk and steepling her fingers under her chin. "Then tell me how his hand became covered in the victim's blood and landed on the gate entrance."

"That . . . I can't explain. But we have to also consider that his handprint on that gate tells us *only* that, at some point after the murders, Dave was physically there. It doesn't tell us that he actually committed the crime."

"Still," she said, "his not going home last night or calling any of us makes him look guilty as hell."

"Or does it?" I asked.

"Are you referring to the traumatized theory again?"

"In a way. What if we're looking at this all wrong? What if Dave *was* there at the time of the murders, but maybe he was hidden in the house and he witnessed who did it and now he's on the run because he's seen too much?"

Candice seemed to consider that before speaking. "That's the best scenario you've come up with yet."

"We have to find Dave before the cops do," I said.

"We do," she agreed, and then her gaze slid to her phone. "This is going to get sticky for our men."

"It's already sticky. Dave's the business partner to two FBI agents who have a connection to the murdered couple."

Candice eyed me sharply. "Did you mention in your witness statement that we arrived at the Roswells' searching for clues about our missing friend who was supposed to do some work at their house yesterday?"

"I didn't." At the time I was interviewed, I was still in a bit of shock about what I'd seen inside the home, and I'd consciously thought to skip over what I'd considered the unimportant details—our search for Dave—to the important details: the dead people inside the home. "All I said was that we'd come to the house as a favor to our husbands, who own a construction company, to check up on some work that was done for the Roswells."

Candice blew out a breath. "I said something similar. But now I'm wondering if that was such a good idea. It could appear like we were withholding information."

"I'm positive it'll appear like that," I said. "And when it does, Dutch and Brice could land in serious hot water both with APD and the FBI."

"Not to mention the potential lawsuit," Candice said.

I felt light-headed. "Lawsuit?"

Candice seemed to sink lower in her chair. "Dave is part owner of Safe Chambers. If he's caught up in this mess and found guilty, the company could be sued into the ground by the Roswells' estate holders."

I gulped. "That sounds very, very bad."

"That's 'cuz it is," Candice said frankly. She then reached for the phone and made the call while I sat miserably in the chair across from her.

Chapter Seven

. . .

Candice called Brice and put the phone on speaker. "Hey, my love," he said warmly when he answered. In spite of everything, that made me grin. Brice was such a tough cookie, but he had the sweetest of sweet spots for his wife.

"Hi," Candice said, reddening in the cheeks a little when I grinned at her. "I've got you on speaker and I'm here with Abby."

"Ah," he said, and I could imagine a slight blush hitting his cheeks too. "What've you two got for us?"

"The bloody handprint on the Roswells' gate is Dave's."

There was a pause, then, "Fuck."

My brow rose. Brice wasn't big on the swearing. That was my job, and one I took seriously. "You're sure?" he said next.

"Yes, unfortunately," Candice told him.

There was some mumbling then, and I thought I heard Dutch's voice in the background mimic Brice's exact sentiment. Then Brice said to us, "That's bad."

"It is," she said. "For a whole lot of reasons."

"We'll have to call APD," he said next.

"I agree," Candice said; then she paused before she added, "And maybe you should also call your company attorney."

Brice grunted on the other end of the line as if he'd been elbowed in the side. "Jesus. This is gonna snowball for us fast," he said. "We'll have to talk to Gaston too. He may pull us off duty until this gets resolved."

Bill Gaston was the regional director for the Austin Bureau. He was Brice's boss, and someone I genuinely liked but was also a tiny bit terrified of.

"Would Gaston really do that?" I asked.

"I probably would if I were him," Brice said.

"We're going to continue to work the case privately," Candice told him.

Brice was silent for a moment, but then he said, "Let me run that by Gaston first."

"You can run anything you like by him, but as a private citizen who holds a PI license, I can investigate anything I want," Candice said firmly.

Brice sighed audibly. "Sometimes I think you try to make my life harder."

"Once you tell the cops that the prints and the truck are a match for Dave, they'll peg him for the killer and they won't look at anybody else. This is the only way we're going to figure out what the hell happened at that residence."

"You guys don't think Dave did this, do you?" Brice suddenly asked.

"No," I said quickly, and glared at Candice when she hesitated to say it too.

"Good," Brice said. "Me either."

"I'm in that camp," Dutch said, and I realized that Brice had switched the phone to speaker. "Something else is going on here."

"All the more reason for Abby and me to continue the investigation, privately."

There was a very long pause on Brice's end of the line. I wondered if he'd put the microphone on mute while he and Dutch discussed it. At last he said, "Fine. But you can't mention to anyone you interview that you're a consultant with us, Candice. You can't link the FBI back to the case."

"I won't," she said. I looked at her sharply because my lie detector had just gone off, big-time.

She ignored me and said that she'd be in touch as soon as she learned something useful, then clicked off so that Brice and Dutch could reach out to APD.

"We can't use our credentials," I told her, reiterating Brice's warning.

Candice folded her hands on the desktop and considered me with a determined expression. "We'll use every means at our disposal to get to the bottom of this case, Sundance. And if that means throwing our FBI consultant IDs around, then I won't hesitate to do that."

"It's too risky."

"It's only risky if we get caught or if Dave actually had something to do with murdering those four people. I don't plan on getting caught, and according to you, he's innocent of that crime. Unless your intuition is telling you something else now?"

I squirmed in my chair. I didn't think Dave had murdered anyone in cold blood, but there was also a lot going on regarding him right now, and I wasn't sure I could pick the pieces apart well enough to understand how he was connected. "I still believe he's innocent and that there's something else going on here."

"Okay, then," she said, as if the matter were settled. "Let's come up with a game plan."

"Where did you want to start?" I asked. I'll admit I was at a complete loss as to how to proceed.

"I think our time of driving all over the city looking for Dave is over, and now it's time to start calling people."

"Who're we going to call?" I asked.

Candice rocked back in her seat. "Anyone who may have a connection to Dave. His friends. His family. His construction crew."

"Do we have all that info?" I asked.

"No, but I can call Gwen and get a list of his friends and have her call his extended family. And in the meantime you can text

Dutch and ask him for a contact list of the construction crew. He should have it, since he does payroll."

"That's gonna be a lot of people," I said with a small groan. Safe Chambers had seven construction crews of three to four guys each.

"I'm sure," she said, already reaching for the phone. "So there's no time to waste, is there?"

I took the hint and got up to head to my office and request the info from Dutch. I also might have held a little pity party for myself while I was at it.

Candice and I spent the whole rest of the day calling everyone on the lists that both Gwen and Dutch had sent us. I think I alone made thirty calls, and not one person had heard from Dave, but several had sent him messages about projects and schedules and he'd never gotten back to them. There was one curious thing, however; it seemed that the last time anyone had heard from Dave was early Saturday morning. One guy from his crew, Alejandro, told me he'd gotten a call from Dave the day before about that time to see if Alejandro could use his magic to fix a rip in the drywall at one of the sites. "I'm very good with drywall repairs," the man told me proudly.

"How did Dave seem on that call, Alejandro?"

"Fine. He was, you know, just normal."

"He didn't seem tense?"

"No."

"What time was this?"

"Oh, I don't know. It was early. Maybe seven?"

"How long did you talk?"

"A couple of minutes," he said. "He wanted to know if I was ready for the baby."

"Baby?"

"Yeah, my missus, she's due at the end of the month."

My mind filled with the image of a blue baby rattle. "You're having a boy."

"Oh, we don't know yet. We want to be surprised."

I felt my cheeks flush. I'd just unwittingly spoiled the surprise, but luckily, Alejandro didn't seem to realize it was a predictive statement. "Well, congratulations," I said quickly. "That's great. But, getting back to Dave, you're sure he sounded normal?"

"Yes, Mrs. Rivers. He was very normal. He even told me a joke."

"He did?"

"Yeah, let me think—it was pretty good. Oh, yeah, what do you get when you cross a crocodile with a cow?"

"What?"

"No idea, but if I were you, I wouldn't try milking it."

I chuckled in spite of myself. And then I felt sad. Dave loved jokes. He usually had a new one every day, and knowing that he was in trouble hit me right in the heartstrings. "Thanks, Alejandro," I said, my voice cracking with emotion.

I think he noticed, because he said, "Don't worry, Mrs. Rivers. He'll turn up."

"Yeah," I said, that knot of worry getting a little bigger in the pit of my stomach. "If you hear from him, though, call me or Dutch right away."

"You got it," he promised.

After hanging up with Alejandro, I found Candice at her desk, with her chair swiveled around to face the window, putting her back to me. I stopped when I heard the distinct sound of a sniffle and saw her wipe her eyes. "Hey," I said softly.

She jumped slightly and wiped her other cheek before turning to me. Adopting a forced smile, she said, "Any luck?"

"No. You?"

The smile vanished. "No. Where could he be, Sundance?"

I shrugged. "I have no idea."

Candice cleared her throat and fiddled with a paper clip from her desk. "Brice called a little while ago. He made one call right

after alerting APD, and that was to a buddy at TSA. Dave Mc-
Kenzie appears to still be in the country. No one using his passport
has flown out of the U.S."

"I take it his name is now on a watch list."

"Yes. If he shows up at any airport, he'll be taken immediately
into custody."

"How did Brice say it went with APD?"

"He talked to Vargas, who said he'd rush the fingerprint analysis on the bloody handprint to confirm it on their end, and he
thanked Brice for the heads-up about the other clues that point to
Dave. He also said he'd keep Brice and Dutch's connection to all
this on the down low until tomorrow morning, which should give
Brice enough time to talk to Gaston."

Instinctively I reached out with my radar to assess how it would
go with Director Gaston. "He's not going to be pleased," I said.

As I spoke, my phone rang and my breath caught when I read
the display. "Speak of the devil," I whispered before I answered
the call. "Director," I said as smoothly as I could.

"Abigail," he replied warmly. Director Gaston is one of the
most formally polite men I've ever met. He's also one of the most
lethal. It's a tricky mix of characteristics that he pulls off master-
fully, by the way. "I trust you're well?"

"As well as can be expected given the circumstances, sir."

"I have no doubt that's true. Which is the reason for my call,
as I'm sure you've already guessed."

"Yes, sir."

"I've spoken to Special Agent in Charge Harrison, and Special
Agent Rivers, and they both believe that, contrary to preliminary
evidence, Dave McKenzie did not commit these murders. They're
basing their conclusions on the long friendship they've had with
him, which worries me, especially given the conflict of interest at
play here."

"I understand, sir," I said. "You think they're biased."

"I don't think, Abigail. In this situation, I know them to be
biased."

"Yes, sir," I said, because I agreed with him.

"What I want to know is, what do you think?"

My brow furrowed. "I'm probably even more biased, sir."

"Of course you are. But your intuition isn't. It speaks the truth, correct?"

"Typically."

"What is it saying about this situation?"

I took a deep breath, gathering my thoughts before replying. "It says that Dave is mixed up in this, but nothing is what it seems. There's much more to this story. How that all shakes out I don't yet know, sir. I'm sorry, I know that doesn't give you a straight answer, but I'm still trying to piece it all together myself."

Director Gaston was silent for a long time. Candice caught my eye while I waited for him to respond, and I could see the worry etched into her expression.

At last he said, "Very well, Abigail. Please give my regards to Ms. Fusco, and tell her that I wish the both of you the best of luck with your investigation into this matter."

I exhaled a breath of relief. "Yes, sir. Thank you, sir."

The line went dead and I set my phone on the desk. "What'd Gaston say?" Candice asked.

"He says he's not going to rein us in. We can investigate on our own, but I don't think we can involve Brice or Dutch until we have something solid to take to them."

"Great," she said. "Or it would be if I knew who else to call or where else to look."

I shook my head. "I'm out of ideas too."

"Feel like eating?" she asked when we both fell into silence.

"Not really."

"Wow. I never thought I'd see the day that you turned down food."

I got up and paced in front of her desk. "I'm too anxious and worried to eat."

Candice got up too. "Come on," she said, closing the lid to her laptop and heading toward the exit. "I have just the ticket for that."

*   *   *

About an hour later, in the basement gym of Candice's condo, she and I lay flat on the floor, our lungs heaving, our hair, tank tops, and leggings soaked with sweat—the end result of forty-five furious minutes alternating between box jumps, dead lifts, pull-ups, push-ups, and wall balls. The workout had been as horrible as it sounds—painful, exhausting, brutal, and seemingly unending. . . . It was exactly what I'd needed.

Feebly, I reached out and tapped Candice's arm. "Thanks," I said.

"Don't mention it."

"I'm hungry now."

She chuckled. "I knew that appetite would kick back in."

"I may be too tired to lift a fork, though."

"I may be too tired to get up off this floor."

I rolled onto my side, still breathing hard. "We could order takeout and have them deliver it."

"Here?"

"Yes. Right here. On this floor, which is my new forever home. And if we get pizza, we won't need forks."

"I thought you were off bread?"

"I am. But I think this is an emergency. I'm, like, *hungry*, Candice."

"Pauline's Pies has a vegan pizza with a cauliflower crust and soy cheese. I've had it and it's honestly good."

"Sold!"

With a small grunt, Candice pushed herself up to a sitting position. "Hey, Siri!" she called.

From the corner of the room a computer-enhanced voice said, "Yes, Candice?"

"Call Pauline's Pies."

"Calling Pauline's Pies," Siri dutifully said.

"I love you," I said to Candice.

"I love you too," Siri told me.

Candice and I both laughed and laughed.

*   *   *

Brice and Dutch found us upstairs in Candice's condo shortly after the pizza was delivered. "Hey," I said when they walked in the door.

"That smells great," Dutch said. (I knew he was talking about the pizza, because I definitely didn't smell great.)

Wrapping a protective arm around the pizza box while using my other hand to hold closer the slice I was currently devouring, I said, "Get your own, cowboy. This here pie's spoken for."

Candice pulled her pizza closer too. She hadn't ordered the vegan pie. She'd ordered something straight off their regular menu. It was crazy rare for my bestie to indulge in anything that didn't come directly out of the ground, so I fully understood her also being territorial with her very unhealthy meat lover's special with extra cheese. I mean, it'd been a long time since I'd tasted anything as good as that kind of pie, and for Candice, it'd been probably three times longer.

Brice looked at us with barely veiled annoyance and turned to Dutch. "We can have something sent up from downstairs."

"They got pizza?"

"No, but there's a chicken pasta that's good."

Dutch's face fell. I grinned at Candice and she grinned back. "Hey, Siri!" she said to the phone on the coffee table in front of her.

"Yes, Candice?"

"We're gonna need you to call Pauline's Pies again. . . ."

I came out of Candice's bathroom just as the boys' pizza was delivered. Rubbing my wet hair with a towel, I sat on the leather sofa next to Candice and sighed. "You have the best shower in the world."

She put a hand on her stomach and groaned. "I shouldn't have eaten that."

"Lightweight," I told her. I'd polished off the whole pie, while Candice had left almost half of hers.

Meanwhile Dutch and Brice had eagerly tossed open the lid of their extra-large Sicilian and weren't even bothering with plates. The smell of their dinner was amazing, and God help me, but I could've gone for a slice of that pie.

"That looks really good," I said, all hinty-like.

"It is," Dutch said, shoveling a bite into his mouth. He and Brice groaned with pleasure. Pauline knows her way around pizza. Word has it she's got a husband and a boyfriend on the side, and she's had that setup for ages. Word also has it that both know about the other. I think they tolerate the situation because Pauline knows that the ultimate love language is a perfectly prepared pizza. Her dough is just a little fluffier, a little lighter, a little chewier than her competitors'. And her toppings . . . don't even get me started! It's like shoveling a piece of heaven into your mouth.

"You guys gonna eat all of that?" I asked, licking my lips.

"It's not gluten free," Dutch said.

"I could probably handle one slice," I said.

Dutch and Brice exchanged a look, and after Brice shrugged, Dutch pulled a piece off and handed it to me. After taking a big ol' bite, I caught Candice staring at me like she thought I was weird. "What?"

"I can't believe you're able to eat that after demolishing a whole pizza."

I grinned and tapped my stomach. "Mad skills, baby."

Candice rolled her eyes and turned her attention to her husband. "How'd it go with Gaston?"

Brice swallowed and dabbed at his mouth with a napkin before speaking. "Better than expected."

"What was expected?" I asked.

"Suspension," Dutch said.

"Suspension? For what? You guys didn't do anything wrong."

"It's about how things look, sweethot," Dutch said, throwing in a little Humphrey Bogart slur. "Right now, Dave looks guilty. He's our business partner, which makes this whole thing very sticky by association. We'll be lucky if Internal Affairs stays out of it."

"Yes, I know, but I still insist that you haven't done anything wrong," I said.

"Again, Cooper, it's about perception," Brice said. "But I'll have to admit that Gaston surprised me on this one."

"By not suspending you?" Candice asked.

"Yes, and because he told us to quietly continue to look into Dave's disappearance."

"Isn't that a conflict of interest?" Candice asked.

"It is and it isn't," Brice said. "Andy Roswell's name was once linked to a Chinese espionage case."

Candice's eyes widened. "He was a spy for the Chinese?"

"No, but his company was named as a valuable target by the Chinese on a list we managed to obtain through counterintelligence."

"How long ago was this?" Candice asked.

"About three years ago. Someone from the Dallas branch met with Andy, briefed him on the threat, and the case was eventually closed. There's been no further action on it."

"So, how is that relevant?" I asked.

Dutch answered me. "It's relevant because we don't know if Andy was perhaps the target of an act of espionage gone bad, or if this had nothing to do with that."

"It had nothing to do with that," I said bluntly. Nowhere in the ether was there even a hint of a Chinese influence.

Dutch waved his slice of pizza at me. "The fact that we can't yet prove it didn't is how Brice and I are still able to look into the case, Edgar."

"Ah," I said. "Okay, so this is your ticket into the case."

"Yes," Dutch said. "But we'll have to tread very carefully. We can't interfere in the APD investigation, and if we find Dave or get a lead on where he might be, we'll need to share that immediately with their team. For now, though, we can continue to use our resources to look into the murder of Andy Roswell."

"Isn't that still a conflict of interest?" Candice asked. "What I'm saying is that Andy was your client, right?"

"He was, which is also our ticket in. Andy knew that Brice and I were FBI. We disclose that to all our clients right up front just in case they happen to place certain illegal substances inside their panic rooms before we're completely off premises."

"Like cocaine," Brice said with a snort.

"Ohmigod, you had a client that had coke in his panic room?" I said.

"We did," Dutch said, shaking his head and smirking. "Luckily, Dave saw it first and ushered Brice and me out of there, but that was a close call. We almost had to arrest the dumb bastard."

"Why didn't you?" I asked.

"Too much paperwork," Brice said with a roll of his eyes. "Plus, the guy we're talking about is a major putz. He's not smart enough to be a dealer. Dave said he saw less than an ounce out in plain sight. That's enough to get him arrested, but not enough to be worth the effort."

"So, back to how you two telling Andy you guys were FBI is relevant," Candice said.

"We could make the case that Andy had suggested he had updated information about the Chinese espionage incident that he wanted to pass along to us right before he was murdered, and now our business partner is missing," Brice said. "We can investigate Andy's murder in an effort to prove there's a connection between the information Andy wanted to pass along and the disappearance of our trusted business partner, who appears to us to have witnessed Andy's murder."

"But none of that first part's true," I said.

"Yes, but Internal Affairs and APD don't know that," Brice said with a bounce to his eyebrows.

"Gaston was the one who came up with that angle," Dutch said.

"Wow," I said. "Go, Gaston."

"It's still tricky," Dutch warned. "Dave's bloody handprint at the scene and the path his truck took on that video make his involvement questionable. We'll be riding the hairy edge of the line on this one."

"Which is why we're so glad you two have volunteered to take point on the investigation," Brice said to us.

"Yay," I said flatly to Candice. "We win again."

Brice wadded up his napkin and threw it on the empty pizza box. "Yes, you do," he agreed. "Which reminds me, did you two get anywhere with the crew?"

Candice sighed. "No. And we called everyone. I spoke to all of Dave's friends, his sister, a couple of his cousins, his mom, and an aunt in Phoenix. No one's heard from him. Abby talked to all the construction crew, and she didn't get anywhere either."

Dutch tossed his napkin on the box too. "If Dave went into hiding, he's hid good."

I shook my head. "It doesn't add up. Dutch, we *know* this guy. Unless your wild theory about some sort of espionage act is true, and Dave is some kind of super sleeper spy, I can't imagine how he could've hidden his true self from us so successfully all these years to then suddenly turn into a killer. I mean, it just doesn't make sense!"

"People can hide their true motives for years, Cooper," Brice said. "Everyone in this room has seen that firsthand. Over and over, in fact."

"Yeah, yeah, but not Dave, Brice. I mean, this took planning, right? And if it took planning, then at some point on this collision course with the Roswells, he'd have to divorce himself from his fake personality, but he didn't do that. He stayed in character until shortly before he showed up at the Roswells'."

"How do you know that?" Dutch asked.

"Yesterday morning as he was headed off to his first appointment, he called Alejandro and asked him to repair some drywall, and then he told him a joke."

Brice elbowed Dutch. "That guy and his jokes. Was it the one about the bullfrog?"

"No," I said. "This one was about the crocodile and the cow." They both cocked their heads at me, so I told the joke and everyone laughed, but we all quickly sobered. "It just doesn't make sense," I said again.

"Is there anything in the ether that can point us in a direction?" Dutch asked.

"Nothing I can tease out yet, and believe me, I've tried. The energy around Dave is urgent, but there isn't much to go on specifically. I can tell he's been involved in an act of violence, but it's almost like there's too much noise and I can't pull out any individual sounds."

Brice squinted at me. "And here I thought I was getting pretty good at deciphering your psychic speech. Do you mean he's in a noisy place?"

I mocked him by rolling my eyes. Translating into English what goes on in my intuitive brain can have its challenges. Mostly my intuition speaks in pictures, physical feelings, emotions, and other, far more intangible ways. It's like telling someone that something *feels* purple rather than describing it simply as, "looks purple." How do you explain to someone that a color has a feeling beyond what it simply looks like?

"It's like this, Brice," I said, closing my eyes as I spoke. "When I focus on Dave, his energy is very swirly and chaotic. That's not normal for him. Normally, his energy hums very steadily, like a gently flowing creek. But right now his energy is more like white-water rapids. When I look at him in his normal state, pulling a detail out of the ether about him would be as simple as peering into that creek, spying an interestingly shaped rock, and lifting it easily out of the water. But if I go looking for something like an interestingly shaped rock now, all I can see is the white water of the rapids. It's too noisy and chaotic."

"Ah," Brice said, nodding his head. "I get it. So, will his energy calm down?"

"God, I hope so," I said. "Otherwise, I'm not sure how much help I can be in tracking him."

"What about you guys?" Candice said. "Did you two have any luck through your channels?"

"No," Brice said. "We didn't finish updating the chief over at APD about the espionage angle and our need to pursue our own investigation into Andy Roswell's murder and Dave's disappearance until almost six, and he was unwilling to share any details with us about where they stand, probably because he thinks our case is bullshit and he doesn't trust us to stay out of the way.

"The truth, though, is that I'm not sure where else we can look," Brice said, his expression frustrated and tired.

"We're kind of out of ideas too," Candice said grimly.

In the silence that followed, I knew we were all trying to think of what stone we'd left unturned to locate Dave, but nobody suggested something that hadn't already been thought of.

At last Dutch stood and said, "It's late. We should let you two get some sleep."

I took Dutch's hand when he offered it to help me up from the couch, and after saying good night to our dear friends, we left.

On the ride home Dutch said, "What's on tap for you tomorrow?"

I knew he was asking about how much free time I had to help with the search, and if we'd had any solid leads to track down, I would've gladly given up my other work commitments and devoted the whole day to finding Dave, but not knowing where else to look, I decided to get on with my day as planned. "I've got clients all morning and early afternoon, but I should free up around three-ish."

"How many on tap for tomorrow?"

"Six, no, wait . . . seven. I've got someone who's doing a makeup session because I had to reschedule them from last week when I had that killer sinus headache."

"That's a lot of clients, Edgar, especially after the long day you've had."

Dutch's concern for me was sweet. "Gotta bring home the bacon so you can fry it up in a pan, my man."

He grinned and we fell into comfortable silence for a bit. Then he said, "Your honest opinion—you're sure Dave didn't murder those four people?"

"My gut says no, honey."

He sighed. "Okay, then. That's good enough for me. Dave's innocent and in serious trouble. I'll put my whole team on tracking him down tomorrow."

"I thought you were going to tread lightly on this." Putting all the agents at his bureau on the case was definitely not treading lightly.

"I've changed my mind."

"But isn't that going to get sticky for you, politically?"

"It's already politically sticky for us, dollface."

"So why take even more risk?"

"Because Dave isn't just my business partner. He's one of my best friends. And he's in trouble, he needs me, and that means that I'll gladly risk my job to find him and make sure he's safe."

I leaned my head against Dutch's shoulder. "Sometimes, I'm so happy to be married to you."

"Sometimes?"

"Yeah. Times like right now. And when you make your beef brisket."

"I do make a mean beef brisket."

"And those times when you step out of the shower and you smell so good and you're all steamy and stuff."

"Steamy and stuff?"

"Yeah," I said with a yawn. "You're like that McSteamy dude from *Grey's Anatomy*, but I'm way more attracted to you."

"But only because I make a mean beef brisket, right?"

I pointed to him. "Bingo."

And that, my friends, is what I truly, truly love about Dutch. He just gets me.

Chapter Eight

. . .

There are days I really like being a professional psychic.

And days I really don't. The next day went down as a check mark in the "don't" box.

I couldn't even blame my clients—normally I might find them all perfectly lovely people, coming to me for advice, but in light of the events of the previous day, all I could think of was how petty their problems were. And my last client perhaps exacerbated that feeling.

"Sorry to be so brief, Dana," I said to the client across from me, after talking for only twelve minutes about the things I saw coming up for her in the next year. In my opinion, the woman had a very neat and orderly life: She was a stay-at-home mom of three grown children and a fourth still in high school. She was in terrific health, and had a devoted husband, good friends, a very secure financial future due to the retirement plan she and her husband had carefully built, with nothing much else to worry about.

Like, seriously, I couldn't even understand why she'd come to me.

"I'll turn it over to you for any remaining questions," I said at the twelve-minute mark, hoping that I'd missed something big that I could talk at length about.

"My daughter, a junior, is dating a senior," she said, as if that were something that should alarm me.

"Okay. And you have a question about their relationship?"

She leaned forward. "Yes. They just seem . . . so into each other."

"Are you worried about them taking things too far?" I asked the question carefully, thinking, *Please don't ask me if they're having sex, because I will have to tell you the truth, and it will freak you out.*

"No, my daughter is on birth control, and she's already told me they've been intimate."

Wow, I thought. She'd seemed so accepting of that. It would've *never* entered my mind to tell my mother that I was having sex with my boyfriend. Of course, my mother wasn't exactly loving and understanding like June Cleaver. She was more like June-wielding-a-cleaver, but I digress. "I see," I said, focusing again on Dana's energy and searching for the essence of her daughter.

This is the part where maybe I should explain how we psychic types look at other people's energy. If I want to look at the significant other of a client, I use the client as a starting point, and sort of bounce off her energy to land on her SO. Think of it like on Facebook you can look at a person's friends by first looking up that person's profile. So, I sort of started with Dana's "profile" and went searching for "daughter energy." I detected three daughter figures for her, and trailed down the energy path until I "landed" on the youngest.

From there I felt out the energy of a bright, energetic, sweet soul. I kept seeing Snow White in my mind's eye, you know, that image of her surrounded by the forest's creatures as she sings to a little birdie. "Your daughter has a real love of animals, right?" I said.

"She does!" Dana said. "She's always bringing home some injured squirrel or stray cat."

"It'll continue to be a passion for her," I said. "She's really, really smart, but you wouldn't necessarily figure that out from looking at her, because I can also see that she's quite beautiful."

Dana beamed. "She's been doing some modeling," she said. "Just local stuff, but we've got a very prestigious talent agent who's super interested in her. He wants her to go to New York and do a couple of shoots. He says Payton has a great look, and she does. I mean, in all the photos she looks twenty-four, not seventeen."

"Yeah," I said, making a face. "The problem is that your daughter isn't that into the modeling gig. Maybe delay the New York trip."

"She hasn't said that to me." Dana's voice took a defensive tone.

"I understand," I said lightly. "But the world of modeling can be really seedy, and not great for building self-esteem."

"My daughter is *very* confident."

But my radar said otherwise. "Has she been dropping weight lately?"

Dana shrugged. "Payton watches her diet. The agencies want the girls on the skinny side."

Jesus. How clueless was this woman? "Okay, so, Dana, I'm gonna give it to you straight: Pushing your daughter into a career as a model is only going to make her miserable, and possibly give her an eating disorder. It's my intuitive opinion that this is a path that's unhealthy for her. She doesn't want to be a model. Sure, it's cool that she's sought after by some bigwig modeling agency, but your daughter doesn't dream of becoming a supermodel. She dreams of becoming a veterinarian, and in the meantime all she wants to do is study hard, get good grades, hang out with her boyfriend, and not have all this pressure on her shoulders to appear older and more sophisticated than she is. You said it yourself—she's not twenty-four; she's *seventeen*. So let her be seventeen."

Dana was clearly unhappy with my answer. "I think it's good for her," she said. "If she'd just dump the boyfriend and agree to let me take her to New York, she could have an exciting life of travel and experiences before she goes off to college. And the money she makes modeling would help pay for her college."

That last line was bullshit, because I'd already had a clear vision of Dana's finances. They were solid. She could afford to send her daughter to any college she got into and barely feel the hit.

But as I looked into the ether a little more, I suddenly saw what was really going on here. Dana was bored. Dana wanted to travel and have a life of exciting experiences. Dana loved having a beautiful daughter to show off, because it gave her importance. And Payton's boyfriend was probably taking up all of Payton's free time, which meant that Dana didn't get to show off her daughter nearly as much as she used to.

"Dana, I'm going to tell you something and I want you to hear me in this: Payton is a different kind of person than your other daughters. She's a different kind of person than you, even. She's not the extrovert the rest of your family appears to be; she's the opposite. She's an introvert who needs quiet, and rest, and think time, and recharge time, and the company of someone who understands that . . . like her boyfriend. She doesn't need to go to a noisy city and be rushed from photo shoot to photo shoot and paraded around in too much makeup and too little clothing. She needs a normal, non-exciting life and she needs to be able to pick her own path.

"I know that you know that, but the thing is, right now your need is so much greater. You need something to focus on. Some excitement in your life. Something to do. You need to become active in a cause that you feel passionately about. You need to meet new people, and travel, and do things that fill you up. And you need to leave your daughter's relationship with her boyfriend alone, because I can clearly see that you're attempting to sabotage it every chance you get."

Dana's mouth had fallen open midway through my speech. Her cheeks flushed and there was barely restrained anger in her eyes. "I'm fine," she said.

"No, honey, you're not," I told her. "You're in desperate need of something to do." I sighed then, because, even after saying that to her, I saw little change in the ether. She was going to hold on to her dream of living vicariously through her daughter until it ruined their relationship, and I knew that's exactly what would happen, because a year ahead I saw Payton moving to Toronto for school, and not coming home so much. You couldn't get a whole lot farther away from Texas than Canada.

Still, I'd maybe pushed it as far as I dared with Dana. She wasn't willing to listen to me anyway, and some people you just have to learn when to let go and move on. So I asked her for another question, but every single one of her remaining questions had something to do with her daughter. I finally ended the session a few minutes early, and wasn't sorry for it. I'd probably never see Dana again, which was a shame, because if she'd been willing to listen, I could've helped her find out how amazing she could be.

After she left, I went to my desk and dug out a Kind bar. I ate it angrily. Then I wandered out of my office into the hallway that connected my office to Candice's. She was there at her desk, tapping away on her computer.

"Hey," I said, knocking on her door.

"Sundance," she sang without looking up. "I heard your last client leave."

I didn't say anything.

"I think the whole floor heard her leave," she added, with a smirk.

"Who knew our door could slam that loud?" I said.

Candice chuckled and sat back in her chair. "You really know how to make friends and influence people."

I walked forward and plopped down across from her. "It's a gift."

"One among many. Care to talk about it?"

"Ugh, *no*. And you know I can't." Keeping my clients' readings privileged was kind of sacred to me. "But her reading did give me an idea."

"Do tell."

"Well, she had asked me to tune in on a family member, and I got a great sense of that family member by bouncing off her energy onto the relative. I think I might be able to do the same thing for Dave."

Candice blinked, clearly confused. "You want to bounce off Dave's energy to look at one of his family members?"

"No, sorry, I meant the opposite. I want to bounce off Gwen's energy to try and get a line on Dave and hopefully discover a clue about where he might be."

Candice sat forward quickly. "Could that work?"

"It could," I said. "As long as Gwen's willing."

Candice shoved her phone toward me. "Call her."

I did and was lucky enough to reach Gwen right away. She seemed to be holding it together pretty well, given the fact that the police had just left her house after conducting a thorough search of it in their efforts to find Dave. "I'm hoping to bounce off of your energy to find Dave," I explained.

"What do I need to do?" she asked me.

"Nothing. Just focus on him and I'll do the rest."

"Now?" she asked.

"Yeah."

"Okay," she said, a quiver in her voice. I took a deep breath and focused first on Gwen while Candice eyed me intently from across the desk.

For a few moments I said nothing; I just got centered and connected to Gwen. As I searched out her energy for Dave, though, some really weird stuff started to come at me from the ether. It was like that rushing white-water feeling I had for Dave had somehow affected her energy too. "Gwen?" I asked.

"Yes?"

"Are you okay?"

And it was like I put a giant crack in her dam and she dissolved into a puddle of tears. "Nnnnnoooo!" she cried.

Candice winced, and mouthed, *Poor thing!*

"Hey," I said, knowing right now Dave's wife needed a hug in the worst way. "Gwen, listen, you sit tight. Candice and I are on our way over to your house, okay?"

Gwen simply cried harder, and I motioned to Candice, who was already up and reaching for her purse.

We got to the McKenzie residence about twenty minutes later. There was a black latex glove on the lawn, the only evidence that the police had been there to search out the house. I've seen search warrants conducted; the police are under no obligation to put things back the way they found them, so I could only hope they'd been kind to poor Gwen.

"The door's open," Candice said as we approached up the walkway.

"She's probably inside cleaning up after the search," I said.

We paused at the door and Candice knocked lightly. "Gwen? It's us."

There was no answer from inside, so we moved into the foyer. "Gwen?" I called, looking into the doorways off the hall. "It's Abby and Candice."

Still there was no answer and Candice and I traded a confused look. I started to notice how utterly silent the house was. There was no music playing, no TV in the background, just . . . quiet.

And then my Spidey sense kicked in, and I started to feel really anxious about where Gwen was. "Gwen?" I called urgently, moving toward the kitchen. "Gwen!"

Behind me I heard Candice's heels on the wood floor. She was moving quickly, and I figured she was covering the other rooms.

Meanwhile I scanned the kitchen. There was no sign of Dave's wife. I moved next to the den at the back of the house, and still no sign of her, even though I kept calling her name. At last I turned back toward the kitchen and saw Candice come from the hallway, shaking her head. I motioned with my chin toward the back door, and we both went to it and out onto the back deck. "Gwen!" I shouted. A knot had formed in my stomach. Something was wrong. She wasn't here—I knew that intuitively just as surely as I was seeing it for myself.

"What the hell?" Candice said after we'd taken in the whole backyard without any sign of Gwen.

"She's not here."

"But the front door was wide open." And then Candice seemed to think of something and she hustled back inside. I followed behind her all the way over to a door off the kitchen, which I suspected led to the garage. Candice unlocked the door and opened it so we could step through. The overhead light came on immediately—probably triggered by a motion sensor. It revealed a silver Ford Focus, which I thought must've been Gwen's car.

Candice walked over to the car and peered inside. Then she opened the door and half sat in the front seat, fiddling with something on the dash. A moment later the trunk opened and I looked at Candice in alarm. "We have to be thorough," she said, walking past me to check the trunk.

I held my breath as she rounded the car and looked inside the trunk. "Empty," she said. I exhaled with relief. Still, as glad as I was that Gwen wasn't dead in her trunk, that didn't change the fact that she wasn't anywhere in the house. "Maybe she just went for a walk or something," Candice said.

I considered that that was possible. I sometimes took walks to help cool down when I was upset about something, or just needed to clear my head. Poor Gwen had been having the worst few days, and she had to be exhausted and at her wits' end. Especially after the cops showed up to search her home for any sign of her husband, whom they had no doubt pegged for a crazed killer.

Pulling up my phone, I said, "I'm calling her."

I listened while the other line rang once, then twice, and then I heard a jingle coming from the kitchen. Candice and I again traded looks before moving back inside. Gwen's phone was on the kitchen counter, ringing away.

I clicked off the call and went to her phone. "Why would she leave her phone here if she was only going for a walk? Especially if she hasn't heard from Dave. Wouldn't she keep it glued to her side at all times?"

"I don't know, Abs," Candice said softly. I glanced at her. She'd squared her shoulders and pressed her lips together. I knew that look. That was a look that said she was braced and ready to kick some ass.

I knew then that we were both thinking the same thing. Gwen wasn't here, not because she didn't want to be. She wasn't here because she'd been forced to leave. Pointing to a nook under the far left cabinet, I said, "That looks like her purse."

"Check to see if her wallet's there," Candice said.

I moved to retrieve the purse and dug inside. Pulling out Gwen's wallet and keys, I said, "Shit."

Candice immediately lifted her own phone and as she dialed, she said, "Don't touch anything else."

"Who're you calling?"

Candice held up her index finger to let me know to hang on a sec. "Hey, babe," she said almost casually into the phone while her eyes roved the entire area of the kitchen. "We're at Dave's house. We were supposed to meet Gwen here, but something's off. She's not here, but her car, purse, and phone are. I think she's met with some trouble." There was a pause, then, "I don't know. Let me check." Putting a hand over the microphone, Candice said to me, "What's your radar say?"

"Danger, Will Robinson."

Candice frowned, and went back to Brice. "Abby thinks she's met with trouble too." Another pause, then, "Okay. We'll wait out front for you."

Twelve minutes later Brice's car roared up the street and braked hard. The car was barely in park when both of our husbands jumped out, along with Oscar Rodriguez—one of the agents at the bureau and a close friend of ours.

All three men had their right hands hovering over their side-arms, and bronze badges swinging from metal chain lanyards around their necks. They approached us quickly, but their eyes roved over every inch of the front yard and house. "Did you touch anything inside?" Dutch asked us.

I held up Gwen's phone and her purse. "I might've put my hand on a door handle or two," I admitted.

"Any signs of a struggle inside?" Oscar asked.

"None," Candice replied. "When we got here, the front door was ajar, though."

"Sit tight," Brice told us, before motioning for Dutch and Oscar to move with him inside.

Candice and I waited maybe three or four minutes before the three men came back out to us. "Have you searched the neighborhood?" Brice asked Candice.

I knew he might've been thinking that maybe Gwen went for a walk and just hadn't gotten back yet. "I took a jog around the block," Candice told him. And she had while I waited in the driveway to watch the house. "There's no sign of her."

"Can I see her phone?" Oscar asked me. I handed it to him. He scrolled through a few screens and said, "Her last couple of calls were from Abby. No incoming calls since yesterday other than that, and nothing outgoing either."

"She probably wanted to keep her phone line free in case either Dave or one of us called."

"Texts?" Dutch asked Oscar.

He shook his head. "Just three, sir, and all three are to someone named Terry."

"That's Dave's sister's name," I said.

Oscar nodded. "The texts from her are asking if there's any news, and Gwen responds, 'None,' each time."

"So she didn't set up a meet with someone," Dutch said.

"It doesn't look like it," Oscar said.

The five of us stood in the driveway for several seconds and looked around the area, as if we could spot the place where Gwen might be hiding. "Let's knock on some doors and see if anybody saw anything," Brice said.

We fanned out in pairs, with Oscar going by himself. Dutch led the way across the street and we started to knock on the doors of the McKenzies' neighbors. Dutch and I found someone home at the house directly across the street. The door was opened by a woman in leggings and a long sweater. She looked like we'd woken her up from a nap. "Hi," I said. "We're looking for Gwen McKenzie."

"Who?" the woman said, blinking and rubbing at her eyes.

"Your neighbor across the street," Dutch said, pointing to the home.

"Oh, I don't know them," she said. "But this morning there were a bunch of cop cars over there. Was there a fight between them or something?"

"No, ma'am," I said. "But we're interested in knowing if you've seen Gwen since this morning. Maybe an hour or so ago?"

The woman looked at the watch on her right wrist. "Oh, wow. I've been out for a while. I was on a flight back from Sydney yesterday and my clock is all screwed up. I've been asleep on the couch for the last four hours."

Dammit, I thought. "Okay, thank you," I said, and we took our leave.

We tried three more doors and only one other neighbor was home to talk to us. He said that he'd been watching TV and hadn't heard or seen a thing. He didn't even seem to know that there'd been a police presence at Dave's house earlier in the day.

Heading back to the McKenzie driveway, we waited for the others, and Oscar arrived first. He shook his head when Dutch asked him if he'd had any luck. "You guys?"

"No," I said, that knot of worry for Gwen getting a little more rope in the pit of my stomach.

Candice and Brice came back a minute later, and they looked like they had news. "The guy next door saw Dave's truck in the driveway about forty-five minutes ago," Candice said.

My eyes widened. "Seriously?"

"That's what he said," Brice confirmed.

I glanced at my phone. I'd hung up with Gwen about fifty-five minutes earlier. "He must've come home right after I got off the line with her."

"So where are they?" Dutch asked.

"No clue," Brice said.

"We should go back inside and see if either of them packed any of their belongings," Oscar suggested.

Candice frowned and glanced at me. I knew what she was thinking. "No way would Gwen pack stuff and leave behind her purse and phone," I said.

"She might've if they were interested in staying off grid," Oscar replied. "You can trace a cell phone, and if they were going off grid, there'd be no need to take any identification or credit cards."

He had a point there. Still, I opened Gwen's wallet and took mental note that there was about two hundred dollars there. My thinking was that someone who's about to go on the lam isn't going to leave behind any cash, no matter how small. She'd need every penny, but then, I wasn't sure what Dave had said to her to get her to leave so quickly. "Okay," Candice said. "Let's go and check it out."

Brice held up his finger to stop us and moved to his car. After retrieving a box of black latex gloves, he said, "Nobody touches anything."

It felt oddly comforting that he was treating the house like a crime scene. We had nothing overtly suspicious in there, except for the fact that Gwen was gone, someone had seen Dave's truck in the driveway, and Gwen's purse and phone had been left behind. It was hardly enough to look more than a bit suspicious, but it was all we knew.

We spent the next ten minutes opening closet doors and searching for any signs that someone had come to collect clothes or personal effects, but there was no indication that anything like that had occurred.

It was obvious that Gwen had spent some time putting things back after the search warrant was served, and I suspected it'd been a task that'd helped her cope. The house overall was neat, orderly, and clean.

The two guest rooms were the only spaces that'd still shown the effects of a police presence, as both duvets had been pulled off the beds, and the closet door and the dresser drawers hung open. Those closets were mostly empty, containing just a few storage items, and the dressers had what looked like excess clothing, mostly for cold weather. Otherwise, nothing much looked out of place.

The five of us met back in the kitchen and Brice said, "We found two sets of luggage in the master bedroom. They're empty."

"The closet and dressers don't look like they're missing any clothes," Candice added.

"The bathroom is stocked with his and her toiletries," Oscar said next.

"Nothing's missing," I said. I knew it in my gut.

Oscar pointed to me. "Can you use your radar to get a bead on what happened to Gwen?"

"Maybe," I said, because I didn't know. Still, I stepped away from the fridge, where I'd been standing, and moved to the center of the kitchen. Closing my eyes, I focused on Gwen. I'd talked to her just a little over an hour before, and I'd been focused on her energy, so maybe it'd be simple to get a bead on her now.

What I felt was a shock. There was this . . . echo in the ether. The only way I can describe it is that it was violent and quick. I felt so strongly that Gwen had been struck down. Like someone had physically punched her and knocked her to the floor, and he'd done it almost exactly where I was standing.

The power of the energy was so strong, in fact, that I stumbled forward and bent down to steady myself with my hands on the floor. "Abs?" I heard Dutch say. Both he and Candice were next to me in a hot second.

"Holy shit!" I whispered, gripping his arm. "Someone punched Gwen!"

"Punched her?" Candice said.

"Yeah," I said. Getting unsteadily to my feet, I let Dutch support me while I looked around. "She was standing here, and I feel like her heart was racing. She was excited, I think, and then all of a sudden she was hit. Hard."

"By who?" Dutch asked me, and there was a flare of anger in his eyes. He had no tolerance for violence against women.

"I don't know," I said, feeling a little woozy. I knew it was the leftover effect of what'd happened to Gwen. I closed my eyes again to try to get closer to the imprint of violence in the ether. I was hoping to discover a clue, but all I could pick up was Gwen's emotion and physical discomfort. I could feel an almost phantom pain in my lower jaw on the left side, and it really did feel like I'd had my own bell rung. There was a faint ringing in my ears, and my balance was off, like I was trying to walk after being on a Tilt-A-Whirl. I also felt as if I were being pulled forward violently. Opening my eyes again, I half stumbled forward toward the front door. And I saw that it was closed, but I swore that it'd been open when Gwen was knocked around.

Dutch stood close to me the whole time, his hand under my elbow to support me should I lose my balance again. There was a lot of sensory input going on in my mind, and I did my best to process it, but it was damn hard. Taking a deep breath, I closed my eyes one more time and started from the beginning.

"Gwen had been excited about something," I said. "She was standing in the kitchen, and she was . . . happy?"

"Happy?" I heard Candice say.

I shook my head, then nodded. "There's a mix here. Something made her feel excited and happy, and then—pow! She got knocked to the floor and I think dragged out of here before she had any chance to fully come to her senses."

"So, Dave came home, then roughed her up and took her with him?" Brice asked.

I opened my eyes, my temper flaring. I wanted to yell, "NO!" because sweet, gentle Dave would never hurt a woman, especially not the woman he loved. But then, I'd never believed Dave would murder someone either, and the four bullet-riddled bodies at the Roswells' house were suggesting otherwise.

With a sigh I said, "God, I hope not."

"Should we file a missing persons report?" Candice asked next.

Brice and Dutch exchanged a look. "Yeah," Dutch said, making the call. "It'll throw some suspicion on Gwen, but it's the right thing to do."

"Wait," I said, that same flash of anger lighting up my insides again. "Screw filing a missing persons report! We need to report Gwen's kidnapping!"

Dutch reached out and took my hand. "Who's going to step forward to say they witnessed the kidnapping, dollface?"

"Me. I can say that I was coming here to talk to Gwen and I saw her being pulled into a truck that looked like Dave's."

Dutch and Brice exchanged another look. "That would be perjury, Cooper," Brice said. "And I can't let you do that."

I rounded on him, all my anger and worry for Dave and now Gwen unleashing like hot lava from a volcano. "Fuck you, Brice! If I want to go on record to say that Gwen was kidnapped, I'm goddamn well gonna do it!"

Brice's eyes narrowed and his jaw muscles bunched, but he kept his cool. Thank God. "I don't doubt you're capable of doing anything for a friend," he said calmly, and with a hint of sympathy that just about broke my heart. "But, Abby, the second you're caught in that perjury, I won't ever be allowed to use you in another federal case again. And APD *will* discover your lie, because when they investigate, they'll hear from the neighbor right next door who not only saw Dave's truck in the driveway, but also caught a clear look of you and Candice pulling up here at four thirty—a full twenty minutes after the truck left. And he'll also say that he saw you two go inside with no sign of Gwen anywhere around. That's what he told me when I knocked on his door, and that's what he'll say to the police."

I ducked my chin in shame. Tears welled in my eyes and the floor blurred. "Sorry," I choked out.

A gentle hand landed on my shoulder. "It's cool," Brice said. "I understand. Really. There's nothing I want more than to find Dave and Gwen, but you risk playing fast and loose with the resources devoted to finding them by setting up a lie that they'll quickly untangle. And then they'll wonder why you lied to them, and maybe they'll devote some resources to trying to find out what you're hiding. It's all a distraction from the objective, which is to find Dave and Gwen. Soon."

I wiped my cheeks and shuffled forward, placing my head in the center of Brice's chest to let him know I really was sorry. He gave me a brief hug—something uncharacteristic for my very always-keep-it-professional boss—and said, "Come on. Let's lock up the house and call in the missing persons report."

Candice was the one who called in the report, for which I was grateful, because I wasn't feeling so good after leaving Dave and Gwen's house. I think I'd been drained from so many clients, and tapping into the violence that'd happened to Gwen afterward was sort of the capper of a craptastic day.

On our behalf Dutch declined Brice and Candice's invitation to go out to dinner, which Oscar had readily taken. "Abby needs some peace and quiet tonight," I'd heard him say. I'd all but shut down in the car, like a computer that was trying to reboot while taking in only the faintest outside signals. Payton and I had that whole introvert thing in common.

We got home and Dutch held the door for me as I shuffled inside. The pups met us at the door, and little Tuttle squirmed and wiggled at my feet until I picked her up and cuddled with her.

Eggy, meanwhile, stood in front of Dutch and gave three loud, demonstrative barks. "Someone's hungry," I said, grinning down at my little guy.

"How come he always barks at me when he's hungry?" Dutch said, picking Eggy up with one hand and carrying him into the kitchen.

"He knows you'll give in first," I said, following behind with Tuttle.

Dutch set Eggy down in his bed by the stove and got busy with the dog bowls, dog food, and a couple of quickly scrambled eggs. My pups *love* eggs, and Dutch always puts a little goat's milk and coconut oil in the scramble to really give them a nutritious boost. Eggy and Tuttle have two of the shiniest coats you've ever seen.

After setting down dinner for the pups, Dutch opened a bottle of red, poured us each a glass, and got to making us dinner. I sat numbly in a chair while he threw some spiralized zucchini noodles into a pan for me, and some pasta on to boil for him, while also heating up his famous meat sauce, which he'd made a few days earlier.

"Hey," I heard him say after a while.

I shook my head, realizing I'd been staring off into space. "Yeah?"

"You okay?"

My lower lip quivered. "Not so much."

Dutch threw the towel he'd been wiping his hands on over his left shoulder and came to me, lifting me out of the chair to hug me. "We'll find them, Edgar. We will."

"I'm as afraid of that as not finding them," I confessed. "I mean . . . what the hell is going on, honey?"

"I don't know. But we'll figure it out. And if there's anything we can do to help them out of this mess, then we'll do that too."

"Promise?"

"Pinkie swear."

"I take it back."

"You take what back?" he asked.

"I don't love you sometimes. I love you all the times."

Dutch chuckled. "Me too, dollface. Me too."

Chapter Nine

* * *

After a fitful night's sleep for me, there was an early morning knock on our door. Dutch and I were in the middle of getting ready for work, after doing our part to conserve water by showering together; hence, we were both naked at the time of the door knock. While Eggy and Tuttle barked crazily in the foyer, my hubby and I did rock/paper/scissors to see who'd have to answer the door.

Dutch lost. *Quelle surpreez*, please. I mean, the guy continually plays these games with a *psychic*. What does he expect?

Still, as he hastily wrapped his lower half in a towel, I threw on a robe to peek out from the kitchen. Dutch must've known I was trying to hide, because with a wicked glance over his shoulder at me, he threw open the door to reveal the caller.

"Detective Grayson," I said, somewhat curious to see her on my front steps.

"Hell—oh!" she said, her eyes going from me to the Greek god in the towel in front of her. Did I mention that Dutch takes amazing care of himself? Did I also mention he's got the body of a Chippendales dancer? No? Well, that's unusual. I totes like to brag about it.

Dutch grinned. "Good morning, Detective," he said. "What brings you by?"

Grayson's cheeks flushed bright red and she shut her eyes, turning her head away from Dutch and back over to me before she opened them again. "I've been assigned to the Roswell case," she said, her words clipped and pronounced with perfect diction.

Gee, it was like she was trying to compose herself or something.

I grinned at her too. I clearly remember the first time I saw Dutch shirtless. I don't remember much *after* he'd taken his shirt off—I mean, that part's fuzzy. Maybe because my thinking brain had traveled straight south to my vajayjay. I gave Grayson props for being able to speak at all, much less remember why she'd stopped by. "Come in, Detective," I said. She walked forward and once she'd passed Dutch, she widened her eyes and mouthed, *Wow!* at me.

My grin got bigger. *I know, right?* I mouthed back when Dutch turned to shut the door.

We offered Grayson some coffee (I didn't think she'd want my caffeine-free tea—call it a hunch), and I shooed Dutch back into the bedroom to put on some clothes before he gave someone a heart attack. Grayson's cheeks bloomed again, but she clinked mugs with me after he left the room. "Sorry to come by so early," she said. "I wanted to catch you two before you both left for work."

"Has there been a development?" I asked, all humor leaving me.

"Maybe. But first I want to ask you about a report that came across my desk this morning. Is it true that Dave McKenzie's wife has gone missing?"

"Yes," I said, wondering how she connected that report to me.

"Your business partner filed the report and named you as a witness to the disappearance. I understand you were headed over to the McKenzie residence yesterday for a meeting with her and when you arrived, she was gone from the house, but her purse, keys, and phone were left behind?"

"That's true."

"Ms. Fusco said that you feel that Gwen has been kidnapped against her will."

"That's also true," I said, because it was.

"Why do you think that?"

I tapped my forehead. "My Spidey sense says so."

Grayson's mouth quirked. "Two years ago I wouldn't have given that Spidey sense of yours much credit. Nowadays, I'm the last person to dismiss it."

I felt my shoulders relax. I hadn't realized I'd tensed up since we started talking about Gwen until Grayson confessed she had faith in me. Given all the years I've faced down unbridled skepticism from the law-enforcement community, it was a damn nice change.

"Thanks," I said.

"No need to thank me. You've proven yourself a few times over. I'm a believer."

"Yeah, well, thanks anyway."

Grayson held up her coffee cup and we clinked mugs again. "What can you tell me about what happened to Gwen?" she asked next.

I grimaced, recalling that punch to the face I was certain Gwen had received. "I think she may have known her kidnapper. I think she let him in, and when she was least expecting it, he clocked her hard. She went down to the floor, he dragged her up while she was still dizzy and disoriented, before she could even cry out for help, and he took her out of the house and away with him."

"That's pretty specific," Grayson remarked.

"When I was in the kitchen trying to home in on Gwen, I just happened to be standing in the exact spot where she got sucker punched. The violence of it left an imprint on the energy and it wrapped itself around me. In essence, I was able to feel what she felt, but perhaps not the full force of the blow."

"Yikes," Grayson said. "That doesn't sound pleasant."

"I imagine it was way worse for Gwen."

"Noted. Okay, so do you think it was her husband who punched her and took her away?"

"No."

"Why not?"

Dutch came into the kitchen and poured himself a cup of coffee. I could tell he'd heard most of our conversation by the subtle supportive look he offered me. I was so grateful for him in that moment. Sometimes I just feel all filled up with love for him. I mean, I'm not the easiest person to live with, let alone love, and during stressful times like these, well, I'm even tougher to be around. But Dutch never wavers in his unconditional love and support for me. In that, he's my anchor. He steadies me and allows me to take a deep breath and focus on the information without feeling overwhelmed by it. "It wasn't Dave," I said, tapping my forehead again. "But I don't know who it was."

"You said it was someone she knew," Grayson pressed.

"*May* have been someone she knew," I corrected. "There was a degree of excitement that Gwen expressed right before she was clocked. I can't account for it, or the fact that there was no sign of forced entry, other than she might have known her kidnapper and let him in."

"But wouldn't she be excited to see her husband?" Grayson said, not letting go of her theory.

"She would, absolutely," I conceded. "But, Detective, if Dave showed up at home and said, 'Babe, we gotta go, right now!' Gwen would go. She wouldn't need to be subdued by a sucker punch. She would've gone with him."

"Even after hearing what he did to the Roswells and their staff?"

I sighed. Grayson didn't know Dave like we did. I tried to remind myself of that before answering. "Dave didn't murder the Roswells or their staff."

"We have a bloody handprint that says different, Mrs. Rivers."

"Please call me Abby," I reminded her. "And the bloody handprint only says that Dave was at the scene sometime between the time of those murders and the time that Candice and I discovered the bodies. It doesn't definitively prove that he did it. And Gwen would undoubtedly think the same thing. She knows and trusts her husband."

"Like you two, right?" Grayson said, pointing back and forth to Dutch and me.

"Yes," Dutch said. "Right now, we still have faith in Dave."

Grayson nodded, but I couldn't tell if she believed us about Dave's innocence. Maybe she'd seen too many "great" guys turn out to be scumbags, but I was still strongly rooted in my belief that Dave couldn't, wouldn't, and didn't murder anybody. Nor had he physically assaulted his wife.

"Am I correct to say that you believe that Gwen's kidnapping is connected to the murders at the Roswell house?" Grayson asked next.

Dutch and I exchanged a look. "Yes," we said together.

"And somehow Dave McKenzie is mixed up in all of this too," she said.

"Yes, but we don't understand how he's connected, yet," Dutch said.

"What's your theory?" she asked him, because, as a fellow law-enforcement official, he would've worked one out by now.

Dutch took a sip of his coffee and shrugged. "Officially?"

Grayson made a face. "No," she told him. "My staff sergeant told us about the Chinese espionage angle you Feds are working, and we all know that's crap."

"Still," he said, "that's our official theory. But because I like you, Detective Grayson, I'll give you my unofficial theory, which is that Dave was at the wrong place at the wrong time. Maybe he witnessed something that scared the shit out of him, and he went into hiding. Maybe the guys who murdered the Roswells and their staff saw Dave before he got away, then tracked down his wife to use as leverage for him to come out of hiding."

Grayson cocked an eyebrow. "That sounds like the plot of a movie."

"I know. But it's a theory that fits with both the facts and what I know about Dave as a person."

Grayson set her coffee cup in the sink before she said, "Okay. Thank you for your time. I'll let you two get on with your day. If you come across any other information on Gwen's whereabouts, give me a call."

After she'd gone, I turned to Dutch and said, "I don't have any ideas left about how to find either Dave or Gwen."

Dutch reached for me and pulled me close. "Me either, dollface. But that doesn't mean something new won't turn up. All we need is one good lead."

I closed my eyes and pressed my cheek against his chest. He was warm and smelled amazing, so I spent a moment filling myself up with his scent and his warmth for strength and courage. "How many clients today?" he asked me.

"Only five. My sixth had to reschedule and I kept the hour free."

"What time are you done, then?"

"Um . . . two o'clock."

"Good. I'd like you to take the afternoon off and come back home to put your feet up and read a good book. You need to recharge, babe. I can tell you didn't sleep well last night."

"I look that bad, huh?"

"You couldn't look bad if you tried," he said, kissing the top of my head.

"Can you be this amazing for the entire rest of our marriage?"

"I will if you will."

"Deal, cowboy."

Later that day, after seeing my last client to the door, I found Candice in her office, studiously bent over her laptop. "How's it going?" I asked.

"Perfectly crappy," she grumbled. "I've called all of Gwen's contacts. No one's heard from her."

"How'd you get a list of her contacts?"

Candice held up Gwen's phone. "This fell into my purse by accident."

"Candice!"

"What?" she said. "I'll give it back to her as soon as she shows up."

"Aren't the police looking for it?"

"Maybe. I told Grayson I'd leave it on the counter for her, and then I made sure to lock Gwen's door. Without another search warrant, she can't get back into that house, and as she's only got our word to go on that Gwen was kidnapped, she can't get another warrant without some hard evidence that Gwen was taken against her will, or that something violent took place in that house."

"So the police haven't been back to Dave and Gwen's home since we were there yesterday?"

"Nope. Or maybe they were there and couldn't get in. Either way, the phone won't turn up missing for a while."

I took a seat in one of Candice's office guest chairs. "I don't have any new ideas about how to find either Gwen or Dave."

Candice eyed me keenly. "Hey, do you believe they're together?"

I blinked. I hadn't actually used my radar to pin that down yet. Taking a moment to focus, I was surprised and frustrated at the answer that came back to me. "Yes," I said. "They're together. But I don't know where."

"Are they being held against their will?"

I focused again. Candice had perhaps unwittingly asked the perfect question. "Yes!" I said. "Yes, they're being held against their will. Or they're being held in check. Someone is using Gwen against Dave."

"Why?"

My eyes flew open. "Because of what Dave knows."

"What does Dave know?" Candice asked next. She was leaning forward over her desk, intently focused on my answers.

"He knows something that someone else wants. There's a secret he's keeping. Something dangerous. Something that would cost him to give it up."

Candice tapped her index finger lightly on the desk. I could tell her own mental gears were spinning. "What would Dave know that could be dangerous and would cost him to give it up?"

I shook my head. That was all I could tweeze out of the ether.

I had all the pieces to form a sketchy outline of the picture, but I needed to put them in the right order to make that picture clearer, and it wasn't an easy thing to do. "It has to do with the Roswells," I said, upset I couldn't provide more than that.

But Candice's eyes were gleaming, as if I'd just said the perfect thing. "If it has to do with the Roswells, then all we need to do is start digging into their lives and see what turns up."

I felt a small sense of relief wash over me. A lead. We had a damn lead to follow. At last. "I'm ready if you are."

"Let's go."

We started by heading to the bureau office. The FBI has access to lots of nifty computer programs that allow them to dig up dirt on people. It'd scare the hell out of me to know this if I didn't work for them. Candice was able to locate lots of very pertinent info quickly. She did this while I made a coffee run. (We all bring our own individual talents to the job.)

"Ahhh, that's the stuff," I said, after delivering hot beverages all around the office and taking my first delicious sip of a decaf green tea latte—a favorite of mine.

"Come on," Candice said, grabbing her cup of tea and her purse on her way out the door.

I'd just sunk into the chair next to the desk she'd been using, and truth be told, I *needed* a moment or two to relax. "I just got comfortable!" I yelled after her.

Without turning around, she waggled her index finger above her head. "You can relax in the car. Daylight's wastin'. Let's roll!"

"*No*body relaxes with you at the wheel, Candice," I grumbled.

"What?" she said as she held open the door for me.

"I'm always relaxed with you at the wheel, Candice," I said with a winning smile.

She narrowed her eyes. "Right. Get a move on, Sundance."

Candice drove us (at an alarmingly high speed) to a modest ranch, north of the city. "Who lives here?"

"Robin Roswell's sister," she said.

"Ugh," I said, knowing how difficult it was to interview loved ones of murder victims so soon after the crime. They were typically in such a state of heartbreak and anguish that it was a terrible thing to try to talk to them. And it was an awful, torturous thing we had to do as investigators, pulling out information from these poor people, knowing that all they wanted to do was curl up into a ball and cry. Sometimes—and I hate to admit this—it's almost better to get to them immediately after the crime, before the news really has a chance to sink in. They're not as anguished or gutted, and it's easier to bear witness to their shock rather than their devastation.

We approached the house from the driveway, as the sidewalk was littered with G.I. Joe figurines. The sight of them was already pulling at my heartstrings. Some little boy would grow up without his auntie, and as the auntie of two amazing tweens, the reality caught me right in the chest like a punch.

"You okay?" Candice said as she reached for the doorbell.

I pulled my gaze from the toys. "Fine," I said, but my voice hitched. I quickly cleared my throat and shook my head a little. It wouldn't do Robin's sister a bit of good if I was emotional.

Our ring was answered by a woman in sweats with salt-and-pepper hair and thick glasses. "Yes?" she said when she opened the door to us.

"Rachel?" Candice said.

The woman seemed confused. "No," she said, without offering any additional information.

Candice looked at the address on the side of the house, then consulted her phone for a moment. "I'm so sorry, but this is the current address I have for Rachel Tibbons. Does she live here?"

"She's inside," the woman said, her arms crossing over her chest defensively. "Are you reporters?"

I held up my FBI consulting badge, and Candice flashed her own badge and her PI license. "No," she said. "We're consultants with the Federal Bureau of Investigation. We're assisting the bureau and the Austin police with an investigation."

The woman's brow furrowed even further. "You're consultants for the FBI and APD?" she repeated. Candice and I held up our badges again.

"Yes, ma'am," I said.

"That sounds like a lot of bull to me," she said.

Candice's warm and friendly smile never wavered. "If you'd like to call the Austin FBI field office to confirm, we can wait, ma'am."

"I don't have the number," she said, even as she lifted the cell phone she'd brought with her to the door.

"I can tell you, or you can Google it," I offered.

She made a stern face at me and said, "I'll Google it."

Candice and I waited without a word as she looked up the number, then called it. I'm not sure who answered, maybe Katherine, the office manager, but within a few moments she'd confirmed our story and hung up to address us again. "Okay, so you're with the FBI. Rachel has already talked to the police and told them she don't know anything, so maybe you should go talk to them."

Candice's smile never wavered from being easy and relaxed, but intuitively, I could sense she was losing patience with this woman. "Yes," she said. "I know she's already been interviewed. All the same, we'd like a few minutes of her time as well."

"She's real upset."

"I can only imagine," Candice said, and it was obviously heartfelt.

That note of sincere sympathy might've made the difference, because the salt-and-pepper guard dog to Rachel's home finally let us in. "You can have a seat in the kitchen," she said. "I'll get Rachel."

We entered the home and sidestepped a few more toys on the floor, making our way to the kitchen, off to the side of the living room at the front of the house. I looked around for any sign of the kiddo, or maybe some siblings, but the house was quiet of children at play, or the sound of a TV.

A few moments later a woman in her early thirties came into view. She was a tall girl, with long spindly limbs and sharp features. Her hair was pulled back into a severe ponytail behind her head, exposing her ears, which were a little big for her face, but otherwise she was a lovely. She looked like a ballet dancer to me, mostly for the long graceful limbs and too-thin frame. Her bodyguard walked with her, supporting her gently, and when Robin's sister saw us, her bloodshot eyes watered a little, as if she expected us to be the bearers of more terrible news.

"Thanks, Nina," she said to the woman, as she let go of the supportive arm and came into the kitchen. She stood in front of us awkwardly, maybe getting the measure of us. "My mother-in-law said you're with the FBI?"

Candice stood up and extended her hand to Rachel, introducing herself. I followed suit and she shook both our hands before sinking down in the chair opposite us. "Thank you for seeing us," Candice began. "I know this is a terrible time for you."

"Is there any news on the guy who killed my sister?" she asked, her voice hoarse with emotion.

"Not yet," Candice said.

"The police brought me a picture of him and asked if I recognized him. I didn't, but I guess he was a contractor who did some work for them."

I felt a jolt of alarm go through me. "The police told you about him?"

"Yeah."

"What'd they say?" I asked carefully.

"They said that he worked for some construction company that installed a panic room in their closet. He was probably just waiting for his chance to break in and kill them. From his photo you could tell the guy probably did drugs."

I felt myself bristle and I had to work at tamping down any

irritation her words had sparked. It wouldn't do at all to defend Dave to her, and it could shut her down altogether if I attempted it. So I willfully kept my expression neutral, because right now what we needed was not to convince her that Dave was innocent—what we needed was information.

I also reminded myself that poor Rachel was still reeling from the blow of losing her sister and her brother-in-law, so her judgments were totally forgivable.

Candice nudged me gently under the table. A show of hidden support for Dave, I thought. "We'd like to hear about what your brother-in-law might've had of value in the panic room," she said.

Rachel sighed, rubbing her temples as if it was hard to think. "I don't know what the hell they had in there. I mean, money? Jewelry? Computers and other valuables? Probably. They loved stuff. Especially Robin. I was always telling her when she said things like 'I love these shoes!' or 'That purse!' or 'This tennis bracelet!' that material things couldn't love her back, but she still collected all kinds of useless stuff anyway.

"Andy was just like her too. They spent money like water on crap that didn't matter." Rachel looked down at her lap and let out another sad sigh. "I guess it made them happy and it was their money, so maybe I shouldn't judge them now that they're gone, huh?"

"It's understandable," I offered.

Rachel lifted her chin to eye us sheepishly, and I gave her a sympathetic smile. I could only imagine that her brain was full of all sorts of angry thoughts and misgivings, which was natural for someone who'd just lost two loved ones.

"What else can you tell us about them?" Candice said.

Rachel's chin lifted a little more to look toward the ceiling. Her eyes watered when she answered Candice. "They were a crazy pair. Big dreamers. Andy was a visionary and really, really smart, but sometimes he was a little too blunt, a little too honest. Robin was impetuous, and fun, and stubborn, and strong-willed, and sometimes difficult, but she loved Andy with her whole heart.

They were each other's worlds. The sun rose and set on the other, so maybe it's a good thing they were with each other in the end. I don't know how Robin would've lived without Andy, or how he would've lived without her." Rachel's voice went completely hoarse then, and she covered her eyes and wept, her shoulders shaking.

I felt terrible for her, so I got up and went to the counter to retrieve a box of tissues and brought it back, setting it down next to her.

"You really loved them," I said as I took my seat again.

She took a tissue from the box with an anguished smile. "She was my baby sister, and he was like my little brother. It's still sinking in. I can't quite wrap my head around what it means to be here without them. Robin was my only blood relative still around. Well, other than my mom, but she's been in a nursing home for the past five years."

My eyes widened. Rachel seemed far too young to have a mother in a nursing home.

"Early-onset Alzheimer's," she said, noticing my expression. "She's in the final stages. She can't even recognize her own reflection in the mirror. It's the only blessing out of this mess. At least she doesn't know that her baby girl's gone."

Rachel began weeping again, and my own eyes misted. God, it was heart wrenching to watch someone in the throes of such grief. "I'm so sorry," I said, reaching out to squeeze her wrist.

She nodded, sniffling loudly. "If it weren't for my husband's family, I don't know how I'd get through the day."

Candice and I were silent for a bit. I thought that neither of us wanted to ask Rachel any more questions, because this was so dreadfully hard, but we needed information, so I knew that Candice would eventually work up the courage to continue with the interview.

At last when Rachel seemed to be able to draw breath without it ending in a sob, Candice said, "Did either your sister or brother-in-law have any enemies?"

Rachel barked out a laugh, as if she couldn't believe Candice

had asked such a ridiculous question. "Of course they had enemies. I mean, Andy had plenty of enemies in the tech world. He
was a freaking genius, and he made a *lot* of money at an early age.
Plus, he married the hottest girl on the block. I know I'm not a
lot to look at, but my sister could stop traffic—she was so gorgeous. And she was full of herself. Women didn't like her because
she spoke her mind, tooted her own horn, and didn't give a shit if
she was nice or not. If you were having a bad hair day, she'd call
you out for it. Andy loved that about her, and encouraged her to
keep it up, which made people dislike him all the more."

It shocked me that Rachel was being so honest about her sister's and brother-in-law's shortcomings. Usually the living tended
to gloss over the more human aspects of their recently deceased
loved ones in an effort to immortalize them. I honestly found
Rachel's straightforwardness about Robin and Andy to be refreshing. At least we had a good understanding about who the couple
really was.

"Do you think any of Andy's or Robin's enemies were capable
of murdering them?" Candice asked.

Rachel blinked. She looked like she didn't understand the
question. "I thought you guys already knew who did it."

Candice and I exchanged a look. We needed to be careful here.
We couldn't very well tell Rachel that we were looking into some
international espionage angle. That lie was already landing our
husbands in some internally political hot water. "Some new evidence has come to light that might suggest there was more than
one person involved," I said. "And since all the known associates
for the current suspect don't lead to anyone we'd consider suspicious, we're thinking that maybe the trail leads in the other direction. With someone linked to Andy and/or Robin."

"What new evidence?" she asked me.

Again, Candice and I glanced briefly at each other before Candice said, "Dave McKenzie's wife has been kidnapped."

"Who?"

"APD's prime suspect," I said. "The hippie-looking dude."

"His wife was kidnapped?" she said.

"Yes. And we have reason to believe that Mr. McKenzie had nothing to do with her abduction. We think she was taken to keep control over McKenzie, which is why we suspect this is much bigger than simply a robbery gone bad. We think that this all connects back to Andy and Robin, either personally or professionally."

Rachel seemed to take that in, and I could tell that what I'd said had rattled her. She'd probably never even considered that someone close to her sister and brother-in-law would be capable of such a violent act against them. "Fuck," she whispered, continuing to blink at the table.

"Yeah," I agreed. Because, well, seriously . . . this whole deal was effed up.

At last Rachel looked at us again. "Lots of people didn't like them, but I can't imagine any of Robin's friends murdering them. I didn't know a lot of Andy's friends. I don't think he had a ton of close personal relationships. He was raised in foster care, and both his parents are dead. I think that experience made it hard for him to hold lasting relationships. I'm sure it was why he loved to collect stuff too. It probably made him feel safe to have lots of material things around him. And he kept Robin constantly interested by giving her his Black Card."

"Black Card?" I asked.

"American Express's Centurion Card," Candice said. "It's their no-limit, invitation-only credit card. Very exclusive. Very hard to get."

"Robin took selfies with it," Rachel said with a sad smile. "Can you imagine? My phone is full of pictures of my husband and kids. Robin's was full of pictures of her with a credit card."

I frowned. Obviously, I hadn't known Robin, but her life seemed so sad to me. And she wasn't even aware that it was sad. Nor would she ever have the opportunity to see it that way now that her short life had been snuffed out. It was incredibly tragic—karmically speaking.

"What about Andy's friends or business associates? Would any of them have a reason to want to murder him?"

Rachel shrugged and shook her head, looking down at her lap again. "Other than his buddies at work, I wouldn't know."

"Where did he work?" Candice asked casually.

"Downtown," she said. "In the One Congress Plaza building." Mentally I called up the redbrick, pyramid-shaped building. I knew it well because it wasn't far from where Candice and I worked. "Andy ran his headquarters there on the twenty-sixth floor."

"We heard he'd sold off the company," Candice said.

Rachel nodded. "Almost. I was supposed to keep this a secret, but now I don't know why it matters. The press got it wrong; the deal between Market Vision and InvoTech hadn't quite gone all the way through yet."

"Really?" Candice and I said in unison. This was news to us.

"Yeah, it was one of those details that was supposed to be hush-hush because of InvoTech's stock being at risk. All the paperwork got signed, but literally right after the deal closed, InvoTech found a small glitch in the code, and they wanted Andy to fix it before they'd wire the funds over. Robin told me that Andy was going to fix it over the weekend, and once he could prove that the code was working properly, then some addendum guaranteeing the code would work was supposed to get signed and that's when the money would get wired."

"So, there's been no exchange of funds?" Candice pressed. "Not even a little?"

"Nope. I talked to Robin Friday afternoon and she was pissed both at the fact that InvoTech hadn't wired over the money and that her husband had to cancel plans to take her to San Francisco in a private jet for dinner. She said he'd locked himself in his home office to work on the code and probably wouldn't be out until Saturday or Sunday. She had a new dress she wanted to wear, and I remember the conversation because she mentioned the price to me and I was floored, because her new dress cost more than six months of mortgage payments for us." Rachel shook her head ruefully. "Sometimes it's like she and I didn't grow up in the same house."

"Do you know if the code was ever fixed?"

"That was the last time I talked to her," she said, her eyes watering.

"Who's running the company now that Andy has passed away?" Candice asked next. She said that like Andy had died peacefully in his sleep. It was unsettling, given what I'd witnessed at the Roswells' home.

"Probably his partner, Stanton."

"Stanton . . . ?" Candice asked, as she wrote the name down.

"Stanton Eldridge," she said. I cocked my head at the sound of the name. "I know," she said, looking at me. "His name sounds like a famous English actor or something, and he's good-looking enough to have made it as an actor, but he's a geek at heart. He and Andy founded their company in college. I guess Stanton is the closest thing to a best friend that Andy ever had."

The phone in Rachel's hand rang and we all jumped. The ringtone was loud and alarming. "Hang on," she said, looking at the screen. "It's the nursing home."

She answered the call and Candice and I waited quietly while she talked. "Oh, hey, Erma, is my mom okay?" There was a pause; then Rachel's face flushed and she got up from the table to walk over to the corner and turn her back to us. "I'm sending you out a check today. I promise. And we'll make up the difference, I swear."

There was another pause, then, "I know, I know, but . . ." Rachel's voice faltered and a sob shook her shoulders. "I'm trying to deal with my sister's death right now too, Erma. Can you just give me a week or two to figure this all out?"

After another moment I saw Rachel's stance visibly relax. "Thanks, Erma. Thank you. My mom needs you guys. I appreciate all you do for her."

After hanging up with the nursing home, she turned back to us, her face still pink. Wiggling her phone as she took her seat again, she said, "Robin was supposed to take care of all of Mom's living arrangements once she got that big windfall. Now it's all on my shoulders. I don't really know what we're going to do. Without Robin's help, we can't swing the nursing home payments."

As Rachel's lower lip began to tremble, I put a reassuring hand on her shoulder. "I have a feeling that Robin isn't through helping you out with your mom," I said, reading the thin line of reassurance in the ether. It was hard for me to tune in on Rachel, because there was so much worry and heartbreak there, but I managed to pull that little tidbit out of the ether.

Rachel nodded. "Yeah, I know I'm the next of kin, but I already know there's no will. I'd talked to them right after my son was born about becoming his guardians if anything happened to me and Allan. You'd have thought I was asking them to put shackles on their ankles, but they eventually agreed. We also mentioned to them that they'd need to get their own affairs in order just in case something then happened to them. We wanted there to be a chain of custody beyond us and them, but they both laughed over the idea of creating a will. That was something that old people did."

"You're sure they didn't create one after your talk?" Candice said. "Sometimes people just need a minute to think about why it might be important."

"If they did, they didn't let us know. My husband talked to an attorney this morning who said that, without a will and with an estate the size of theirs, it could be years before it's settled and we see any money from it. The only good thing he told us is that we should be able to take custody of the house once the police release it. I do know that Andy paid cash for it, and the attorney said although I can't sell it until the estate is settled, I can rent it out and charge a fee back to the estate for managing it as an income property. But who would want to rent that house after what happened there?"

I grimaced. I couldn't imagine anyone who'd be willing to rent or buy that home now.

"What about life insurance?" Candice offered.

Rachel wiped her eyes. "I don't even know," she said. "Maybe. The attorney my husband spoke to is going to help us with all this. He's going to look into the estate and also see about suing that company where that guy worked."

My back stiffened. "What company?"

"The construction company. The police said that the guy who killed my sister and Andy was on the job at the time he killed them. My attorney thinks I can sue his employer for wrongful death."

My mouth went dry and I felt the blood drain from my face. Candice reached for my hand and squeezed it. Standing up, she said, "Thanks, Rachel. You've been super helpful."

Rachel nodded, then sighed tiredly, getting to her feet too. "I'll walk you out." Right before we left, she reached out and caught Candice's arm. "Catch these people, would you? One or all of them," she said, anger in her eyes that was so intense it was scary.

Candice paused to cover Rachel's hand with her own. "Count on it."

Chapter Ten

· · ·

Later, when we were alone in the car and cruising back toward downtown, I said, "Well, that was sobering."

"Try not to sweat the threat of a lawsuit too much, Sundance."

"She's got a case, Candice."

"Only if Dave was responsible, which we're going to prove he wasn't."

I inhaled a deep breath and let it out nice and slow. It was a little selfish of me to focus on a potential lawsuit when Rachel had just lost her sister and brother-in-law. "That poor woman."

"Yeah," Candice agreed. "She's got it rough."

"I can't decide if it's a good thing or a bad thing to hear that Robin and Andy weren't well thought of in the community and potentially had made a few enemies."

"It's good news for Dave, assuming he's caught and charged with the Roswells' murder, but bad news for us, because it means that the suspect pool has widened considerably."

"I'm assuming we're going to talk to the business partner?"

"Yeah," Candice said, focusing on swerving into the next lane to pass someone daring to go the speed limit. "I want to know more about this big merger between InvoTech and Market Vision that didn't officially go through."

The car behind us honked. I glanced in the side mirror. The

driver was giving Candice a little piece of his mind. She ignored him and swerved again, punching the gas to put some distance between our car and his. Meanwhile I did my level best to hold down my lunch.

Amazingly, we arrived in one piece at Market Vision's headquarters, and Candice was nice enough to hold the door open for me as I passed through on shaky legs. "You okay, Sundance?" she asked me. "You look a little pale."

"We need to start driving separately."

"Aw, I'm not that bad."

My jaw dropped. Did she actually *believe* that? Looking at her expression, I'd have to say that she did. Swell. "Who exactly taught you how to drive?" I asked.

"My grandmother," she said proudly.

Ah. Well, that explained it. Madame Dubois had been a force of nature and someone I'd known only long enough to completely adore and never fully understand. Her French accent had been impossibly thick. She'd been a very unique woman, headstrong and marvelously unaffected by whatever drama was happening in the world. If I remembered correctly, Madame's pink Cadillac had had more than a few dents in it before she'd passed away. It was no wonder that her granddaughter drove like a crazy person.

Candice stepped up to the reception desk and passed her credentials forward, asking to see Mr. Eldridge if he was available.

The receptionist, a lanky young man in an oversized shirt and a poorly assembled tie widened his eyes when he saw the ID. He told us to have a seat and he'd inquire about Mr. Eldridge.

We took a seat and I looked around the Market Vision offices and wasn't all that impressed. For a company that'd been about to close a big deal, it was a pretty cheap setup. There were the typical millennial twentysomething workers, almost all of whom were wearing Beats headphones and typing rhythmically on laptops. A few of the workers were actually sitting on those big round rubber balls that're supposed to be good for your back. Or your butt. I never remember which, but you wouldn't catch me on one. I have a penchant for falling off unsteady objects and I like the back of my head too much.

The office itself was painted a rather dreary teal gray. Almost like the color started out very cheery until some crab ass at the paint factory felt it was too optimistic and needed a dose of *reality*.

Otherwise, the space was fairly Spartan. Desks were spaced close together, and the company logo was plastered on teal gray plastic water bottles and coffee mugs littering most of the desks. There were no plants or motivational posters, and very few windows.

Silently I thanked my lucky stars I didn't work in a place like this. It looked and felt like a place hope went to die.

And then something on the wall next to where I was sitting caught my attention and I got up to inspect it. "Hey," I said over my shoulder to Candice. "Look at this!"

Candice got up and came over. "Huh," she said when she saw the framed cover of *Texas Monthly* on the wall. It was the same issue that Safe Chambers had gotten the nice write-up in. On the cover was the familiar photo of the man with brown hair and matching eyes, standing confidently next to a whiteboard with lots of zeros and ones. I'd never really considered the cover's lead story, preferring to devote all of my attention to pages 36–40, which'd been dedicated to Safe Chambers. But now that I was really looking at the cover, I realized who the man in the photo was by way of the caption under it: "Is This the Next Bill Gates? Meet Austin's Own Whiz Kid, Andy Roswell!"

"The issue must've been how Andy first heard of Safe Chambers," Candice said.

"Whoa," I said breathlessly. If not for the chance coincidence of Andy and my husband's company being featured in a local magazine together, maybe Dave would never have gone missing. I wasn't sure if Andy would still be alive. . . . It was still too soon to tell.

"Pardon me, ladies," the receptionist said to get our attention. "Mr. Eldridge can see you now."

Candice and I stood and walked toward the desk. "He's through there," the receptionist said, pointing to a hallway off the lobby. "He'll be in the last office on the left."

We walked to the corridor side by side and passed only one other office, with a large glass window along the length of it, allowing us a view of the interior. Inside that space the furnishings were gorgeous: white walls, dark chestnut wood floors, a chrome and white leather seating area, and a huge lambskin rug in the center of the room.

The office was a big departure from the dull and depressing atmosphere out in the main work area.

One additional feature made it especially interesting, however. On the far wall, spaced between two exterior windows, was an enormous, framed, black-and-white photograph of an absolutely gorgeous woman. She was seductively posed on a lounge chair, her knees touching but her ankles splayed, her chest leaning forward as her décolletage spilled out of a loosely buttoned man's shirt—which was all she wore—and her full lips pouting in a come-hither expression. She resembled Rachel Tibbons enough for me to conclude the portrait was of Robin Roswell, and the office had no doubt belonged to her husband, Andy.

At Andy's desk, however, sat a nerdy-looking man with thick glasses and hunched shoulders. He was typing furiously on a laptop and seemed unaware of our presence as we passed him on our way to the end of the hallway.

It made me feel a little icky that someone had already taken over Andy Roswell's space. I knew the company had a business to run, but the guy had been dead for only two days.

We found Stanton Eldridge at the office next to Andy's, which wasn't nearly as nicely appointed and seemed to have been thrown together as an afterthought.

Stanton was indeed a very good-looking man, as Rachel had suggested. When we walked into the open doorway of his office, we found him hovered over his laptop, momentarily typing before lifting his chin to observe one of three monitors, one at a time.

Candice cleared her throat to get his attention, but he didn't look up from the screen. "Mr. Eldri—"

"One sec!" he interrupted sharply.

Candice turned at me and raised a brow, like, *Really?*

I gave a one-shoulder shrug like, *Yeah, but what can you do?*

She rolled her eyes like, *Whatevs. He's a douche.*

I nodded like, *True dat.*

Sometimes Candice and I have whole conversations without ever actually speaking. We have these most often in the company of our husbands, but that's probably just a coinkydinky.

We waited silently while he continued to type and consult his screen. I became aware of the passage of time. I checked my watch, then rocked back and forth on my heels, rolling my own eyes to let Candice know I thought his douchiness was surpassing even my early expectations.

She shook her head slightly, and I knew *that* was trouble. For the most part, my best friend and partner is the calmest, most levelheaded person I know. Until you're openly rude to her. Repeatedly. And then she'll do something—usually physical—to make you regret that decision. I worried that Eldridge was quickly approaching the "deep regret" segment of his day, so, to spare us from continuing to wait, as much as his as-yet-unbroken pinkie finger, I said, "Mr. Eldridge, we understand that you're busy, but we have just a few ques—"

"I said hold on!" he snapped again.

Out of the corner of my eye I saw Candice set her jaw and square her shoulders.

Uh-oh . . . , I thought

Before I could do much else to defuse the situation, she had stepped forward to pick up one of the gray plastic water bottles bearing the Market Vision logo from the side of Eldridge's desk. Unsnapping the plastic cap before holding it above his keyboard, she flashed him a wicked smile. Meanwhile, he'd frozen in place, moving only his eyes to look at her with a shocked expression. Candice's smile got bigger and a little more wicked. She then slowly, deliberately began to tilt the water bottle over the central monitor, which I could now see was also the desktop computer. There was a crack in the panel above where she held the bottle.

I couldn't help it. I smiled a little wickedly too.

"What're you doing?" Eldridge barked as he got to his feet.

"Getting your attention," she replied. "Do I have it?"

His face flushed with anger. "You know I can have you thrown out of here, right?"

"Of course you can," she said. "But I'm afraid that anyone who lays a hand on my arm might cause me to drop this very full bottle of liquid all over your computer. It'd be a shame if that ruined your productivity."

His hands balled into fists. "You wreck this computer and I'll sue you into the ground."

"I have no intention of wrecking it. But I have every intention of holding this water bottle right here for as long as it takes for you to answer a few questions."

He glared hard at her, refusing to speak.

"Dude," I said to him. "I'm only an observer here, but I think the safest and quickest path to letting you get back to work might be to talk to us."

Eldridge ignored me and began to reach for his phone. Candice wrinkled her nose and sniffed loudly. "Oh, man! I think I'm allergic to something in here. I'd hate to sneeze right now. It might cause my arm to jerk."

Eldridge backed his hand away from the phone. "I already talked to the police," he said, his voice so low it was hard to hear him. "And I'm on a deadline. You two are just going to be wasting my time."

"Really?" Candice said. "Assisting with the investigation into your business partner's murder is a waste of your time?"

Eldridge put the heels of his hands against his forehead and slumped back into his chair. For several seconds he just sat there, pressing his hands to his head. "I'm sorry," he finally said. "It's been a really bad past two days, and I don't want to be here, but there're things that have to get done before I can take a few personal days to mourn my friends."

He spoke with such mournful sadness that it was hard to stay angry at him. "We understand," I offered, because I knew we both did.

Eldridge took his palms away from his eyes and his whole expression had changed. "Please forgive me. How can I help?"

Candice nodded as an acknowledgment of his apology, but she didn't lower the water bottle. "We understand that the deal with InvoTech didn't go through as planned due to an issue in the software code."

Eldridge's expression changed yet again to one of alarm. His gaze moved to the open door of his office and he said, "Would you please keep it down? That's not common knowledge."

"So it's true?" Candice pressed.

Eldridge was about to answer her when there was a knock on the door behind us. I turned to see the nerdy-looking man from Andy's office standing there, and the expression on his face was a mixture of worry and regret. "Stanton?" he said.

"Greg," Eldridge said, his voice tense. "Did you find anything?"

"No," Greg said. "I looked through every file. It's not there."

My attention turned back to Eldridge. The color had drained from his face and he seemed on the verge of crying. After a hard swallow he reached over to the side of his computer and pulled out a flash drive. "Here," he said. "There's a shitload of data on here, which I've been trying to sort through all morning. The first section of code we need is in the very first file. Beyond that, we'll need the next three sections, which have to be somewhere in the remaining files."

Greg pushed up his glasses with his index finger and came forward to collect the flash drive. He snuck a wide-eyed look at me and Candice before ducking back out again.

After Greg left, Eldridge sat back in his chair with a heavy sigh and stared at his central computer monitor. Tears formed in his eyes and threatened to spill down his cheeks, but he sniffled loudly and rubbed his eyes to wipe them away. His cheeks reddened and he seemed embarrassed to be so upset, but I thought there was no way he couldn't be, given what'd happened over the weekend.

Meanwhile, Candice had already lowered the water bottle back to the desk and put the lid back on too. "You okay?" she asked Eldridge.

A sound escaped him, almost like a strangled laugh. "No," he said. "Far from it. In fact, today is looking like it'll be the second worst day of my life.

"Yesterday, two detectives came here to inform me that my best friend and business partner had been murdered along with his wife—another of my closest friends—and the fix to the code that Andy *promised* me was on his computer . . . isn't. So, a two-hundred-million-dollar deal that was supposed to go through on Friday is dead on arrival today because only Andy could've repaired it. InvoTech now has grounds to sue us, which will put us out of business and everyone here will lose their jobs. Including me."

Candice frowned, and I could tell she was feeling bad about torturing Eldridge with the water bottle. "We're very sorry to hear about your troubles," she said gently. "But I'm sure InvoTech will understand, given what's happened to Mr. Roswell."

Eldridge looked up at her as if she'd just given him something to hold on to. "God, I hope so," he said.

And then Eldridge lost the battle to hold his emotions in check, and tears slid down his cheeks. He turned away from us for a moment, to collect himself, and Candice and I exchanged uncomfortable looks.

After a few more sniffles and lots of wiping at his cheeks, Eldridge swiveled back to us and apologized again. "Sorry," he said. "This is all hitting me at once."

Candice took a seat in the chair across from Eldridge and motioned me to do the same. "We know this is very hard," she began. "And we're very sorry for your loss and the worry over your company. We have only a few questions for you, though, and normally we would never press, but time is of the essence here. If we're going to catch Andy's killer, we need as much relevant information as possible."

"I understand," he said, closing the lid to his laptop and focusing on us. "What did you want to know?"

"How about we start with the basics—what can you tell us about Andy and Robin?" Candice said.

Eldridge sighed and his shoulders sagged. It seemed like he aged ten years in that moment. "They were great people. Everybody loved them."

My intuitive lie detector went off, but it didn't really tell me anything other than Eldridge was naturally trying to put the best face on a young couple murdered in their prime.

"How long had you known Andy?" Candice asked.

Stanton blew out a breath. "I've known Andy since my freshman year of college." He used the present tense, as if his mind hadn't fully accepted that Andy was gone. "We were roommates at Boston College. He was there on a scholarship. Brilliant guy. Seriously brilliant. One of the best coders I've ever known. He triple-majored in marketing, computer science, and behavioral science. On the surface, those things might not seem related, but Andy put them together in such a remarkable way. He used everything he learned about human behavioral patterns and marketing to create predictive product algorithms."

"Predictive product algorithms?" Candice repeated. "What're those exactly?"

"They're computer code for predicting how people will respond to a given product or design based on a whole host of variables like color, shape, size, ease of use, expected PFT—"

"What's PFT?" I interrupted.

"The positive feeling trend of a product." Pointing to the Apple Watch I wore on my right wrist, he said, "How often do you check the activity app on that watch? Or track your workouts?"

I smiled. I checked my watch a lot throughout the day. "Often," I said.

"And you feel good reaching the goals your watch sets, right?"

"I do," I admitted.

"Yeah, the Apple Watch's activity app has a PFT of, like, six point eight. Anything over five would be considered by us to have enormous market potential.

"Identifying the PFT was key to Andy's success. He'd use it to make investments in the market, and either short a company making a product, or buy lots of shares, then sell it as soon as the PFT had leveled off. He could assign the PFT to whole groups of users, and he was also able to generate algorithms to predict market saturation for any demographic."

My eyes widened. "Whoa," I said. "So, Andy basically invented the holy grail for market research."

"He did," Stanton agreed. "An algorithm like that is what every single consumer-based company lives for. The kind of insight he created could save millions in lost revenue from poorly conceived or flawed products."

"I'm assuming everyone wanted the algorithms?" Candice said.

"They did," Stanton said. "And for a price, they could have an analysis of their product that would evaluate its PFT and saturation points. Our clients could also bundle several products together if they wanted to for a larger fee, and if one of their products scored a low PFT, if they made improvements to it, then we would reevaluate it for a lesser fee than if we were simply analyzing a new product."

"Why'd you decide to sell off the holy grail?" Candice asked next.

Stanton shrugged. "I could tell you that it was for the money, but that's not really the reason why. Like I said, Andy and I had pretty spectacular success operating with limited staff and not a lot of overhead for years. Our employees became very good at assessing the most important identifiers to plug into the algorithm and obtain a score that we could be confident about. We likened the process to what the credit bureaus do to create a FICO score for potential borrowers.

"Our algorithms couldn't guarantee the success of a product

with a high PFT, but our math came very, very close. The system worked well; companies who got an analysis from us had valuable information and they made better products to offer to the marketplace. Over the course of the last decade, we've had an outstanding reputation, and we've made a lot of money for both ourselves and our employees. I thought Andy was happy. I know I was. But about a year ago, he came to me and said that he'd reached his own happiness saturation point. He wanted out."

"Out meaning he wanted to sell his company? Or do you think he was depressed?" I asked.

"Out meaning he wanted to sell the company," Stanton clarified. "He said he wasn't finding any joy in it anymore, and he wanted to spend more quality time with Robin. He wanted to travel with her. See the world. And he was tired of Austin's traffic."

Candice asked the next question, which was one I was also curious about. "It took you a year to find a buyer?"

Eldridge shook his head. "It took us a year to find the right buyer. We didn't want to sell Market Vision to someone who was going to dismantle it. And it was fine that Andy wanted out, but our staff was going to suffer for it. Most of these guys have been with us for nearly a decade, and they're highly specialized. Finding a job after us in such a competitive tech industry would prove challenging. So we decided to find a company that would agree to let Andy leave and allow me to stay on as president.

"So, we investigated various companies, and entertained a host of generous offers, but InvoTech came out as the clear winner. They met our terms and offered us quite a bit more money than any of the other firms."

"How much is quite a bit?" Candice asked.

"Just over two hundred million."

I whistled in appreciation. "That's a nice chunk of change."

Eldridge gave a one-shoulder shrug. "It was pretty close to our true valuation, all things considered."

"What happened with the deal?" Candice asked.

Stanton sighed. "InvoTech discovered something they didn't

like about the code, and after learning about it, I can't say that I blame them."

"What does that mean?" Candice asked.

Eldridge sighed again. By way of explanation he said, "As much as Andy wanted to let go of the company, it was still hard for him. He built it from nothing, after all, and he just couldn't let it go without leaving a little bit of himself behind. So, without telling me, shortly after signing our portion of the paperwork, he tunneled his way into the code."

"I don't understand," I said.

"Along with being one of the very best coders in the world, Andy was also one of the best hackers," Eldridge said. "He used to brag that there wasn't an encrypted system around that he couldn't figure out a way into."

"That kind of thing could get you arrested," Candice said.

"It could, and I have no doubt that Andy stopped just short of abusing it—that is, until we were closing on our deal with InvoTech. I doubt that they would have been the wiser had not someone on their side actually been inspecting the code just as Andy opened up a back door. He left it open too, just so that he could look at it or manipulate it at a later date."

"Is that even legal, contractually speaking?" Candice asked.

"No," Eldridge said, and he looked irritated about it. "Like I said, Andy did this without telling me. If he had told me, I would've called bullshit and stopped him, which is why he did it in secret."

"But why?" I asked. "Why would Andy want to sneak back in to mess around with the code he sold for hundreds of millions and claimed that he wanted to leave behind?"

Stanton smiled and traced a circle on his desk with his index finger. "I don't know for sure, but I suspect it's because Market Vision was his baby—his virtual house. And he wanted a set of keys to that virtual house for those times when he was traveling far from home and feeling nostalgic. I think he also wanted to make sure that the code was being used properly, and not for counter-competitive reasons."

"Counter-competitive?" I said. "What's that?"

Stanton leaned back in his chair and laced his fingers together. "We've always likened our company to Switzerland during World War Two. We're neutral. If Coke and Pepsi both came to us at the same time with similar-tasting sodas they wanted to launch, we'd generate PFTs for them without ever divulging that we'd run algorithms for both companies, and we'd do that without slanting the results one over the other, because we have to be neutral to be true to the marketplace. That's our real customer. We want to avoid the Edsels, Betamaxes, and Google Glasses of the world. But as you yourselves pinpointed, we hold the holy grail of information for product developers. Our algorithms could be used to either offer confidence or force companies to abandon a product they believed would be a market failure. That kind of information is incredibly valuable and in the wrong hands could be quite destructive."

"In other words," I said, "if Coke came to you guys and said something like, 'We'll pay you ten million dollars to rig the PFT results for Pepsi's new cola product,' and you took the money and did that, you could keep a potentially great product out of the hands of consumers, and give Coke a leg up in the competition."

"That's exactly it," Stanton said. "And that's what Andy was most worried about. Corporate espionage is a very real thing and obtaining a competitor's PFT or even manipulating that score is something we're constantly having to fight against. Over the years we've had to fend off attacks on our systems from both foreign and domestic aggressors."

I remembered what Dutch had said about the FBI speaking with Andy a few years earlier about an espionage threat from China. Apparently it was true.

"Andy was nervous that InvoTech hadn't taken the threat seriously enough," Stanton continued. "He told me after I confronted him on Friday about the back door that he wanted a way to police the code from the back end to make sure no SEC rules were broken and that the technology wasn't being used for corrupt purposes."

"How were you first alerted to the fact that Andy had tunneled his way in?" Candice asked.

"I got a call from Chevy Zeller, the CTO at InvoTech. He told me about the tech on his staff who saw it open up in front of his eyes, and was able to quickly put a trace on it back to a familiar IP address, which routed back to us. I knew there was only one person here who could've been responsible.

"Anyway the whole deal almost blew up then and there, but I was able to talk Zeller down off the ceiling and got him to agree to let us fix it. He put a lock on the wire of funds for the sale of our company until we could remove the back door and hand over all of the source codes that had been contracted originally to stay here."

"What did that mean?" I asked. My head was swimming with all this tech-speak.

"It meant changing the terms of the sale," Eldridge said with a heavy sigh. "InvoTech would get to store the source code—the original code that Andy created when he invented the PFT rating system—which would prevent it from being duplicated or tinkered with by anyone here, including Andy. Once they took possession, all InvoTech had to do was to change a small part of the source code on their end, and we'd be locked out indefinitely.

"It also probably meant that I'd lose my job as president of the company and that InvoTech could easily lock out all the employees too. Holding on to the source code would've prevented InvoTech from dismantling us."

"Were you mad about the compromise?" Candice asked carefully.

Eldridge rolled his eyes. "Of course I was mad," he said. "But as long as the deal goes through, I'll be fine, financially speaking. It's the staff that I'm worried about. These guys have been very loyal to us, and if we close on this thing with InvoTech, they could be out of a job by the end of the summer."

"Why not just let the sale blow up, then?" I asked. "I mean, you said earlier that Andy promised you'd shut the back door, but I'm guessing by your conversation with that other man who came in here that he didn't?"

"No," Eldridge said with a hint of anger in his voice. "He didn't. And letting it blow up exposes us to litigation from InvoTech. They'll sue us and collect damages. Probably heavy damages."

"Yikes," Candice said. "What're you going to do?"

Eldridge shrugged. "Work through it," he said. "But with Andy's sudden death, this is all going to be an uphill battle."

"Who gets the shares of the company now that Andy's passed away?" Candice asked.

"Most of the shares revert to me," Stanton said. "With ten percent assigned to Robin or her next of kin. But with this back door still open and our flanks exposed to litigation from Invo-Tech, it won't matter how many shares come my way if I don't find a way to close it."

"In other words, you're basically screwed," Candice said bluntly.

"Beyond screwed," Stanton agreed. The stress of what he'd already been through and what he was facing was etched clearly in the lines of worry on his forehead and the dark circles under his eyes. No wonder he'd snapped at us.

"Getting back to Andy and Robin," Candice said. "What can you tell us about their enemies?"

"Enemies?" Stanton repeated. "What do you want to know that for? Aren't you guys looking for that construction worker?"

"We are," she assured him. "But we have reason to believe there's more to the story."

"What does that mean?"

"It means we're convinced that there were more people involved, and that the motive wasn't simple robbery," I said.

Stanton gulped and seemed to take that in. "You think Andy and Robin were targeted for some reason besides money?"

I looked at Candice, who answered, "Possibly. We're not sure yet. If the deal with InvoTech never went through, and the money wasn't transferred, then how much money could Andy have had in his panic room for thieves to steal?"

"Millions," Stanton said bluntly. "Andy kept a personal stash of two million on hand at his house at all times."

My eyes bugged. "Two *million* in cash?"

"Yes." Eldridge affirmed it casually, like it was an everyday thing to have two million dollars just lying around the house.

"Did you tell the police this?" Candice asked.

"I did. I spoke with Detective Grayson this morning. Haven't *you* guys talked to them?"

"We have," I said. "This morning, just like you, but Detective Grayson never mentioned that the Roswells had that kind of cash on them." (What? It wasn't a lie. Grayson never mentioned it when she was asking us about Dave.)

"That's a lot of money to keep in a house," Candice said. "Why would Andy and Robin want that kind of stash anywhere other than a bank?"

"There was a hell of a lot more in the bank," he said. "Andy was worth about fifty million even before the sale of Market Vision. But, to answer your question, I think it made him feel safe. He grew up in the foster care system, and as a young man there were times when he literally survived on pennies a day. He told me the first time he'd had more than fifty dollars in his wallet was when he was a senior in high school and earned his first paycheck at a grocery store. Having cash on hand made him feel safe in a way, and I know that Robin liked to have it around too."

"How'd you get along with Robin?" I asked, curious about his feelings for his partner's wife.

Eldridge smiled, and it was sweet and sad. His eyes misted again and he ducked his chin to wipe the moisture away. "She was one of my best friends."

"She was?" Candice said, unable to keep the surprise out of her voice. Maybe it was because the picture Robin's sister had painted of her was of someone so shallow and materialistic.

"Yes," Eldridge said, either ignoring or not noticing her reaction. "Robin was the first person I came out to. She made me feel safe, and after my declaration, she made me feel accepted. Hell, she made me feel special. I come from a very religious Southern Baptist family. My parents still don't know I'm gay, although I think they've figured it out by now."

"I'm sorry you can't share it with them," I said. I could clearly see the burden of guilt on Stanton's shoulders. It's a heavy thing to be denied the opportunity of acceptance from those who should love you unconditionally. And I knew that firsthand.

Eldridge made a gesture like it was nothing, but I could see the pain in his eyes. Pain of the rejection he was certain to face from his parents if he ever came out to them. Pain from the accepting friend he'd lost. "Anyway," he said. "Lots of people didn't like Robin, and I get that. The woman was a first-class bitch, but she was also fabulous, fierce, and her own person. She didn't put up with shit, and if you were screwing up your life, she'd get in your face and tell you to get your shit together. I loved that about her most of all."

"Was there anyone specifically who you think might've had it out for her?" Candice asked next.

Eldridge appeared troubled, as if he knew of someone but didn't want to say the name. "Robin's ex might've been capable of doing something like this," he said at last. "In fact, before Detective Grayson said they were looking for the construction worker who worked on Andy's house, I would've told her to look in another direction."

"Can you tell us his name?" Candice pressed, getting ready to tap out the name on the notes section of her phone.

"*Her* name," Eldridge said. "Robin dated a woman prior to committing to Andy. Her ex was a certified psycho."

"Okay," Candice said, rolling with that added twist. "What's her name?"

"Murielle. Murielle McKenna."

I will admit that at this moment I just about fell out of my chair. "Are you serious?" I gasped. "Robin dated *Murielle?*"

He blinked at me. "You know her?"

"We do," Candice said. "We were under the impression Ms. McKenna was only fond of men."

Stanton snorted. "Murielle is fond of anyone beautiful. She likes men. She likes women. She likes a mix of both at times. I've often worried about my dog in her company."

That got my attention (and made me go *eww*, to boot). "So you know each other socially?"

"We do. We would often"—Stanton paused to use air quotes around the next word—"*bump* into Murielle when the three of us were out or at a party. She was clearly stalking Robin, and it got pretty creepy after a while."

"How long had Robin and Andy been married?" I asked. I'd gotten the impression they'd been together for a long time, but maybe I was wrong.

"The first time or the second?"

Candice and I looked at each other. She said, "They've been married to each other twice?"

"Yes," Stanton said. "They were married for four years, then split because of Murielle, whom Robin had a torrid affair with. She left Andy for Murielle, spent two years with that bitch before she wised up and came crawling back to him. Andy never dated anyone else, and he moped around here for those two years. He was happy to have her back, and I think that's part of the reason he wanted to sell off the company and leave town. He was sick and tired of having Murielle show up everywhere they went."

My toe began to tap under the table. I'd known that Murielle McKenna was no good the second she'd laid eyes on him! I mean, *I'd* laid eyes on *her*. (Okay, *and* she'd laid eyes on my husband . . . whatever . . .)

Meanwhile Candice continued to press Eldridge. "So you really believe Murielle was capable of murdering Andy and Robin?"

Eldridge leveled a look at her. "You've heard she's connected to some serious money, right? And you've also heard that her family is much feared in their home country, right? You don't cross Murielle without incurring consequences. You don't leave her and you don't cross her."

"She would've killed them just because Robin left her?" I asked. Something about the motive wasn't sitting well with my intuition.

Eldridge sagged in his seat and let out another long sigh. I thought the exhaustion and the stress and the sadness were finally catching up to him. "I think to understand, you have to know that Robin had acquired some insurance against Murielle when she left."

Candice cocked her head slightly. "What kind of insurance?"

"The video kind. She'd secretly taped Murielle begging her to stay and confessing to all sorts of personal failings. I saw the video. Murielle was a drunken, sniveling, sobbing mess. It was pathetic. And it would've humiliated Murielle if it was ever released to Robin's Facebook page—they share a lot of the same friends.

"Robin told Murielle that if she did anything to hurt her or Andy, she'd ensure the video would go viral. Murielle was enraged because she had no play other than to back off and let Robin go.

"And if Robin had been smart, she would've just packed her shit and left, but Robin wasn't always so smart, and as a parting gift to Murielle, she convinced a few of McKenna's staff members to go with her. As you can probably guess, Murielle is a nightmare to work for, but most of her staff is too afraid to leave. Robin convinced a few of them to come work for her and Andy, and Murielle knew that if Robin could pull away a few allies from the house, they'd be able to back up any story that Robin wanted to tell about Murielle."

I sucked in a small breath when something clicked in my mind. Candice turned to look at me at the exact same moment. She'd had the same epiphany. *The maid and the gardener!* I mouthed.

Candice nodded.

There was a knock on the conference door then, and a young, bearded, hipster-looking dude in a knit cap stuck his head in. "Sorry, Stanton, but InvoTech keeps calling about the code. They want you on the phone, uh . . . now."

Eldridge visibly paled. "I'll be right there, Jerrod."

"We'll leave you to it, Mr. Eldridge," I said, gathering my things. "Good luck today."

"Thanks," he said. "I'll need it."

Chapter Eleven

. . .

"Come on, Sundance! Bring it home!"

"Fuck . . . you . . . Candice . . . ," I huffed as I passed her on the high school track. She'd brought me out here for a "light" run, which, apparently, was Candice-code for "sprint until you vomit, then keep going until you faint, then wake up and keep going until you die."

I was currently on the die portion of the run and it was making me *reeeeally* pissy.

"Two more laps! Keep pushing!" Candice called after me, clapping her hands enthusiastically.

It's like she had a death wish or something. Well, maybe I'd die before I reached her at the last lap. She still had hope, if her overall chances weren't so good.

Maaaaaaaany minutes later, she wrapped an arm around me and said, "How's the smoothie?"

I sucked down some banana-yogurt-strawberry goodness and narrowed my eyes at her. "You're lucky I'm too winded to hit you."

"Well, at least you're making sense now. Right after that run I was worried I was going to have to call an ambulance."

So was I, but it hadn't been to take *me* away. Ah well, we were back to being besties. "What time are the boys meeting us?"

"In less than an hour," Candice said, looking at her watch. "We should head back to your place and get cleaned up."

"I don't know why they won't let us interrogate Murielle without them," I grumbled, getting into Candice's car.

"We have to be careful, Abs," she said. "If Murielle really is the killer, then she's got some serious anger and firepower. No way are the boys gonna let us go in there alone."

"I still can't figure out how Dave fits into all of this!" I said irritably. (Maybe my blood sugar levels hadn't gotten completely back to normal yet.)

"I wish I knew," Candice said. "He did meet Murielle, though."

"He did?"

"Yeah. Brice told me about it. She called Dutch to complain about Dave. I guess Dave showed up from another job to take some measurements, and at the time he was looking less than professional, or that's the way Murielle described him. Now, did they meet secretly later and plan to murder Robin and Andy Roswell? That I don't know, but would really like to find out."

This whole new angle wasn't sitting well with me. I didn't like all the coincidences. I didn't like them one bit. And we were still no closer to knowing what'd happened to Gwen, other than my radar's insisting that she'd been abducted. "I can't believe that with all of us looking for Dave, nobody's been able to spot him since this thing went down."

Candice appeared unsettled, and I could tell she was thinking about something she didn't really want to voice out loud. "What?" I asked her.

She made a twitchy motion with her lips before answering. "Dave wouldn't have to work very hard to change his looks, you know."

"Come again?"

"I'm saying that, if he was somehow mixed up in all of this, and wanted to get out of town without being seen, he could've ditched his truck, shaved his mustache, beard, and sideburns, then cut his hair, and presto—he's unrecognizable to most of the people who know him."

Candice had a solid point. A point I didn't like. Not one bit. "It wasn't him," I said moodily.

I was going to remain loyal to Dave until he sat down in front of me and said, "Abby, I did it. I murdered those people." Anything other than that and Dave would always be innocent in my mind.

"Okay," Candice said when I crossed my arms and turned my head to glare out the window. "Hey," she said, laying a hand on my arm. "We have to explore all of the possibilities, Abs. Including the ones we're uncomfortable with."

"I understand, Candice, but he *didn't do it*."

"I believe you," she said. Then she subtly picked up what was left of my smoothie from the cup holder and handed it to me. "How about you polish this off and I'll fix you up a nice chicken salad to eat on the way over to Murielle's, okay?"

I frowned and in a stilted, grumbly voice replied, "Well, that would be very nice of you and I would probably like that."

We met Brice and Dutch at the entrance to Murielle's Mc-Mansion. Dutch was out of the car and heading over to the call box when we pulled up behind Brice's car. "What's he doing?" I asked.

"He's probably giving the request to talk to her the personal touch," Candice said.

I swiped a lock of loose hair out of my eyes and rubbed my glossed lips together. For once, I was wearing makeup. And my hair wasn't in a ponytail. And it was clean. And styled. To be honest, it was a departure from the "ready to work out" look I typically sported. Not that the thought of visiting with Murielle again had *any*thing to do with that. I usually look like this on the third Tuesday of the month. Pinkie swear.

"What's taking him so long?" I asked as Candice and I waited silently for Dutch to finish his conversation with the call box.

"He's schmoozing his way inside," Candice said with a grin.

I narrowed my eyes at her. "You could at least be on my side, you know."

She chuckled. "I'm always on your side, Sundance."

Dutch abruptly stood tall and stepped away from the call box. The gate began to open and he offered us a thumbs-up, which

Candice returned. I might've been too busy clenching my fists to offer a similar gesture.

With the help of the house staff we gathered in Murielle's office again. And again she kept us waiting. Dutch sat next to me, his muscled arm draped heavily across my shoulders, and his free hand firmly holding mine.

Candice sat smirking next to us.

That won her a look from me, which only made her smile widen.

Murielle finally found the time to grace us with her presence and she walked into her office looking and smelling like a million dollars. Which, I suspect, was how much it took to maintain that kind of perfection.

Dutch squeezed my hand and allowed his face to fall into a flat expression. My heart kinda skipped a beat, because I knew that expression. It's very close to his cop face, but with an undercurrent of annoyance. "Dutch," she said huskily the moment she saw him, her whole face lighting up like a kid at Christmas. The rest of us might as well have been invisible chopped liver. "How lovely of you to come see me in person. Is this a social visit, I hope?"

Dutch never let go of my hand. "No, Murielle, we're here on official business."

Murielle sagged into her chair dramatically, but held the playful smile she'd walked in with. "Oh, that sounds so boring. I already told you I've withdrawn my complaint from your company. You and your people can carry on with the construction of my safe rooms."

"We're not here on that business, Ms. McKenna," Brice said.

Murielle never took her eyes off Dutch. "What other business do you and I have together, Dutch?"

"*You* have the kind that involves murder," I said, maybe a weensy bit smugly.

To my surprise, Murielle chuckled. She then reached into her desk drawer and withdrew a silver (or maybe platinum . . . it looked damn expensive) cigarette case. She tapped out a white cigarette and held it elegantly between two fingers before reaching for a lighter.

After taking a long pull from the cigarette and blowing it skyward, she motioned to me but said to Dutch, "That one is a little theatrical, no?"

"That one is my wife, Murielle," Dutch replied, his tone dangerously low and even.

Murielle rolled her eyes but kept the smile in place. After taking another long puff of her cigarette, she said, "Who was murdered and why do you think I had anything to do with it?"

"What do you know about the slaying of Robin and Andy Roswell and two of their staff?" Dutch said.

Murielle crossed the hand holding the cigarette over the other, and bounced her foot a few times while she considered Dutch. "I heard they were riddled with bullets. The scene must've been particularly grisly."

A trickle of fear slid like an icicle down my spine. Not only was Murielle unmoved by the news that her former lover had been brutally murdered, but she almost seemed to enjoy the idea of what the aftermath must've looked like.

"You say that like you might've had a glimpse of the scene," Brice said.

Murielle shrugged noncommittally.

"We thought you would've been more upset by the news," Candice said.

"Upset? Why would I be upset?"

"Didn't you and Mrs. Roswell have a relationship at some point?" Candice asked.

Murielle stopped bouncing her foot and took another drag from her cigarette without responding.

"See, we heard that you two had quite the affair," Candice continued. "And that things didn't end well. There's talk that a video was made. One that maybe you didn't want anyone else to know about."

Murielle narrowed her eyes at Candice and they were clearly the eyes of a cold-blooded killer. "Get out," she said ever so softly.

Candice and the rest of us sat there for a few beats.

Murielle reached over and lifted the landline phone from her desk to speak into the receiver. "Gustavo, would you please come and escort my guests from the property? Make sure they leave with the card to one of my attorneys, who will be filing suit against them in the morning."

"Well, that went well," Brice said once we'd been shown the exit by a big, scary, face-tattooed behemoth who probably had a yeti for a first cousin.

Candice looked ready to punch someone. Like herself. "Dammit," she muttered. "I'm sorry, you guys. I pushed her too hard."

"She would've clammed up like that sooner or later," Dutch said.

But I wasn't so sure. Murielle seemed to be the type that liked a good game of cat and mouse. What she didn't like was being disrespected, which I felt Candice had done, but I sure as hell wasn't going to point that out to her and make her feel worse than she already did.

"No, it was my fault," Candice said. "She might've tipped her hand a little more if I hadn't gotten up in her grill."

"She's not someone you get a confession out of, love," Brice said.

Candice offered him a grateful half smile. "I wasn't looking for a full confession so much as a clue to follow. If I'd reined it in a little, I could've asked her about Dave."

I turned to look at the front of Murielle's estate, wondering if Dave and Gwen might be nearby. Flipping on my radar, I searched for them in the ether, but I couldn't say for sure if they were somewhere hidden behind that giant facade, or maybe somewhere else far away. "What do we do now?" I asked.

"Now we start looking into Murielle's life," Dutch said. "Which isn't going to be easy, because with as much money as she has, her financials are probably made up of lots of shell corporations with offshore account numbers."

"In other words, trying to follow the money for any assassins she might've hired is gonna require a whole lot of effort with little result," Candice said.

"Yep," Brice agreed.

I looked again toward the estate, and my gaze drifted over to the set of windows that marked Murielle's office. To my surprise, she was standing there at the window, glaring in our direction with a cigarette dangling from her long fingers and smoke curling up around her head.

The funny thing was, I felt so strongly she wasn't glaring at us as a group. No, I felt so certain she was instead looking meanly at *me*.

So I looked meanly back. I mean, fuck her, right? She offered me her middle finger, and I will admit to having a moment where I *almost* lost my cool and went marching back through the front door to give her a sample taste from my personal can of whoop-ass, but then I remembered the yeti inside, and considered that, mad and pumped up with new muscle as I was, I still probably couldn't take him on.

"We might want to take a look at her security guy," I said, purposefully turning away from the window to focus on the riddle at hand. "He seems like just the guy you'd hire to cut a couple to ribbons with an AR-fifteen."

"What was his name again?" Brice asked as he pulled out his phone to make a note.

"Sasquatch," I said.

"Gustavo," Candice corrected with a friendly nudge to my shoulder.

"He did look like he's related to a yeti," Dutch agreed.

I beamed at him. "I love that you get me."

He wrapped an arm around me and I leaned into him, lifting my chin back to the window to offer Murielle a smug smile.

She puffed out a big plume of smoke and turned her back to us.

"I think we should get going," Dutch said when the front door opened and the yeti stuck his head out like he couldn't believe we were dumb enough to still be standing around in Murielle's driveway.

"Fine by me," I said, heading to Candice's car. For once I didn't mind her speedy getaway.

We all met back at our offices and came up with a game plan. "So our focus is going to be on Murielle," Brice said. "She's the most likely suspect in this scenario."

"Did you see the look she gave me when I asked her about the video?" Candice said. "We're all lucky to have made it out of her estate alive."

"I saw that," I said supportively. "That woman is totally capable of killing. Or at least hiring someone to kill."

"And her motive is, what? The video?" Brice said.

I sat forward when a small ping to my radar went off in my mind. "Ohmigod, do we even know where the video is?"

Candice's brow furrowed. "It's probably on Robin's cell phone."

"Okay, so where's her cell phone?"

Everyone looked at one another.

Dutch pulled out his own phone and said, "I'll call my buddy at APD. It'll be inventoried unless the killer or killers took it with them when they robbed the place."

I put a hand on his arm to keep him from dialing the phone just yet. "Does APD know exactly how much cash was taken out of the Roswells' safe room, Dutch?"

"Want me to ask?"

"Yes, please." There was something that was nagging me about the crime scene. Something that I couldn't quite place, but wanted to.

Dutch got up and went to make the call while the rest of us talked about Murielle as a suspect.

Candice moved to her computer and began to poke around in Murielle's social media accounts. "Whoa," she said almost right away.

"What?" Brice and I asked.

"Come here, you two," she said. "Look at this."

Brice and I moved to just behind Candice's shoulders and peered at her screen. She indicated a photo on Murielle's Instagram, which mostly showed the heiress posing alluringly in front of the camera, but behind her were two familiar faces. "That's Robin and Andy Roswell," I said of the couple in the background, who were actually glaring at Murielle.

"It gets better," Candice said, and she began to scroll forward through the pictures. Time and time again when Murielle was taking a selfie, Robin and Andy could be seen in the background. The settings and outfits varied, so that we knew these were all taken on different nights at different places, and the hashtags associated with each photo indicated that Murielle, Andy, and Robin frequented the VIP rooms of all the hottest Austin nightspots.

"It almost looks like they're stalking her," I said.

Candice winked at me. "That would be the obvious point here, Sundance."

"What do you mean?"

"Murielle is making it look like she's the one being stalked by Andy and Robin, not the other way around. See how she always gets one shot where she's rolling her eyes with the camera pointed mostly over her shoulder at them? She's creating a visual story to tell people of that social circle that she's the victim."

"Whoa," I said. "That's like . . . diabolical."

"Do we know that's not the truth?" Brice asked. We all stared blankly at him. "What I'm saying is, do we know that they *weren't* stalking her to every bar in town?"

Candice shrugged. "No, but you've met her, Brice. Do *you* think she's someone worth stalking?"

"Hell no," he said, then nodded to his wife. "Okay, point taken. Also, I wouldn't want to mess with her because rumor has it that her family's connected to the mob."

"How come you guys decided to do business with her if she's supposedly connected to the mob?" Candice asked. "Doesn't that cross your line of Boy Scout ethics or something?"

Brice smiled at his wife. "It does, and trust me—before we agreed to work with her, we did our homework. She came up squeaky clean on our background check. If she's involved in something illegal, no federal branch has any record of it. There was no reason to deny her a contract for the safe rooms."

Dutch came back to us, pocketing his phone before sitting down. "Sorry that took so long. I was on hold a while. APD has Robin's cell. It was on the counter in the kitchen."

"Have they checked the photo library?" I asked. "Is the video of Robin dumping Murielle there?"

"APD is still going through the evidence," Dutch said. "My contact said he'd check for us, though."

I frowned. "I'm not sure that it matters if it's there or not."

"Why wouldn't it matter?" Candice asked.

"Because even if it's not there, and Murielle's motive for killing Andy and Robin was revenge for Robin leaving her, recording their breakup, and taking two members of her staff, Murielle couldn't know that there wasn't a copy of that video on Robin's cell or up in the cloud somewhere, right? At the very least, whoever killed the couple should've grabbed the cell and turned it off—especially since these days all you need to alert nine-one-one is to give a shout-out to Siri."

Dutch eyed me thoughtfully and nodded. "You're right."

"And another thing," I continued. "The killer should've taken the phone and forced Robin to give up her password to the cloud, so that, if it was backed up there, the video could've been erased on both the phone and the cloud. In other words, no way would Murielle's hired killer leave Robin's cell behind."

"I agree," Dutch said while both Candice and Brice nodded.

I got up to pace the room then, because so much wasn't making sense here and I was getting all sorts of weird, mixed signals. It was hell trying to untangle them. "As much as I hate to admit it, I'm not sure I'm buying the story of Murielle seeking revenge for being dumped and made a fool of. The Roswells' murders feel like overkill. It's as if the killer or killers didn't just want them dead—they wanted them annihilated. Obliterated. Disfigured, dismembered, and destroyed."

Brice crossed his arms over his chest. "That's what happens when you bring an AR-fifteen to the party. No one ends up in an open casket."

But I shook my head. "No, it's more than just that, Brice." I stopped pacing to stand still and close my eyes to better concentrate. "The people that did this to the Roswells, they don't feel *connected* to them, you know? Like there's a level of removal with them."

"Hadn't we already established that if Murielle is the killer, she would've hired someone to kill Robin and Andy?" Candice said.

"Yeah, yeah," I said, frowning and opening my eyes again. "But that's not what I mean. I'm trying to say that this was a pretty sloppy job when you think about it, right?"

For effect I looked at Dutch, Brice, and Candice with meaning. I wanted them to feel what I felt in the ether so that maybe they'd understand what I was trying to get at.

Brice offered me a slight one-shoulder shrug. "Like I said, it wasn't the cleanest of hits."

I went with that and made my next point, which was what was really bugging me. "Not only wasn't it the cleanest of hits, Brice, but there was a shit ton of evidence left behind, including Robin's cell phone, and all of that speaks to an amateur job."

"I guess I still don't understand your point, Edgar," Dutch said.

I turned to him. "Murielle doesn't strike me as tolerating sloppy, babe. She strikes me as the type who'd hire a professional to get the job done right. She sure as hell wouldn't let a trail lead back to her, and she had to at least suspect that there might be video on Robin's cell phone or up in the cloud somewhere where we in law enforcement could eventually find it. If the Roswells were murdered on Saturday, and Candice and I didn't discover the bodies until Sunday, that would've given Murielle plenty of time to send the killers back to the house and retrieve Robin's cell phone."

"That's true," Candice agreed.

"Right," I said. "So why didn't she?"

"Good question," Brice said.

"Also," I said, pacing again because I was on a roll, "this whole connection to Dave is really weird. I mean, *why* would Murielle want to either recruit Dave or frame him for the murders?"

"To throw suspicion off her?" Candice tried. "He would've had easy access to the property. The Roswells knew him."

"Yeah, but how would that matter to Murielle? She knew a lot of people who knew them. She floated in their same circles, after all. And she was constantly showing up where they were, so she had to have known a little bit about their schedules."

And then I snapped my fingers and pointed to Dutch. "And how was it that Murielle came to Safe Chambers, anyway? You think it was a coincidence that she decided to use the very same builder as the one that Andy and Robin used?"

"She floated in the same social circles," Candice reminded me. "I'll bet you that Robin bragged about her new safe room to some mutual friend or posted something about it on her social media page and Murielle picked up on it and made the call. Plus, to your earlier point, if Murielle knew the Roswells' schedules—and it seems like she knew their schedules enough to continue to stalk them across the Austin area club scene—then she could've easily figured out or found out that they were home on Saturday."

I frowned. "Okay, so even if she did know they were home, why would she pick Saturday afternoon of all times to send in her hit squad? My point is, she'd be far more likely to schedule something for after an event she was certain they had all attended, both to create a legitimate alibi for herself and to easily track the two of them back to their place. The timing of the actual hit suggests that at best she'd have to guess that Andy and Robin would be home, and she'd have to hope that her hit man or hit men didn't make too much noise, and if they were bringing AR-fifteens, then of course they'd be making some noise. No, this type of hit makes more sense for the early morning hours on Saturday, not one o'clock in the afternoon in broad daylight."

Everyone was silent for a few moments before Brice said, "While persuasive, all of that still doesn't mean that Murielle isn't behind the hit, Abby."

I sighed and sat down. "You're right, Brice."

"Is your intuition saying that she didn't have something to do with it?" Candice asked gently.

I shook my head. "I gotta admit, this thing is so muddled and so complicated that I can't tell which end is up. Did Murielle order a hit on Robin and Andy? I have no idea. I just can't tell. What I can say is that this thing isn't nearly as simple as we want it to be."

Dutch nodded toward me. "To Abby's point about it being complicated, now that Robin and Andy are dead, we need to ask ourselves how Dave was mixed up in all this, and why was Gwen kidnapped?"

"That's right," I said. "We all believe Dave is innocent and that he's being used against his will, which is the only reason it would make sense to kidnap Gwen. The killer or killers need something from Dave, and they're using Gwen to control him."

"So what could Dave do for them?" Candice asked.

Across from me, Brice's face drained of color and he looked sharply at Dutch, who also looked shocked and upset. "He could open doors," Dutch said softly. "He probably knows the security codes to dozens of our customers."

It was Candice's turn to look alarmed. "Which means he could open doors to some of the wealthiest houses in Austin."

"Dammit!" Brice swore, before getting quickly to his feet. "We need to call all our clients."

What followed was several hours of somewhat panic-driven phone calls to every client Safe Chambers had ever had. We couldn't reach a lot of them, which wasn't really surprising because this was a class of people who were probably too busy to answer their own phones, or were jet-setters, off in the world somewhere, yachting and working on their tans.

The fact that we couldn't reach almost half of them bothered me. A lot.

Still, we left everyone messages and asked them to call us, day or night. We got a few immediate calls back, which was good, but there were still about twenty people on the list whom we couldn't reach.

"What are we telling people?" I asked, my hand covering the microphone on my phone when I'd gotten my first client on the line.

Dutch appeared in the doorway to my office. "Tell them we've recently let an employee go who may have accessed our client's private security data. They'll need to change their security system codes immediately, just as a precaution."

I jotted that down on the notepad in front of me and said it to every person I spoke to. No one seemed particularly upset or alarmed, which also bothered me. I wanted them to be worried enough to change their security codes ASAP.

As darkness settled onto the city, the four of us met back in Candice's office. Brice, Dutch, and Candice each wore a frustrated, worried expression—likely mirroring my own. "I feel like we haven't done enough," I said.

Brice paced the room like I had an hour earlier. "We need to consider calling APD about this."

"I agree," Candice said.

"Me too," said Dutch.

"Me three," I agreed, and everyone looked at me. "What?"

"Nothing," Dutch said. "I just didn't expect you to be on board with getting APD involved before we've had a chance to track Dave down."

I shook my head. "We've got to protect these people, honey. And I don't like how the ether is feeling right now."

"How's the ether feeling right now?" Candice asked.

"Bad," I admitted. I'd had the most anxious feeling creep over me the past hour and a half. Something terrible was going to happen, or maybe it'd already happened; I couldn't tell.

"I'll make the call," Dutch said, tapping his phone to pull up his source at APD.

"Call Detective Grayson," I said before he could place the call to his buddy.

Dutch paused with his finger over the screen of his phone. "Grayson?"

"Yes. Call her."

Dutch clicked back to his contacts list, but before he found her number, his screen lit up with an incoming call. "Whoa," he said, holding it up so that we could see. "It's Grayson."

I moved to a chair next to Candice and sat down heavily. "Then it's already happened," I said.

"What?" Candice said as Dutch answered the call.

"Whatever terribleness comes next," I whispered.

Chapter Twelve

. . .

Dutch hung up the phone and we all stared hard at him, trying to piece together what'd happened from the snippets of conversation he'd had with Grayson, which was impossible, because mostly Dutch had stuck to cursing under his breath and putting a hand up to his forehead in distress.

"What's happened?" Candice asked.

I felt my stomach muscles clench. I almost couldn't stand to hear what he was about to tell us.

"Who had Chris Wixom on their list tonight?"

I glanced at the piece of paper Candice had printed off with a list of Safe Chamber's clients. "That would be me," I said, remembering the name as someone on the list I'd set up an appointment for on the previous Saturday—the same guy whose house we'd driven by on Sunday right before we discovered the victims at the Roswell residence. "I marked him as unavailable, but I left him a message."

Dutch's expression was unreadable, but his eyes held such worry, I almost couldn't take it. "Earlier tonight, Chris was shot in his home by Dave McKenzie," my husband said, his voice rough with anger.

Brice sucked in a breath and Candice let out a small gasp. "How do they know it was Dave?"

"Chris is still alive. Before being taken away in an ambulance, he identified Dave as the shooter."

A disconnected feeling washed over me at the news. It was almost as if this reality was too much for me to handle, and I mentally backed away from it. Whatever Candice, Dutch, and Brice discussed after that, I don't remember, because I was too busy trying to deny what I'd just heard. "It's not possible," I heard myself say after a bit. And just like that, I mentally checked back in again.

To my surprise, I realized that Dutch was squatting down in front of me, concern in his eyes. "It's true, dollface," he said, reaching up to tuck a lock of my hair behind my ear. "And we've got to get to the crime scene. I'd have Candice drive you home, but I think I'm gonna need you there, unless you really don't want to come?"

"I'm okay," I said, taking a deep breath and getting to my feet. "I just . . . it's . . ." I couldn't even put into words my disbelief over the fact that Dave, of all people, had tried to murder an innocent man. Nothing from what I knew about my friend, either anecdotally or intuitively, made logic out of that.

"I know," Dutch said, his expression a little anguished. "I can't make sense of it either."

"Come on, guys," Candice said gently, motioning to us from the doorway. "We've got to get down there and talk to Grayson before she leaves."

We arrived at the scene about twenty minutes later.

Chris Wixom's house had been the last stop before Candice and I had driven to the Roswells' residence. It'd been the one that'd had all the blinds drawn and no cars in the driveway.

The fact that Wixom's house was hit made some sense; if they'd discussed the security code, then Dave would've had it fresh in his notes, whereas he might've long forgotten the security codes of many of the other clients of Safe Chambers. I could see how suspicious it was that Dave had arrived Saturday to take measurements and talk about the panic room with Wixom. They could've talked about the security system already in place, about what time Wixom activated it each day or night, and where Chris's valuables were stored. Dave could've tweezed all sorts of secure information out of Wixom without the homeowner ever being the wiser. It made me shudder to think how vulnerable we all were because of what Dave appeared to be up to. Barring another explanation, which I was at a loss to come up with, this current crime spree of Dave's would ruin all four of us, both financially and emotionally. We'd be sued into the ground, and I couldn't imagine that Brice and Dutch would survive with the bureau after a criminal investigation into the business practices of Safe Chambers was launched. I had no doubt that would follow too, because the people being targeted were the kinds of powerful folks with even more powerful political friends, and they all protected their own.

The ride over had been dead silent, as I'm sure the same thoughts were ricocheting around in everyone else's minds. When we pulled up to Wixom's street, it was awash in red and white strobe lights that danced and bounced across the surrounding area, lending the scene an extra dose of urgency.

We parked behind a patrol car and walked up to the yellow tape strung across the road where an officer was standing guard. Brice and Dutch flashed their badges and we were allowed to pass.

Grayson was squatting in the doorway of Wixom's front entrance, eyeing a red swath of fresh blood on the slate next to her feet. She held a flashlight in one hand, and a small notepad in the other.

Dutch called out to her and without looking up, she said, "I figured I'd see you four here sooner or later."

"We want to help," Brice said, stopping at the walkway.

Grayson eyed him slyly. "I'll bet."

"Is there any word on Wixom?" I asked, because I was very concerned about him. I remembered speaking to him the week before, and he'd sounded like a nice man. I hated that he'd been targeted like this.

"He's in surgery," Grayson said, getting to her feet and stepping carefully across the blood trail. She walked to us then, and I could tell she was mentally calculating how to get the most information out of us while appearing to fill us in on what'd happened.

"I saw your number on Wixom's landline caller ID, Abby. I tried calling you a couple of times and when I couldn't reach you, I called your husband."

I had a moment of panic as I searched my purse for my phone; then I remembered that I'd left it on my desk back at the office. It'd been nearly out of its charge, so I'd plugged it in and obviously hadn't heard it when Grayson had called me. "My phone is back at the office."

Grayson turned to look at the house. "You called right in the middle of all of this going down," she said. "Weird timing, don't you think?"

I felt my shoulders tense. Did she think we had something to do with this?

"We were calling Wixom to warn him about McKenzie," Brice said. "We realized too late that if Dave really was responsible for the murders at the Roswells', our other clients were also vulnerable."

Grayson turned to Brice. "I'd say so."

Brice cleared his throat uncomfortably. "Can you run us through what happened?"

"Sure," the detective said. "About seven thirty this evening, Wixom says, his doorbell rang. He checked through the peephole and saw Dave McKenzie standing on his front steps. Because he recognized McKenzie, he opened the door and that's when he got a gun shoved in his face. He says McKenzie was with another male, and the pair pushed their way in and ordered Wixom to get down on the ground with his hands behind his head. As Wixom was crouching, about to get on the floor, his landline rang—that was your call, Abby—and when McKenzie and his partner turned their heads in the direction of the ringing landline in the kitchen, Wixom started to bolt toward the front door, when he was popped twice in the back. The first bullet went through and through; the other's still inside him. He fell in the front foyer and blacked out. He thinks McKenzie left him for dead, and went on to rob the place. At some point Wixom woke back up, somehow managed to get to his feet, and stumbled down his driveway to the neighbor across the street. They were the ones who called it in."

I glanced at Dutch. His face was expressionless, but the vein at his temple was throbbing. Hearing what Dave had done to Chris Wixom was killing him.

I reached for his hand and found his fist clenched, but he relaxed it when he felt my fingers and looped his around mine. "What'd they get away with?" he asked Grayson.

The detective glanced at her notepad. "Looks like a lot of cash and a few valuables. Wixom collected expensive watches. His whole collection seems to be missing. We'll get a better idea of what they took off with when he comes out of surgery. Assuming his wound isn't fatal."

"Was he shot with the same caliber as the Roswells?" Brice asked next.

"No," Grayson said. "He was shot with a thirty-eight. We think that's the only reason he survived the shooting. The AR-fifteen at close range would've ripped a hole in him too big to plug."

"Did you talk to him?" Candice asked the detective.

"Wixom?"

"Yes."

"I was the first detective on scene," she said. "In fact, it was a tie between me and one of the patrols."

"How'd you get here so fast?" Candice asked curiously.

"I was down the road at the Roswells' place, going over that crime scene one more time, and heard the home invasion call come in through dispatch."

"Weird timing," I said to her, just to be snarky.

Her mouth quirked slightly. "We're on the same team, you know," she said.

"I do," I agreed. "I just wanted to make sure you knew it too."

Grayson crossed her arms. "I have no reason to suspect any of you had anything to do with either the murders at the Roswell residence or what happened here tonight. But I am a little worried you've been trying to protect your friend Mr. McKenzie, and I'm also worried that even after tonight, you might not fully cooperate with our efforts to locate him."

I made sure to look Grayson right in the eye when I said, "Nikki, I want *nothing* more than to find Dave. And Gwen while we're at it. Please trust me on that. And if you guys find them first, then I'm okay with it. In fact, if there's any way we can help you locate Dave before he gets himself killed, then just say the word. We'll do whatever you need us to."

She squinted at me for a half second before offering a congenial nod. "Okay, Abby. I believe you."

"Can we take a look inside?" Brice asked.

Grayson frowned. "No way," she said. "I can't. There's too much of a conflict of interest here given that McKenzie works for your company, Agent Harrison. And don't even start with the Roswell-foreign-espionage angle—there's no way that applies here, or even over there anymore, really."

Candice pointed to Grayson's cell phone, which was clipped to her waist. "Can we at least look at the photos you took of the scene inside?"

Grayson's mouth quirked again. "What makes you think I took photos of the scene inside?"

Candice smiled back at her. "Because you're a damn good detective, Grayson, and that's what I'd do if I was in your shoes."

Grayson chuckled softly and unclipped her phone. "I can show you a couple of the photos," she said. "But when I show you, your own cell phones need to be in your pockets. No taking shots of my shots, got it?"

Candice pocketed her cell, and Brice and Dutch did the same. Satisfied, Grayson called up several of the interior images of the home, which was brightly lit and sparsely furnished.

One particular series of photos was of Wixom's bedroom,

which had obviously been ravaged. Clothes and dresser drawers lay strewn on the floor, and the closet door was open to reveal an area in the wall about three feet wide and two feet high that was nothing more than a large gaping hole. "Wall safe," Grayson said, pointing to the hole. "We think they pulled it out with the use of an ax or maybe a sledgehammer. They took it with them, and they'll probably get it open one way or another."

"How much was in the safe?" Candice asked.

Grayson turned the phone back to click off the pictures. "That was the last question I asked Wixom before he was taken away in the ambulance. He says he had close to a hundred thousand in cash, his mother's engagement ring, and some bonds in there."

"What's with these people hiding so much money in their homes?" Candice muttered.

I was with her on that one. Dutch and I weren't superrich, but we were well-off, thanks to the profits from his security business, and at the very most, we kept only about a grand in the house at any given time.

Candice too kept a reserve of petty cash at her place, but it was only about five thousand, and I knew that because I'd seen her get paid that in cash for a job once and she'd stuffed the money inside the small floor safe in her condo, where she kept her valuables; I knew the cash was still there, as I'd seen her open that same safe a few times since.

For the most part we all put our serious money where it belonged—in the bank.

"Wixom's positive it was Dave, though?" Dutch asked.

"He is," Grayson said. "He told me at least three times it was McKenzie."

"Any idea who his partner was?" Brice said.

"No," she said. "He blacked out as I was asking."

I looked anxiously toward the front door of Wixom's house again. I badly wanted to go inside and get a feel of the ether in there. Something was way off about all of this. It was like I was looking at all the pieces to a puzzle that everyone was saying was a zebra, but all I could see in the image was a polar bear. The pieces were identifiable, but the picture wasn't.

"Nikki," I said softly. "I know you don't want your crime scene compromised, but, please. I *need* to get in there and feel out the energy."

Detective Grayson considered me for a long moment before answering, and I could see how torn she was about the decision. If Dave was in fact responsible, and the defense found out that I'd been inside the house after the crime went down, they could throw serious shade at any evidence collected, suggesting that I'd compromised the scene to protect myself and my husband's business from any civil suit brought. "It's out of the question tonight, Abby," Grayson said, and my hopes fell. "But meet me at the APD substation tomorrow morning at nine, and I'll bring you two out here to walk you through the house. If you let on to *anybody* that I allowed you inside, though, I'll have the prosecution treat you as a hostile witness and you'll never make your way onto any APD crime scene again. Got it?"

"I do," I said, relieved. "And I won't tell anyone. I promise."

Grayson looked meaningfully at Brice, Dutch, and Candice too, and they each held up their hands in surrender. We all understood the stakes.

"Good," Grayson said when she was satisfied. "Now get the hell off my crime scene, and if you hear anything from or about McKenzie, you call me immediately."

Brice dropped Dutch and me off at our car and Dutch drove us home in somber silence. After greeting the pups and getting them watered and fed, he pointed me to the master suite and told me to take a bath while he warmed up some leftovers for us.

He didn't have to tell me twice, and I sat in the huge garden tub while it filled with hot, soothing water and created some terrific suds as my favorite scented candles infused the air with jasmine. Leaning my head back in a contented sigh, I powered up some soft music on my earphones and calmed my nerves with a big ol' goblet filled with red wine that I'd nicknamed Big Mike. I'm not sure how long Big Mike and I were alone together, but at some point the bathwater was disturbed by another guy nicknamed Big, who made me forget all about Mike.

Twenty minutes later I lay against Dutch's chest with a soapy-dopey, satisfied smile on my face. "I think I'm hungry, but I'm not sure I care about eating."

"I warmed up some leftovers for us," Dutch said lazily. "They're probably cold again."

My soapy-dopey smile grew bigger. "I've got something you can warm up a second time."

He chuckled, low and deep. I think Dutch's laugh is the sexiest thing on the planet. It sends a shiver of pleasure right down to my hoo-ha every time. "Again?" he said. "You're insatiable."

I inched up his chest and wrapped my arms around his neck. "Lucky man."

"Don't I know it," he said, leaning forward to kiss me slow and deep.

Forty minutes later my soapy-dopey smile was a full-on perma grin, and I didn't even care that the water had cooled. Dutch got gingerly out of the tub and reached for a towel before lifting me out with ease.

For the record, there's nothing sexier than being lifted out of the tub by a big, strong, sexy man. Okay, so maybe being lifted out of the tub by a big, strong, sexy man with a throaty chuckle is sexier. . . . Uh, oh. There goes my hoo-ha again.

Anyway, Dutch finally got me to stand on my own wobbly legs while he wrapped a towel around me and led me to the kitchen. We ate the leftovers cold, and no, we didn't even mind. Then we went to bed, but neither one of us could sleep.

In spite of our romantic time in the tub together, what was going on with Dave had crept back into the front of our thoughts and we needed to talk it out with each other. "Are you worried about Safe Chambers getting sued?" I asked Dutch.

"Very," he admitted. "I don't see how it'll be able to survive this mess, Edgar. The business is finished."

The ether was filled with all sorts of terrible possibilities. None of them felt set yet, but there were so many roads that led to rough financial waters for us that I didn't have any faith that we'd be able to survive it either.

"How bad could it get for us?" I asked, almost afraid of his answer.

He hugged me a little tighter. "Bad," he said. "Robin Roswell's sister and Chris Wixom could come after us personally if our liability insurance won't settle the case to their satisfaction."

"What'll we do?"

Dutch sighed. "Ride it through. What's going to be will be."

We were both quiet for a bit before Dutch said, "I'm less worried about the money and more worried about Dave and Gwen, though. Especially Gwen."

My radar pinged with urgency. "I'm really worried about her too."

"You think she's still in danger?"

"I do. And Dave's in danger as well. I have a terrible feeling in the pit of my stomach about what they're both up against right now. I suppose the only good thing is that I very much feel that they're both still alive."

Dutch scratched at the stubble on the side of his face. "I can't understand what would make Dave shoot Wixom. I mean, what the hell, right?"

I shook my head, which was awkward, because it was resting on Dutch's chest. "It's so completely out of character. I want to say he was forced to do it, but hearing Grayson recite Wixom's account of how it went down, it doesn't sound like Dave was forced to do anything."

"I want to know where he's hiding," Dutch said. "Both our guys and APD have been combing through security footage from all the traffic cams and toll roads, and there's no sign of Dave's truck. I don't understand how he's getting around."

"Grayson said he was with someone else. Maybe they ditched the truck and are driving something new."

"Yeah, maybe," Dutch said. We were quiet for a long time and I began to fall asleep when Dutch whispered, "I'm not gonna rest until we find them, dollface. One way or another, I'm bringing Dave and Gwen home."

Candice and I met Detective Grayson at her cubicle located at the North APD substation off Lamplight Village Avenue. It's typical for a publicly owned and funded building: lots of concrete and the personality of a discarded refrigerator box, but everyone inside is friendly enough. Well, unless you're on the wrong side of the law. Or had ever been on the wrong side of the law.

Candice and I made sure to step lightly.

"Morning," Grayson said when she walked in, wearing a slim-cut charcoal suit and a bright raspberry silk top that made her skin tone pop.

I noticed that she seemed to have taken special care with her makeup, and her hair was down and styled. A sly smile tugged at the corners of my mouth. "Hot date tonight?" I asked with a little bounce to my eyebrows.

Grayson's cheeks tinged pink. "Shut that shit down, Abby," she said, pointing to my forehead.

I rocked back and forth on my heels, greatly amused. No way was I stopping. "He's supercute. And I see he also works with the law, but his employment has to do with books and there's a connection to government. City attorney, by chance?"

Grayson's cheeks warmed to a deeper hue and she looked around to see who might be listening. Of course *everyone* in the area—about six detectives in total—was staring at us curiously. "I could arrest you, you know."

"Second date?" I said, completely unfazed. I've been to jail. It ain't no thang. "Looks like you might get lucky if you play your cards right."

Grayson narrowed her eyes and reached into her side drawer to withdraw a set of handcuffs. "I'm not playing, Cooper."

I laughed and Candice covered her lips with a finger to stifle a giggle. "Okay, okay," I said, holding up my hands in surrender. "But for the record, you look gorgeous today. Stunning, actually. He'll be lucky to be seen out with you."

Grayson pocketed the cuffs before tugging at the front of her blazer, but I could tell she was pleased by the compliment. "Can we just focus on the Wixom and Roswell cases this morning?"

"Of course," I said. But then one more thing occurred to me, and I almost hesitated mentioning it, because it was early and I knew that Nikki would be disappointed.

"What?" she asked me, noticing I was trying to say something else.

"Probably nothing," I said, but it wasn't nothing, and it was bumming me out.

"Spill it," she said, her hand finding her hip.

"It's just . . . this guy, he kind of plays the field. I'm sensing he's got a bit of a wandering eye."

Nikki shifted on her feet. I got the impression she wasn't aware of that. "He's a good-looking man," she said with a shrug. "And we're not exclusive."

"Yeah, okay," I said, but I didn't like what I saw in the ether with the detective's love interest. He seemed ready to disappoint her, and I liked Nikki. I didn't want to see her end up with some jerkwad.

The three of us fell into an uncomfortable silence until Candice made a waving motion toward the elevators to get us back on course. "After you, Detective."

"Hold on," Grayson said. "The reason I wanted you two to come down here instead of meeting me at the crime scene is because there's something I want to show you."

"What's that?" Candice asked.

Grayson tucked her purse into her desk drawer, retrieved a key card on a lanyard, picked up one of the two coffee cups she'd carried in, and said, "Follow me."

We headed away from the detectives' area back toward the elevators, took one down to the first floor, where we walked through a windowed corridor and finally through a set of double doors with the words CRIME LAB posted on them.

Grayson had to swipe her key card to gain access to the doors, and she held them open for Candice and me. I have to admit that I was very curious about what she wanted to show us, and my gut was telling me I was about to learn something crucial to the case against Dave.

The brightly lit lab itself was a large room with several work-stations, and crime techs in lab coats and rubber gloves were al-ready hard at work on various cases identifiable by the clusters of brown paper bags on the long tables at each station. Only one or two of the dozen or so techs in attendance looked up as we en-tered; one was a statuesque blonde, with an absolutely beautiful heart-shaped face, full lips, a shapely figure, and angular black-framed glasses.

She was like something out of a nerd's wet dream. "Nikki," she said warmly as we approached.

"Good morning, Sienna," Grayson replied, offering the tech the cup she'd brought with her. "Mocha chai latte, right?"

Sienna's beautiful face lit up with a smile. "Thank you!" she said, grabbing for the cup and taking a sip. "Yeah," she added, closing her eyes with pleasure. "That's the stuff."

When she focused on us again, Grayson motioned to Candice and me. "These are the two I was telling you about."

Sienna looked from me to Candice. "Which one is the psychic?"

I raised my hand. *"Moi."*

"Huh," Sienna said, as if my admission had disappointed her. "I gotta admit that I don't really believe in psychics, but word around here is that you've got some sort of talent for seeing stuff on cases that no one else hits on."

My smile tightened. For the record, it's SUPER rude to tell someone that you don't "believe" in their profession. I mean, even if you don't, don't fucking say it to their face, okay?

"Yeah, I get that a lot," I told her.

"Get what a lot?" she asked.

"Doubt. But the doubters always seem to come around after I say something like, 'Gee, I hope you like that new black SUV you're driving. It's a real improvement from the dull white sedan you used to drive. Oh, and while I'm at it, sorry about the breakup you just had with your significant other. I know it got really ugly there at the end, but now that you took a little break to visit with your family on the East Coast . . . somewhere in the Carolinas, and he's moved out, you're actually finding yourself relieved about his absence and ready to spend some quality time working on yourself.'"

Sienna's mouth fell open and she simply stared at me for five or six wide-eyed blinks. Finally, she switched her gaze to Detective Grayson and mouthed, *Whoa!*

Grayson shrugged her shoulders in an I-told-you-so way and Candice nudged me slightly with her elbow to let me know she liked what I'd just done.

But I was still a bit annoyed. My life is a never-ending battle to prove myself, over and over, and over again, and it got really wearisome and old after a decade and a half at it.

"How did you know all that?" Sienna asked once she'd recovered herself.

"How do you think?" I replied.

I could see the mental gears turning while Sienna considered how I might logically know several very intimate and personal details about her without ever having met her, and I'm pretty sure she was thinking that I'd either spied on her prior to this morning or gleaned the info from the Interwebs.

To my relief, Detective Grayson said, "Sienna, just so you know, Abby had no idea I was bringing her to you, and I doubt that she's ever even heard of you. To my knowledge, she's never even been down here, right, Abby?"

"Right," I said, without taking my gaze off Sienna.

"That's what I thought," Grayson said. "So, there's no way she would've had an opportunity to investigate you prior to following me down here just now."

Sienna seemed troubled, and I suppose I could understand.

These science people are the hardest to convince because they can't measure or quantify the type of energy I interact with. It doesn't compute in their minds.

A long moment of silence followed while the crime tech continued to process what had to be, in her mind at least, an impossibility, and then Grayson said, "I brought Abby and Candice down here to have them hear about what you discovered last night on the Roswell case."

The set to my shoulders eased. I loved that Grayson was so obviously on my side when it came to supporting my talent in the face of skepticism. She'd almost always proven herself to be a terrific ally to me and Candice, and I found myself feeling a little guilty for having teased her about the new beau in her life.

Sienna nodded, but I could tell she was still slightly thrown by what I'd said to her. There was a flush to her neck as she moved away from us to retrieve a thick, tan case file. "I received confirmation on the blood sample taken at the Roswells' home and the hair sample supplied to me from the search warrant as being from the same individual."

My brow furrowed, as did Candice's. "Which blood sample?" I asked.

"And which search warrant?"

Sienna was flipping the case file pages up as she read the notes. "The blood sample taken at the security gate of the Roswells' home, and the hair sample retrieved from the ponytail holder confiscated at Dave McKenzie's house."

It was my turn to let my jaw hang open. "The bloody handprint with Dave's fingerprints was also made up of Dave's blood?"

Sienna pushed at the nosepiece to her glasses. "Yes," she said. "If it's truly Dave McKenzie's hair from the ponytail tie—"

"His wife claimed it was his and we got it from his side of the bathroom," Grayson interrupted to confirm the origin of the hair tie.

Sienna nodded. "Right, then the DNA from the ponytail holder matches the blood sample taken from the gate."

"So it wasn't the Roswells' blood, or Rosa's, or the gardener . . . what was his name?" Candice asked Grayson.

"Mario," Grayson said. "Mario Tremblee."

"Yes, if it wasn't Mario's blood either, then that could only mean that Dave was wounded when he left the Roswells' house."

"That's what it looks like," Grayson said.

I felt that awful sinking feeling in the pit of my stomach again, especially when I remembered the handprint. Dave's hand had to have been covered in blood. "He'd have to have been hurt pretty badly," I said.

"Yes," Grayson said. "From the blood trail leading to the handprint and the amount of blood recovered on the gate, that's what it looks like."

"Did you check the hospitals?" Candice asked. "To see about any men matching Dave's description who might've sought treatment in the past couple of days for a severe injury?"

"We did," Grayson said. "No one matching his description has sought any medical attention for a wound bad enough to cover his hand in blood."

"It could be the reason Gwen was abducted," Candice said to me. "She could've patched him up."

I remembered Gwen telling us she was a registered nurse, so Candice's point was a valid one. Gwen possessed the skills to provide at least some level of aid to Dave.

"Was he shot?" I asked the group.

"Given the amount of blood on the palm print and the droplets we recovered from the driveway, he certainly could've been," Grayson said. "It could've been a ricochet, though, as all the bullets fired at the Roswells' house came from two guns."

"Uh-uh," Sienna corrected. "There were three guns involved, Detective."

Grayson motioned to her. "Yeah, sorry. Three guns. I forgot about Tremblee. He was shot with a forty-five."

"A forty-five? That's different than the thirty-eight used to shoot Chris Wixom last night," I said.

"It is," Grayson said. "Rosa Torrez was shot with an AR-fifteen, as were Andy and Robin Roswell, but there appears to have been an additional AR-fifteen used to shoot them as well."

"Two killers," I said. "Both using AR-fifteens to kill the home-owners."

"Yes," Sienna said.

"So the point was to cut them to ribbons," Candice said.

Sienna's expression turned grim. "It appears that way. With two of those weapons turned on them, they had no chance of survival."

"But Mario was shot with a handgun," I said. "Along with Chris Wixom, but not the same handgun."

"Yep," Grayson said, and I could tell that it troubled her as well that none of the same guns had been used at both scenes. The inconsistency was hard to explain.

"Any prints on the casings?" Candice asked next.

"We found an index fingerprint and a partial thumbprint on the casing that came from the bullet fired at Tremblee, but none on the casings of the AR-fifteens. The prints don't match anyone in the system either," Grayson said.

"They're not Dave's?" I asked just to be sure.

"No, which leads us to the next puzzling bit of info."

"Which is?" I asked when she fell silent.

Sienna answered the question for her. "We found a set of prints on the casing recovered at the front door of Wixom's house. It doesn't match the print from the casing at the Roswells', but we did get a hit in the system for it."

"Who?" Candice and I asked together.

Sienna pulled out a mug shot from the file she was holding and handed it to me. The guy in the photo was a seriously bad-looking dude. His mug shot had him at above six feet tall, with stringy long hair, a thick beard, a mustache, and mean beady eyes.

Candice, who was looking over my shoulder, said, "He looks a little like Dave."

I'd seen the resemblance too, but it went only as far as height, hair, and maybe general scruffiness. Next to each other, however, these guys were as different as night and day. It was in the eyes, I reasoned. Dave's eyes were bright blue with a twinkle of good humor. The guy in the mug shot had the eyes of a killer. A guy who'd shiv an old lady for getting in his way.

A guy who'd murder four people in cold blood.

"Who is it?" I asked, because there was no name to go with the mug shot.

"Gene Gudziak," Grayson said. "He goes by the nickname Snake and he's wanted in Arizona, New Mexico, and now here. He served twenty years of a forty-five-year sentence for murdering his landlord in Phoenix back in the early nineties; then he violated his parole by skipping town and is the key suspect in a double murder in Albuquerque and a sexual assault in Santa Fe."

I shuddered as I stared at Gudziak's photo. I've looked at the mug shots of lots of wicked men in my time. Men who've done heinous things, unspeakable really, but almost none of them gave me the shivers like Gudziak did.

"There's more," Grayson said in a quiet tone, and I understood that she'd saved the worst for last.

"Tell us," Candice said, and I could tell she had steeled herself to hear something terrible. Much like I was steeling myself.

"It appears that Robin Roswell was violently raped before she was murdered," Grayson said even more softly. "The DNA recovered from her attacker matches Gudziak."

I shut my eyes against the imagery of Robin Roswell's final hour on this earth. "Jesus," I whispered.

Candice swore softly and I felt her lean against me. She was imagining the horror Robin must have endured too.

And then Gwen's image came to my mind's eye and I felt a renewed sense of panic. "We have to find Gwen," I said, opening my eyes.

"Do you know if Dave has any association to this guy?" Grayson asked me.

"None," I said.

Grayson looked to Candice and she backed me up. "No way," she said. "There's no connection."

"And yet," she said, "the evidence from the casing suggests he was with McKenzie at Wixom's attempted murder."

"I still don't believe Dave did this voluntarily," I snapped.

Grayson shook her head and crossed her arms. "When I spoke to Wixom, he didn't hesitate to implicate McKenzie had been the one to shoot him with little provocation."

"That's not the Dave I know," I insisted. And then I turned the mug shot of Gudziak toward the detective. "And I know you see the resemblance between this guy and Dave. What if it was Gudziak who shot Wixom, but Wixom got confused and fingered Dave as the shooter? In fact, what if Dave was this guy's hostage, forced to ride along with Gudziak, who was really in charge?"

But Grayson seemed unconvinced. "Abby, I know McKenzie is your friend, but up close McKenzie and Gudziak couldn't be mistaken for each other."

My lips pressed together. I knew she was right, but I still wanted Wixom's statement to be a mistake. The Dave I knew just couldn't have pulled that trigger.

"Listen," Grayson said, seeing that I was still stubbornly holding to the faith of my friend. "I know you want to believe he's innocent, but I've got two separate connections to him at two violent home invasions. He was at both places, and he wasn't some innocent bystander at the second one. He *shot* Wixom."

Candice crossed one arm over her torso, resting the opposite elbow on her wrist, to tap her lip with her finger. It's a mannerism she adopts every time she doesn't agree with an argument. I call it her Sherlock pose. "Detective," she said formally. "You told us the casing retrieved from the bullet that went into Wixom had Gudziak's print on it, right?"

"Yes."

Candice took the mug shot from me and waved it at her. "Then isn't it more likely that Gudziak shot Wixom and not Dave? After all, wasn't Wixom shot in the back?"

"Yes, he was shot in the back, but no, Wixom told me he saw McKenzie step up to him when he was lying on the floor and fire the second shot. Gudziak's prints on the casings only mean that Gudziak loaded the gun."

"Okay," I tried, thinking of a different angle. "Wixom said that two men entered his home and attacked him, right?"

"Yes," Grayson said with a small sigh.

"So, what did the other guy look like?"

"What do you mean?"

"I mean that Wixom identified Dave, but since last night has he been able to give anyone a physical description of the second man?"

Grayson pressed her own lips together. "No," she said. "Like I told you, he blacked out before I had a chance to ask him."

"Did he make it out of surgery okay?" Candice asked carefully.

Grayson pulled up her cell and tapped at it. It looked like she was searching for a text. "He did. The hospital has listed his condition as stable, but he's on a lot of pain meds right now."

"Can we go talk to him?" I asked, meaning the three of us.

Grayson frowned. "I'd prefer to speak to him alone."

"Oh, come on, Grayson!" I said, frustrated that she kept blocking my efforts to figure out what was going on.

"No, Cooper," she replied calmly. "I'm not compromising this case just because you want to try and find a hole in Wixom's story. He's on painkillers and subject to suggestion. I'm not going to have you plant a different suspect in his mind."

My chest got hot with anger, but I stifled the retort I wanted to spit back. Mostly because she was right. If I were in her shoes, I'd have made the same call.

"So why show us all this?" Candice asked.

Grayson sighed again. "Because none of the evidence is stacking up in a way that's making sense. I'm bothered by the fact that everyone I talk to tells me that Dave McKenzie is this sweetheart of a guy who wouldn't hurt a fly, but who actually once threw a man down a flight of stairs and killed him."

"He did that to save my life!" I yelled, unable to hold in the outburst.

"I know," Grayson said, offering me a sympathetic look. "Which is why I brought you two here this morning. I don't believe that people simply snap after fifty-eight years and become cold-blooded killers. McKenzie's profile suggests he's a good guy. He's hardworking, loyal, stable, steady, colorful, and honest. He pays his taxes and his bills on time. He's been with the same woman for thirty-two years. He donates to six different charities and volunteers at Austin Pets Alive."

"He does?" I said, honestly surprised. I had no idea Dave was a volunteer at the shelter.

"He does," Grayson said with a slight smile. "The shelter staff love him. He walks every single dog in the place even if it takes all day every Thursday, which I understand is his one day off a week. He plays fetch with the pups, cuddles with them, and comforts the ones who've been the most neglected. That's not a guy who's going to suddenly snap and pick up an AR-fifteen to murder four people in cold blood. There's something seriously wrong with the witness statements I have for everyone who's ever spent time with him, and what the evidence shows, and for the life of me I can't understand the incongruity of it."

"The evidence is wrong," I said. Handing her the mug shot of Gudziak, I added, "Ask Wixom if Gudziak was there. Maybe he was forcing Dave along. Ask him if Gudziak was the one who was really in control."

Grayson took the mug shot. "I'll show him a six-pack," she said, referring to a grouping of mug shots shown to witnesses to avoid implying the guilt of any one potential suspect. "But I'm not putting any kind of suggestion into his mind. He'll tell me only what he remembers, and I'm going to proceed based on that."

"Can we at least ride along with you and wait in the corridor or something?" Candice asked.

"I thought you wanted to take a tour of Wixom's crime scene," she said.

"We do," I said. "But we also want to be there when you follow up with Wixom."

She frowned, undecided.

Sienna, who'd been largely silent for the past few minutes, said, "It couldn't hurt for them to wait in the hallway, Nikki."

I smiled at her gratefully, and just like that, she and I made peace.

"Fine," Grayson said. "But you're not to say a single word when I talk to Wixom, understand? Not. One. Word."

I held up my little finger. "Pinkie swear."

Chapter Thirteen

. . .

Grayson called over to the hospital and discovered that Chris Wixom was being visited by his mother, so she decided that in the meantime we should head over to the crime scene. We rode along in her car, which was a welcome change, as she drove at the posted speed limit and didn't take the turns on two wheels.

I didn't even have to pray to make it to our destination in one piece.

We arrived to find Wixom's house barricaded by a patrol car and a whole lot of yellow crime-scene tape. The patrolman on scene waved Grayson into the drive after she flashed her badge, and we parked right at the front door.

Getting out of the car, we stood for a moment in front of the house and I steeled myself for the second time that morning. I didn't quite know what I'd be picking up intuitively inside the house, but I wasn't especially looking forward to the task.

Grayson looked to me to see if I was ready, and after a brief nod we stepped forward to the front door. Nikki handed us blue booties to put over our shoes and some black rubber gloves to wear before she punched in a code to the lockbox placed on the handle, then retrieved a key, and we were in.

I came into the coolness of the front foyer and was jarred by the violence that was still reverberating in the ether. It hit me hard and I looked down and found that I was standing in a big patch of dried blood.

I shuddered and hopped to the side. It was awful to look at, but even worse to be standing on top of.

"Where was he shot?" Candice asked, making a motion across her body.

"Once in the upper back, which went through and came out just under his clavicle, and then again in the lower back near his left kidney," Grayson told her.

"It's a miracle he survived," I said.

"It is," Grayson agreed. "The second bullet did the most damage. It took out a kidney, missed his liver by less than an eighth of an inch, and completely destroyed a good chunk of his small intestine before ricocheting off his pelvis and getting lodged in a rib."

"Ouch," Candice said. "Poor guy."

"Barring an infection, his surgeon told me, he should make a full recovery," Grayson said, moving to the far side of the foyer to allow Candice and me room to look around.

Well, Candice did the looking, I mostly lifted my arms a little away from my body and stood still, literally feeling out the ether.

"They were in a hurry," I said, moving away from the front door to follow the trail of what felt like hyperactive energy. No one commented, so I continued to move along the central hallway, which had several rooms jutting off from it.

To the right was a dining room, beautifully decorated with a large stone table and high-backed gray suede chairs. The hyperactive energy lingering in the ether suggested the intruders had never entered here. Moving down the hall, I passed entrances to the living room, a giant kitchen, a den, and finally the master bedroom. I paused at each doorway and sensed that the only room the thieves had entered was the master bedroom.

Doubling back along the way I'd come, I found Grayson and Candice still in the foyer, patiently waiting for me. Ignoring them, I went to the staircase, which presumably led to the upstairs bedrooms, but the energy of Gudziak and his partner had never taken even one step up there.

"They definitely knew the layout of the house," I said, feeling a weight settle into my chest. Dave had been here just a few days ago. He would've known the home's blueprint, and he probably would've taken some notes on it and maybe even drawn a diagram. I felt so strongly he'd been the source of how Gudziak had known exactly where to look for Wixom's valuables.

Heading back to the master bedroom, I entered it cautiously. Don't ask me why; I think it was simply that the energy in the house was wigging me out and putting my nerves on edge. I didn't know how Chris Wixom was ever going to be able to come back to this house, because this kind of energy can linger for decades. Then again, not everyone is as sensitive as I am, so maybe he'd come back and have only the demons of his memory to battle.

Edging beyond the doorway, I looked around. The scene was the same as it'd been in the crime-scene photos, with furniture, clothes, and personal effects strewn about to create a mess. Drawers had been pulled out and their contents rummaged through. A large mahogany box lay on the ground, as though it'd been tossed there hastily. Moving over to squat down and inspect it, I saw that it was lined with foam, and indented with a series of round imprints.

This must've been the case that'd held Chris's prized watch collection, I thought. Standing up, I moved to the bedside table, where a charger indicated some electronic gizmo might've been on the nightstand getting charged. I didn't know if it'd also been stolen or was perhaps in another part of the house.

My gut said it'd been taken.

Finally I moved to the closet, which was a large walk-in. This would've been where Wixom would've wanted his safe room, I thought.

Straight across from where I stood in the doorway was that sizable square hole we'd seen in the photos on Nikki's phone. White chunks of drywall were scattered all over the bare wood floor, which was the only residual evidence of how forcefully the wall safe had been removed.

I walked forward and touched the edges of the hole in the wall. Standing there, I felt the height of the hyped-up energy left by the two intruders. What struck me was that not even one ethereal thread of it felt like it belonged to Dave.

For as long as I'd known the handyman, his energy had always been gentle, strong, stubborn, and filled with mirth and mischief. This energy . . . well, it wasn't any of that.

Stepping away from the hole, I stared mournfully at the drywall littering the floor. Dave hadn't been here. No way. I was absolutely convinced of it.

"Hey," I heard Candice say behind me. "Anything?"

"He wasn't here, Candice."

"Dave?"

"Yes. There were two men, but neither of them was Dave."

Candice was silent for a long minute. "Then it'll be really interesting to hear what Wixom has to say."

I turned and moved toward the exit. "Yep." Nothing else needed saying.

Before entering Chris Wixom's room, Candice went over the logistics with Detective Grayson. "We'll be right outside the door, but we promise not to say a word."

"You probably won't be able to hear much anyway," Grayson told her. "I doubt Wixom is going to be able to project his voice loud enough for you two to hear."

Candice frowned. "Good point." Fishing out her phone from her purse, she dialed my number and pointed at me to answer the call.

Puzzled, I tapped at the screen and said, "Yeah?"

"Don't hang up," Candice instructed; then she handed Grayson her phone and grabbed for mine. "We'll put this on mute, but you keep my phone on speaker, okay?"

"That'll work," Grayson said.

Candice then dug into her purse again and pulled out her iPad. "If I need to ask Wixom a question, I'll text it to your phone, Detective, and if you think it won't compromise your case, you can ask him."

Grayson's brow furrowed. "Fine," she said after a bit of consideration. "But if I don't ask him your question, don't try and sabotage my interview by busting in and asking him anyway, you got it?"

I lowered my lids and looked to Candice. "It's like she doesn't trust us."

"Right?" Candice said. "And we're so trustworthy too."

Grayson rolled her eyes. "I'm serious," she said.

"So are we," Candice and I said together.

Grayson sighed. "I'm going in there before his family gets back from lunch. You two stay put and don't interrupt."

I saluted and Candice followed suit. Grayson made a face at both of us and turned away toward Chris Wixom's room.

After she disappeared through the door, Candice pulled out a pair of earbuds and connected them to my phone. Then she handed me one of the buds and we put our heads close together so that we could each hear.

"Good morning, Chris," Grayson said. "I'm not sure if you remember me. We spoke last night. I'm Detective Grayson."

"Detective," said a hoarse voice. "I'm glad to see you."

"Oh, yeah?" she said. "That's nice to hear. Most people aren't so happy to see me when they're in the hospital."

There was a sort of snort like laughing and Chris said, "The last time we met, I remember thinking you might be the last person I talk to. I wanted to make sure you knew who'd pulled the trigger if I didn't make it."

Grayson's voice softened a bit when she said, "I'm sorry you had to go through that, but I really appreciate how helpful you've been in identifying the man that shot you."

"Dave McKenzie," Wixom said, like he was afraid she'd forgotten it. "That son of a bitch. Did you catch him yet?"

"Not yet, Chris," she said.

Standing next to Candice, I could hardly hold still. I wanted very much to rip out my earbud and stomp away, because I knew Chris Wixom was lying. I'd felt the ether, and no way had Dave been there, but I couldn't figure out why he kept insisting that it'd been Dave who'd shot him. But that wouldn't help Dave or Gwen, so I kept my temper in check and waited to hear where Grayson took this.

"Chris, you said to me last night that there were two men who invaded your home. Did you happen to get a good look at the other man?"

"Yeah," he said, but then paused to cough and moan slightly. "Sorry," he said. "My lungs are full of junk from that anesthesia, and it hurts like hell to cough it up."

"Don't worry about it," Grayson said. "I'd give you another day or two to recover before pressing you on this, but the more information we have on these two armed and dangerous criminals, the more quickly we can hunt them down and prevent them from hurting anyone else."

"It's fine, Detective," Wixom assured her. "I want to help. Anyway, the second guy wasn't anyone I recognized. He was big, maybe six-two or six-three and two hundred seventy pounds. Maybe even two eighty. Built like a linebacker."

"Hair color?"

"Dark. He had long curly hair, tied back."

"Ethnicity?"

There was a pause, then, "Honestly? He looked like a native Hawaiian, or maybe he was from Samoa."

"He was Polynesian?"

"Yeah, that's it. Polynesian."

"Any other distinctive features?"

"He had a bunch of tattoos on his arms and his neck. The one on his neck, I remember that one—it was a dollar sign."

I imagined what Wixom's attacker must've looked like as I listened to his description, and I was even more convinced that Dave hadn't been at Wixom's house the night before. I'd never seen anyone resembling a large Polynesian man with a neck tattoo of a dollar sign around Dave. None of his workers or friends fit that description.

"Did McKenzie maybe say the name of the other guy?"

Wixom was quiet for a moment; then he said, "I think he called him Cap. Or maybe Captain. Something like that. I can't really remember. I was trying to play dead and hold still so they wouldn't keep shooting me."

"Cap or Captain," Grayson repeated. "That's great, Chris. You've given us a lot of detail. It should help us isolate a list of potential suspects. Speaking of which, I was wondering if you could look at a six-pack for me—it's a photo lineup—and see if you recognize anyone."

A small jolt of excitement went through me. I knew that Grayson was about to show Wixom the set of mug shots containing Gudziak's picture. I was very interested to hear if he'd pick him out of the photo lineup. "Okay," Wixom said. We heard a bit of rustling of paper, and then a very long pause before Wixom said, "I don't recognize anybody here."

My hopes sank. "Dammit!" I muttered. I wanted for him to recognize Gudziak.

But then Grayson surprised me by saying, "Okay, so how about in this six-pack? Recognize anybody here?"

Immediately Wixom said, "There. Right there! That's McKenzie!"

"That one?" Grayson said. "You're sure, Chris?"

"Positive. That's the asshole who came to my house last week and took measurements for my safe room, and that's the son of a bitch who shot me last night."

Candice and I glanced at each other nervously. Neither of us had known Grayson was going to pull out two six-packs, but then, that was often done these days because eyewitness testimonies were surprisingly unreliable, and witnesses were usually far more likely to point to someone—anyone—in the first set of photos than they were in any subsequent photo lineups. We figured that Grayson was simply making sure that Wixom saw whom he said he saw, and that his memory hadn't been distorted by his ordeal.

"Okay, Chris, that's great," Grayson said, and there was more shuffling of paper before she added, "You look exhausted. How about I let you get some sleep, and I'll check in on you tomorrow?"

"Thanks, Detective," Wixom said. "I am pretty wiped out."

Abruptly, the phone disconnected and Candice pulled out her earbud and I did the same. A moment later Grayson appeared in the doorway of Wixom's hospital room and motioned for us to follow her.

She moved quickly and I could feel the sense of urgency coming from her. Finally, she stopped at the entrance to a small, empty waiting room, and turned to us. "You two may be on to something," she said.

"How's that?" Candice asked her, while I tugged at my jacket anxiously. I knew she had something, but I didn't quite know what yet.

Grayson pulled out two photo lineups and showed them to us. In the upper left corner of the first set of photos was Dave's driver's license photo. In the lower right hand corner of the second set of photos was Gudziak's mug shot. "I showed this one to Wixom first," she explained, tapping the lineup with Dave's picture in it. "He didn't recognize McKenzie, but, as I'm sure you heard, he nailed Gudziak immediately in this second set of photos, fingering him for McKenzie."

"I knew it!" I exclaimed, slapping Candice on the upper arm.

"So it wasn't Dave," she said, glaring at me while she rubbed her shoulder. "He wasn't the shooter."

"Not according to Wixom," Grayson said while she continued to compare the six-packs. "Still, McKenzie and Gudziak do kind of look alike. And Wixom's on a lot of painkillers right now. He could be mistaken."

"Oh, come on, Grayson," I snapped. "Gudziak's print was on the casing found at the scene, and Wixom picked him out of the six-pack while ignoring Dave's photo. I doubt that's a giant coincidence."

"I doubt it's a coincidence too, Abby, but it wasn't Gudziak's bloody handprint we found at the scene of the Roswells' murder. *That* was Dave McKenzie's."

"So what're you thinking?" Candice asked.

Grayson sighed. "I'm thinking we have a lot of loose threads here and nothing that ties them all together yet. Even if McKenzie wasn't at Wixom's house last night, it doesn't mean he didn't have a hand in it. He could've orchestrated the whole thing for all we know."

"All *you* know," I muttered. "Not all *I* know."

"Okay, so what do you know, Cooper? I mean, enlighten me on how all this fits together."

I stared hard at her, angry that she wouldn't drop the theory that Dave was guilty. "You really want to know?"

"Yes, yes, I do."

My temper was flaring and my radar was wide open, reaching for the answer, when all of a sudden I had it. "Holy shit," I squeaked when it came together in my mind.

"What?" Candice and Grayson both said.

I held up a finger to get them to hold on a moment and quickly pulled out my cell to make a call. "Hey," I said when Dutch answered the call. "I need you to do something right away and don't ask me any questions about it—just do it, okay?"

"Deal. What do you need?" he said.

"I need for you to send some of your private security to the homes of Roger Mulligan and Sylvia Ramirez. It needs to happen *immediately*, Dutch, and they need to be armed."

"I'm on it," he said, without argument or a single question. "I'll text you when the security teams check in."

"Thanks. I'll call you in a while and explain."

"That would be great," he said, and clicked off the line.

When I pocketed my phone, I looked up to see both Candice and Grayson eyeing me with raised brows. "Private security for three other clients?" Candice asked.

"Yeah," I said, seeing in my mind's eye so clearly what must've happened. "They're the most vulnerable."

"Why's that?" Grayson asked.

"Because they're the three clients along with Chris Wixom who met with Gudziak when he was impersonating Dave, whom Gudziak and his buddy carjacked earlier that morning."

"Come again?" Grayson said.

But Candice's eyes went wide with understanding. "The accident!"

Grayson blinked. "What accident?" she said.

I pointed to Candice to let her know she got the answer right before I explained it to Grayson. "There was a report called into APD that a truck resembling Dave's went off the road on Lost Creek Boulevard. We went there to check it out, but only saw a few signs that anything had occurred. When your patrol car arrived on scene, Dave's truck was already back on the road."

"What if," Candice said, taking over for me, "Dave didn't drive off the road? What if he was run off the road and abducted?"

"He'd be no match for the two guys that Wixom describes," I said. "Dave's fairly tall, but he's skinny. If Wixom is right in his description of the tattooed assailant, then Dave would've been easily subdued, especially if he was rattled after having been run off the road."

"Where's the proof, though?" Grayson said to us, adding, "I remember that call. The guy on the line didn't mention anything about another car."

"True, but he also sounded under the influence and nervous about being identified. Maybe he was trying to give as few details as possible so that he wouldn't be tracked down for his statement."

"Or maybe he didn't see the other car," said Candice. "Maybe he only saw a partial view of the accident and didn't see Gudziak and his accomplice come up behind Dave."

Grayson rubbed her temples, and I suspected she was starting to get the first part of a headache. "You guys are chock-full of hypotheticals. But I still don't see any evidence to back up this theory."

"Okay," I said, trying to see it from her perspective. "How about you lend us the benefit of the doubt and concede that there might be more to this story, Nikki?"

"I'll concede to that," she said. "But you need to show me something, *anything*, Abby, that backs up your theory before I lend you any more leeway here."

"Cool," I said. "I can work with that. And I'd love to show you something to back up my theory. The place that I think we need to start is at the beginning."

"Where's that exactly?" she asked.

"The scene of Dave's accident," Candice said, and I was grateful she was right there with me on how to proceed. "We need to look for evidence of another car."

Grayson's crossed arms remained crossed and she tapped her arm with her index finger, all the while looking super annoyed. "Tell me you guys didn't know I used to work accident investigations."

My brow shot up. "You did?"

She rolled her eyes.

"Seriously?" I said. "We didn't know, Detective. I swear."

With a heavy sigh she turned and began walking away from us. Over her shoulder she said, "Best come with me, ladies. Daylight's a-wastin', and we've got an accident scene to process."

"Found something!" I yelled an hour later while standing on the rocky, dry ground of the place where Dave's truck had gone off the road.

Detective Grayson moved to my side and squinted at the piece of clear plastic I held in my hand. "Yep," she said. "That's part of a headlight. Problem is, there's no way to know how long it's been here."

"Why can't we just assume it's from the car that ran Dave's truck off the road?" I whined. So far I'd found four pieces of similar size and shape to the one I currently held, and she'd said the same thing for each piece.

"Because there aren't any skid marks or paint chips or pieces of metal from another vehicle lying on the side of the road to indicate that another car was involved, Abby. It's all circumstantial evidence right now, and it's flimsy at best."

At that moment Candice—who'd spent much of the time we were there on the phone—waved to us. "You guys!" she called. "Come here!"

Grayson and I picked our way over the terrain to her and she covered the microphone with her hand to say, "I called Brice and told him to head to APD to put some pressure on the brass there to trace that recording," she said. "He was able to get the gears greased and he's been in with Seabright and the phone companies ever since, working to find a trace on the call. He just called to say they may have gotten a hit on the number."

Candice moved her hand away from the microphone to say, "Yes, Brice, I'm still here." Grayson and I waited while Candice listened; then she said, "You're sure you got the right name?" Another pause, then, "Okay, I believe you. Send me the address and we'll run it down and get back to you."

After clicking off the call with Brice, Candice said, "The call originated from a cell phone belonging to a woman named Helen Leggero."

"You're kidding," I said.

"Nope. Brice and Officer Seabright had the carrier double-check it just to make sure."

"But the caller was a man," I reminded her.

She rolled her eyes. "I know, Sundance, which only means that someone borrowed or stole her cell phone to make the call."

"Let's hope it's borrowed," Grayson said.

"Only one way to find out," Candice replied, wiggling her cell when it pinged. "That's Helen's address. Let's go talk to her unless you two want to continue to dig around in this scrub."

"We're good," Nikki and I said together.

Candice grinned. "Let's roll."

Chapter Fourteen

. . .

Helen Leggero lived in a two-story stone house with big planters filled with overflowing vines and hardy flowers. She answered our knock carrying a cane, looking a bit sleepy and rumpled, as if we'd just woken her up from a long winter's nap. Also, she was like eleven million years old.

We introduced ourselves to her, and she eyed us quizzically, then held up one finger and disappeared back into the house, only to reappear a few moments later shoving a hearing aid big enough to be mistaken for a pancake into her ear. "Can't hear nothin' without my aids," she said, her voice crackling with phlegm. Pointing to the badge displayed at Grayson's waist, she said, "What's my great-grandson done this time?"

I rocked on my heels. *Jackpot!* I thought.

"Your grandson?" Grayson said, playing dumb. "What makes you think we're here about your grandson?"

"Great-grandson," Helen corrected. "Little shit's always getting into trouble and expecting me to bail him out. That's why I assume you're here, cuz it can't be for me. I haven't left the house in a month, not since my daughter had a stroke, and her daughter ain't around to take care of either of us or her own kid. Now there's nobody to take me to get my lottery tickets. Not even that worthless little moron Kramer, who's always busy every time I ask."

"Kramer," Grayson said smoothly. "Kramer's last name is . . . ?"

"Kissinger," Helen said. "No relation."

I suspected Helen was referring to the former secretary of state, but why she'd think that we'd think that her great-grandson was a relation was a mystery to me.

"Helen, did you happen to give Kramer your cell phone?" Grayson asked next.

Helen dug into the pocket of her housedress and came up with a giant flip phone, which she'd probably gotten before Kramer was born. (Maybe around the time that Kissinger was secretary of state.) "No," she said. "It's right here."

"Did you by any chance get him his own phone on your account?" Candice asked.

Helen scratched her head. "Maybe," she said. "His grandmother took care of all that before she had the stroke."

"We're trying to get in touch with Kramer," I said, pushing a big pleasant smile onto my face. "Do you know where we can find him?"

Helen made a motion with her thumb to the back of the house. "He's got that room above the garage," she said. "He's up there most days when he's not in school."

"How old is he?" I asked.

"Twenty-eight," she said. My eyes widened. She laughed like she knew what I was thinking. "Yeah, I've got a twenty-eight-year-old great-grandson. My daughter is seventy-four, and my granddaughter is forty-nine."

"That'd make you . . . ?" Grayson said.

Helen laughed again and tapped her cane. "Ninety-two. I'll be ninety-three next month. I want to live to see a hundred, but who knows if I'll make it?"

I grinned at her, liking her spirit. My gut said she'd be around to make that birthday and then some.

We took our leave of Helen and walked the driveway to the rear, where an unattached garage stood sentinel over the backyard. There was a doorway into the side of the structure, and I noticed that an AC unit was perched in an upstairs window.

Next to the garage, an old, white Volvo sat dripping oil onto the grass. The car had a certain smell to it—one that might invite a search by a certain APD officer if she was so inclined.

Grayson stopped at the driver's side door to peer inside the car, and came up smiling. Pointing to the passenger's seat, I clearly saw an apple that'd been turned into a bong not long ago. It looked like there were still a few hits left, judging from the contents in the small well where the cannabis was kept.

Grayson then walked back down the drive and motioned for us to follow. We did and in the shadows of a row of crepe myrtle trees she made a call back to her department for a records search on Kramer Kissinger. We waited while she listened to the info; then she gave us a thumbs-up and finally disconnected. "Kissinger's got a prior for possession," she said. "He's been on probation for the past year, was court ordered to take a drug test every month, which he has, and he's passed each one. His last one before his probation ends at the end of the month was this past Friday."

"Ahhh," I said as Candice's face lit up with recognition too. "So, Kramer takes his last drug test, and has a couple of hits to celebrate."

"Looks like it," Grayson said. "Too bad for him he's still got a little over twenty days of probation left."

"But lucky us," Candice said with a knowing wink to Grayson.

"Yep," Grayson said, motioning for us to follow her back down the drive to Kramer's door, which she gave several good whacks to.

"What?" we heard someone yell from inside.

"Kramer Kissinger?" Grayson asked through the door.

Silence followed. I suspected Kramer was right now creeping along the floorboards to the window to peer down at whoever had called his name in such an authoritative voice.

I looked up, as did Candice and Nikki, and a moment later we saw one lever of the blinds pulled aside and an eye and a partial glimpse of a nose peek out. "Yeah?" he asked when he saw us looking up at him.

Detective Grayson flashed him a toothy grin and her shield.

"Aw, shit!" he said, disappearing from the window.

Candice moved away to look at the rear of the garage; she then turned back to us and shook her head. The door Grayson and I were standing in front of was the only way in or out, excluding of course the big garage door, but Kramer would have to raise it up or wait while it rose up to scuttle under and make a run for it. I was almost hoping he'd try it, because we'd easily catch him.

For a long time there was only silence from Kramer's side of the door. Grayson knocked again and called to him, but he wasn't responding. At some point we heard a toilet flush, and Grayson rolled her eyes. Eventually we heard loud footsteps descend the stairs and on the other side of the door Kramer said, "I didn't do nothing."

"We believe you," Grayson said, shaking her head and rolling her eyes at me to let me know she thought him a liar, liar, pants on fire. "We just want to talk for a few minutes."

"Okay, so talk," he said, without opening his door.

"Is that your car right here on the lawn, Kramer?" Grayson asked.

A long pause followed, and finally he said, "Yeah?"

"Cool. Is that your apple on the front seat? The one with what looks like cannabis still in it?"

"No," he said. "I don't know where that came from."

"Really?" she said. "Kramer, you know you're still on probation, right? Which means I don't need probable cause to search your car, your house, or your person. Nor do I need a reason to haul your ass downtown for a drug test, which I doubt you'll pass, which would be a real shame as you passed the one on Friday with flying colors."

"Shit!" Kramer swore again. "Goddammit! I didn't hurt anybody! This is bullshit!"

"Yeah, I know, kid," Grayson said, as if she had all the sympathy in the world for the fact that he'd been caught with a bong on his front seat. "But here's the deal. We're not here to check up on you or arrest you for your drug use. We're here about the call you made to APD the other day. And you can come out here to talk to us, nice and calm, or I can call for backup, bust down this door, haul you into custody, and send you to prison for a few months— or years, depending on what else I find inside your car or in the pipes leading from your toilet. I'll search it all if you don't come out right now, Kramer. Play nice with us or accept the consequences. The choice is yours."

There was a pause, then a mechanical sound as the lock was released. The door opened a fraction and Kramer's one eye peered out at us, squinting in the daylight. "How do I know you won't try and arrest me after I talk to you?"

Grayson crossed her arms casually. "You don't, kiddo."

Kramer rolled his eyes and stood there defiantly without coming out or saying another word, so Candice said, "You were right, Grayson. He's not going to cooperate. I'll keep watch on the door while you call for backup."

Grayson reached for her cell and Kramer's one eye widened— along with the door, revealing a lanky, scruffy, bearded young man in a dirty T-shirt and saggy shorts. "Okay! Okay!" he shouted, holding up his hands in surrender. "Fine, okay? I should've stuck around until you guys got to that accident, but the guy seemed okay—I mean, his car didn't roll or anything. And there were the two guys in the other truck that stopped! What about them, huh?"

I stiffened. "What two guys in the other truck?" I asked him.

He pulled his angry gaze away from Grayson to vent his frustrations at me. "Aw, man! You don't know about them?"

"No," I said. "So tell us."

"Two guys in a black truck pulled over to help the guy in the silver truck. If they didn't wait around for the cops either, then that's not on me."

Grayson said, "Of course it's not on you, Kramer, but we still need your full statement, because the guy in the silver truck was hurt a lot worse than you might've thought. Which is why we need you to tell us *exactly* what happened on that road, starting from the beginning."

Kramer sighed dramatically and looked away like talking to us was *such* a chore. I barely resisted the urge to grab him by the shoulders and shake his strung-out, skinny ass for all it was worth until he started talking.

As it turned out, I wasn't the only one who was feeling a little impatient. Candice stepped up to Kramer, grabbed him by his grubby T-shirt, and got right up into his face. "Listen, you skinny little shit," she hissed. "I am *not* playin' around here, you feel me? You start telling us what happened on that road last Saturday, or I will personally use your face as a scrub brush on that toilet upstairs to see what traces of drugs might stick to your beard!"

Kramer threw his hands up in surrender again and yelled at Grayson. "Hey! This is police brutality! You gonna stand there and let her threaten me?!"

"She ain't police," Grayson said. "And all I see is a fellow citizen helping to straighten out your attire."

Kramer's mouth fell open and his big eyes swiveled from Candice to Grayson, and finally to me. By this time, I'd had enough. *"Talk!"* I shouted.

Kramer began shaking, but at least he also started talking. "I was driving home from a gig," he began. "I play bass in a band, and we went pretty late. We usually practice in my buddy Grady's garage, so none of us even knew what time it—"

"We don't care about that!" Candice interrupted, tightening her grip on his T-shirt. "Get to the accident and don't leave out a single detail."

Kramer gulped. "Okay," he said, blinking his eyes rapidly. "It was morning, I think, like around ten or maybe a few minutes before. I was pretty fried, but . . . uh . . . I was being *really* careful about driving when I heard this loud sound behind me—"

"What kind of a loud sound?" I asked.

Kramer frowned. "I don't know, like a bang."

"Did it sound like a collision?" Candice asked him.

Kramer seemed to mull that over. "Well, yeah, I guess it could've been that."

"Then what happened?" Grayson said, making a slight motion to Candice, who eased up on her grip of Kramer's T-shirt.

"Well, it was loud, so I don't know. I think I ducked and my car swerved a little, and behind me I hear tires squealing, so I glance in my side mirror and I see this big silver truck, like, fly off the road and down this embankment. It bounced a couple of times and then it stopped kinda hard. I think it might've hit a rock."

"Then what?" Grayson asked. I saw that she was taking notes on notepad.

"Well, then I pulled over to see if the guy was all right, and I called nine-one-one and while I was on the phone with them, I saw a black truck pull over right where the silver one had gone off the road. While I was talking to the nine-one-one operator, I saw two guys get out of the black truck and run down to the silver truck."

"Did they see you?" I asked.

Kramer shrugged. "I dunno for sure, but I don't think so."

"So what happened next?" Candice asked.

"Next? Nothing. I hung up with the operator and saw that the guys from the black truck were pulling the dude from the silver truck out of his cab, so I took off."

Grayson finished typing on her phone and looked up at Kramer. "Anything else?"

"No. That's pretty much it. I got back on the road and drove home. I figured the cops were on their way and they'd send an ambulance and a tow truck."

"Okay," Grayson said. "Can you describe everybody involved?"

"Uh . . . ," Kramer said, scratching his disheveled head of hair and rolling his eyes to the sky while he tried to remember. "Like, the guys in the black truck were big dudes. One had a beard and long hair, a white guy, and the other had lots of tattoos. He was, like, maybe Hispanic or something." I looked meaningfully at Grayson. They sounded suspiciously like Gudziak and his accomplice.

"What about the guy in the silver truck?" Candice asked.

"Hmm," Kramer said, thinking hard on it again. "He kinda

looked like the one white guy from the black truck. He had a beard and long hair pulled back in a braid."

"Did he appear injured?" Candice asked, her face a mask of concern.

Kramer tilted his head from side to side. "He seemed pretty woozy when they pulled him out of the truck. They might've been a little rough with him too, but maybe they were worried the truck would catch fire or something."

I closed my eyes for a moment, imagining the scene. Poor Dave had been run off the road by Gudziak and the tattooed man, and then they'd nabbed him. I knew that's what'd happened.

"Did you see anything else that we should know about?" Candice asked him.

Opening my eyes again, I could see that Kramer looked uncomfortable, or at least a little hesitant to say something else. "What?" I said to him.

"I don't know," he said. "I . . . it . . . listen, I don't want to get involved or anything."

"Involved in what?" Grayson pressed him. When he didn't immediately reply, she added, "Kramer, I really don't mind hauling your ass downtown for another possession charge. I've got all day to file the paperwork, son."

He glared at her, but then he said, "The two guys in the black truck . . . I kinda thought . . . I mean, for a minute I thought maybe they were cops."

"Why would you think that?" I asked, genuinely curious.

"Well," he said, "maybe it's cuz they both had holsters strapped to their chests. I couldn't say for sure that they were wearing guns, but it looked that way to me. And I swear, just before I took off, I saw some kind of automatic in the cab of their truck. The door was open, and I could see that something that looked like an assault rifle was in the front of the cab. That's why I got the hell out of there. I mean, I was really tired, you know? And I didn't need any hassle from the cops."

"Tired, huh?" Candice said skeptically.

Kramer's face reddened. "Yes," he sneered. "I was tired."

"Wait a second," I said. "You saw that those two men had weapons? And you didn't think to say that to the dispatcher who took your call?"

Kramer broke out into a small sweat. "Listen," he said. "I didn't know for sure if they were cops, but they could've been cops. I did my part—I called it in. After that, I thought I'd let you guys figure it out."

Grayson fished around inside her purse and came up with the two six-packs containing Dave's photo and Gudziak's picture. "Anyone in either of these lineups look familiar?" she asked him.

He surveyed both sets of photos, his brow lowered as he focused on the faces. Pointing to Dave's picture, he said, "He looks like the guy who was in the silver truck." Then he pointed to Gudziak's image and said, "And that guy looks a whole lot like the guy who was in the black truck."

Grayson pocketed the photos and her cell. "Okay, Kramer. Thanks. That's all helpful information."

His eyes widened and he appeared dumbstruck. "That's it?" he said, like he couldn't believe she was just going to let him off the hook like that.

"That's it," she said, turning away, but then she stopped and looked over her shoulder at him. "In the next day or so I may want you to come down to the station to look through some mug shots."

"For who?" he asked.

"For the guy with all the tattoos," she said.

Kramer gulped. "I'm pretty busy the next couple of days," he said.

Grayson shifted her gaze to Kramer's car. "Yeah," she said. "Well, I've got loads of free time. You know what I like to do in my spare time, Kramer? I like to sit on the ass of lowlifes like you, following them around town, and see what they're up to. I like to make my presence known too, so that all their friends, and maybe the dealer who gets them their drugs, know what a bad boy they've been. You feeling what I'm saying here, Kramer?"

The blood drained from Kramer's face. "I get it," he said. "And I'll come down."

"Good. Oh, and take your great-grandma to get her lottery tickets, you ungrateful freeloader!" she snapped, then moved away.

Candice and I had little choice but to follow; however, before we left him, Candice leaned in and actually growled in Kramer's face. He trembled and backed up against the garage, and it was enough, I thought, to let him know he'd been very, very lucky today, and not to push that luck any further by being uncooperative when we called on him to help us identify Gudziak's accomplice.

Once we were all back in Grayson's unmarked car, she turned to us and said, "Okay, so, you two *might* have a point."

"How do you think we only *might* have a point?" I demanded, knowing she was referring to my theory that Dave had been run off the road and abducted. "Because, from where I'm sitting, we *definitely* have a point."

"Kramer didn't say he saw the black truck run Dave's truck off the road," she said. "He only said he heard a loud bang. The bang could've been a blown tire."

"What difference does it make whether it was a blown tire or Dave was run off the road?" Candice said. "Either way, Gudziak and his buddy abducted Dave, then impersonated him to Wixom."

"It makes a difference, Candice, because I'm still not sure how Gudziak knew where to find Dave last Saturday morning. So, either Gudziak was following Dave when his tire blew and he ran off the road, becoming disoriented after his car came to a sudden stop, and forcing Gudziak to take over the role of Dave, *or* Gudziak and his accomplice were tailing Dave with the intention of driving him off the road, abducting him, and then impersonating him on the rest of his appointments."

I frowned. Grayson was right. I hadn't even thought about that first angle. "I think he was purposely run off the road," I said. "In fact, that's what my gut says, so it's less of a thought and more of a knowing."

Grayson nodded to me. "Okay, Abby, so let's say that Dave was run off the road—that Gudziak and his accomplice had targeted him and were tailing him, waiting for an opportunity to take him off the road. How did they know where to find him? And how did they know where he was going? And how did they know that he'd be headed to the Roswells' place? Because that scene was an assassination if ever I've seen one."

"In other words," Candice said, "how did Gudziak learn about Dave and Safe Chambers?"

"*Texas Monthly,*" I said immediately. "Dave was photographed standing next to his truck. All Gudziak had to do was read the article."

Grayson frowned. "So, what's the personal connection between Gudziak and the Roswells?"

"Does there have to be one?" Candice asked. "The same edition of *Texas Monthly* that featured the story on Safe Chambers also had Andy Roswell—whiz kid—as the cover story. Maybe it was simply a crime of opportunity."

"There were four other opportunities prior to their house, though," I said. "To Nikki's point, the violence of the crime at the Roswells' house . . . it's overkill."

"Yes," Grayson said. "Exactly."

"It'd be interesting to know if Murielle has a subscription to *Texas Monthly,*" Candice said. "I wonder if they'd ask us to provide a warrant to look that up for us."

Grayson looked from Candice to me, then back again. "Who?"

Candice and I filled her in on our theory about Murielle ordering the hit on Andy and Robin Roswell, Rosa Torrez, and Mario Tremblee all out of revenge.

"Hold on," Grayson said when we were finished. "You mean *the* Murielle McKenna? The woman whose house we had to provide extra security detail for when President Bush visited her here in Austin? *The* Murielle McKenna the governor and the mayor both interrupt meetings for whenever she calls?"

"Yep," Candice said. "*That* Murielle McKenna."

Grayson eyed both of us like we had to be insane.

"You guys must be crazy," she said. "No way would you ever get a warrant to look into Murielle's *any*thing in this town. Especially not when you have no evidence other than a couple of Instagram photos where it looks like the Roswells are actually stalking *her*. And besides all of that, you'd have to also find a connection between McKenna and Chris Wixom for your theory to work. Why would she order a hit on Wixom?"

"She didn't," I said. "I think Gudziak and his partner hit up Wixom's home because that actually *was* a crime of opportunity. I think Gudziak and his accomplice grabbed Dave on his morning route at the point where they weren't likely to be seen. Lost Creek Boulevard doesn't get a lot of traffic, and they almost carjacked him without being seen, and certainly got away before the police arrived. From there, Gudziak was able to impersonate Dave and case all the homes on his roster before he got to the Roswells'."

"And maybe the other homes were both an incentive and a payment for the hit," I added. "Not only did they get to keep the money from the Roswells' safe, but they would've gotten plenty of other goodies if they went back and hit up the other homes."

"That all sounds very risky," Grayson said, and I could tell she wasn't buying my theory.

But I knew I was closer to the truth than not. It just felt right in my gut. "Carjacking and assassinating four innocent people is probably a bigger risk," I said. "Gudziak obviously likes to push the line."

Candice turned to me. "Which reminds me, did you hear back from Dutch yet? Has he set up security for all the other clients Gudziak went to on Saturday?"

"Yes," I said, holding up my phone. "He's got guards posted at all the other locations. He said he sent a team to Chris Wixom's house, but the patrol is still there."

"They'll be there until we release the crime scene, which won't be for a couple of days," Grayson said.

My radar pinged with a thought. "Nikki, do you guys still have a patrol guarding the Roswell residence?"

"Yes, but only through the end of the day," she said. "We collected a mountain of evidence and we won't release that scene until all of the evidence has been processed, but Sienna's team is almost finished and she told me she'd send word to release the property between three and five today."

I sat with that silently for a minute, struggling with the uneasy feeling I had.

"What is it?" Candice asked, and I knew she was reading my body language.

Instead of answering her, I directed my next question to Grayson. "Can you do me a favor?"

"Depends on what it is," she said warily.

"I need for you to keep a guard at that scene for an extra couple of days."

"Other than the fact that it's already putting a serious dent into APD's budget, my butt would be on the line if I put in a request like that, Abby."

"I know, which is why I'm asking for the favor."

"Can you tell me why?"

I shook my head. "I have no idea. Yet. But you still need to keep that patrol posted, twenty-four/seven."

Nikki frowned. "Why can't your husband's company just send a team over like he's doing with the other clients?"

"I don't know," I said honestly. "Like, that would've been the logical next step, but my gut is insisting that APD not release the scene and continue to stand guard over that house until we figure this out."

Grayson blew out a sigh. "Fine," she said to me. "I'll pull some strings and send over the paperwork, but you should know that I'm only assigned to the Roswell case as an extra detective. I'm not the lead on it, so if I get overruled, there'll be nothing I can do."

"Please try, will you?" I said.

Grayson pulled up her cell and made the call. We listened as she spoke first to Sienna, who seemed reluctant to sit on the last few pieces of evidence and drag out the forensic analysis, but at last she agreed, and then Grayson called the lead detective and used her considerable charm to convince him not to make a big stink about how long the crime lab was taking to process the evidence.

The second she hung up with the lead detective, I felt a huge sense of relief. "Thank you," I said.

"I bought you forty-eight hours," she said. "Tops."

"I'll take it," I replied. "Hopefully, that'll be all we need to find Dave and solve this thing."

Grayson frowned. "Assuming Dave's still alive—"

"He is," I said. I'd checked on his image about an hour before as we were driving to Helen's, and he was still alive according to my sixth sense, but his energy spoke of immanent peril.

"Okay," Grayson acknowledged. "We need a lead to find Gud-ziak. Let's head to the substation and see what we can dig up."

"Sounds like a plan," Candice said.

As Grayson turned around to put the car into drive, however, I put a hand on her shoulder. "Nikki," I said, sensing something in the ether. "I keep getting the feeling that if you go back to work, you'll get pulled off course."

"Pulled off course?" she repeated. "What does that mean?"

"I'm not sure," I said. "Maybe you'll be redirected by your superior. There're a few more detectives than you working this case right now, correct?"

"Counting me, there're five," she said. "I was the last-minute add-on, which is why I was made the lead on the Wixom case. I'm the bridge between the two cases."

"Ah, well, I'm sensing that you might be the last-minute add-off and redirected. We can't go back to the substation, where you can be pulled off this case. We need you to stay on it."

"What would you suggest?" she asked me, looking a little exasperated.

"We could head to the bureau," Candice said. "Brice and Dutch have loads of investigative power at their fingertips. Let's loop them in and see if we can't utilize the FBI's tools to help come up with some leads."

Grayson didn't look happy. "Fine. But they'd better not try and take over the Wixom case. He's all mine and we clearly have jurisdiction."

"They'll behave," Candice promised. "Or they'll have me to contend with."

I smirked. They'd behave all right.

"Good," the detective said, and then she switched her gaze to the digital clock on the dash. "I've got . . . plans at six. So we need to work quick."

"You'll make your date," I promised, trying to sound reassuring. Trouble was, that's not at all how I felt.

Chapter Fifteen

· · ·

"Hey! Hey! Hey!" Agent Oscar Rodriguez yelled across the room. Everyone looked up from their computers, where we'd all been buried in case files and information looking for any connection between Gudziak and some guy with a neck tattoo of a dollar sign. Oscar, who had his hand over the mouthpiece of his phone, said to the suddenly quiet room. "Got him!"

I stood and trotted over to Oscar's desk, as did Brice, Dutch, Candice, and Grayson. "Who is he?" Dutch asked.

"Kaapo Hekekia," Oscar said, swiveling his computer screen so that we could see the man.

As I stared into the eyes of a seriously mean-looking individual, Grayson said, "Wixom said he thought Gudziak called the other guy Cap or Cappy."

Oscar, wearing a look of triumph, said, "Kaapo is a Hawaiian native. Moved here in two thousand six. He's been in and out of jail since then for everything from possession to human trafficking. For his last stint he was shipped out of state to Phoenix, where he served eight months of a nickel sentence for the latter."

"That's where he met Gudziak," I said.

"Yep," Oscar said. "The two were in the system at the same time."

"I don't see the dollar sign tattoo," Grayson said, pointing to the mug shot on the screen.

"That's new," Oscar said, with a smug knowing smile. Pulling up his sleeve to reveal a tribal tattoo, he added, "Turns out, me and Kaapo share the same tattoo artist, Chris Ellis, from Badass Tattoos. Chris is the best artist in Austin, a favorite of a lot of gang members."

"And you go to this guy?" I asked.

Oscar smiled. "Chris doesn't know I'm a Fed. He thinks I'm a reporter for the *Statesman*."

"You get away with a lie like that?" I asked.

Oscar bounced his eyebrows. "It's not like Chris reads the paper, Cooper. He's too busy sleeping, drinking, chasing girls, and working. Anyway, I called him and told him that I sat next to a guy at a bar who looked like he was from the islands, and he had a dollar sign tattoo on his neck that I thought looked like Chris's work. I also told him that if he had done the work, I'd want to interview his customer for a piece I'm doing in the *Statesman*. Chris remembered the guy right away and told me his name is Kaapo something—he couldn't remember the last name. He said that he and Kaapo talked a lot about Oahu while Chris worked on him, and the tattoo is actually a two-headed dragon, snaked into the shape of a dollar sign. Anyway, I did a first-name search in the system and found Hekekia right away."

"So that's our man," Dutch said beside me. "He lives here, Oscar?"

Oscar tore off a piece of paper with some numbers written on it. "This is his last known address."

Dutch put a hand on Oscar's shoulder. "Good work, buddy."

"So what do we do?" I asked.

Dutch and Brice moved away from me. In fact, everyone seemed to be in motion at once. "What's happening?" I asked, still standing by Oscar, who had gotten up out of his chair and was reaching into his desk to retrieve his gun.

"We go get the son of a bitch, Cooper," he said.

"Oh," I replied. "Okay." But then I didn't exactly know what to do. I mean, it's not like I carry my gun around in my purse. (It's at home, locked in a box under my bed, if you must know.)

"This is my collar!" Grayson said loudly when Dutch and Brice appeared from their offices, donning Kevlar vests and guns.

"Of course it's your collar," Brice assured her. "We're just backing you up."

Grayson nodded, but she still looked troubled. I had a feeling that protocol dictated that she call in the address and request her own backup, but everyone knew that the minute she did that, she'd be pulled back from the scene and made to take orders from someone else. "We'll need a warrant," Grayson said, looking a little defeated as she spoke the words.

"Yes," Brice said. "And if you call in for one, it won't be your collar anymore."

Grayson eyed Brice shrewdly. "What would you suggest?" she asked him.

"Let me call in for the warrant. Gudziak and Hekekia's crime spree has now crossed state lines, which makes for a great case for this to be our jurisdiction. I'll give you all the credit for the collar, though, if you'd prefer."

Grayson's mouth quirked into a crooked smile. "Okay, Special Agent Harrison. Have it your way."

"Good," Brice told her. "Good."

Candice and I sat in the van and watched on a digital monitor as our husbands, our friends, and Detective Grayson descended on a shabby-looking house south of downtown. They made quick work of surrounding the house, and Oscar and Dutch were the first two through the door.

Even though I'd checked the ether all the way over to Hekekia's place to make sure nothing bad would happen to any of the people I cared about, I still braced and held my breath as they went through the door.

For a long series of tense moments we couldn't tell what was happening. No sound came back to us, so we didn't know if they'd found the two men, or if the house was empty, but soon every single agent had filed into the home and was helping in the search.

I glanced at Candice and she appeared as tense as I was. "What do you think is going on?" I asked.

She shook her head, but then, all of a sudden, her hand grabbed onto mine, and with the other she pointed to the screen. From the corner of the screen where she was pointing, I saw a figure dart out of a doorway from the house next door and dash across the porch, followed by another larger figure.

Before I could even connect the dots, I realized that either Oscar had written the address down wrong, or Hekekia had given a false address, because our two suspects were right now flying away from the scene.

Candice was in motion well before I was. She flew to the back of the van, flung open the doors, and launched herself out onto the street. The image of the Roswells' bloody bodies bloomed horrifyingly in my mind, and all I could think was how dangerous it was for Candice to go after those two giant, violent men alone. "Hey!" I shouted, chasing after her. "Stop! Candice, *stop*!" But she wasn't listening, because she kept going as fast as those long legs of hers could carry her.

"Goddammit!" I yelled, hitting the street and giving chase. *"Dutch!"* I screamed, flying past the house where the boys had entered. *"DUTCH!"*

I had no idea if he heard me, but I couldn't let Candice go after Gudziak and Hekekia by herself, so I kept going.

As did she.

As did they.

Candice and I gained easily on the men—which just goes to show you the power of the workouts that my BFF puts us through. Within fifty yards she caught up to Hekekia, but he must've heard her coming, because he swiveled midstride and drew a giant gun from his waistband, taking aim right at her face.

If I haven't mentioned it before (or enough times), let me state that Candice has the reflexes of a cat. Or maybe a ninja. Or if a cat could become a ninja, she'd have those reflexes.

Just as Hekekia's gun came level with her face, Candice's arm whipped up, swatting the gun out of his hand *as* the gun went off! I heard the bullet ricochet off the pavement right next to me and felt the spatter of gravel against my pant leg.

When I looked up again, I saw Hekekia bring his other fist around, but his aim was off and it landed on Candice's shoulder. The blow spun her around hard and made her stumble. Unable to regain her footing, she went down.

Watching the big Hawaiian shoot and strike at my friend triggered an outraged response from me. With a bloodcurdling war cry I quickened my steps, hurdling over Candice's rolling body, and launched myself at him, leaping onto his back and wrapping my legs around his torso. *"You son of a bitch!"* I screamed. *"You son of a stinking, ugly, bat-faced bitch!"*

No disrespect to Hekekia's actual mother, who I'm sure is simply a *lovely* woman, but I may have been a little hyped up on adrenaline when I tackled him. Also, I was scared enough to wet myself, and yelling obscenities and insults helps overcome the pee-my-pants impulse when I'm afraid.

For his part, Hekekia didn't seem quite so terrified. He reached up over the top of his head to try to grab my shirt and pull me off him, but his hands were slick with sweat and he fumbled the hold. Meanwhile I had him gripped so tight with my legs, I was definitely restricting his airflow, but that position also allowed me to beat him with my fists and scratch him with my nails. *"I will shiv you!"* I screamed, pounding on him for all I was worth. Forget the fact that I wasn't packing a knife—the crazy talk was giving me much-needed courage. Like I said, despite my rabid attack on the man, I was scared shitless of him.

Pummel!

Punch!

Scratch-scratch-scratch!

"I will shiv you and gut you like a fish, you worthless trout!"

Punch! Punch! Punch!

Meanwhile, Hekekia's own hands were slapping at me, and by now he'd stumbled to a not-so-stable walk. Unable to fill his lungs with air, he was sweating profusely and gasping for air. "Get . . . the fuck . . . off me!"

I renewed my efforts to beat him senseless. *"Go fuck yourself!"* I roared while I beat and scratched and pulled hard on his ears. He swatted at me, and it hurt, so I grabbed his nose and pulled it to the side. He cried out in pain, but I didn't let up. Instead, I took a new tactic: I went for the fucker's eyes. Like, I literally went all *Game of Thrones* on his ass and tried to jab my fingers into his eyes—I was so angry and hyped up on adrenaline.

Hekekia came to a full stop, needing to shield his eyes from my assault with one arm, and I saw him ball his other hand into a fist right before he sent it up toward my face. I leaned hard to the side to duck the blow and it threw him way off-balance. We both went down.

My left leg and hip took the brunt of the blow, which hurt like you *cannot believe*, but I clenched my jaw, sucked it up, and kept attacking. No way in hell was I giving up until one of us was dead. Preferably him.

And then I heard someone yell, "Freeze, motherfucker!" and Hekekia and I both went perfectly still.

Panting, shaking, and still gripping a fistful of the man's long black hair, I looked over to see Candice planted at my side with the barrel of the Hawaiian's gun kissing his temple. She looked mad enough to pull the trigger too, which, I will admit, in that moment, I badly wanted her to do.

I don't know how she held back, but she did, and she motioned for me to release my death grip on the man's torso and move away from him.

But suddenly, I didn't know if I could. It was as if all the adrenaline and energy evaporated from me in the blink of an eye, and I sagged to the ground, gasping for air.

Then there was a sudden pounding of footsteps behind me, and strong arms hooked under my armpits to pull me away from the Hawaiian. "Jesus . . . Christ!" Dutch panted, after he'd freed me. "What the hell . . . were you *thinking*, Edgar?!"

He didn't give me a chance to answer. He simply scooped me up, held me tight to his Kevlar vest, and walked away. I was never more glad for his presence in my life, and I clung to him out of both pain and exhaustion. I'd fractured my pelvis a couple of years before, and that fall with Hekekia really rattled the six pins I've got lodged in my pelvic bone.

"Hey," Dutch whispered when his labored breathing had normalized. "Edgar, it's okay. Don't cry."

Belatedly I realized tears were leaking out of my eyes and streaming down my cheeks. "I'm not crying," I whimpered.

"Of course you're not," he said, a smile in his tone. "You took a pretty good fall there, though. You okay?"

"N-n-n-no," I blubbered. "It hurt!"

"I'll bet," he said, coming to a stop next to the van.

"That son of a bitch!" I wailed, burying my face in Dutch's chest. "I thought he was going to kill Candice!"

Dutch stroked my hair and kissed my cheek. "And here I thought he was going to kill *you*."

I took a deep breath, collecting my emotions. "Nah," I said, wiping my eyes. "I had him right where I wanted him."

Dutch chuckled and kissed my cheek again. "Sure you did, dollface. Sure you did."

"Is she okay?" I heard Brice say. He sounded winded too.

I squinted up at him. "I'm fine. Just spent. And a little bruised."

Brice wiped his brow. He looked at me with wide, somewhat crazed eyes. I'd never seen him look like that. "Do you need a ride to the hospital?" he asked me.

My brow furrowed. "No. Do I look like I need a ride to the hospital?"

"Maybe the mental ward," he snapped.

"Hey," Dutch said quietly. "Brice. Easy."

But Brice was too wound up to listen. "What the fuck were you and Candice thinking, Cooper?!" he shouted.

I glared at him. I don't much take to being yelled at. "Oh, I'm sorry, *Special Agent* Harrison. Did our collar of *your* suspect perhaps make a dent in your manhood? Well, sorry, not sorry!"

"Hey!" Candice yelled behind Brice. "What's the matter?"

Brice glared at me but rounded on her. *"What were you thinking?"*

Candice smiled at him, cool as a cucumber. "I wasn't, sweetheart. I saw the bastards make a run for it and I reacted. It was pure instinct."

Brice breathed loudly in and out of his nose for a moment, his face crimson and the vein near his temple throbbing. And then he opened his arms wide and reached for his wife, pulling her to him in a crushing embrace.

I rolled my eyes and looked at Dutch. He shrugged and said, "We saw Hekekia draw on Candice, and from our view, it looked like he'd shot her. When she went down, we thought he'd killed her."

"Ah," I said, all the anger I'd had toward Brice evaporating. "Okay. Well, then his attitude is understandable."

"Yeah, but your actions aren't so much," he said, cupping my face and forcing me to look at him. "Don't ever do anything so recklessly stupid again, okay?"

"Okay," I said. "I won't. I promise."

Dutch held my gaze. "I feel like that's not a promise you'll be able to keep."

"It's like you know me."

He pulled me to him again and held me close. "I guess you missed the fact that Kaapo had a knife strapped to his belt, huh?"

"He *did*?"

"Yep. We all saw him trying to grab for it while you were riding him like some whacked-out rodeo cowboy, but then you started gouging him in the eyes and he abandoned the effort. I don't think I've ever run so fast in my life."

"Yeah, well, it's probably a good thing that Candice got to us first."

"It is," Dutch said. I glanced up at him and saw him staring over my shoulder. When I looked, I saw him and Candice smiling at each other.

Several minutes later, while Dutch and Brice were searching Hekekia's house for evidence and any trace of Dave and Gwen, Candice and I, standing outside by the van, saw Agent Rodriguez and Detective Grayson come around the corner with Gudziak in cuffs between them. Oscar and Nikki appeared winded, but Gudziak looked barely able to walk. He was stumbling and coughing and nearly unable to keep moving forward. "You got him!" I called as they approached.

Nikki pushed Gudziak hard, a big old smile on her face. "We did," she said. "Mostly thanks to you."

They stopped in front of us, and we waited for them to bend Gudziak over the back of one of the sedans parked on the street, and while Oscar patted Gudziak down for weapons (he had several), Grayson talked about the capture.

"The idiot's gun jammed," Grayson said, a huge smile on her face. "He drew it and tried to fire on us, but nothing came out. He got so mad he threw it at us, and then he ran face-first right into a light post!"

Candice and I laughed as we imagined the scene, but Grayson laughed the hardest, having witnessed it firsthand. Oscar was chuckling pretty hard too. The only one not laughing was Gudziak. He was still a bit wobbly on his feet, and truth be told, he looked slightly disoriented. "My chest hurts!" he squawked.

At first, none of us paid him any attention—we were too busy laughing at Grayson while she pantomimed Gudziak kissing the light post—but when the fugitive said it again even more urgently, my Spidey sense went off with a sudden alarm bell.

Turning away from Grayson to focus my radar on Gudziak, I immediately knew he wasn't kidding around. The energy of a heart under duress is quite distinct. I can pick out high blood pressure in a person easily. It's a distressing condition; the pressure of the blood coursing through someone's cardiovascular system sends out a sort of pulse. A throbbing, if you will. I could feel this throbbing energy from Gudziak, but it was super intense.

Lifting up a hand, I shouted, "Hold on!"

Nikki stopped midsentence. "What's the matter?"

I pointed to Gudziak. "He's having a heart attack."

She looked over at him. "Aw, he's all right, Abby. He's probably just faking."

Candice, however, knew me well enough to know that I was picking up on an intuitive feeling, and not going by Gudziak's word. "Oscar!" she said urgently. "Lay him on the ground!"

Oscar stood up from the squat he'd been holding as he made sure to clear Gudziak's legs of weapons, and he looked at us quizzically. "Say what?"

Before we could explain, Gudziak's knees gave out from underneath him and he sank to the ground. "Call for an ambulance!" I yelled, rushing to the killer's side. I wasn't concerned for him in the slightest, in case you're wondering, but I was very worried for Dave and Gwen.

Minutes earlier, Dutch and Brice had done a quick search of the house that the two felons had come out of, and there was no sign of our two friends. Brice had tried to get Kaapo to talk, but he'd completely clammed up, yelling, "Lawyer!" as he was put into the back of Agent Cox's car.

I realized that Gudziak might be our only shot at finding Dave and Gwen. Or finding out what'd happened to them.

When I reached Gudziak's side, he was sucking in small gasps of air, as if he couldn't fill his lungs all the way. I tugged on his shirt and used my knees to elevate his head. "Lift his feet!" I yelled to Candice, who was next to me in a quick flash.

"Son of a bitch!" Nikki said somewhere behind me. "He *can't* be having a heart attack!"

"He is!" I insisted. "Call for an ambulance!"

"I'm on the phone with nine-one-one!" Oscar told me.

"Shit, shit, shit!" I said as Gudziak struggled to take a few more gasping breaths. And then the gasps stopped and his face started to turn blue. *"Candice!"*

She scooted up to his head as I got out of the way, and then she tilted Gudziak's chin toward the sky, opening his airway. She then moved down to his chest and began compressions.

Nikki and I watched helplessly for about two minutes, until the sweat began to pour down her temples. "Here!" I said, moving in next to her. "Let me take over!"

I pushed up and down on Gudziak's chest as rapidly as I could. For the record, performing CPR is incredibly taxing. It's nearly impossible for a lone individual to maintain the rhythm for longer than a few minutes. It takes a lot of physical strength to push on a diaphragm locked behind a sternum and the armor of a rib cage.

"My turn," Grayson said when I was panting so hard I thought I might pass out.

I let her take over; then it was Oscar's turn. The whole time Gudziak's face remained blue and his eyes stared listlessly skyward.

I was trembling as I watched Oscar's determined efforts, and he went far longer than any of us had. In fact, he was relieved only by the paramedics who finally arrived, and they tried four times to get Gudziak's heart to start with paddles. But as they loaded him into the ambulance, I knew without a doubt, he was dead.

And I could only wonder if our chances of finding Dave and Gwen alive were equally as hopeless.

Chapter Sixteen

· · ·

As evening fell, we got word from the hospital that Gudziak was DOA. The news struck all of us like a punch to the gut, because Hekekia had, unfortunately for us, witnessed Gudziak's death right next to the sedan he'd been cuffed inside. The second we got Kaapo back to the bureau's offices, he started doubling down on his calls for a lawyer and telling us that he wasn't going to talk to us without his attorney.

For an hour after getting back to our offices, we talked to Nikki about keeping the jurisdiction with us, instead of turning him over to the APD. "I told you guys he was my collar when we started this," she said the first time Dutch brought it up to her. "I've got seven or eight charges I need to file on him for the Chris Wixom home invasion and attempted murder alone."

"And he is your collar, Detective," Dutch said smoothly. "But if we turn him over to your custody, what're the odds that your prosecutor is gonna put pressure on you to keep the focus on Hekekia's involvement with Wixom and not work extra hard to make the case for his involvement in murdering the Roswells?"

I considered that for a minute, and had to concede that Dutch was probably right. Murder cases were crazy expensive for the state to take to trial. The investigation alone would cost a cool half million, and the trial was sure to cost double or even triple that, if history was any indicator. All we had at the moment to connect Hekekia to the Roswells' murder was his connection to Gudziak, who was no longer able to either admit nor deny that Hekekia had been with him when he'd murdered the Roswells.

There was no circumstantial evidence that'd turned up at the Roswells' house that could connect him to their murder, not even the unknown fingerprints on the casing of the bullet that had killed Mario Tremblee, but there was plenty that connected him to Chris Wixom's home invasion. Not only was Hekekia wearing one of Wixom's watches, but we'd also found the rest of the collection and what remained of the wall safe that'd been ripped out of Wixom's closet in the garage of the home he and Gudziak had raced out of. Oh, and about fifty thousand in cash, and a nice stash of narcotics that looked recently purchased.

All of that was enough to build a slam dunk case, probably even without the fact that Wixom was sure to ID him, especially with that prominent dollar sign tattoo on his neck.

Our dilemma was that if we turned Hekekia over to APD, we'd never be able to leverage the information we really needed from him, which was for him to tell us what he and Gudziak had done with Gwen and Dave.

Dutch reminded Nikki of all of that, and I could see her steely determination to keep the case with APD begin to waver. "We need to find Dave and Gwen, Nikki," I said softly after Dutch was through. "The only chance we've got is if we keep the pressure on him to tell us where they are, and the only way to do that is to try and build a federal case against him."

"On what charge, though?" she asked. "I'm all for helping you guys out, Abby, but what federal charge trumps attempted murder?"

I turned to Dutch and held my hands up. I had no idea.

"Nothing on our end trumps what you could charge him with," Dutch admitted, which surprised me. It sounded like he was giving up. "So, I'm asking you for time. Give us a couple of days to hold him in our custody and we'll keep working to try and make you a case for his connection to the Roswells while also working to locate our friends."

Nikki crossed her arms and shook her head while she stared at the ground. I knew we were putting her in an awful position. She'd have to be the one to call her superiors and convince them to let us have the case for a couple of days. They'd ask her why, and if she told them the truth, they'd probably refuse to grant us the favor. So she'd have to lie. Or we'd have to come up with something pretty good for her to take to them.

Finally, however, she glanced at her watch and said, "It's almost six. My CO is probably getting ready to head home for the day."

Dutch's mouth quirked at one corner. "Think you can wait to talk to him until morning so that we can come up with a charge?"

She sighed, lifting her chin to frown moodily at him. "I guess. But you know I'm gonna get my ass chewed for this, right?"

"Not if we help you connect Hekekia and Gudziak to the Roswells' murder," I said. I had a feeling we'd be able to pull that off. What I was less confident about was if we'd find Dave and Gwen in time. And that was something that my gut was saying was in extra short supply. Dave and Gwen were running out of time. Fast.

"Fine, but I want a crack at him when you interrogate his ass," she said.

"Done," Dutch assured her. "I'll call our federal prosecutor and see what we can make stick on our end."

As it happened, Matt Hayes—our local federal prosecutor— was close to our office when Dutch called, so he stopped in to help us work up something to hold Hekekia.

But after Matt showed up, it was like pulling teeth to get him to even consider filing a charge against our suspect. "Guys," he said after we'd all had a go at trying to convince him to help us, "this is going to cost me politically, and I know you're worried about your friend, but why can't you just turn Hekekia over to APD and ask them to let you interrogate him after they're done?"

"He's already called his attorney," Candice said. "You think the attorney is going to let him talk to us after the state files an attempted murder charge on someone from the wealthiest zip code in the county? Hekekia will be lucky to escape the death penalty. No way will his attorney want to add any more charges if he can avoid it."

Matt bit the inside of his lip, thinking. At last he pointed to Candice and said, "Were you working on this case in an official capacity?"

Candice in turn looked to Brice. "She was," he said without hesitation. "And I can have her submit an invoice before we head home tonight."

"Good," Hayes said. "Then I can make a solid case for Hekekia's assault and attempted murder of a federal employee. And I'll file a few other charges too, just to make it look scary. Along with the drug trafficking charges for the narcotics you guys found in the garage. Is there enough to make a case for trafficking, Agent Harrison?"

"It's close, but we could fiddle with the scale to make it work," he said without pause.

Matt nodded. "Okay. We'll go with that, but don't tell me you fiddled with the scale, got it?"

"What scale?" Brice said innocently.

"Good," Matt said, moving off to a cubicle to set up his laptop.

I breathed a sigh of relief. It'd buy us some time. Not much, I knew, because APD was sure to demand we turn Hekekia over to them for Chris Wixom's case, but maybe it'd give us a day or two. I could only hope that was enough.

"We need Hekekia's attorney to get here so we can see what he knows," Candice said, eyeing her watch.

Dutch looked over her shoulder. "We also need to order something in for dinner."

I didn't need to know the time. My stomach had been rumbling for at least an hour.

"He got his phone call as soon as we got here," Oscar said.

"Do we know who's representing him?" Matt asked, lifting his chin from the computer screen.

"No clue," Oscar replied.

Just then the main door to the office opened and in stepped a seriously striking-looking man in a perfectly tailored suit, with a flashy watch, a superexpensive-looking briefcase, and shoes that probably cost more than my monthly mortgage payment. "Hello," he said when we all glanced his way. "Zane Maldonado. I'm here to see my client, Kaapo Hekekia."

No one spoke for a moment; we all simply stared. I mean, the guy was, like . . . breathtaking. Tall, with chiseled features, startling ice-blue eyes, and light blond hair slickly combed and parted to the side, he looked like someone fresh off an *Esquire* magazine cover shoot.

Zane smiled knowingly. It was pretty clear he got that reaction a lot. "Is he in a room somewhere?" he asked, wagging a finger to the right and left.

"I'll show you," Candice suddenly volunteered, getting up to step forward with a winning smile and an outstretched hand.

My eyes widened (more than they already were) and I glanced at Brice, who was also staring at his wife with a bit of shock.

"He's back here, Counselor," Candice said, in a husky, rich voice that I'd only ever heard her use for her husband.

"Thank you," Zane said, his own smile broadening while he took in her lovely form. "You have amazing arms, by the way. You work out, right?"

"These?" she said coyly, flexing one biceps. "They're the result of clean living and a virtuous lifestyle."

"I'll bet," he said, chuckling, while turning to offer her his arm.

To my stunned amazement, Candice took Zane's arm in a gesture that was maaaaaaybe a weensy bit too flirtatious before she led him to where Hekekia was currently handcuffed to a chair in one of the conference rooms. In that moment I also saw Brice's whole countenance change.

And it wasn't pretty.

Even Dutch winced at the sight.

The rest of us? We sorta made ourselves busy. Or scarce.

"Who wants coffee?" I asked, grabbing my purse.

"I'll drive you," Oscar said, grabbing his keys.

"We should order some takeout," said Dutch, grabbing his coat.

"I'll drive you," said Matt, grabbing his laptop.

"I've got a dinner date to cancel," Nikki said, grabbing her cell.

Nobody, and I mean nobody, grabbed the opportunity to comment on what'd just happened between Candice and the hot-looking attorney.

Well, except the new guy. Idiot.

"Do they know each other?" Agent Howell asked Brice, referring to Candice and Mr. Hot-guy-attorney.

Brice rounded on Howell (appropriately named) and lit into him. *"Where's that report on Gudziak's vehicle?"* he roared. *"Didn't I ask for that two hours ago, Howell?"*

Nikki made a beeline for the large conference room on the opposite side of the office. Oscar and I broke into a trot to get out the door. Dutch and Hayes were right behind us.

Downstairs in the parking garage I turned to Dutch and said, "How long should we stay outta there, do you think?"

"Give him at least a half hour to calm down," Dutch said.

"Okay. Usual order for you?"

"Yeah. But text the guys individually to see what they want."

"Got it."

"Matt, you okay with Thai food?" Dutch asked.

"Works for me," he said.

"Oscar?"

He gave a thumbs-up. "Great. We'll get a half-dozen orders of pad Thai."

"Awesome. But no pad Thai for me," I said. "I'd like—"

"Steamed veggies with chicken over brown rice," Dutch said for me. Does he know me or what?

I beamed at him. "You're a prince of a man, you know."

He bounced his eyebrows smartly. "I heard a rumor like that, once."

"See you in forty-five minutes or so," I said, leaning in to give him a kiss.

Before I could complete the deed, he pulled back and said, "Did you think that guy was good-looking?"

(Uh. Oh.) "What guy?"

Dutch thumbed over his shoulder. "That guy. The attorney. What's his—"

"Zane?" I said—too quickly. (Double. Uh. Oh.)

Dutch's eyes narrowed. "Yeah," he said. *"Zane."*

I gulped. Behind me I heard a car door open and close. Oscar, sensing danger, had taken cover. Over Dutch's shoulder I saw Matt follow suit and get into his BMW. Sons of bitches, deserting me in my hour of need. "Well, he was *okay*," I said. "I mean, if you *like* that look."

"Look?"

I shook my head, and felt heat rise up from my belly. Dutch had me all flustered and for the life of me I couldn't think of an easy way out of this conversation. "You know . . . ," I said, pushing playfully on his shoulder.

My husband's eyes narrowed a little more.

"That—that—that . . . look," I stammered, *literally* starting to sweat and unable to come up with any kind of "look" that might put Dutch off this line of questioning.

"Uh-huh," he said, turning away from me.

"Shit," I muttered. "Babe, he's not nearly as good-looking as you!"

And then I blinked because my inboard lie detector hadn't gone off. I realized that, as model beautiful as Zane was, he was no match in my heart for my husband. "Hey!" I said, reaching out to grab Dutch by the arm. He stopped and looked back at me, his lips pressed to a thin line. It killed me to see the hurt in his eyes. "No!" I told him, pulling him toward me and forcing him to see the truth in my own eyes. "You don't get it, honey. My lie detector didn't even go off when I said that! I seriously, seriously mean it that, sure, he's a good-looking guy, but he's no . . . you. You take my breath away. You always have, and you always, always will."

Dutch's scowl remained for a moment, but then he softened, and then he smiled and leaned down to give me a light peck on the mouth. "Peace," he said.

"Peace," I agreed.

He released me and I got into the car with Oscar.

"You good?" Oscar asked as I buckled myself in.

"Peachy," I said a bit stiffly.

"Man," said Oscar. "Who knew one guy walking into an office could cause so much trouble?"

And then I sat forward, because something clicked in my memory. "Hang on," I whispered, digging for my phone.

"What's up, Cooper?" Oscar asked, braking on his way out of the parking space.

"Nothing," I said, waving at him to carry on. "I just need to check something."

Forty minutes later Oscar and I were back with hot beverages, and some pretty interesting new insights. Of course, we walked in to find Brice's office door closed and the blinds drawn. No doubt he was in there sulking. Meanwhile, Candice was busy typing on her computer with a decidedly unhappy expression. Nikki looked up from her laptop and rolled her eyes before motioning in first Candice's then Brice's direction.

Meanwhile, all the other agents had their noses glued to their computer screens. *Yikes,* Oscar mouthed to me.

I sighed and started handing out the coffees. When I got to Candice's desk, I stood there with my cardboard tray and two remaining drinks. "Hey," I said.

"None for me, thanks," she said woodenly, without even looking up.

"Oh, you're drinking this," I said angrily. Reaching down to grab hold of her arm, I added, "And you're coming with me."

"Sundance," she sighed, pulling away from me. "I'm not in the mood."

"Don't really care, Cassidy. I'm serious—you need to come with me."

She glared up at me, but I continued to stare expectantly at her and she finally caved.

With another gigantic sigh she pushed back from her desk and got up to follow me back to Brice's office. I didn't even knock when I went in.

"Busy, Cooper," Brice said, brusquely.

"Don't care, Harrison," I said.

His head snapped up as I waved for Candice to come in. She did, but she wouldn't look at Brice. Instead she took a seat at his round conference table, crossed her arms, and her legs, then bounced one foot up and down in agitation.

Focusing on Brice, I said, "Did she tell you?"

He looked at me blankly. "Tell me what?"

"About our good friend Zane?"

Brice's expression darkened. And his reply was clipped and short. "What?"

"Oh, I *tried* to tell him, Sundance," Candice said behind me. "But the idiot wouldn't listen."

I set Brice's coffee down on his desk, and walked over to hand Candice her cup. She took it with a muttered, "Thank you," and the room fell silent again.

I took a seat across from Candice but turned to speak to Brice, who was still at his desk glaring at his wife. "Zane's the missing link we've been looking for," I said.

"What's that supposed to mean?" he asked.

I turned to Candice, waving at her to take over. I'd put it together in the car, and actually felt bad for ever doubting her. "Zane is one of Murielle's groupies," she said, glaring at her husband. "When we were looking for a clue on Murielle's Instagram page to link her to the Roswell murders, I remembered seeing him in several of the photos she took out on the town with her posse."

I'd remembered him too, but belatedly when I was in the car on the way to get coffee. When I'd viewed her Instagram account, I'd been so focused on the fact that Murielle had taken every photo to make it look like the Roswells were crashing her scene that I hadn't given a ton of thought to the extra people in her group. But Candice had, which is why she's such a good investigator.

At the news that Maldonado was part of Murielle's posse, Brice's brow furrowed. And his mouth opened as if he had something to say, but then it closed again and it took a minute for him to actually speak. "Wait . . . he's . . . what?"

Candice turned her phone so he could see the image on the screen. It was a shot of Maldonado with his arm slung around Murielle at some nightclub. "He and Murielle are super chummy. I recognized his face and thought that appearing friendly and flirtatious might help get a little info out of him. As I was showing him where to find his client, I asked him about Murielle. He told me that they go way back, but he wouldn't give up much more than that. Since dropping him off at Hekekia's door, I've been researching him. He costs five fifty an hour to retain. Five hundred and fifty bucks an hour," she repeated for emphasis, and I had to agree that it sounded ridiculous to pay that much for an attorney. My own attorney was less than half that, actually.

"How the hell can Hekekia afford him?" I asked. "I mean, all the cash we recovered from the house he was in with Gudziak was confiscated. He wouldn't have access to it to pay for Maldonado."

"I doubt he's got the money to afford him," Candice said. "But Murielle sure can."

"Do we know she's paying for him to represent Hekekia?" Brice asked.

"How could we know that?" Candice asked. "Without a warrant for her finances, we can only guess. Even so, I find the link between Murielle and Hekekia through Maldonado pretty interesting."

I smiled smugly at Brice once Candice was through explaining. I hoped he'd notice and walk back his jealous hissy fit.

For his part, Brice appeared to be struggling with a whole bunch of emotions and thoughts. Mostly he looked confused and embarrassed. As if to cover it up, he took the coffee I'd brought him and peeled back the tab on the lid to sip at the black liquid. I wondered if he was stalling for time to come up with an appropriate apology. Instead—and in perfect Brice fashion—he ignored the fact that he'd been a complete jackass and focused on just the facts. "Even knowing we're hard-pressed to get a warrant for her financials, would Murielle be stupid enough to send in her own attorney to represent the guy who'd murdered the two people we suspect she ordered the hit on?"

"She would if she wanted Hekekia to keep quiet about it," I said. "It's sorta perfect when you think about it. I mean, if she pays for Hekekia's counsel, she can control what he admits to through Maldonado. And *he's* not going to let the scumbag talk. He'll convince Kaapo to keep quiet about anything relating to the Roswells and wait for us or APD to put enough together to form a case."

"Which will be hard, as we currently have shit to tie Hekekia to the Roswells," Brice said.

"But maybe we can use Maldonado's connection to Murielle to throw him off-balance," Candice said, with an extra bounce to her knee. "Maybe before we try to interview Hekekia, we toss out the fact that we suspect Murielle is behind the financing of Kaapo's defense."

"How much do you think she's willing to spend to keep him quiet?" I asked. At $550 an hour, the tab would run up pretty fast.

Candice waved her hand casually. "I doubt Murielle is concerned about the cost. The woman's worth about a billion dollars, right? She has money to burn, especially to keep any mention of her connection to the murders of the Roswells and their staff under wraps." And then Candice seemed to think of something else and she asked me, "Hey, do you think the guy she was talking about when she asked you to use your radar to focus on that employee she didn't know if she could trust—could that have been Maldonado?"

I snapped my fingers and pointed at her. "It absolutely could've been him! Wow, I hadn't even made that connection. He's certainly pretty enough for her to want to jump into bed with, and he strikes me as the kind of oily narcissist that totally fits the bill of who I was describing."

I turned my attention to Brice then. "Is there any way we could force Maldonado to tell us who's paying his tab?"

He shook his head. "Nope. That falls under the scope of attorney-client privilege. He's under no obligation to tell us, and we can't look at Murielle's finances without a warrant, which we don't have anything to go to a judge and get, especially not with her money and influence. Any kind of a warrant for her is going to require a smoking gun with her prints on it or something just as compelling."

"This case is so frustrating," I grumbled. "We have all these disconnected pieces and no way to bring them together."

"So we'll have to be clever in that interview room," Candice said, once again focusing on her phone. Then she looked up and said, "Hey, Sundance, feel like running a quick errand with me?"

My stomach grumbled. Dutch was due back with our dinners any minute, and I was fast approaching the hangry zone of the evening. "How quick?"

"Fifteen minutes, tops."

I sighed. "Fine. But if we see Dutch between here and the garage, I'm grabbing my dinner and eating it in your car."

Candice had a rule about eating in her Porsche: No one was allowed to unless it was an emergency. It's crazy how many times feeding me has been deemed an emergency. "Deal," she said. "Let's go so we can get back before Maldonado finishes talking to Hekekia."

On the way out, Candice pointed to Nikki, who was looking majorly bummed while staring at her phone in one of the free cubicles around the office.

"Hey," Candice said, snapping her fingers to get Nikki's attention. "You. Come with us."

"Where?" she asked.

"It's a surprise," Candice said, moving past the cubicle toward the door like a woman on a major mission.

Nikki fell into step with me and said, "I've got nothing better to do tonight anyway."

I cut her a sideways look. "The hot date cancelled?"

Nikki pocketed her cell. "I texted him to see if we could meet up later because I'm stuck here for at least another two hours, and he texted back to say that he already had plans for later."

I winced. "Ouch."

"It might not be with another girl," she said, squaring her shoulders.

I didn't say anything. It was clear to me that this player had made a second date with the girl he planned to get lucky with tonight. Meeting Nikki for dinner had simply been his warm-up act. Douche bag.

I was suddenly glad that Candice had a little excursion to help take Nikki's mind off things, but I still had no idea what Candice had up her sleeve.

A short time later we walked into her condo, following her right to her closet, and it sort of came together about what she might be thinking.

"I'm not wearing that," I said, standing defensively with my arms crossed while Candice basically shoved a slinky, low-cut, impossibly tight outfit at me.

"Put it on, Sundance," Candice said firmly.

"I'll wear it," Nikki volunteered.

I made a gesture to indicate she should by all means take the outfit, but Candice shook her head. "I've got something better for you, Detective." Candice tossed the tight, slinky thing onto my head as if it was a foregone conclusion that needed no further argument.

I pulled it free so that I could scowl at Candice, who was reaching back into her closet to take out a gorgeous powder pink pantsuit, cinched tight at the waist and flaring slightly in the pant leg. "Oh, come on!" I yelled. I would've worn that in a heartbeat.

"It'll look better on her," Candice said.

Nikki grabbed the outfit greedily, and after Candice motioned toward the master bathroom, she trotted happily off to change.

I continued to glare at Candice. "Why do I have to wear the slinky outfit and you two get all the class?"

Candice smiled sweetly. "Maldonado has already seen what I'm wearing, but I don't think he really took you and Nikki in. We need a little distraction in that interrogation room, Sundance. You in that outfit will be a terrific diversion. And Nikki's skin tone is sure to bring out the best of the other outfit. Maldonado might not even be able to think straight with all the bombshells in the room."

I arched a skeptical eyebrow. "That seems a little desperate, don't you think? I mean, would this guy really be that easily distracted by such an obvious ploy?"

Candice pulled out her phone and showed me a few of the pictures highlighting Zane in the background of Murielle's photos. In every single one he had his arm wrapped around a beautiful woman in a tight, cleavage-baring outfit, and always his eyes were roving to about midchest. The guy was an obvious Lothario.

"Great," I said woodenly. I'd be the only one of the three of us with lots of cleavage showing, which was a problem, as I didn't have lots of said cleavage to offer.

Candice seemed to understand the dilemma, because she walked to her dresser and opened the drawer. "Here," she said, tossing me a push-up bra from the collection. "And I've got some falsies to help fill you out."

I was about to protest when the door to the bathroom opened and Nikki stepped out, looking so radiant it was a wonder I'd ever thought about taking that pink number away from her. "Candice, I *love* this outfit!" she exclaimed.

"I figured you might. You can borrow it too, if you'd like. Wear it to your date with the new guy."

Nikki blushed, and my chest tightened because she still looked so hopeful whenever anyone mentioned the guy. "I couldn't," she said, even though her expression turned eager.

"Yes, you should," Candice insisted. "Especially since you're going to be taking hell from your CO tomorrow. Consider it my way of saying thank you."

Nikki smoothed her hand over the waist of the pantsuit. "You're sure?"

"Positive," Candice said, and it was decided. Then she turned back to me and pointed to the door. "Get dressed. Now."

With a growl I headed off to the bathroom and put on the outfit she'd handed me, which—shocker—didn't look slutty at all. Okay, so maybe it honestly looked amazing on me, and maybe I felt stupid for making such a fuss about it, but hell if I was going to let Candice know that.

I came out of the bathroom to find Candice working on Nikki's makeup. The girls both let their mouths drop when they took me in. "Whoa," said Nikki. "You look so beautiful, Abby!"

"Nice," said Candice, offering me a satisfied smile. "All that working out has really paid off. Your bod is absolutely gorgeous, my friend."

I grinned. Okay, so maybe I'd let on that I liked the look too. "You guys think it fits okay?" I asked, tugging at the hem, which was midthigh.

"It fits you better than it does me, so you can also borrow that one," Candice said. "In fact, Abs, why don't you just go ahead and keep it?"

"Really?"

"Oh, yeah," she said with a light laugh. "I don't think Dutch would forgive me if I took that back after he sees you in it."

"Maldonado's going to have a hard time keeping his head in the game," Nikki joked. "We should be able to ask Hekekia anything we want."

"We'll see," Candice said. I was with her. Maldonado was pretty, but he sure as hell didn't strike me as stupid. He'd certainly be distracted, but I doubted he'd let us run roughshod over his client.

"We should be able to push the envelope a little at least," I said.

"Assuming the boys let the three of us go in together to interrogate Hekekia," Candice remarked.

"Oh, crap," I said. I hadn't even thought of that. By rights it should've been Nikki and maybe Brice, or maybe Nikki, Brice, and Dutch. We'd have to get their permission to allow us into the room with Nikki.

And then it hit me that maybe that was also part of Candice's plan. With the three of us showing up like Charlie's Angels, we had a better chance of getting all the men to see things our way.

Candice fluffed Nikki's curls and said, "Okay, beautiful, move over so I can get to work on Sundance."

"Oh, boy," I sighed, and my stomach gave another rumble. This had already been longer than fifteen minutes and I had a bad feeling my dinner was quickly getting cold.

"Sit," Candice said when Nikki got up. "I promise, this won't take long."

Chapter Seventeen

. . .

Candice kept her word and in five minutes I was primped, fluffed, pushed up, and primed—ready for a night out on the town . . . or, you know, to interrogate a killer and his suave lawyer.

We arrived back at the office and walked in with all the drama that three gorgeous girls exerting major *va-va-voom* power would. Walking side by side, and stepping in time down the main aisle among all the cubicles, I think, we needed only a big fan to pull off the Hollywood crime-drama walk.

Even without the fan, jaws dropped all around. Oh, and I didn't really look, but I swear there were a few men in the room who gave at least a little salute to our entrance.

We stopped in front of Dutch's desk, and my hubby stood there a bit stupidly, one hand stuck in a large take-out bag, the other holding a plastic set of utensils, his mouth a big round O.

"Hey," I said, giving him a little lift of my chin.

"H-hey," he said, blinking hard. "You . . . you . . . wow."

I smiled coyly. "You okay with the three of us taking first crack at Hekekia?"

"Hell, no!" we heard, and I turned to see Brice standing in the doorway of his office, that jealous, angry look back on his face.

Candice stepped away from Dutch's desk and approached her husband. Her walk was full of extra bounce and even though I couldn't see her face, I had a feeling she was turning on her considerable charm as she approached him.

Sure enough, Brice's expression wavered when she neared him, but then he shook his head as if to clear it and said, "I'm serious, Candice. No way."

She didn't say anything; she simply stopped in front of him, took his hand, and led him into his office. The door was shut a moment later and at first we heard Brice's muffled and slightly raised voice, but then it softened, and then there wasn't much noise at all. A few moments later the door opened again and Candice stepped out triumphantly.

Brice came out adjusting his tie, but he still didn't look happy.

I grinned at Candice. There are days I'm so grateful she's on my side.

I was so full of adoration for her I almost didn't notice when she got up next to me and lifted the container of Thai food that I was greedily about to dive into.

"Later," she said.

I grabbed the container back. "I'm hungry!"

"Three bites," she ordered. "No more."

"Why?"

Candice's gaze dropped to my belly. "You really want that big meal hitting your stomach about the time we walk into that interrogation room?"

I looked down. My getup clung tightly to my body. Hell, you could see the outline of my belly button. "Dammit," I muttered, shoveling three huge bites of chicken and rice into my mouth, chewing quickly, and setting the rest aside.

At least those three bites were enough to take the edge off. "Okay, let's do this," I said. Dutch was still staring at me with lustful eyes. "We'll be back," I assured him, patting his shoulder and following Candice and Nikki toward the conference room where Hekekia and his attorney were.

Candice looked back over her shoulder toward the boys and

said, "Oscar, give us two minutes to square it with Maldonado and then hit the cameras, okay? We'll want to record this."

"You got it," Oscar said to her, but his eyes never left Nikki. The poor boy looked like he was honestly lovestruck.

Huh, I thought. *Interesting.*

Oscar was my buddy at the bureau. He and I had been through a lot together, and our bond was pretty tight. I adored him and we got along like brother and sister, always looking out for each other.

Now, Oscar didn't know that I knew he'd been recently dumped by a beautiful girl I'd really thought was going to work out for him. He'd told no one, but broken hearts are pretty easy for me to pick out of the ether, and one morning about a month earlier when he'd offered me a breakfast burrito from one of our favorite local restaurants, I'd seen it written all over his energy. Outwardly, he'd shown no sign of the breakup. And I hadn't mentioned it, because, well, the boy should have some privacy. When he was ready to share his relationship status with me, he would.

So far he was still keeping mum about being single again, but there were signs. He'd removed his girlfriend's photo from his desk, for one, and he'd stopped talking about her altogether, which was another. For the past few weeks I'd felt so bad for him, because Oscar is one of those really great guys that can't seem to find lasting love.

Looking to Nikki as she stood in front of me, I realized that was her exact issue too.

I glanced back at Oscar and waited for him to notice that I was staring at him. When he finally did, I offered him a smile and a knowing wink. He blushed and I motioned with my chin toward Nikki, then winked again, silently promising him that I'd put in a good word for him and see what little fires I could start for these two.

Oscar's face reddened even more, but a sweet, grateful smile spread across his face, so I knew he was on board at least.

In answer to Candice's knock, Maldonado opened the door to us and took a step back, his expression one of surprised delight.

"Are you ready to get this thing going?" Candice asked in that same rich, husky voice she'd used before. Before he could answer, she used her thumb to point to me and Nikki. "We've got plans later, and we'd like to wrap this up in the next hour or so if possible."

Maldonado's gaze traveled from Candice to Nikki and settled on me, where it lingered for an uncomfortable few seconds before he said, "You three are doing the interview?"

"We are," I said, forcing myself to hold his gaze. I'll freely admit that it felt really weird to appear so openly provocative to anyone but my husband.

Maldonado opened the door wide. "Please come in, ladies," he said.

Candice went in first and took the chair to the left, Nikki took up the middle, directly across from Hekekia, and I took up the end, directly across from where Maldonado had placed his briefcase.

No surprise, the attorney moved his briefcase to the floor, and took up the chair across from me. Again I held his gaze as he sat. His eyes cut to the sizable emerald engagement ring on my left hand, and the wedding band with matching emeralds that hugged it.

I allowed a small smile to form on my lips, and moved my fingers subtly to shift the rings, hoping his interpretation was that I wasn't as committed to my husband as my wedding set might suggest.

Maldonado sat back in his chair and puffed his chest out. All the unspoken messages in the room were saying more than actual words could.

To Maldonado's right, Hekekia sat with his mouth agape. He was moving his eyes from the three of us to his attorney, then back to us, like he had no idea what the hell was going on.

It was exactly where we wanted the two men to be. Thrown off and distracted. Nikki started by opening a thick folder she'd prepared and pulling out a photo of Chris Wixom. "Remember him?" she said to Hekekia.

The Hawaiian didn't even look at the photo, but he did glance at his lawyer, who was still staring at me like he couldn't wait to get me alone somewhere. "No," Hekekia said when his attorney said nothing.

"He remembers you," said Nikki. "Picked your mug shot right out of a six-pack, Mr. Hekekia. He says you were the person who shot him and stole his property."

Hekekia blinked lazily. "He's lying."

"Really?" she said. "Why would he do that?"

Hekekia shrugged. "Maybe he's confused. You should ask Snake about him."

"Snake," she said. "You mean Mr. Gudziak?"

"Yeah," Hekekia said. "He might know that guy."

"I'd love to ask Mr. Gudziak about him, but your friend didn't survive his heart attack."

"Huh," he said. "Too bad."

"Yeah," Nikki agreed. "A real tragedy."

Nikki then pulled out two more photos: one of the set of watches that'd been in Wixom's home, the other a photo of the watch that'd been on his wrist before being confiscated. "How about these timepieces?" Nikki asked. "Recognize them?"

Hekekia peered at the images and said, "Yeah. Those are the watches that Snake brought over to my place yesterday."

"He brought them to you?" Nikki asked.

Maldonado kept his leering, smiling eyes on me as he said, "Asked and answered, Detective. Move on."

So he was paying attention. "And what about this, Mr. Hekekia?" Nikki asked next, showing him a photo of the wall safe that had been found dismantled in his garage.

Hekekia looked to Maldonado, who merely nodded. "Snake showed up with that too."

"Where'd he say it came from?"

Hekekia shrugged. "He said he found it in the middle of the road along with the watches."

"What road?"

"He didn't say."

"So, let me get this straight," Nikki said. "Your friend, a fellow felon, shows up at your door with a wall safe and some stolen watches, and you just let him in and tell him to make himself at home?"

"Hey, I didn't know he was a felon," Hekekia said. "Man, I met him a couple weeks ago at a bar."

"Don't you mean a couple of *years* ago, Mr. Hekekia?" Candice interrupted. "Didn't the two of you serve time together in the Arizona State Prison Complex?"

Hekekia scratched his head like her question was a real thinker. "ASPC is a big place. Over six hundred bros run through there. But you can check my records to see that we never shared a cell or work duty or anything like that."

My eyes narrowed. His answer sounded very confident and rehearsed. He wasn't lying about never having shared a cell with Gudziak, but every single other thing he said was total bullshit.

Nikki pointed to the three of us. "So you expect us to believe that the first time you met Gudziak was at a bar here in Austin, population nine hundred thousand, and not under the roof of the same penitentiary where you both were serving time?"

Hekekia shrugged. "Yeah," he said simply.

I shook my head subtly. What a load of crap.

"What bar?" Nikki pressed.

"Don't remember."

"Okay, then *where* was it located? Maybe we can Google it."

"Don't remember," Hekekia said. "I only remember being at the bar when he sat down and we had a drink and started talking."

"And the subject of your mutual time in prison never came up?" Nikki said, as if she couldn't imagine that wasn't a topic of conversation between the two.

Maldonado tore his eyes away from me to look at Nikki. "He

didn't know he was associating with a felon, Detective, which, if he had known, would've been a clear violation of his parole."

"Yes," she said. "It would." Still, she let the topic drop and reached back into the folder to pull out a photo of the drugs confiscated from Hekekia's garage. "Know what is also a clear violation of his parole, Counselor? This."

Nikki slapped the photo down on the table, but Maldonado gave it no more than a cursory glance. "Kaapo, tell them about the drugs."

"They were Snake's," Hekekia said. "He bought them, used them, and didn't tell me he'd hidden them in my garage. When I found out he had them in there, I told him to take his shit and get out of my house."

"Really?" Nikki said, as if she were fascinated by all the tall tales. "And did he?"

"No. He started giving me a story about how he stole the drugs from some drug dealers and was afraid they'd followed him to my place. That's when we heard the yelling outside and saw you guys breaking into the house across the street. We thought you guys were the drug dealers and that's why we ran."

Candice shook her head and rolled her eyes. "You thought *I* was a drug dealer?" she said.

"Yeah!" he insisted. "I don't know who you are if you don't say something like, 'Stop! Federal officer!'"

My eyes narrowed again. I realized that Maldonado had coached Hekekia pretty well before our interview. Candice had never called for Hekekia to halt, or announced herself as a federal employee. She'd just raced after him until he'd pulled a gun on her.

"You tried to kill her!" I spat, pointing at the despicable criminal.

"I thought *she* was trying to kill me! And then, *you* went all crazy on me! Pulling my hair, scratching me! *Biting* me!"

I felt my cheeks redden and my attention was momentarily diverted to Maldonado. He'd lowered his lids seductively and mouthed, *Wow,* to me.

I nearly punched him in the piehole, but managed to keep my

cool. "Sounds like you've got an explanation for everything, Mr. Hekekia," I said.

"It's the truth!" he replied.

Of course, it wasn't the truth. It wasn't even in the same neighborhood as the truth, but Hekekia had probably been lying and manipulating people his whole life. Truth meant little to him; in fact, it became whatever he said it was. I realized quickly that he'd *never* admit to wrongdoing and go to his grave denying he was involved in any crime whatsoever.

Still, Nikki asked several more questions, trying to get Hekekia to crack, but he stuck to his story that he'd innocently offered a down-on-his-luck friend a place to stay for a little while, and said friend had turned out to be nothing but bad news, which was really a shame because Hekekia was now a model citizen trying to turn his life around.

"Where's Gudziak's truck?" Nikki asked him.

"What truck?"

"Gudziak drove a black pickup, right?"

"He didn't have a truck," Hekekia said. "Or a car. He showed up at my place on foot."

"With a wall safe weighing over forty pounds and a collection of watches?" Nikki reiterated.

"Asked and answered, Detective," Maldonado said, his eyes roving the V-neck of my outfit as if he could find an angle to allow him to see inside my bra.

Nikki shook her head and went back to her folder. She pulled out several gruesome photographs that I immediately recognized, and laid them out in front of Hekekia. "Remember this?"

"Oh, man," said the Hawaiian. "That looks rough."

"You should know," she said. "You were there."

Maldonado diverted his attention from my bustline to the photos. "You have proof linking my client to the Roswells' murder?"

It surprised me that he would recognize where the gruesome images had come from. Andy and Robin Roswell had been rendered unrecognizable after such a violent death. "We're working on the connection," Nikki assured him, keeping her focus on Hekekia.

Kaapo shrugged again. "Don't know 'em," he said. "Or what happened to them."

Nikki produced more photos of the scene.

I couldn't help but glance at them all too. My stomach muscles clenched and my appetite disappeared. I'd seen the scene up close, but the trauma of it had blocked out almost all the worst memories of it until I saw the photos spread out on the table.

For his part Hekekia kept his eyes staring sightlessly ahead. He made no effort to take a closer look as Nikki set out photo after photo on the table. She finally ended by setting down a photo of Andy Roswell, so handsome in life with a beaming smile, and next to it one of his beautiful wife, Robin. "Look!" she demanded, as she slapped down the photos. "Andy, Robin, and their faithful employee, Rosa Torrez, who'd been caught fleeing for her life just past the stairs . . ."

Hekekia cast a lazy glance at the photos being slapped onto the table, doing his best to look bored.

". . . and Mario Tremblee, who'd been innocently working in the backyard and probably never even knew you and Gudziak were inside killing the couple he worked for! You were there, Kaapo! You and Snake."

I was watching Hekekia as his gaze moved across the photos and then there was something about his expression that shifted for a moment when his eyes rested on the Roswells' gardener. I glanced quickly at the image of the very handsome young man with deep, soulful eyes and black hair, and when I looked back up to Hekekia, I couldn't really say for sure, but as he took in Mario's image, all of a sudden he seemed to look confused. Or maybe surprised. It was hard to say. It was over in a flash, however, and it left me wondering if I'd really caught a reaction or not. Maybe he'd just been reacting to what Nikki was yelling at him, and that made me wonder if he'd actually been there. I mean, we didn't know for sure that he had. We were only fairly certain that Gudziak had been involved, given his meeting with Chris Wixom when he was impersonating Dave the day of the murders at the Roswell residence.

"Detective," Maldonado said in a commanding voice. "My client has already told you that he has no knowledge of these murders, or the attempted murder of Chris Wixom. And you have no proof to tie him to them, so shall we move on?"

"No proof?" she said, her eyes sparkling with anger. "You mean, other than Chris Wixom's witness statement that your client was one of the men who violently invaded his home, shot him in the back, and looted his house of personal items?!"

"You have the word of a man who's been through a terrible trauma, and is probably still high as a kite on painkillers. How trustworthy is his eyewitness testimony?" he asked. "And my client has already given you an explanation for how Wixom's belongings ended up in his home. He had no idea these items had been stolen. Or that Mr. Gudziak—a man he barely knew—was a felon."

Nikki furiously gathered up the photos and put them back into the file. I could see how frustrated she was because we hadn't gotten anything useful out of Hekekia. He was, after all, a seasoned criminal who knew how to come up with explanations that would cast doubt on the evidence, and he had a really good lawyer. Distracted as he was, Maldonado was still very much a player in the interview, which made me even more worried about how talented he might be in a courtroom.

Nikki retrieved two last photos and laid them on the table. "We need to find these two," she said simply.

Dave's and Gwen's driver's license photos stared up at us from the tabletop, and I felt my eyes well. It was an emotional thing seeing their photos being presented to one of the men responsible for abducting them.

I think we were all a little surprised when Hekekia put his finger on Dave's picture and said, "I've seen this guy," he said. "His name's McKenzie, right?"

"Where have you seen him?" Candice demanded.

Hekekia tapped the photo again and said, "He's a friend of Snake's. Or he was. Maybe he was part of all this stuff you guys are trying to accuse me of."

My breath caught in my throat. Sweet Jesus, Hekekia had just played us brilliantly. Chris Wixom had already given a statement to the police that Dave McKenzie was the man who'd tried to shoot and kill him, and even though we knew that Gudziak had been impersonating Dave on the initial visit to Chris's home, Maldonado was certainly going to insist that Wixom hadn't been mistaken about Dave being the one to invade his home and attempt to kill him. He'd been mistaken about seeing Hekekia there.

Further, it would give even more credit to the theory that Dave and Gudziak had both murdered the Roswells. Gudziak's fingerprint on the casing at Wixom's house, and Dave's bloody handprint at the Roswells'.

Suddenly, I could see it clearly through the eyes of a jury, and knowing that Hekekia could very well get off for the crime of attempted murder while Dave was found guilty was like being splashed in the face with ice water.

"Where can we find this guy?" Nikki pressed, tapping Dave's photo herself.

Hekekia scratched his head. "I think he left town."

"Why do you think that?" she pressed.

"Something Snake said. He told me that he and McKenzie had a fight and McKenzie left town."

"And where did he say that McKenzie was going?" Nikki said next.

Hekekia gave another one of those lazy shrugs. "No clue. If Snake were still alive, you probably could've asked him."

Maldonado rested his laced fingers on the table and eyed the three of us smugly. The interview had been a huge mistake; I could see that now. Not only did we have nothing to gain from it, but Hekekia and Maldonado had just played us by inserting a connection between Gudziak and Dave into the official record.

Still, Nikki continued to try to get something, anything, out of Hekekia for the next forty minutes, but eventually, Maldonado's constant, "Asked and answered, Detective, move on," was the only thing coming from their side.

Finally, Nikki packed up all her photographic evidence and glared moodily at Hekekia. We all knew the interview was over, and even though we'd still charge Hekekia with everything we could think of, we'd be leaving the interview the definite losers.

Candice spoke before we officially ended it, though. She said, almost casually, "I've seen you out and around downtown, haven't I, Counselor?"

Maldonado was packing his legal pad and pen into his brief-case. "Maybe," he said. "I get out when I can."

Candice snapped her fingers, as if she suddenly remembered something. "I know where I've seen you. You were at Murielle McKenna's birthday party at . . . where was it? Oh, yeah, at Back-beat, right?"

Maldonado smiled wide. "That was a great night," he said with a fond shake of his head. "But I should've remembered seeing you there."

She laughed like they were old friends. "I think you were busy with some triplets."

Maldonado's grin turned wolfish. "Like I said. Great night."

Candice nodded, and next to Maldonado, Hekekia showed the first signs of becoming uncomfortable with the direction of the conversation. "Yeah," Candice continued, "you looked like you were having the time of your life. Not sure about the triplets, but I'm sure you were everything they expected that night."

"And more," he said, his voice low and sounding pleased with himself.

Candice laughed lightly. "You know," she said, "Murielle is sure a great party to be around. How does one get invited into her in-ner circle?"

Maldonado's eyes narrowed suspiciously. He seemed to know what she was up to. "I'll never tell," he said, getting up and scoot-ing his chair in. "Attorney-client privilege, you know."

"Oh, we do," Candice said, all friendly pretense gone. Focusing on Hekekia she said, "We're going to nail you. And we're going to tie your wealthy benefactor to the crime as well, but she'll probably evade the death penalty, because, you know, she's got big money. But you . . . now, you're gonna take the fall. You know what the state of Texas does to murderers like you, right?" For emphasis, Candice slid one finger across her throat.

I watched Hekekia closely. He stared at Candice with half-lidded eyes, but I could see she'd gotten to him. At least a little.

"I'm assuming charges are coming soon?" Maldonado said impatiently.

"In the morning," Nikki said. "Both state and federal."

With that, she got up and headed out the door. Candice and I followed without another word. Or a look back.

Chapter Eighteen

• • •

We gathered in the larger conference room to commiserate on the disaster that Hekekia's interview had been. "I fucked it all up," Nikki said miserably.

"Not true," Brice was quick to say. "You had no chance with him, Detective. His lawyer was too good, and he's too seasoned a criminal to give you much even without Maldonado's coaching."

Nikki offered Brice a grateful smile, but I could tell she was still disappointed in herself.

"So where do we go from here?" Oscar asked.

"We press charges for what we do have," Brice said simply. "It'll be enough to get him locked up, and maybe we can work on him in the meantime. There's nothing like jail to make a criminal think about bettering his situation."

"We don't have that kind of time," I said, knowing for certain we didn't. "It'll be too late by then to help Dave and Gwen."

"So what do we do, Abs?" Dutch asked gently. I glanced at him and saw that he wasn't so much asking for my personal opinion as asking for my intuitive guidance.

I took a deep breath and closed my eyes, trying to feel out a solution. "We're missing something," I said as a series of images started to fill my mind's eye. I noticed almost immediately that they were memories of the images I'd seen when scrolling through Murielle McKenna's Instagram account. Focusing on the memory of the photos I'd seen, I just allowed my intuition to speak to me in its own language, which is a combo of images and flashes of insight along with simply "knowing" something without an actual context.

The vision appearing in my mind's eye was pulled directly from my memory banks the day before, right after we'd met with Murielle and we'd been gathered in our office, snooping through her Instagram. The pictures scrolled across the screen in my inner eye, one after the other, like a speedy slide show, without ever really forming into solid detail. And then two interesting things happened. The photos began to spin around, almost like pinwheels, but they also continued to slide on by. Occasionally, one of the images would stop spinning, and come to rest upside down, but the detail of what was in the photos was still just out of my reach.

The other interesting thing was that out of the void producing the photos emerged a big, black iron key. It simply appeared, fully formed, and floated to the space above the pinwheels. The key captured my immediate attention, because it was accompanied by a strong sense of urgency. And then, almost abruptly, the spinning photos disappeared, and my mind's eye was filled with the image of what I'd seen in the safe room at Robin and Andy's home. Mentally recoiling at the memory, I was still able to take note that the big iron key hadn't gone away. It continued to float there above the bodies of Andy and Robin and I worked hard to piece together the clue it was offering.

Once I thought I had it, the scene in my mind changed one last time, morphing into the image of Dave and Gwen's house. The key moved to the front door, then floated down to the keyhole and inserted itself, twisting in the lock until the door clicked open.

After it swung wide, instead of the inside of Dave and Gwen's house, the interior was just one large, empty, and windowless room, with a lone full-length mirror propped up on the wall facing the door.

Perhaps because it was the only thing in the room, I focused on the mirror, and to my surprise, Dave's reflection appeared there. He was so vivid in my mind's eye that I could see him as clearly as if I were peering at him through a peephole in a wall. But seeing him there brought me no relief, because he was a terrible sight to behold.

For starters, he was pale, sweating profusely, and bleeding from the hip. Seeing him propped against the wall opposite the mirror, I could tell that his chest was heaving while he tried to suck in enough oxygen, but his lungs didn't seem to be able to hold on to any of the air he was sucking in. Then there was the terrible look of pain pulling at his features, which caused me to literally wince and wish that I could reach through the ether to find him and get him some help.

But the image was already losing its clarity, the edges of the vision softening and Dave's features becoming blurry.

Frantically, I tried to hold on to the image, to look at it for the clues I knew it wanted to offer up, but it continued to fade until Dave was nothing but a fuzzy patch of light in a nondescript room. That sense of urgency that had hit me in the gut when it first showed up in my mind's eye also came back in full force.

The iron key, however, made one last appearance in my mind's eye, emerging from the mirror and zipping over to the right, past my nose, and forcing my perspective to turn with it as it sailed by me, back out the front door of Dave and Gwen's. In my mind's eye I moved forward to follow it out onto the front porch. From there I saw the key float over to the side yard, then to the back of the house. I waited on the porch for it to come back, but it didn't.

At last I opened my eyes, seeing that everyone had been silently watching me, waiting for me to speak about what lay in the ether. I thought about telling them all of what I'd seen, but I decided against it. The vision had contained three separate components, which I felt needed to be pursued in order. Giving the group the full report of what my intuition had shown me might only confuse and muddle things. We couldn't afford any more delays; of that I was certain.

"There's something in the photos from Murielle's Instagram that is the key to this whole case," I announced into the expectant silence.

"You mean how Murielle took so many photos with Andy and Robin in the background?" Candice asked.

I shook my head. "No. No, there's something else there. There's a clue in the images that can help us."

Candice got up from her chair. "Okay, give me a few minutes. I'll be back."

After she left our presence, Dutch tried to push my cold dinner in front of me again. I'd shoved it away as soon as we'd all sat down. I was no longer hungry, and certainly not for cold chicken and rice. "I can warm that up in the microwave," he offered when I made a face at the food.

"It's okay," I told him. My mind was still buzzing with the images from Murielle's Instagram. Something within those photos was out of place. Or maybe, I thought, completely upside down. "I think we're looking at this case all wrong." As I spoke those words, I had a bit of a eureka moment.

"What's that mean?" Oscar asked.

"I don't really know," I confessed. "But nothing about this case is actually what it seems. That's the only thing I can say. How we're looking at it is all wrong."

"How are we looking at it?" Nikki asked me.

I shook my head. I didn't yet know. What felt right side up was actually upside down, only I didn't know how to translate that for the rest of the group.

"But you still think Gudziak and Hekekia killed the Roswells, right?" she pressed.

"Oh, yeah," I assured her. "Of that I have no doubt."

"Then how could we be looking at it all wrong?" Dutch asked.

"It's not about who did it," I said, trying to puzzle out what I intuitively knew to be true. And then I had it. "It's not the who we need to focus on. It's the why. It's about motivation."

"Money?" Nikki said.

"No," I told her, staring off into space for a moment to call home what I thought the case actually revolved around. "It's about revenge." And then I thought about it some more, and added, "Okay, yeah, it was about money too, but revenge first and foremost. Revenge was the driving force, the reason for the crime, but the money figures into this too. I just don't know how."

"Revenge," Dutch repeated. "Makes sense, I guess. We've been assuming that Murielle wanted revenge against Robin for leaving her."

And that was the part that bothered me. It fit, but it didn't. There was something else. Something I couldn't quite put my finger on.

Candice came back into the room at that moment, carrying a large stack of printouts. "Here," she said, laying out the photos she'd printed from Murielle's Instagram account. "I'm printing off all of Murielle's photos from the past three months leading up to the Roswell murders. These are the first ones off the printer."

I scanned the pile of photos she dumped onto the conference room table. "There's *more* than this?" There had to be a couple hundred pages in the pile.

"This is just the first two and a half weeks," Candice said with an annoyed shake of her head. "There're thousands of photos. The woman is a true narcissist."

My shoulders slumped. "Great," I muttered as everyone in the room gathered a small stack to study.

"So, what're we supposed to be looking for here?" Oscar asked me.

I sighed and grabbed the last handful. "I have no idea. But I'll definitely know when I see it."

"Abs?" Candice asked.

"Yeah?"

"It's cool that you'll know, but . . . will the rest of us?"

I lifted my head to see everyone looking at me expectantly. My shoulders slumped again and with a weary groan and a wave of my fingers to call their pages forward, I said, "Probably not."

Everyone began to put their pages back into a center pile in front of me, their relief evident because looking through Murielle's selfies was gonna be sooooooo boring. And annoying. And maybe even a little depressing.

When the pile was back together, once again everyone looked at me as if to say, "What're we going to do next?"

I inhaled deeply, trying to think, but it was late and it'd been a long-ass day. I was damn tired. Not to mention that Candice's push-up bra was really starting to dig into my rib cage.

"Let's call it a night," Dutch said, like he was reading my mind. "We'll pick this up fresh in the morning."

"Detective," Brice said to Nikki as the rest of us grabbed up our things. "You're sure you can keep this case with us for a day or two?"

"I'm gonna give it my best shot, Agent Harrison," she said, and I knew she would. "Still, I'll probably need one of you to make the case for temporary jurisdiction to my CO after I give him my pitch."

"Hey, Oscar," I said, before Brice could speak. "How about you meet Nikki at the substation tomorrow, and make our case to her superiors?"

Oscar's mouth was open a little, and his eyes moved nervously between Brice and Dutch—his superiors and the two men who by rights should've been there to make the pitch to APD in the morning.

Hedging off any protest, I added, "My gut says Oscar and Nikki will be able to convince APD to give us the case for a day or two."

Dutch and Brice exchanged a look, but then Dutch shrugged. "If Abby thinks it's better for Rodriguez to be on point in this, I'm good."

"Fine," said Brice, but I could tell he knew I was up to something. Of course, the slight smirk his wife was wearing didn't help any. Nor did the red tinge to Oscar's cheeks. Or Nikki's suddenly flushed face.

Matchmaker, matchmaker . . . , I thought, with a slight smirk of my own.

Chapter Nineteen

· · ·

We heard early in the morning that Oscar and Nikki had been successful in getting us forty-eight hours to have Hekekia all to ourselves without their interference. As a bonus, Nikki had been reassigned to focus on Chris Wixom's attempted murder and ordered to work alongside our bureau while building her case. It couldn't have worked out better, actually.

Nikki and Oscar met us at our offices after the meeting with APD's brass, and they found me and Candice sitting on the floor in Candice's office, going through pages, and pages, and *pages*, of Instagram photos.

We'd been poring over the photos for hours, but nothing was jumping out at me. It was beyond frustrating. I kept waiting for my eye to hit on that "thing" that would ignite a *PING!* from my intuition, but there'd been nothing in any of the photos so far that seemed to tug at my radar in a "This is it!" kinda way.

And yet, I knew I was on the right track. There was something we were missing. Something vital.

"You guys gonna look through those all day?" Oscar asked, after holding the door open for Nikki, who was looking radiant in a sleek charcoal suit and long silver earrings.

I let the photos in my hand fall to the floor and then I lay down on my back and rubbed my temples. "This sucks," I groaned. "Whatever is in here, I'm not seeing it."

"Maybe it's because we've been at it for three hours straight," Candice said, continuing her slow, meticulous observation of each photo in her stack.

"How many pages did you print out?" Nikki asked, squatting down next to me to poke at some of the photos.

"Three thousand, six hundred, and thirty-eight," Candice said.

"Whoa!" Nikki said. "That's a *lot* of selfies."

"A lot of self-love," I muttered. "God, I hate that woman and her obsession with herself."

"So you guys are gonna keep going with the photos, huh?" Oscar said again.

I sat up. "No. I need a break. And I need to come at this thing from a different angle."

"I thought that's what we were doing?" Nikki said, indicating the photos.

"True. Then we need a different-different angle."

"What'd you have in mind, Sundance?" Candice asked.

I shook my head, recalling the vision I'd had the night before. The first thing that came to mind was the memory of the Roswells' murder scene. Lying back on the floor again, I swept an arm over my eyes, knowing what I needed to do. "I think we've got to revisit the murder scene."

"The Roswells' place?" Candice asked me.

I nodded. I didn't want to give a verbal yes, because the thought of going back to that house and recalling that scene was almost more than I could bear. I didn't want to stand in that energy, or soak in that ether, or experience any of that horror. Ever. Again.

But I was starting to feel very strongly that I had to go back.

"You guys haven't released the scene yet, right?" I heard Candice ask Nikki.

"No," Nikki said. "I checked in with Sienna right before we came here. She said she can stall through today, but after that, she'll have to order up the release or her ass is going to get chewed out by the brass."

"Good," Candice said. "Can you get us in to have a look around?"

"I can, but it could be tricky depending who's been assigned to keep watch over the house. Let me make a call."

Nikki stepped out into the lobby to make a call and I sat up again. Oscar had also squatted down next to me and was poking at the photos strewn out on the floor. "It's a shame, you know," he said.

"What?" I asked.

Oscar held up a photo of Murielle, staring into the camera with lowered chin and a come-hither expression, as if she was trying to seduce the whole world in that one photo. "All looks. No substance."

I watched while Oscar set the photo back down and turned his attention to where Nikki's muted voice was floating back to us from the lobby.

"Whereas she's the whole package," I said, thumbing over my shoulder toward the detective.

Oscar grinned and winked at me like I'd winked at him the night before. It was nice to see him with a light on again behind those heartbroken eyes.

"Am I missing something?" Candice asked us.

Oscar's grin only widened, and I laughed. "Definitely!" I said.

Nikki came back into the room again. "I know the patrol officer. We're good."

"Great," I said, getting up and not even bothering to neaten up the photos on the floor. Candice looked at me pointedly, so I added, "I'll pick these up when we get back." Her pointed look continued, so I bent down and sort of squished them into one big pile and let that be enough.

We arrived at the Roswells' home and were met by an APD officer who was parked at the foot of the entrance to the drive. He leaned into Nikki's open window and said, "Detective Grayson. You're on this case?"

"Hey, Baker," she said. "I'm wrapping up a lead before the house gets turned over to next of kin. Can you let us in?"

"Sure," he said. "But I'd hurry. Someone was here about ten minutes ago, royally ticked off that she wasn't allowed inside."

I leaned over in the passenger seat to address the officer. "Who was it?" I asked.

Officer Baker looked at me as if to ask who the hell I was. Nikki said, "This is Abby. She's on the Feds' team. We're doing a joint investigation."

"Fed?" Baker said, his brow shooting up. "I didn't know it'd gotten into all that."

"It's complicated," Nikki told him. "Who was here to take over the house, Paul?"

Baker turned slightly, as if looking for whoever had come to try to gain entrance to the home. "The wife's sister," he said. "She said she's been waiting for the scene to be released for the past couple of days. She tried to give me a lecture about how I work for her when I told her the house wasn't going to be released until tomorrow and I couldn't let her beyond the yellow tape."

Nikki snorted. "I bet that went over well," she said. "I love the 'I'm a taxpayer and you work for me' speech."

Baker shrugged with one shoulder. "As speeches go, hers was pretty uninspired. I think she was headed off to raise some hell, though, so I'd get in and get out while you can."

She gave him a two-finger salute and Baker backed away from the car, moving over to the gate to unlock it and let us in.

We entered the house single file, Nikki handing out booties for us to put on in the front foyer.

The house was brightly lit with late-morning sun bouncing off the gleaming white walls. Well, the sections of wall where no fingerprint powder had been brushed on. There was a stillness here too; it mirrored the one from the other day when Candice and I had first gone inside, before we'd discovered the bodies up the stairs. But this silence was almost . . . peaceful.

It was odd, because I didn't expect that. I expected instead to feel the violent energy echoing and reverberating off the walls that had all but assaulted me when I'd first entered the house a few days earlier.

But it'd dissipated. Significantly. Which was good, because it meant the structure had hope. To recover. To not be so scarred by the events that'd taken place inside the walls that it was forever cursed to make anyone who entered here feel unsettled. Uncomfortable. Unsafe.

"You okay?" Candice whispered, as she was putting on her booties.

"Fine," I said, squeezing her arm to let her know I really was. Then I squared my shoulders and said, "I'm going to let my radar guide me. You guys can follow me, or look around yourselves."

Candice, Oscar, and Nikki all exchanged a look, and no one needed to speak to know that they'd all arrived at the same conclusion. Candice would go with me, and Nikki and Oscar would stay in the foyer, supportive, but out of the way.

I turned to the stairs and got on with it, moving slowly through the foyer along the very same path that I'd moved with Candice the previous Sunday. Heading up the steps, I braced myself when I entered the central second-story corridor. It was a good thing I did. On the floor was a large, deep, rust-colored stain.

Rosa's body had obscured the extent of her blood loss. It was so upsetting because, judging by the size of the stain, her heart had continued to pump well after she'd been shot. I've seen a lot of crime-scene photos, and it's never hard to tell who died within moments of being stabbed or shot, and who'd continued to suffer until they'd bled out.

I had no idea of the full extent of her suffering, but I did know it'd been a terrible thing to endure. Moving to just the edge of the stain, I knelt for a moment and closed my eyes, sending up a small prayer to her. It just felt right to pay homage before continuing forward.

Candice put a hand on my shoulder, and when I glanced behind me, I saw that her eyes were also closed. My dear friend understood.

Moving into the master bedroom after that was . . . hard. The sense of peace that'd begun to take over the house again ended at the foot of the door leading into the master suite.

The second I was past the threshold, a wave of nausea hit me like a punch in the gut. I even grunted from the impact.

"Abs?" Candice asked, and once again I felt her hand on me, gently placed on my lower back to steady me should I need it.

"It's fine," I said, straining to speak. "But, sweet Jesus, it's thick in here."

"We can leave, you know."

"No," I said, forcing myself to move into the room. The chaos of energy only got worse. It was like being in the middle of a bar-room brawl. The crisscrossing of panic and violence and hatred and anger coalesced into one large swarm of horribleness. It was hard for me to breathe. To see. To remain standing. It just assaulted me from every angle.

"Dammit," I said through clenched teeth.

"Talk to me, Sundance," Candice said, that hand on my back never wavering.

I blinked several times, and took deep breaths, but I couldn't seem to shut out the barrage of energy swirling and battering against me. "I'm fine," I said, my voice even more strained.

Pressing forward another couple of feet, however, I was stopped dead in my tracks. Ahead was the safe room that Dave had built for the Roswells, and straight ahead of where I stood was a full-length mirror much like the one from my vision. A flood of images and emotions pretty much overwhelmed me in that moment. "I need some air," I said, and bolted from the room.

Tearing down the hallway and the steps, I heard Candice's footfalls behind me, but I didn't pause or wait for her. Instead I went right down the stairs, turned the corner somewhat blindly, and entered the kitchen. Ahead was a door leading to the outside, and I rushed to it. Twisting the dead bolt and yanking the door open, I dashed through to the outside.

For a minute all I could do was try to take in oxygen and have it stay in my lungs. This proved challenging, so I started walking forward, attempting to calm the hell down. Man, it was tough. Tears leaked out of my eyes and I wiped at them in annoyance. "Hey," Candice said when I'd stopped at last to bend at the waist and rest my elbows on the tops of my knees. "Sundance, what can I do for you?"

I wiped my eyes again. "I'm okay," I lied. "I was just trying to . . ."

"I know what you were trying to do," she said kindly. "And I have no idea how someone as sensitive to energy as you are could find the courage to walk into a room that'd recently been filled with that kind of violence, and remain sane."

I stood up and took one last deep, cleansing breath. "Who're you calling sane?"

"Not you," she said, a relieved smile appearing on her lips. "Obviously."

I wiped my eyes one last time with my sleeve. "Yeah, not one of my brighter moves."

"Did you get anything?"

I shook my head. "No. It's a mess up there. All I could feel was their panic, fear, and pain with an extra layer of hatred hanging in the ether, and that was all before I felt the violence of the bullets hitting their targets. It's overwhelming."

Candice's eyes pinched with sympathy. "Let's get out of here," she suggested.

"Okay," I agreed. I was ready to quit this house forever. But then I realized where we were and looked around. "Hey," I said when I saw that Candice had already begun to walk her way to the back door.

"What's up?"

I pointed to a flattened section of grass right in front of a tall grouping of shrubs. There was some crime-scene litter on the ground too. A pair of black gloves. The backing to an evidence label. And the noticeable presence of black flies. Which is always, by far, the creepiest thing about crime scenes. The first and last on scene are always the flies.

"This is where Tremblee was murdered, right?"

Candice came back over to me and stepped back a pace or two. "I think so," she said.

In my mind's eye I remembered the last part of my vision, where the key had come out of the mirror, past me, and had gone back out the front door of Dave and Gwen's to disappear around the corner of the house.

To the backyard.

It suddenly dawned on me that in bringing me here, maybe my intuition was trying to get me to this exact spot.

But why?

"What'cha thinking?" Candice asked as I simply stood staring at the flattened piece of grass.

"Why was Mario killed?" I said. Candice didn't answer me at first, so I turned to her and repeated the question.

"Gudziak and Hekekia got rid of all the witnesses," she said simply.

I pivoted back to the flattened patch of grass. I could just make out the faint outline of a body there. I went back over the details of his murder as I remembered them. He'd been shot once in the back of the head with a forty-five caliber. He'd died with his ear-buds in.

And that's the part of the scenario that wasn't working so well for me, because as much as I wanted to imagine it differently, what I kept seeing in my mind's eye was this young man trimming some shrubs while someone snuck up on him and shot him at point-blank range assassination-style.

Either the gunshot should've alerted the people inside that someone was outside shooting off a weapon, or Mario should've been alerted to the sound of gunfire from inside the house and he should've gone for help. At the very least, he should've run away as fast as he could.

Then again, what if the volume was up so loud on the earbuds that he couldn't hear the noise from the AR-15 going off inside? That seemed unlikely, though, given what I know about the sound an AR-15 makes.

"How high was the volume turned up on his earbuds?" I asked Candice.

"What?"

I tore my gaze away from the ground to look at Candice in earnest. "Do we know how loud the gardener's music was when he was murdered?"

She eyed me quizzically. "That's a question for Grayson, I think."

"Yeah," I said, leaving the trampled grass to head back toward the house.

We found Nikki and Oscar talking quietly together still in the front foyer. "Hey," I called to Nikki.

"You done?" she asked when she saw us.

I ignored her question and went for the one I needed answered. "How loud was the gardener's music turned up when he was shot?"

She blinked at me a couple of times, probably not understanding the context of my question. "I don't know," she said. "Need me to find out?"

"Yes," I said, my radar humming, as if I was on the trail of something big.

Nikki took out her cell and said, "Give me a minute."

We waited in silence until Nikki came out from the kitchen where she'd made her call, an odd expression on her face. "Okay, so it's weird that you should ask that, Abby, because Sienna says that Tremblee's music was actually up to almost full volume when he was shot. His phone had died, but she was able to plug it in, using her own charger, to see how high the volume was, and it was nearly at max."

"Wow. That's loud," I said. I often wore headphones when I

did housework at home, and I could never take the volume much past a low setting.

"Maybe he had a hearing issue," Candice said. We all looked at her. "He was a landscaper, right? He would've been around loud mowers and leaf blowers all the time."

I nodded, something sliding into place in my head. That made sense.

"Why was that important to know, though?" Nikki asked me.

I frowned. "I'm not sure yet. It's just one more thing that's a little off about this case. There's something I can't quite put my finger on, and it's bothering me. The fact that Tremblee's music was at max volume and he probably couldn't have heard the commotion from inside is bugging me."

"Why?" Nikki pressed.

"Because there was no reason to kill him," I said. "And yet, he was shot execution-style, in the back of the head. He wasn't corralled into the safe room like Andy and Robin. He wasn't shot in the hallway like Rosa. He was shot outside, where the sound of the gunshot would've carried and maybe even been reported by neighbors."

"It actually *was* reported by a neighbor," Candice reminded me. "The guy with the video camera that caught Dave's truck cruising by said he heard a firecracker going off and complained to the neighborhood association about it."

I pointed to her. "Exactly. In other words, it was super risky to murder him."

"But what does that tell us?" Candice said.

"Again, I don't know. Still . . ." I looked over my shoulder back toward where Tremblee had been shot, and my radar just didn't want to let go of the man's murder. My intuition was practically insisting I look into him. "I want to do a little digging into his background."

"Tremblee's?" Oscar asked.

"Yes," I said.

"Okay," said Candice. "I'm game."

I turned my attention to Nikki, but she seemed troubled. "I'm going to drop you guys back at your offices. There's a lead that came in that I need to follow up on."

"What's that?" Candice asked.

"It's connected to the Roswells," she explained. "I should turn it over to one of the guys still assigned to that case, but I think I want to check it out first."

"What's the lead?" Candice repeated.

"I put a monitor on all of the Roswells' accounts to alert me in case one of their credit cards was used."

"You got a hit?" I said, surprised.

"Yeah. Twenty minutes ago Robin's Amex card was used to ring up a hundred twenty thousand dollars in merchandise."

My eyes widened. "Whoa! A hundred and twenty grand?"

"Where?" Candice asked.

Nikki shook her head. "That's the part I'm not sure of. The code on the transaction is weird, so I've got to head back to the substation and do some research."

"All right," I said. "Go. But take Oscar with you. He's good with stuff like that."

Nikki's brow lowered a little, and I could see that she was about to tell me she could handle it just fine when Oscar said, "Detective, can I buy you lunch while we track this new evidence down?"

Nikki appeared a tiny bit flustered by his sudden proposal. "Um . . . okay," she said, tucking a strand of hair behind her ear. "I guess. I mean, we've gotta eat, right?"

"We do," he said pleasantly.

"Lunch sounds good," Candice said, and I wanted to slap her.

"I'm not hungry," I said loudly. Everyone looked at me. No one believed me. Clearing my throat, I added, "What I mean is that I'm anxious to get to the investigation into Tremblee. I don't think we have time to eat, Candice. Or at least not a sit-down meal. We should grab a to-go order from someplace. Maybe there's a salad food truck you can find for us."

Candice rolled her eyes and turned her head away from Nikki

and Oscar to whisper in my ear, "You need to stop meddling in other people's love life."

I beamed innocently at her. "Fat chance of that ever happening."

She shook her head and muttered under her breath as she walked away.

Nikki and Oscar headed to the substation after dropping us at our offices, and I bought Candice lunch before she lectured me again about meddling. The ploy worked, and she didn't bring it up again. Maybe she was also happy to see the bud of new romance, especially for Oscar.

Anyway, we started our new investigation by setting up a little experiment; Candice and I went to the outdoor shooting range, where she got to target practice and I wore my earbuds with the volume turned up as loud as I could stand it. "Did you hear the shots?" Candice asked me after she'd killed about five paper posters.

"Not well," I admitted, twirling the earbuds in my fingers. "These things work pretty effectively if the volume's turned way up."

"So what does that tell us?"

"I think it tells us that Tremblee probably didn't hear the Roswells being murdered."

"I doubt anyone heard them being murdered," Candice said.

"What's that mean?"

"The acoustics in that safe room are solid. The walls are thick as hell and I doubt a lot of sound came out of there. Certainly not enough for a neighbor to hear."

"But wouldn't he have heard Rosa Torrez being murdered?"

"Maybe. But she was only shot once or twice, right?"

"I don't remember," I said, tucking the earbuds into my purse as we got into the car.

"I think the report said something like that," Candice said. "Anyway, my point is that she was shot once or twice in an interior hallway of a house with good insulation and the closest neighbor a half acre away. Probably nobody heard her murder except for the people inside at the time."

"God, this is a depressing topic," I said. Poor Rosa. Nobody should have to die like that.

"It is, but we have a chance to bring some justice if we can figure out how these puzzle pieces fit together. Now, to your point about why Tremblee was murdered, it might have something to do with the fact that he was part of Murielle's staff that went with Robin when she left."

"We know that for sure?"

"No, but that's my theory and one that I think we should follow up on."

"Where do we start?"

Candice zipped up the case she used to carry her gun and tucked it under her seat. "I've been thinking about that, and I've decided we should start by treating Tremblee's murder as a separate event from the others. You keep singling him out for some reason, and I think that's your intuition telling you to do that."

"I love that you get me."

She laughed, and pulled her laptop out of the backseat. "Okay, so let's look him up and see if he had any relatives in the area that we can talk to."

Using her phone as a hot spot, Candice conducted a few searches before she said, "Got him. Mario was sharing a residence with a Walter Abbott, age fifty-two, on the east side."

"Father?"

"Don't think so. He's got a different last name. Let's go check it out."

We arrived at the address Candice had looked up and were surprised to discover how lovely the home was. A sloping roof angled down to offer plenty of shade to a wide front porch that extended the length of the house.

Two flowering trees stood sentinel in the front yard, and between them, perfectly framed, was a porch swing with several colorful pillows and a side table ready for a pitcher of iced tea or lemonade.

There was something so welcoming about the setting. It was inviting, comfortable, and elegant. Not at all the kind of environment I'd expected a young landscaper to live in.

A shiny red Mustang sat in the front drive, indicating someone was likely home. "You ready?" Candice asked me.

I took a deep breath and steadied myself. I had a feeling this was going to be a difficult interview, much like the one with Robin's sister had been hard. Like I said before, it's an awful thing to witness people in the midst of their grief, struggling to give you information that they know you need to help bring their loved ones some justice. They want desperately to help, and you can see that little bit of hope in their eyes, like if they supply you with the right answer, then some of their pain will lessen. And sometimes, it does work. They give you some clue, something that you need to connect the dots, but it's never enough to suspend them from the terrible anguish they're in the throes of experiencing.

And while we didn't know how this Walter Abbott figured into the picture, he'd probably at least be sad that Mario had died so senselessly.

Candice stepped up to the door and rang the bell. We heard it buzz and stood back, waiting. There wasn't any noise coming from inside. The house was silent, as if its grief was so deep that it couldn't bear to be conscious.

We were about to turn away when the door was opened and in the doorway stood a man who was shocking for both how beautiful he was and how destroyed he seemed.

He had the most regal features: stunning gray eyes deeply set into a square face, an unlined forehead, and a straight, elegant nose with a small crease at the start of his brow—making him appear like a man who spent a lot of time thinking deeply.

Other than that, his shoulders were broad, his waist was trim, and his general countenance was one that stood out. He'd be noticed in any room simply for walking into it. Mentally I compared him with Zane Maldonado, and found this man to be the far more handsome of the two. But it was his expression that was the most telling. There was so much sorrow there. So much unmasked heartbreak. It was easy to see he'd recently been crying. "Yes?" he said, his voice hoarse and raw.

Candice spoke to him first. "Mr. Abbott?" He nodded and only then did his eyes narrow slightly, wary and suspicious. Candice was quick to hold up her PI badge. "I'm Candice Fusco, and this is Abigail Cooper. We're working with the FBI and Austin PD on the murder of a resident of this home. We were wondering if we could ask you a few questions?"

"Mario?" he asked us, his voice cracking again on a barely veiled sob. "You're working on Mario's case?"

"We are," I said, drawing his attention to me. And then, right there, I understood. He and Mario had been in love. "May we talk to you?"

He nodded, but it was a moment before he seemed to be able to connect that he should invite us in. "I'm sorry," he said, his cheeks flushing. "I've just been calling and calling to see if they found that madman who killed my . . ." Abbott paused to put his fist up to his mouth, struggling with his emotions. At last he cleared his throat and added, "No one seems to care about Mario. They won't tell me anything."

"We'll talk to you," I assured him. "We'll tell you what we can if you'll talk to us about Mario."

Abbott stepped aside and made a motion with his hand. "Please. Come in."

We gathered in the living room, which was a space I could've visited every day of my life and never grown tired of. It was beautiful, full of soft, warm hues, a cozy sitting area, and bookshelves crammed with books lining almost every wall.

Nowhere in sight was there a TV, a computer, or a tablet—just books and soft music coming from a set of speakers above the sofa.

There was also a stone fireplace opposite the sofa, and on the mantel was a large, framed black-and-white photograph of an ex-quisite male form, naked and arching back on one foot with one hand high in a beautiful ballet pose that elevated his chest like an offering to the sun god. No face on the model was visible, and nothing too private was exposed, just his elongated legs, arms, and gorgeously chiseled torso.

The way the sunlight was hitting his exposed skin was evoca-tive and moving, and if that weren't enough of a dramatic effect, he was posed at the very edge of a cliff face, with the photographer likely positioned several hundred yards away on a rock outcrop-ping of equal height.

There was so much to take in about the natural beauty of the scene, and yet the viewer's eye was immediately drawn to and captivated by that model.

I pointed to the photo. "That's amazing."

Abbott made a small choking sound and I looked over at him to see that his eyes were welling again and he'd put a hand to his mouth.

"I'm so sorry, Mr. Abbott," I said quickly, not understanding what I'd said to upset him.

He waved his free hand at me and closed his eyes to inhale a ragged breath and collect himself. At last he wiped his eyes and said, "It's all right, and please call me Walter. I don't mean to keep falling apart like this—it's just . . . that's my favorite photo of Mario. He would've been so pleased that you noticed it."

Candice and I both turned back toward the photo, then ex-changed a look as if to say, That's *Mario?*

"I didn't realize he was a model," I said, finding a place to sit on one of the Eames-style chairs to the side of the sofa.

Walter swallowed hard and sniffled. "He wasn't a professional. But he could've been. He only modeled for me."

"You took that?" Candice asked him, referring to the photo again.

"I did," he said, without a hint of pride. His voice sounded so eminently sad, especially as he gazed at his creation across the room. "I dabble in photography. It's a hobby."

"You could've fooled me," Candice said. "Looking at that, I'd say you're better than most professionals I've seen. It's hard to believe you produced something so exquisite from just dabbling."

Walter chuckled and it seemed to surprise him that a laugh had come from his own throat. "It took us two whole days to get that shot. Mario was such a trouper. He could see what I was going for and he kept working his way through poses, trying to give me something great. That was taken at noon. It was the last shot I took, because I knew immediately that I had it."

Walter got up then and moved over to a closet on the other side of the wall containing the fireplace. He dug around inside for a moment before he brought out a large leather-bound portfolio. "Here," he said, swiveling it to show us the collection of photographs inside. "These are all him. My sweet muse." Walter's voice broke again and while I turned pages and Candice looked over my shoulder, Walter cleared his throat several more times, bravely attempting to collect himself.

"He's beautiful," I said, meaning it. Every single photo threatened to steal my breath away; they were so gorgeous. Mario was like something divine: chiseled, radiant, innocent, powerful, and alive. Except to my eye, whenever I saw his face, it took on a subtle two-dimensional quality—for me, the tell for when someone had passed away.

Even with my inner tell, the photos weren't any less lovely. Candice seemed to agree, because she reached out to run her finger along one of the photos—a close-up of Mario's face, his skin and hair dotted with droplets of water and his eyes half-closed and his gaze downcast. His lashes were impossibly long, his skin smooth and imbued with the beauty of youth. "He was so gorgeous, Walter. You really bring out his spirit in all of these."

Walter dipped his chin in gratitude and I closed the portfolio. I realized, as I did so, that I felt profoundly sad for Mario and especially for Walter. His devastation wafted off him in turbulent waves that disrupted the ether and washed over me like a sad rain. I wanted so much to offer him words of comfort, but he was beyond any words at the moment. I knew that. But still . . .

"How long had you and Mario been together?" Candice asked gently.

Walter lifted the portfolio from my lap and hugged it to his chest. Walking over to the sofa, he sat down with a heavy sigh and said, "Six months or so."

That surprised me. The way he was grieving felt like someone who'd lost a mate of many years. "Only six months?" Candice said, probably thinking the same thing I was.

Walter's lips twitched at the corners and he shook his head ever so slightly. "I know," he said. "You'd think the way I'm carrying on that we'd been together forever, but no. Our May-December romance began last August."

"How'd you meet?" I asked.

Walter set the portfolio on the sofa next to him, smoothing his hand over the cover. "My friend Robin introduced us."

Candice glanced at me, and I nodded. We knew this. Robin had stolen Mario and Rosa from Murielle. "You mean Robin Roswell, correct?" Candice asked.

Walter was staring at the portfolio, his mind no doubt drifting back to the moment he and Mario had met. "Yes," he said before closing his eyes as if he was suddenly pained. "Robin and Andy were my dear friends. I can't believe they're gone too."

"I'm so sorry, Walter," I said. I knew then just how difficult it was for him to talk to us.

He reached for a tissue on a side table to wipe at his eyes; then he waved that hand again. "It's fine," he said. "Please go on with your questions."

"How long had you known Robin and Andy?"

Walter barked out a laugh, and again it seemed to surprise him. "From the beginning," he said. "I introduced them."

"You did?" I said.

"Yes," he said simply. "Robin used to work for me, you see—"

"I'm sorry," Candice interrupted. "What do you do, Walter?"

He made a sweeping motion with his hands to indicate the room we were sitting in. "I design," he said simply.

"You're an interior designer?" she asked.

"Yes. Been doing it a very long time. Maybe too long. Anyway, Robin worked for me as my assistant, but she had real talent. She had an eye for both the dramatic and the sublime. She could switch between two styles as easily as you could turn a light switch on and off. Most of us can't do that. Well, I can, but most designers pick a style that becomes their brand and you never see anything unique or different afterward. Think Ralph Lauren and you'll know what I mean."

I smirked. I'm not a fan of the Lauren. Never was. Never would be.

"Anyway, one fine day," Walter said, scratching the stubble on the edge of his chin, "this nerdy-looking young man waltzed into my studio and said that he needed some help. My first thought when I looked at him—dressed in a hoodie and high-tops—was that I don't do charity cases, but . . . I don't know. There was just something about him. Something that suggested he was more than he appeared. After I looked him up, I knew there was more, so I took him on as my pet project. But my pet project turned into Robin's pet, and before I knew it, the two of them were running off together to get married. The rest is a rather rocky road of history."

"Why do you say 'rocky road'?" I asked.

"Oh, there was a breakup in the middle of their love story. Robin was seduced by a dreadful woman. A she-devil if ever there was one. My little protégé left Andy for a year or two before the smart part of her brain took over again."

"You're referring to Murielle McKenna," Candice said.

Walter pointed at her. "The very bitch," he said with a mean glint in his eye.

I glanced up at the photograph above the mantel. "Did you ever have any run-ins with Murielle?"

That humorless bark returned. "Plenty," he said, and then he abruptly got up and headed to the kitchen, only to return with a small stainless steel garbage pail. "Like this one, for instance." Reaching in, he pulled out several torn pieces of paper, but when he laid them on the ottoman in front of me, I realized they had been a greeting card. I assembled the pieces and inhaled sharply when I saw that together they formed a group of laughing hyenas like from *The Lion King*. I unfolded the creases to what would've been the inside of the card and reassembled them to see that Murielle had written, *Soooooo sorry for your loss, Walter. Really. Truly. Cross my heart and hope to laugh and laugh all day long about it. Love, Murielle.*

"Ohmigod," I said breathlessly.

Candice leaned forward and I twisted the pieces so that she could see how the card had come and what it'd said. Candice's eyes narrowed and her mouth pressed into a thin, dangerous line. I didn't think I'd ever seen her so angry. Or . . . lethal.

If Murielle had been standing in front of us, I had no doubt that bitch wouldn't have been standing for long.

Walter bent forward and swept the pieces back into the pail before wordlessly walking it back to the kitchen. When he returned, he didn't so much sit as deflate on the sofa.

"She's hateful," I said to him. "Despicable."

He nodded dully. "There would've been a time I might've been amused by something like that," he said, his hand reaching for the portfolio again. "But not now. Not after falling in love with Mario."

"Walter," Candice said after a moment. He lifted his chin to her and she continued. "Do you think Murielle could've been behind Robin, Andy, and Mario's murders?"

He blinked, as if confused by her question. But then he seemed to think on it and after a bit he said, "She's capable. But I can't say for sure that she had a hand in it."

"Even with the card?" I pressed. That thing felt like a barely veiled admission to me.

Walter held his hands up in mild surrender. "That's typical for Murielle. She's cruel. She likes being cruel. And she looks for every opportunity to punish anyone who's ever stood up to her. I've got a long track record of standing up to her, so she's using the opportunity to kick me while I'm down. It's war."

"Robin stood up to her," I said. "And so did Mario. Maybe she did more than kick at them."

"What do you mean, 'so did Mario'?" he asked me.

My brow furrowed. "Didn't Mario leave Murielle's employment to go with Robin when she went back to Andy?"

Walter shook his head slowly. "No," he said. "Mario was fired by Murielle, for something trite of course, and Robin felt sorry for him, so she called her ex, Andy, and asked if he would hire Mario to work on the grounds at his place. That's what got them talking again, actually. It was Robin trying to help Mario that opened the door for her to see what she'd lost by letting Andy go. They were back together a few weeks later."

"Is it possible that Murielle blamed Mario for being the catalyst that led to Robin leaving her?" Candice asked.

Walter frowned. "It's possible," he said. "But I never got the impression she cared anything about Mario or where he went to work after she fired him. After all, in her eyes he was just a landscaper."

"But the card?" I said, pointing back toward the kitchen.

"I believe Murielle meant Robin and Andy when she was talking about my loss," Walter said. "She might've known that I also lost my lover. . . . That hag seems to know everything, but I believe she was mostly referring to the death of my dear friends."

I took in everything Walter had said, but something still nagged at me. "Assuming Murielle had a hand in the murders, is there any reason you can think of why she would've specifically targeted Mario?"

He sighed and leaned back against the cushion. "Nothing comes to mind," he said. "Even though Mario was with me out and about, he was little more than a serf or a slave in Murielle's eyes. She would've considered him my plaything if she considered him at all. He had no power. And if they ever did have words or hard feelings, Mario never mentioned it to me."

"What did Murielle have against you?" I asked curiously.

Walter rolled his eyes. "I worked for her, very briefly, a decade ago, right at the end of her breakup with her husband. Because I was often there, I'd see her in her most vulnerable moments. There were a lot of pills and alcohol and seething anger and even some award-winning self-loathing. Murielle doesn't handle break-ups well. Unless of course she's the one doing the breaking up. Anyway, when her husband left her, she told me things. Secret things. Things she never wanted another living soul to know. Years later, when Robin confessed to me that she was thinking of leaving Murielle to go back to Andy, I told her what I'd seen, and I advised her that if she told Murielle they were done, she needed to get it on film."

I sucked in a breath. "The infamous video," I said. "We've heard about that."

Walter smirked. "Everyone's heard about it. And everyone has yet to see it. I know it exists because Robin often referred to it. It was her insurance policy—to an extent. Murielle still sniped at her, but it prevented her from going after Andy the way I know she wanted to. She would've loved to have destroyed them both."

"Maybe she did," Candice said pointedly.

Walter paled. "Maybe," he conceded, as if the full realization was dawning on him.

"And maybe . . . ," I said, hating myself for what I was about to say. "Maybe, Walter, Murielle destroyed Robin, Andy, and you for giving her lover the idea to use the camera and for telling Robin all those dirty little secrets. Maybe she knew more about your love for Mario than you're giving her credit for, and exacted her revenge on you as well."

Walter's face grew paler still, and he put that hand back to his mouth again, his eyes darting back and forth as he sorted through that thought. "Oh, God," he whispered.

For a long moment, no one spoke, because what more was there to say, really? We were saved by the chirp of Candice's phone. She lifted it to glance at the screen before she said, "We've got to go."

"We do?"

"Yes," she said, getting to her feet. "Walter, thank you very much for your time. We appreciate it so much more knowing how difficult this all must be for you."

"Wait," he said, getting to his feet as well. "What can you tell me about the investigation?"

Candice smiled gently at him, but she took the time to say, "The Austin police are still hunting for their main suspect. There's been no sign of him anywhere in the Austin area. We're hunting down other leads to see if perhaps this was more than a home invasion gone very bad."

"The Murielle McKenna angle," he said.

"Yes."

He drew in a deep breath, lifting his chest and slumped shoulders as he did so. "I'll tell you this," he whispered. "If that hag had *anything* to do with Mario, Andy, or Robin's death, APD won't have to arrest her."

"Why's that?" I said, almost too afraid to ask.

"Because I'll kill that bitch myself before they ever get close enough to put handcuffs on her."

Candice stepped up to our host and laid a gentle hand on his arm. "Walter," she said firmly. "I promise you that we will get to the bottom of this and find out who's responsible, and we'll find out why they murdered Mario and your friends, but if you go making threats like that, you'll only slow us down and distract us from our course. I need you to promise me that you won't do *anything* to tip Murielle McKenna off that we're digging into her history for a connection to these murders. Okay?"

Walter stood rigidly in front of Candice for a long moment, but then he seemed to falter and his eyes welled. "All right," he said, so softly that only the tiniest sound came out.

Thank God my lie detector didn't go off in that moment, because I didn't know if I could've told Candice that he'd lied to her face about keeping his word. Part of me, the ugly, angry, vigilante side of myself, wouldn't have batted an eye if Walter had raced out of his home with a loaded gun, ready to hunt Murielle down.

People like her always deserve what they get in the end.

Chapter Twenty

• • •

"What'cha got?" Candice asked as we hustled into the substation in response to the text Nikki had sent Candice, requesting our immediate presence.

Oscar was seated next to Nikki in her cubicle. The pair looked a bit cozy, and that's not just my opinion; all the other detectives in the area were currently giving Oscar the stink-eye.

"You're not gonna believe this," Grayson said, waving a piece of paper at us.

I reached Nikki first and took the paper, scanning it for details. "Wait . . . what?"

"See that code at the top?" Nikki said, referring to an abbreviation at the top of the page.

"Yeah?"

"That's an acronym. It stands for Silver Woods Hospitality."

"Okay," I said, reading the text below the acronym, which spelled it all out. Then I realized what I was looking at. "Someone charged one hundred and twenty thousand dollars to Silver Woods Hospitality?"

"Must've been some party," Candice said.

"Oh, it's not a party planning company," Nikki said, handing us another piece of paper.

Candice read over my shoulder the printout of what appeared

to be a pamphlet. "'Silver Woods Hospitality, where your family becomes ours.'"

Synapses fired like alarm bells in my brain. "It's a nursing home!"

"Yep," Nikki said, a look of triumph on her face.

"Why would someone charge a hundred and twenty thousand to a nurs—," Candice began, and then abruptly stopped as she put two and two together.

Turning to me, she said, "Robin's mother!"

I pumped my head up and down, then turned back to Nikki. "She's got Alzheimer's, right?"

"Yep. And she currently resides . . ." Nikki leaned forward to tap the paper in my hand with her pen.

"So . . . wait . . . ," I said, trying to think it all through. I still felt like I wasn't seeing the whole picture. "Robin's Amex Black Card was charged for her mother's stay at Silver Woods?"

"A year of residency," Nikki confirmed.

"When did the charge go through?" Candice asked.

"This morning. About ten a.m."

"Did Robin set it up in advance to be charged today?" I asked, still working to put it together.

"Nope," Nikki said, swiveling back and forth in her chair.

Candice crossed her arms, her patience waning. "How about you just tell us what's going on so we don't have to keep guessing?"

Nikki waved her hands in apology. "Yeah, sorry. Okay, so Rachel Tibbons, Robin's sister, used the card to charge a year's residency this morning at a little after ten. I spoke with the nursing home's clerk, and she said that the card was used to pay the entire invoice online, and the username to log in to the payment system was Rachel's."

"You can pay for an entire year's residency at a nursing home online?" I asked.

"You can pay for most things online these days," Candice said, her focus still on Nikki. "Is the clerk going to reject the charge?"

I understood what Candice was asking. The card clearly didn't belong to Rachel Tibbons, and she had no legal right to use it, so she'd probably purposely made the payment online hoping it would go through without question, since, likely, both Rachel and Robin were listed at the nursing home as their mother's next of kin.

"I asked the clerk not to take any action at this time," Nikki said. "She's willing to cooperate and she's not going to question the charge for at least a few days."

My brow furrowed and I looked at Nikki in puzzlement. "Why is this so significant?" I asked. "Wouldn't Rachel stand to inherit lots of money now? I mean, I know it was wrong of her to use the card, but I could see how she'd be pretty desperate given the fact that we overheard her on the phone with the nursing home the other day and it sounded like they were getting ready to evict Rachel's mother. Plus, she'll definitely be able to pay off the balance once Robin and Andy's estate is settled."

"You're right," Nikki said, her eyes gleaming with the hint of more information. "I'm sure she'll be able to pay off the balance. As long as she's not in jail for murdering her sister."

Candice took a step back. "Whoa, what?"

Oscar spoke next. "When APD did their inventory of the Roswell home, the Amex card wasn't recovered. It's why Nikki—I mean Detective Grayson—thought to put a marker on the card to see if there'd be any attempts to use it. We think it was taken at the time of the home invasion."

"Couldn't Robin have given her sister the card to use for that purpose, though?" Candice asked.

"No," Nikki said. "Robin used her card ten minutes before Dave's truck drove past the neighbor's security camera. She bought ten thousand dollars in luggage from Louis Vuitton."

"Ten grand?" I said. "What'd she get? A toiletries case?"

"Compact mirror and lipstick holder," Candice quipped.

"Change purse," I countered, poking Candice in the ribs with my elbow.

We chuckled heartily until we saw Nikki and Oscar looking at us like they couldn't believe we were making light. Sometimes gallows humor is so unappreciated. "Sorry," we both said.

"*Any*way," Nikki continued, "I'm reasonably sure that Robin had that card in her possession in the minutes before she was murdered."

"So how'd Rachel get it . . . oh!" I said. "Oh, oh, oh!"

Nikki stabbed the air with her finger. "Exxxxactly."

"Is it enough to get a warrant?" Candice asked. "And will APD want to? I mean, this blows the whole theory out of the water that Dave McKenzie acted alone."

"It's enough for you guys," Nikki said. "It's electronic fraud, after all. Plus, we also have this."

Nikki handed us another piece of paper and Candice and I studied it. On the paper was a grainy photograph of Rachel Tibbons, standing at an ATM, counting out some bills. "She used the card to withdraw cash," Candice said, a smile spreading to her lips.

"Yep. About a half hour after making that online payment to Silver Woods, Rachel went to visit her mother, and stopped at the Bank of America across the street to withdraw eight hundred dollars."

"Even if she lied and said someone else used the card and her username to make the payment for her mother, the photo is proof that she committed fraud," I said, a smile emerging on my own lips.

"It is," Oscar agreed. "I've already e-mailed Harrison a copy of what you're holding there. He's working on both the arrest and search warrant. We'll go when he gives the okay."

Rachel Tibbons was arrested and brought to our bureau field office for questioning. There was some debate as to who would get to interrogate her, and I was somewhat buoyed by the fact that there was a unanimous call to have me be in the room while the interview was being conducted. The advantage of course was that my lie detector would hopefully allow us to know when Rachel was being a big fat fibber.

Finally, Brice made the decision. "Let's go with the girls' team again," he said. "Nikki. Candice. Abby. Get prepped."

"You want me in there?" Nikki asked him, and I could see that she'd lost some confidence since our interview with Hekekia.

"Of course," he said without hesitation. "You're good, Grayson. I'd have you on my team anytime."

Nikki beamed before turning away to prepare for the interview, and I could've hugged Brice right then and there. God . . . am I lucky to work for a guy like that or what?

I was about to say as much when he leaned over and whispered in my ear, "Try not to let her screw this one up, okay, Cooper?"

Well, so much for thanking my lucky stars.

When we entered the conference room where Rachel Tibbons was seated, she started and wiped her cheeks. I wasn't surprised that she'd been crying. I wondered if they were tears of regret for her sister, or for herself.

"Rachel," Candice said smoothly, sliding into the chair directly across from her. Nikki took up Candice's left side, and I took up her right. We'd already spoken about strategy, and all three of us were wearing small earpieces connected to either Oscar, Brice, or Dutch, who were watching the feed from cameras placed in the corners of the room.

"There's been some kind of mistake!" Rachel said immediately. I noticed she was trembling from head to toe. "I've never committed fraud in all my life!"

Oscar and Agent Cox had arrested Rachel and brought her downtown. They'd told her only the charge of fraud. They hadn't given her any of the details.

"Someone must've stolen my identity!" she continued, her voice cracking with barely restrained panic.

Candice calmly opened up the cover of a blue folder embossed with the FBI's logo. On top of a stack of papers was the famous Amex Black Card, secured in a plastic evidence bag. "Look familiar?" Candice asked.

Rachel's lids fluttered. And then her brow lowered and she went from staring at the credit card to Candice and back and forth. "Where'd you get that?" she demanded.

"It was in your purse," I said.

"You had *no right* to search my purse!"

"Ah, but we did," said Nikki, and she motioned to Candice, who then pulled out the snapshot taken from the ATM where Rachel had withdrawn the cash advance.

Rachel's mouth hung open. "*That's* what this is about?"

"Yes," I said. "See, it's against the law to use someone else's credit card without their written authorization, and since you withdrew funds from a federally insured institution, you actually committed a felony. Also, you used this same card to pay for your mother's residency for the next year at Silver Woods. At a hundred and twenty K, we're now possibly talking grand larceny."

Rachel crossed her arms and legs, the fury on her face plain for all to see. "You people!" she snapped. "My sister is *dead*! By all rights that card *belongs* to me!"

"Ah, see, but it doesn't," Candice told her. "The court has yet to award you anything from your sister's estate, Rachel."

"I've already contacted Andy's attorney, you idiots!" Rachel spat. "He said that the court would grant me custody of the house and everything in it just as soon as it's released from the police department."

"Yeah, that may be true, but there's the problem of timing on this one," Candice said. "See, the court hasn't made a decision yet, and Andy's estate attorney hasn't actually handed over anything to you proving that you're entitled to their property and everything in it. That won't be decided until probably Monday."

"*What difference does it make if it's Monday or today?!*" she shrieked. "My sister *gave* me that card to use as I saw fit, okay?"

My lie detector went off big-time. I tapped the table twice with my index finger to let the girls and the boys know I'd just picked up Rachel's first big lie. "Can you prove that?" I asked.

Rachel glared meanly at me. "No," she said. "And you can't disprove it either."

"Actually . . . ," Nikki said, leaning forward and motioning again to Candice, who took out another piece of paper from the file and moved it across the table to Rachel. "See that?" Nikki asked.

Rachel's eyes were scanning the paper, and I could tell she didn't know what she was looking at. "I don't know what this is," she said. Beads of sweat had broken out across her brow.

"That's a printout of purchases your sister made from Louis Vuitton, and that IP address belongs to Robin's laptop, which we did find at the scene. The time stamp shows that Robin completed her purchase at one oh seven p.m., which was maybe four or five minutes before her killers arrived. So, either you were there at the time she was murdered, Rachel, or you stood next to her as she completed her online purchase, got her permission to take the card, then bolted out the door before the killer or killers arrived. And, I gotta tell you, that's the sort of timeline that we in law enforcement like to call 'suspicious.'"

Rachel's eyes were wide and she began to chew on her bottom lip. You could practically see the wheels turning inside her head, searching for an explanation that would put her in the clear. At last she said, "I'd like to make a phone call, please."

In my ear I heard Dutch say, "You can press her, Abby. She hasn't actually asked for her attorney yet."

"We'll let you make that call just as soon as you tell us how you came to have this card in your possession," I told her.

Rachel leaned forward to get up into my face as she shouted, "Lawyer!"

Magic word spoken, the three of us got up and began to walk out.

"Hey! Are you going to give me a phone?" she said.

I handed her my cell. There wasn't anything important on it

except some amazing sudoku and Candy Crush scores, and I'd know if she went snooping around anyway. "Here," I said. "Take all the time you need."

In my ear I heard Dutch say, "Cut the audio, Webber, but keep the feed going. We can't listen to her call, but we can watch her."

I shut the door behind me and followed Nikki and Candice to the large conference room where the boys were monitoring Rachel.

We gathered around the table and watched as Rachel got up and began pacing the room. It looked like she was yelling at the person on the other end of the line just like she'd yelled at us. "That girl is definitely unstable," Candice said.

"Yeah," Nikki agreed. "I could see her snapping and taking an AR-fifteen to her sister and brother-in-law."

"She's been under significant financial strain," I said, still watching Rachel pace like a caged tiger. "Which makes me wonder why Robin, with all her wealth, never ponied up the funds for her mother's nursing home."

"Maybe they didn't get along," Candice said.

I could understand that.

Rachel spoke angrily one last time into the phone and then clicked off the call. She tossed the phone onto the table like she didn't care about cracking the screen. "Hey!" I said. "That's my freaking phone!"

"Best get in there and retrieve it, then," Candice told me with a hint of a smile.

I rolled my eyes and went to get my phone. When I opened the door to where Rachel was, I found her standing in the corner, her arms wrapped tightly about her and that same tremble radiating up and down her limbs.

There was almost a moment when I thought to offer her a word of comfort, but then I remembered the scene at the Roswells' house and all the sympathy for her evaporated.

A moment later I had my phone and was gone.

"So now what?" I asked when I was back with everyone else.

"Now we wait until the lawyer gets here to see if we can have another crack at her," Brice said. "Only this time, Dutch and I will take point."

Candice arched an eyebrow as if to question the change of team midplay, but she didn't argue with him.

I could see Brice's reasoning, though. He'd want it to appear that we weren't about to let up on the pressure just because she'd called an attorney. And since Rachel was financially on thin ice until she got some money from her sister's estate—if she ever got that money, that is, and if we could prove our case, she wouldn't—then her attorney was bound to be cheap and not very good.

"Hello?" called a voice from outside the conference room.

We all looked at one another. The voice sounded . . . familiar.

No way, I mouthed to Candice.

She looked ready to spit nails and she and I were the first two out the door. Zane Maldonado stood in the middle of the large room, looking about. When he saw us emerge, he brightened. "I was wondering if the office had been abandoned," he said.

"Maybe he's not here for her," I whispered to Candice, but we both knew why Murielle's favorite pet had just arrived at our bureau offices.

"My client?" Zane said when no one greeted him or inquired why he was there. "Rachel Tibbons? I'm here to see her."

"You sure get around," Dutch said, coming to stand next to me before he spread his legs in a powerful stance and crossed his arms, flexing his biceps, which strained against his dress shirt.

My husband, the caveman, ladies and gentlemen.

Zane didn't seem to notice the flexing and posturing. Or pretended not to notice. "I *do* get around, don't I?" With a shrug he added, "It's work."

"She's in the same room as your last client," I said. God, I hated the smugness of that man.

"Wonderful," he said, turning sharply on one heel and heading off to find Rachel.

Brice walked back to poke his head inside the conference room with the monitors. "Webber, cut the feed. We'll wait on Maldonado to let us know when she's ready to talk to us."

Zane was in with Rachel for only twenty minutes before he popped out and said, "We'll talk to you now. Oh, and if you wouldn't mind bringing in my client's iPhone, which I'm sure you confiscated along with the other contents of her purse."

Oscar moved to his desk and handed Brice Rachel's cell; then he and Dutch began to move toward Zane, but the attorney abruptly held up his hand. "Oh, I'm sorry, gentlemen, but Mrs. Tibbons has expressly requested to be interviewed by the women." For emphasis he made a sweeping motion toward me, Candice, and Nikki.

My lie detector went off as he'd spoken, though, and I subtly shook my head at Dutch. It wasn't Rachel who wanted us in there. It was Maldonado. Probably so he could try to get a peek down our cleavage again.

"Tell your client she's not in charge," I said loudly, glaring hard at Zane. "We make the rules here, Counselor. Not you, and not her."

A sly smile spread across Maldonado's face and he looked at me wolfishly. I glared back and tilted my chin up. Fuck him and his intimidation tactics. I wasn't playin'.

"As you wish," he said at last, and disappeared back inside the room. Brice and Dutch squared their shoulders and walked through the doorway. The rest of us bolted back to watch the monitors.

"Turn the sound up!" I said to Agent Webber, who was working the feed. I didn't want to miss a word.

Brice and Dutch were just taking their seats. "My client has informed me that you intend to charge her with fraud, grand larceny, and possession of stolen property."

Dutch opened the same folder that Candice had carried into the first interview. "That's true," Dutch said, holding up Robin's credit card. "But we're about to share our discovery with APD, and I have a feeling the charges will extend to murder in the first."

Maldonado chuckled like he thought that was very funny. When the smug son of a bitch collected himself, he said, "As my client has already explained to you, Agent . . . what's your name again?"

"Rivers," Dutch said. "And that's *Special Agent*, Counselor."

"Ah," Maldonado said, placing a hand on his chest like he was aghast he himself had been so rude. "Special Agent Rivers, what my client has already explained is that her sister gave her that credit card with the express order to use it as she saw fit. After suffering the unbearable loss of her sister just days ago, my client set about to honor what were some of the last wishes of her dearly departed sibling by using the card to ensure her mother's care was paid for, and to retrieve some cash to be used on flowers for the funeral of Andy and Robin Roswell."

Brice leaned forward, placing his laced hands on the tabletop. "See, here's where it gets tricky, Counselor. We think your client's lying. We think that Robin never gave her the card. We think she stole it."

Zane nodded gravely. "I see. Can you prove that?"

"As a matter of fact," Dutch said, pulling the same pieces of paper out of the file that Candice had, "these tell us that Robin still had physical custody of her credit card in the minutes leading up to her murder."

Zane turned his head so that he could peer at the evidence being presented, then used his hand to swivel it around to face him. After a moment he said, "All this tells me is that Robin Roswell knew her credit card's number by heart, and she entered it along with the expiration date and security code into the computer when she made her online purchase."

My gaze drifted to Rachel. She'd stopped trembling and was now sitting next to her attorney with a mean smug smirk of her own.

"Could be," Dutch said, agreeing with Maldonado. "But it could also be that your client was there at the time of her sister and brother-in-law's murder."

Zane shrugged one shoulder. "Again, gentlemen, there's the question of proof. I've offered our version of events and as far as I've seen, you cannot prove otherwise, so . . ."

"She still made unauthorized purchases against a financial institution," Dutch insisted. "We've still got her on fraud."

Zane rolled his eyes. "Mrs. Tibbons will be granted custody of her sister's estate Monday morning. I'd like to see a judge hold her accountable for using money and property a few days before it was officially awarded to her."

"Dammit," Candice muttered.

My thoughts mirrored hers. Zane had us and he knew it. Everything could be explained.

"Still," Brice said stiffly. "We'd like to hear Mrs. Tibbons tell us where she was last Saturday afternoon, say around one p.m.?"

Rachel opened her mouth, but Maldonado placed a hand of warning on her arm. Pointing to her cell phone, which rested in front of Dutch, he said, "May I?"

Dutch slid it across the table and Maldonado handed it to Rachel. She quickly began tapping at it and then showed her attorney the screen. He in turn swiveled it around so that Brice and Dutch could see. "Rachel was grocery shopping across town at the time her family was murdered. Completely unaware of the course of events taking place at the Roswell residence. She was buying a long list of groceries, and she used these seventeen coupons, which were each redeemed with a time stamp on this handy little coupon app she downloaded."

We couldn't see the screen, but we could see Dutch and Brice squint at it, and frown. "Security footage at the HEB supermarket on Interstate Thirty-five should give you all the verification you need as to my client's whereabouts."

"Just because she wasn't there doesn't mean she doesn't know something," I said. The more I looked at Rachel, the more convinced I was that she had a hand in all this. She'd lied about the card—I *knew* that—and the only reason to lie was to hide something.

Later, after Rachel and her attorney had gone (Matt Hayes refused to file the fraud charges, given the alibi Rachel had provided and the fact that she'd have her hands on Robin's estate in a matter of days), we gathered once again in the large conference room to talk about what to do next.

"I'm out of ideas," Nikki said. She appeared tired and stressed. And then I realized that we all looked that way. "If she's got the shopping alibi, then there's no way to prove that she got the card at the time of the murder."

"Someone could've given it to her," I suggested. "The killer could've given it to her to use."

Oscar rubbed the top of his head and yawned. "You think Hekekia and Gudziak gave it to her?"

I had to shake my head. No way would either of them have given up access to an Amex Black Card.

"Even if they had, we'd still have to solve the puzzle of why," Candice said. "Why give Robin's sister the card?"

That one really stumped me. I was absolutely convinced that Robin had used her credit card in the minutes leading up to her murder, and that it'd been stolen from the scene, but the only ones we were fairly certain had been there were Hekekia and Gudziak, and they weren't talking—albeit for different reasons. Still, we'd gotten all we could out of Hekekia, especially now that Maldonado represented Rachel too.

"The common link in all of this is still Murielle," I said. "She's the center that everyone pinwheels out from."

"Through Maldonado," Candice said, picking up on what I was thinking.

"Yes."

Brice stood up and stretched. "So, Murielle hires Gudziak and Hekekia to murder Andy and Robin, but she couldn't have been there, could she? Wouldn't that be too big of a risk for her to take?"

"It would be," I had to concede. "But maybe they were too afraid of her to disobey a direct order."

"What're you thinking?" Nikki asked me.

"Well," I said, trying to puzzle it out, "Murielle would definitely have had someone else do her dirty work, and Hekekia and

Gudziak are good for the job, but maybe she tells them to bring her everything after they're done. Maybe they were under orders to bring her all the loot they took."

"But where's all the money?" Candice said. "Where's the millions of dollars that were taken from Andy's panic room? We only found fifty grand at Hekekia's house, and that was probably what remained of what they stole from Chris Wixom."

"I don't know where all that money went," I said on a sigh.

"And what happened to Dave?" Dutch said.

I wanted to slap myself. In the complicated fallout from this terrible case, I'd all but put him out of my mind for the day. "I don't know that either," I said, closing my eyes against all that guilt. In my mind, however, the vision I'd had the day before returned. I saw the photos from Murielle's Instagram scroll quickly across my inner vision, and then I saw that key emerge from the mirror before flying out and around the back of the house again.

"Abby?" I heard my name called.

I jumped and opened my eyes. Everybody was staring at me. "What?"

"You okay?" Dutch said. "Brice asked you a question three times and you didn't respond."

"Oh, sorry. I'm . . . distracted."

"Want to share?" Candice said.

"Not really. I keep having this same vision and I can't figure it out. It's like I'm on the verge of putting it all together, but connecting the dots isn't happening."

"I repeat, wanna share?" Candice said with a kind smile.

I shook my head. I didn't feel she'd be able to make any sense of it either. It took an expert in the lingo to be able to puzzle it out. What can I say? It's an intuitive thing. "I'll work on solving it tonight."

Brice looked at his watch. "It's already night." When nobody said anything else, he added, "Okay, gang, here's the plan. Everybody go home, get some dinner, and meet back here in the morning with ideas for a plan. We've only got Hekekia for another eighteen hours and we'll need to make good use of that time. We'll hunt down any lead we can to make his connection to either Murielle or the Roswells."

"Or Rachel," Candice said. "Even though it's a long shot, let's not forget about her."

"Deal," Brice said, and we headed out.

Chapter Twenty-one

• • •

At two a.m. the next morning I was ready to wave the white flag on making it to Snoozeville. Next to me in bed, Dutch's soft snores let me know I was alone in my struggle.

Easing out of the bed as gently and quietly as I could, I grabbed a sweatshirt and headed to the living room. Eggy roused from his doggy bed and came over to cuddle in my lap as I sat on the couch staring listlessly off into space. He gave the only comfort I'd found in the past several hours. I just couldn't get my mind to settle down, or really to focus the way I needed to. I could feel Gwen's and Dave's lives hanging in the balance, and in my gut I knew that we were at the very end of the time we'd been granted by fate to find the both of them.

I was nearly insane with worry that it might already be too late. And all of it rested on my shoulders, because I also knew in my gut that I had everything I needed to solve this case if *only* I could connect that one crucial dot. "What the hell am I missing?" I said softly.

Eggy lifted his chin and I stared down into his soulful brown eyes. I could see his faith in me. His love. I wondered, if he knew why I was so troubled, would he still look at me that way?

"Where's Dave?" I said to him almost absently.

Eggy's expression perked up and I realized that my sweet

pup knew Dave by name. They went way back and were very good friends. His tail began to wag too, and it nearly broke my heart. "I know, boy," I said, pulling him close for a hug. "I'm trying."

As I held Eggy, my eye drifted to a photo of me and Dutch taken on our wedding day. We were standing with our arms around each other's waists with our foreheads touching and enormous smiles on our faces. I'd been blissfully happy that day, and judging by the look of him, he'd felt the exact same way.

And then something sort of pinged in my mind. It wasn't so much a realization as it was a sense that I needed to get my ass down to the office to take yet another look at those Instagram photos, pronto.

Lifting Eggy away to hold him up in front of me, I said, "Want to go on a field trip, buddy?"

Eggy's tail wagged like mad.

Forty minutes later I was on the floor of the office sorting through the photos. Eggy was curled up in a ball on my coat, snoozing away and keeping me company. At last my mind felt able to focus in a way it hadn't before. I could feel my intuition heightening, like a battery charging with energy, ready to offer up the current.

I allowed it to guide me as I sifted through the photos; at each one I paused to look at it, waiting to see if it rang any intuitive bells, and then set it aside. I was trying to keep my mind as blank as possible, holding back on the urge to roll my eyes at Murielle's every pouty pose. And then . . . and then . . .

There was one photo that didn't necessarily bang a gong of *Eureka!* But it sure held my attention.

Murielle was front and center, as per her usual photo pose, and to her left, carefully framed, were Andy and Robin, seemingly in deep conversation, but over to Murielle's right was another couple, standing with their foreheads pressed together, holding each other in the exact way that Dutch and I had on our wedding day.

"That can't be a coincidence," I murmured. My radar was practically crackling with energy now.

And then I realized I recognized the couple. "No way . . . ," I said, smoothing my hand over the profiles of Walter Abbott and Mario Tremblee.

Quickly I reached for all the other photos from that night, but only two contained the faces of Mario and Walter.

In those additional photos, both men were obviously in love. Besides Andy and Robin, they appeared to be the happiest couple in the room, and again that nagging sensation from my radar urged me to look deeper.

I studied first Walter, then Mario, noting that Mario was so much more beautiful than his driver's license photo had indicated. He was breathtaking on the arm of Walter Abbott.

Drumming my fingers on the floor next to me, I started to gather other photos, searching for the couple and going back from most recent to least.

That's when I *finally* heard my radar ping.

And boy howdy . . . *what* a ping it was. Because, in that moment, absolutely everything else from my vision slid neatly into place.

"Abby?" I heard from the other side of the door.

"Open up!" I said loudly, giving the door another good pounding.

The door was opened by a clearly disoriented and super-disheveled Brice Harrison. He took one look at me and said, "You can't have dogs in here."

"Get dressed!" I said, brushing past him as I walked with Eggy into his condo.

"Morning, Sundance," Candice said in that lazy drawl she likes to use when she's amused. "Eggy," she added when she noticed him wagging his tail at her. "What brings you by?"

I waved the photo I'd brought from the office and said, "Dutch is going to be here any minute. You guys need to get dressed and come with me!"

Brice rubbed his eyes. "It's four in the morning, Cooper," he said, annoyed.

"Four-schmore!" I said loudly. I maaaaaaaaaay have stopped for a quick cup of coffee from the gas station on the corner on my way here. It maaaaaaaay have been supercharged with caffeine. And I'm pretty sure the Red Bull chaser hadn't helped to chillax me either. Shooing them both toward the bedroom, I said, "Go! Now! Get dressed!"

Brice ground his teeth and sent a scathing look toward his wife. "Don't look at me," she said, then waved a hand in a circular motion toward me. "I had nothing to do with this."

"I'll make coffee!" I announced, turning my back to them. "Oh, and we should call Nikki!"

"I'm firing Abby the second she saves all our asses on this case," Brice muttered.

"Oh, please. You fire me every other day. We all know you don't mean it," Candice said, and disappeared into their bedroom.

Dutch arrived just as the coffee stopped brewing. I'd thoughtfully combed the cupboards for every travel mug I could find, and laid out the cream and sugar on the counter assembly-line-style. "Let's go, let's go, let's go!" I said, waving my mug toward everyone as they gathered once again in the living room.

Candice eased the mug from my rather shaky fingers. "How about we get you a cup of decaf?" she said.

"I love stimulants!" I yelled. "Man! I haven't had coffee in *ages*! Why'd I give it up, Candice? Why?"

She raised her brow. "No idea, Sundance. But how about we not make up for lost time all at once, hmm?"

"Okay, but we've got to go!"

"Seriously, can I fire her now?" Brice said.

"No time for firing!" Scooping up Eggy, I moved to the door. "*¡Vámonos!*"

*   *   *

We met Nikki and Oscar (his presence was *very* interesting for two reasons—one, I hadn't called him, and two, he was still wearing the clothes from the previous day . . . mmmhmmm) at the Roswells' residence.

A patrol officer met us there, and much to my relief he said that there were no signs of forced entry past the lock APD had on the front gate. I'd been hopeful that would be the case, as I figured that Rachel wouldn't have wanted to risk drawing any more suspicion to herself by trying to break and enter into her sister's house when she simply needed to wait until the next morning when the key would be handed over to her. Especially if Zane Maldonado was working on her behalf to arrange it, which I had no doubt he was.

"Hi!" I said, greeting Oscar and Nikki.

"Morning, bright eyes," Oscar said with a chuckle. "You feeling okay?"

"Definitely!" I said. "I feel ahhhhhmazing!"

"She's had coffee," Candice said.

"Did she flavor it with cocaine?" Nikki asked.

"Red Bull," I told her.

"Ah. Tomato-tamahto," she quipped.

"Oscar," I said, turning my attention to him.

"Yes, Cooper?"

"Hold my dog." Slipping Eggy into Oscar's arms, I marched forward toward the house and waited impatiently for the APD officer to pull open the gate for us.

"You really ready to go back in here?" Candice asked, sliding up next to me.

"As ready as I can be," I said, waiting to see if she understood.

"Ahhhh," she said. "The coffee."

"Yeppers." Knowing I'd have to come back to this house, I'd prepared by loading up on the caffeine, which I was hoping would serve as a buffer to all that swirling energy. If my physical senses were too busy twitching from all the caffeine I'd pumped into myself, then I might be able to ignore all the other swirling messy energy radiating from that upstairs bedroom. "In any case, we won't be here long," I said, as much to shore up my courage as to let Candice know this was a get-in-get-out mission.

"What're we looking for, again?" Brice called from behind me.

"Money, honey!" I said, wagging a finger over my shoulder. "And maybe something even more important. Something worth kidnapping Dave for."

Candice eyed me curiously, but I didn't explain. I'd never been more certain of a hunch in my life. It felt marvelous! Or maybe it was the coffee . . . hard to tell.

I didn't pause to reflect on it in any case; I just made my way inside after Nikki got the front door open and then straight to the kitchen at the back of the house. There on the kitchen island was a MacBook, its lid closed and dusty with fingerprint powder. Next to it, as if casually tossed there, was an ivory Hermès leather bag. The chair at the counter in front of the computer was pushed back, as if hastily exited.

I looked from the chair to the back door, which was all of six to eight feet away. A large window dominated the door, allowing a spectacular view out to the garden.

"Yep," I said to the scene. "Just like I thought."

"What?" Dutch said over my shoulder.

Instead of answering him, I merely turned on my heel and snapped my fingers. "Everybody follow me!"

Heading through the crowd that'd lined up behind me, I gathered speed as I neared the stairs and trotted up them with purpose. I didn't stop until I was moving through the doorway into the master suite, and even there I didn't hesitate; I just braced for the impact and I stepped across the threshold, walking quickly all the way to the mirror inside the closet. Standing in front of it, I said, "We need to get this opened."

Everyone coming in behind me stopped short, looking at the mirror, then back at me as if to say, "Um . . . say what, now?"

I felt around the trim of the full-length mirror and found the trigger. Clicking it, I pulled on the mirror's frame and it opened to reveal a small inset with a hidden safe. The safe's door was slightly ajar, and then I really knew why Dave was still alive.

Only he'd known about the secret panel and the safe that held Andy's most precious material items. My radar buzzed and I glanced at the ground in front of me. My mind filled with the image of Andy, kneeling there as if he was putting something away. And as he was doing that, there'd been a loud pop from the backyard. Maybe he'd paused then to listen, trying to figure out what the noise was. Maybe he'd called to his wife too, because something might've caused Andy to be on guard.

And then he'd of course heard a commotion at the back door and his wife's scream. Thinking of her, he hadn't taken the time to close and lock the safe; he'd merely slammed the mirror door shut, and run to her aid.

I imagined he'd come into the hallway to see Hekekia and Gudziak shoot Rosa as they'd come up the stairs. Behind them, a familiar face, along with that of his wife as a hostage. I could then imagine Andy had stopped there, paralyzed by the sight of his wife held by that awful man Gudziak. Gudziak had then likely moved off with Robin, and it pained me deeply to think that Andy had been forced to listen to the sound of his wife being raped while he was pumped for information. He'd given the killer enough of what they'd wanted to satisfy any thoughts of an extensive search of the safe room, but he must've known that neither he nor Robin would survive the day.

That had to have been an awful moment for him. But he'd protected the contents of the safe, which had to have more importance than money. There was something tucked inside that was worth dying for.

Truthfully, I wasn't completely certain how it had all actually gone down, even though my radar was pretty awesome at filling in the blanks, but I did know two things that were vital to this case: One, whatever super-important thing the killers had been after was still inside the safe at my feet, and two, Dave was still alive. I'd looked at his photo only minutes before arriving back at the Roswells'. Of course, that wasn't enough to raise my hopes too high, because I also understood the noose was tightening, and the puppet master—the orchestrator of all of this—would make a hasty exit even without the thing in the safe and the additional money if things started to look like they were going south.

Speaking of money, when I pulled open the safe door, there was a whole lot of green exposed. Literally *millions* of dollars. "Whoa," I heard a few of my companions say when I swung the door open.

But I'd known I'd find the bulk of Andy's cash hidden there. What I still wasn't sure of was what else I'd find. Getting down on my knees, I rooted around in the large safe, first pulling out a cell phone. An old iPhone 4 by the looks of it, with a solid pearl cover. I smirked when I saw it, because I knew exactly what was on it. Setting that aside, I continued to fish around and then I found the flash drive. Or what looked like a flash drive with some weird-looking gizmo attached to the tip. Maybe it was a fancy flash drive, but I held it up and offered it to Brice. "This is why Andy was killed," I said.

"What is it?" he said.

"A key," I said, my eyes finding Candice's.

"To what?" she asked.

"To the back door," I said, my voice cracking with excitement.

Brice took the flash drive and turned to his wife. "She makes less sense the more she talks."

But Candice's eyes were bright with understanding. "No. Freaking. Way!" she exclaimed.

"Way," I told her. "Way, way."

* * *

Several hours later, but still morning by the read of the clock, I stood, all smiles and excitement, in front of Brice while he fired me.

A glance at Candice revealed that she was taking her termination with the same level of good humor. "Sign here, please," Brice said to me.

I took the pen he offered and scribbled out my name on the dotted line with a flourish. Matt Hayes peered over my shoulder. "Good. Mrs. Harrison, if you would?"

Candice stepped forward to sign her resignation and Matt took up the papers to reread over the termination-of-services agreement one last time. He wanted to make absolutely certain we couldn't act as agents of the FBI from that moment forward.

Everyone waited until he seemed satisfied, and then he handed the papers back to Brice. "Scan those and send them straight to D.C. Then call and make sure your wife's and Ms. Cooper's status is showing terminated on all HR databases."

"Got it," Brice said.

While Matt instructed Brice, I flashed a smile to my hubby, who was sitting moodily in a chair a few feet away. He looked ready to punch someone. "Will you please stop worrying?" I told him.

"No," he replied. "I don't like this, Edgar. And I especially don't like that it was your idea."

I rolled my eyes. "Protest noted. But it's the only way, love."

Dutch ground his teeth. "That's where I think you're wrong. It's too dangerous. A thousand things could go wrong."

"Or everything could go right," Candice said simply.

Dutch offered her a look of exasperation. "And when has *that* ever happened where you two are concerned?"

"Plenty of times," I said. And by plenty I meant at least once or twice . . . maybe.

Oscar walked to us, his phone in his hand. "Tech at HQ says that flash drive you found, Cooper, is blowing their minds."

"In what way?" Candice asked.

Oscar pointed to me. "Cooper was right to call it a key. It's some sort of encryption lockpick. You stick that thing into any system, open or closed, and it'll create a back door for anyone who knows about it to just walk through. No need to get past firewalls or encryption codes. It'll create a door just like that."

"How'd we figure out what it does?" Candice asked. "Doesn't the key need a password or something to work?"

Oscar shook his head. "Nope. It's plug and play. You plug it in and you're in. The only catch is that you have to be physically present to gain access to the system. It's not hacking remotely— it's hacking up close and personal."

"I'm still not following how that would be worth killing someone for," Candice said. "Any top-level government facility or valued commercial target would have all kinds of security to watch out for suspicious characters attempting to plug in a flash drive."

"That's true," Oscar said. "But it would take very little effort to send in a mole as a low-level job applicant and, after he or she was hired, to instruct them to plug the key into the system for thirty seconds, which is how long it would take to create a back door. It wouldn't matter if the mole had a low-level security clearance, like the receptionist or data entry person; it would only matter that the mole got the key into one of the system's computers. From there the entire system could be hacked."

Intrigued, I said, "If it's plug and play, then how specifically does it work?"

Oscar reached into his desk drawer and pulled out a flash drive. He stood up, walked over to Candice, and plugged it into the hard drive on the desk next to her. "If that were the key, I'd be in," he said. "From the moment I plug it in, it begins to run and piggy-back off the entire network's IP, always looking for a higher link up the food chain. After it reaches the very top, which would take about ten seconds, it'll start downloading any information marked important or classified. Then it'll quickly backtrack through the same links down the network's chain before finally shutting the door behind itself but leaving two extra zeros in the code to mark its place. The whole process would take no longer than two to three minutes. Tops.

"After downloading all the information it can grab, the flash drive ejects itself to let the mole know that he's free to walk out the door and hand the drive to an operative, who could then freely access the cyber back door from a laptop across town or across the world any time he or she wants. The geek I spoke to says he's never seen anything like it."

"Wow," Candice said. "That *would* be worth killing for."

"Yep," Oscar agreed.

"We're using a dummy drive today, though, right?" Candice asked. I could understand her nervousness. That thing had already cost several people their lives.

"We are," Oscar said, reaching into his pocket to pull out a very good replica of the little gizmo I'd taken out of Andy Roswell's safe.

Nikki walked into the bureau offices then and came right over to us, holding out two thin manila packages. "Here," she said. We took the packages and then she offered us a folder. "The agreements are inside. Just sign and we'll be good to go."

Candice and I took the packages and the paperwork over to a nearby desk, each of us signing on the dotted line and handing the paperwork back to Nikki, who, having witnessed both, pocketed them back into the folder. "Welcome to the team, APD informants."

I grinned. "We'll change and be right back," I said.

Candice and I headed off to the ladies' room and shrugged out of our tops and bras. "Wow," I said, pulling out the contents of my package. "They've done an awesome job of hiding the cameras."

"Look close at the top button," Candice replied from the next stall.

I did and only then did I spot the slightly grayer hue to the middle of the button stitched there. And then I also realized that I had the camera pointed at my bare chest. I didn't know if the camera was currently being monitored, but I probably made some APD tech's day with an up-close shot of "the ladies."

After quickly flipping the top around toward the wall, I hung it on the hook while I wriggled into the bra. There was a microphone hidden in the underwire, but I had to admit that it felt no different from any other time I'd worn it.

Candice and I emerged from our respective stalls at the same time. "Ready?" she asked.

"Freddy," I replied. I was as ready as I could be.

Before we exited, however, she reached into her purse and said, "Hey, I want you to wear this."

"Oooooh," I said, looking at the oval onyx and diamond pendant she was offering me. "That's nice. But why am I wearing it?"

She smiled slyly. "Think of it as a distraction, or even a decoy."

When we walked back into the offices, we found Dutch arguing with Brice. And Matt. And anybody else that would listen. Of course, he'd been arguing about our plan since I'd first mentioned it, but that's a little par for the course with my husband. He's a bit overprotective. And, okay, so maaaaaaaaybe I don't have the best track record, but that's beside the point. This was the only way we'd be able to draw out a confession and nab ourselves the mastermind in all this.

It was also the only way we could save Dave.

"I'm telling you, Matt, if we dispatch a team to that house, we'll *find* you a reason to get inside and conduct a search!" Dutch was saying. (Or yelling. It was probably a yell to everyone's ears but Dutch's.)

Matt looked at my husband calmly and said, "If you drum up an excuse to break into that house, Rivers, then I guarantee you, our whole case goes up in smoke, along with the APD's. *Anything* you find in there will get kicked out and the fact that you're even suggesting this course of action is enough to get you fired."

"Then let me have a crack at the interrogation!" Dutch said/ yelled next.

"You'll be talking to a wall and you know it," Brice countered. "Maldonado will shut his client down in two seconds."

"Then let *me* go have a chat with the other—"

"You can't," Matt said. "You'll have to identify yourself as FBI, and the second you do, she'll call her attorney. If you force her to talk without her attorney present, not a thing she says will be allowed in court. And after she calls Maldonado, he'll make another call and then it's game over. We have enough to form a suspicion of conspiracy, but that's it. Nothing that'll sway a judge or hold up in court to get us into that house, Rivers, and if we're going to find Mr. McKenzie and his wife—alive—then any move you make will greatly reduce those odds."

Now you know why Candice and I had been terminated by the FBI. We couldn't act as their agents or consultants in any respect because we'd have to confess to our suspect that we were acting in that capacity, and as acting consultants with the FBI, we'd probably have to inform our suspect about pesky things like Miranda rights. At least, that's what Matt suspected Maldonado would argue when his central client was brought to trial. The *second* we acted on behalf of the FBI in any capacity, our suspect would know that we'd figured out the motive, and Dave's life, already hanging by a thread, might well be over before we could do a thing about it.

No, if we were going to save Dave, the only thing we could do was draw out enough of a confession to invoke probable cause. We had the bait; we just needed to place it ever so carefully so the trap would spring.

"Honey," I said, laying a hand on Dutch's arm when he continued to protest. "This is the only way."

He turned to me, that vein in his temple throbbing, and grabbed me in his arms. "I don't like it," he whispered into my ear.

"I know," I said. "But it's a good plan, and it'll get us to Dave and Gwen. You've got to trust me."

"You're not the one I don't trust."

The door to the offices opened and an APD detective wearing a blue jacket poked his head in. "We ready?"

Nikki looked to me and Candice. "Ladies?"

"Freddy?" I said, with a grin to my partner.

"Freddy," she said, and held out her fist for a bump.

With that, we all followed Nikki out the door for a drive across town, with of course one stop along the way for our ace in the hole.

Chapter Twenty-two

. . .

I walked into Market Vision with barely a tremble. True confession, I'm *way* more courageous with Candice at my side than I am on my own, which is why I held tightly to the MacBook tucked under my arm, not caring if I got a little black powder on my clothes. "Hi," I said to the lanky young receptionist behind the front desk. "I'm here to see Stanton Eldridge."

Lanky blinked at me. "Do you have an appointment?" he asked in that way that said, "You don't have an appointment."

"Oh, I don't think I need one. I think Stanton will be more than happy to make room in his busy schedule to see me."

Lanky's mouth curved down into a frown, as if he felt sorry for me for thinking that. "He's really very busy today."

"I'm sure he is. But if you could tell him that Abigail Cooper is here to return the key to his back door, I'd appreciate it."

Lanky's brow knit together, and I could tell he was wondering if I'd taken an extra spoonful of crazy in my coffee that morning (if he only knew), but he wisely picked up his phone and turned away from me to speak quietly into it.

I perched my butt on the corner of his desk and waited. *Three, two, one . . .*

"Oh!" I heard him say. "Yes, sir. Yes, sir, I will."

Setting the phone down, Lanky turned with that same knit

brow to me. "He'll meet with you in the conference room. I'll show you the way—"

I hopped off the desk and waved dismissively. "No need. Just point me in the direction and I'll find my own way."

Two minutes later I found Stanton alone in the conference room, his back to me when I entered. "Close the door," he said after I walked in.

I did.

He turned slowly around to face me and I was struck again by the difference in this Stanton versus the one I'd met several days ago.

That'd been the clue that had finally jumped out at me when I'd looked at Murielle's Instagram reel. I'd gone back through her timeline to that first picture of Walter and Mario, sitting so snugly on some sofa in a bar where Murielle was stalking the Roswells. The group had all been huddled with their heads together, talking intimately, and Mario had been holding tightly to Walter's hand, leaning in against him in that way that people who are in love do, and behind them, just to the right of the couch, had been someone I'd barely noticed. Someone I hadn't initially recognized. Someone looking on at the four of them with such open hatred that, once I noticed it, it seemed impossible to have ever missed.

Stanton had stood there, consumed with jealousy and rage, unaware that anyone was noticing. But the lens on Murielle's phone had.

Her camera had also caught other moments from a year or so ago when Mario was captured standing next to Stanton in a not so much intimate way, but nonetheless definitely suggested the two had been a couple.

I'd confirmed it with Walter that morning, just to make sure. Mario and Stanton had had a long affair, but it'd been a hard one on Mario. Stanton had a temper, so it seemed, and he liked to control Mario's every move and belittle him publicly.

Robin had no doubt felt a bit of compassion for the lovely young man, having come from a terribly controlling and abusive relationship herself, and she'd made a point to introduce Mario to her dear friend Walter.

Maybe she'd known they would hit it off; maybe she'd only thought that his influence might give Mario some much-needed confidence. Whatever her primary motivation had been hadn't mattered in the end. She'd been responsible in Stanton's eyes for Mario's leaving him for Walter.

That's why he'd killed him first when he, Gudziak, and Hekekia had stormed the property. Dave had been the key to getting them in through the front gate, and Stanton would've known all about the panic room that Andy had built. They were best friends and partners after all, and Stanton of course knew about Andy's key and how dangerous and valuable it was. On the international espionage market something like that could make a person a *very* wealthy man. And using it to close the back door on their deal with InvoTech would also assure Stanton of riches.

The whole plan had probably come together fairly easily; there was the issue of *Texas Monthly* featuring Andy, which had been the very same issue with the article and photo spread on Safe Chambers to give Stanton the blueprint for his scheme. He'd just needed to bide his time and wait for the opportunity, which maybe he wouldn't have gone through with if Andy hadn't been so eager to test out the key at InvoTech and blown the lucrative deal. With the gambling debts we found racked up on Stanton's credit cards, it was no wonder he was anxious to collect his millions.

My gut said that he'd even overheard the call between Andy and me setting up the appointment days earlier—I could even remember from my first visit with Stanton in his office how he'd been nervous that the nerd in Andy's office would overhear us. Maybe Stanton had hired Hekekia and Gudziak to trail Dave the previous Saturday, telling them to pick a spot to force his truck off the road and kidnap him, and, to keep everyone from suspecting anything amiss, I imagined he'd instructed Gudziak to impersonate Dave on a few of his appointments with the incentive being they could go back and rob the places they visited at their leisure. Certainly no better opportunity to case wealthy homes would so readily present itself to the likes of them.

But at the Roswells' on that Saturday afternoon, the front gate had been opened and in had driven three killers. Somewhere on the route Gudziak had ditched his truck and Stanton had joined them in the cab of Dave's vehicle and off the three of them had gone to carry out their plot.

Stanton had wanted two things: revenge and Andy's key. He'd gotten one.

I had the other.

"How's the FBI?" he asked me when at last he spoke.

"If, by that, you mean where my lying, cheating soon-to-be-ex-husband works, I have no idea. They are two consultants lighter, this morning, though."

"What's that supposed to mean?"

"It means that your friend Murielle sure gets around. She'll sleep with anyone, apparently."

Stanton's eyes narrowed. I could tell he didn't believe a word I said, but he didn't really need to. Yet.

"She slept with my husband and my partner's husband," I continued. "Maybe they all got cozy together."

I had to suppress a grin at that moment, because, well, I could just imagine the side-eyed looks *that* comment was getting from Dutch and Brice.

"If you don't believe me, you could make a few calls," I offered when Stanton simply continued to glare at me. "I'm sure someone like you, Stanton, has powerful governmental connections. You could find out if I'm telling the truth."

Stanton took out his phone from his back pocket and turned away to walk to the corner of the room. I waited patiently where I stood, hearing small bits of the murmured conversation before he pocketed his cell again and came back toward me. "Why are you here, exactly?" he asked, his tone clipped. I could tell he was a little thrown off not only by my appearance, and the fingerprint-dusted MacBook I hugged to my chest, which was clearly Robin's, but also by the fact that so far my story checked out.

"I want to make a deal," I told him.

"Or entrap me," he replied.

"Or entrap you," I agreed. "But if you'll hear me out, maybe you'll see that I'm not feeding you a line of bull."

For a long time Stanton simply stared at me. Then, slowly, he turned toward a credenza that was behind him, and after opening the drawer, he reached in and lifted out a gun. Pointing it at me, he said, "Open your shirt."

I'd been expecting him to pull something like that, so I wasn't too surprised when the gun appeared. Still, it wasn't the highlight of my day to unbutton my blouse and flash my cleavage at gunpoint.

Eldridge moved forward, that gun holding steady on the center of my chest while he used his free hand to feel all along the underside of my bra. I wanted to chuckle at him, because wires these days are so small that they're easily hidden between the underwire and the seam in a bra. Plus, the Victoria's Secret number I was currently wearing had lots of lace that helped to obscure any bump a wire might form.

Stanton removed his hand after a thorough groping and moved up and down both of my legs. Then he peered at my necklace—the one Candice had given me—and he backed up. "Take that off," he said.

"Why?" I said, my hand going to the necklace protectively, just like we'd practiced on the way over.

Stanton's expression turned ugly and he reached forward to yank the thing from my neck.

For the record, having a necklace pulled from your neck hurts like a bitch. It's not like in the movies where it barely causes a flinch when it easily breaks. Stanton literally pulled me off my feet when he yanked hard on the chain, and I went down on one knee and one arm while still clutching the laptop.

I muttered a few expletives and rubbed the back of my neck as I got up; the chain had cut into my skin before the thing broke.

Meanwhile, Stanton had tossed the necklace to the floor and he stepped on it with his heel until it crunched. Then he motioned for me to button up, which I did. "Satisfied?" I asked him, a little bitter about the pendant. It'd looked expensive.

"No," he said. "But give it your best pitch."

"Like I said, I have something you want."

"What's that, exactly?"

I reached into my pocket, ignoring Stanton's stiffening posture, and pulled out the cell phone with the ivory case. "Recognize this?" I asked.

Stanton eyed the iPhone, his expression unreadable.

"It's Robin's," I said helpfully. "Know where I found it?"

Stanton's gaze moved slowly, predatorily, from the phone to the laptop, then up to my eyes. I swear to God in that moment, as realization dawned, he was a breath away from pulling that trigger. "Now you know," I said softly, trying not to send him over the edge. "You do something for me, and I'll do something for you. We'll make an exchange and everybody wins."

"Where's the key?" he asked, the knuckle on his trigger finger whitening with tension.

"It's with a friend of yours," I said. "Someone you trust. Or someone you've been forced to trust."

Eldridge's eyes narrowed again. I could see he wasn't sure he understood. I decided it might be best to get to the point and help make it crystal clear for him. Carefully placing the laptop on the conference table, I said, "May I?"

He hesitated, but finally tilted his head slightly to indicate I could proceed. I opened up the laptop and said, "I need a Wi-Fi password to make the connection."

Stanton dictated the password and I sent out the call. It was answered on the third ring. "Hi, Rachel," I said, waving to her as she came into view.

Robin's sister was perched on the edge of her couch, her features tense. Next to her sat Candice, and around Candice's neck was a necklace at the end of which was the duplicate to the key we'd taken from Andy's safe.

Eldridge peered at the screen, and I could tell he'd spotted the key right away. "How did you find it?" he asked me, his voice hard and angry.

"I'm not sure if you know this about me, Stanton, but I'm a professional psychic by trade. The other day when I was trying so hard to find Dave McKenzie and his wife, Gwen, I had a vision. The vision was of a full-length mirror, and out from the mirror came a large iron key. When Candice and I discovered the bodies of Robin and Andy, I remembered that there'd been a big full-length mirror in their panic room slash closet. So, last night after we discovered proof that our husbands have been cheating on us with Murielle, well, we hatched a plan to sneak inside Andy and Robin's place, and see if my vision was right."

"You snuck in?" he said skeptically. "APD just let you walk right past their patrolman?"

I laughed lightly. "Do you know of a Nikki Grayson? She's a detective with APD and a good friend of mine. All we had to do was call her and ask her if it was okay for me to take one last look around the place to see if my intuition could pick up anything useful, and she was all, 'Go for it, and let me know if you find anything!' See, everybody trusts us, 'cause of who we're married to and all the work we've done for the bureau over the years."

"And you expect me to believe that now you're just throwing all that away?"

"Oh, no, I don't expect you to take my word for it. I expect you to take their word for it." I pointed to the computer screen, and Candice, right on cue, swiveled her computer to the side, revealing a huge pile of cash.

"It's real, Stanton," we heard Rachel say.

Candice swiveled the screen back and we waved to each other. "She's right," I said to Eldridge. "It's real. Well, at least Rachel's half is. We're taking the other half. You're not getting any of it, though, which is a bummer, but these are the rules."

Stanton inhaled deeply and let it out slow. I had a feeling he was thinking through his options, and I figured one of those options that was starting to look really good to him was to shoot me in the face for taking his money.

"This is how this is all going to go down," I told him before he had a chance to consider that option much longer. "I'm going to give you this cell phone. You're going to upload all of Murielle's dirty little secrets onto her social media accounts, and you're going to create a few more so that she can't simply delete them."

"We want her ruined," Candice said.

"Yep," I said. "And then, you're going to make an anonymous, nontraceable call to APD and tell them where they can find Dave McKenzie and his wife. I suspect my friends are trapped somewhere close to you, Mr. Eldridge. Maybe at your house. I'm not sure if you have a panic room or not, but I know you've got Dave locked up somewhere without windows or any chance of escape. And I know you know all about Dave McKenzie, because Andy was featured in the same edition of *Texas Monthly* that Safe Chambers was in. A photo of Dave standing next to his silver Ford F-one-fifty is on the second page of the article and there's a short bio and interview of him there too."

"Great article," Candice quipped.

"It was," I said. "It's where you learned all you needed to know to hatch your plan to kill your best friends, am I right, Stanton?"

From the computer there was a small gasp. Rachel. I ignored her and kept talking. "You wanted that key, didn't you? Andy probably showed it to you, and showed you how it worked. He might've been getting ready to deliver it to someone here, like the CIA, or he might've been getting ready to sell it on the international market to make himself a bajillionaire. My gut says he was about to deliver it to someone at the CIA to use against the Chinese who'd tried to steal his secrets years ago, but who knows other than you?"

"How about you get to the point?" he sneered. I knew he was trying to provoke some fear into me, and trust me, he'd get a "Mission accomplished!" on that score, but it did me no good to show him that I was one gun wave away from peeing my pants.

"Yes, sorry," I said, collecting my thoughts to give him my best pitch. "Where was I going with all that? Oh, yeah, you knew about the key and you knew where Andy was going to take it after he sold off Market Vision, and you started to think about how valuable that key was, and maybe you were a little too curious about it? Maybe you asked Andy one too many questions, or maybe he left his laptop here one night and saw signs that you were trying to discover the key's secrets.

"That's probably why he created a duplicate that wasn't so much a duplicate as a decoy. I remember the other day you told your office geek that the first part of the code was on what you thought was the key, but it wouldn't work for you, would it? Andy gave it up to you to save his wife, though, and because you'd allowed Gudziak to rape her while demanding the key from Andy, you thought no way could he be lying. But he was lying, and that's why I think Andy was a good guy after all. I think he developed the key for his own government to use as revenge against the Chinese government for trying to steal his trade secrets. He wasn't interested in selling it on the black market, where it could be used against U.S. companies. He wanted it used to level the playing field when it came to corporate espionage. But you have no such morals, Stanton. You just wanted the money to continue to feed your gambling addiction.

"So you took the key he offered up without question, and from his home office, you took his laptop—the one APD suspected had been stolen, as they found the power cord still plugged in and some papers on the desk were shuffled around. Of course you assumed the original code for the key could be found on the laptop, but it wasn't there, was it?"

I paused here to see if Stanton would maybe say something in the form of a confession, but he remained stubbornly, irritatingly silent. I continued trying to provoke him. "It must've excited you to kill Andy. You'd get the key, close the InvoTech deal, and mete out some revenge."

"Like I asked you before," he snarled. "What. Do. You. *Want?*"

"Ah, yes, well, like *I* said before, we want to take our half of the money we found in Andy's safe, and for you to point APD to Dave and Gwen, and after we hear that Dave and Gwen have been found, we'll tell Rachel that it's okay to give you the key."

"You can then close the back door on Market Vision's code, and close your deal with InvoTech," Candice said, her voice sounding out loudly from the computer. "And that will allow you to collect all those hundreds of millions of dollars for yourself."

I glanced at the screen and saw Rachel looking absolutely terrified of the track the conversation was taking, but Candice had also noticed and she added, "Of course Rachel isn't about to ask you to share the money from the deal with InvoTech, Stanton, because, like we've said, she already knows you're capable of murder. It was okay when it was her ungrateful, selfish sister, but when she or her family become the next target, well, things get a little dicier."

"Which is why we're sharing half of the contents of Andy's safe with her," I said. "That's her consolation prize for giving you the full share of the deal with InvoTech and leaving her alone for the rest of her—hopefully—long life. After all, it's the least you can do for her after convincing her to hand over the house key to Robin and Andy's home the second it gets turned over to her by APD, and you'd head over there with Dave and Gwen and force him to tell you where the hidden safe is. And for incentive with Rachel, you gave her Robin's Black Card, didn't you? She was able to save her mother from certain eviction on the last day the nursing home had extended her, which was so nice."

"I—I—I don't know what you're talking about," Rachel stammered. I could see how scared she was, and I didn't care. She'd made a deal with the devil, and she deserved to feel terrified.

"Oh," I said to her as I wiggled my cell phone. "I think you do, dear. See, when I let you make that phone call using my phone, I simply assumed you'd called Maldonado directly. Imagine my surprise when you dialed this number instead. . . ."

With a little twirl of my finger I pressed the recently placed number and a second later Eldridge's butt began to ring. He reached into his back pocket, pulling out his phone, and silenced it.

"There's a flaw with your plan here, ladies," he said.

"What's that?" I asked him, all innocence and confusion.

"McKenzie," he said.

My heart skipped a beat.

"Once he's free, he'll talk," Stanton continued. "His wife too. They can't be released. They'll have to be eliminated."

I felt a flood of relief, but we weren't exactly out of the woods yet. We had enough now to obtain the warrant for our team to storm Stanton's home and search it for Dave, but there was no way to know if Dave was actually there. I had to try to tease more information out of him by continuing to gain his trust, but I couldn't seem too eager. "No," I said to him. "Eldridge, these are my friends. You're not going to kill them."

He shrugged as if he didn't give a damn. "They'll point the police to me. It's nonnegotiable."

"What if you wait to make that anonymous phone call until the funds on the deal with InvoTech have been transferred?" Candice suggested. "That way you could be on a plane out of the country before anyone even thinks to come looking for you."

"Oh, *and* in the meantime, by uploading the video on Robin's cell, you can continue to paint Murielle as the main suspect out for revenge against the woman who had all of her secrets. Speaking of which, I have to hand it to you, that whole gig was a stroke of genius. Knowing how Murielle stalked the Roswells for all those months, pointing us in her direction subtly by telling us about her relationship with Robin, then hiring Maldonado—a member of Murielle's posse—to represent every suspect in the case and make it look like she was behind it all . . . well . . . that was sheer brilliance."

Stanton's shoulders lifted slightly. I knew he was proud of that one.

Feeling overly confident, I maaaaaaaay have then taken it one teeny-weeny step too far. "You had the bureau field office convinced she was the puppet master. The whole team is *still* trying to nail her for those crimes, actually."

Stanton's smirk dissolved slowly, like the blood draining from my face as I watched his reaction. "Your two husbands have been trying to nail her for murder *and* they've been sleeping with her?" he asked.

Gulp.

"They slept with her way before they were trying to pin her for the murders," I said quickly. Too quickly.

"Abby!" I heard Candice shout as Stanton moved fast toward the laptop, slapping the lid closed with a loud bang. He then picked up the computer and threw it against the wall, breaking it into several pieces.

Meanwhile, I heard a flurry of pounding feet coming down the hallway a second before he reached me.

Chapter Twenty-three

. . .

Stanton held the gun to my temple and used me as a human shield to address the eight hundred law-enforcement folks who'd flooded his conference room.

Okay, maybe not eight hundred, but the room was *packed* with people. And guns. Mostly guns. Literally *all* of them pointed in my direction.

I'm nothing if not a glutton for attention.

"Can we talk about this?" I squeaked. Stanton had me around the throat and he was cutting off some of my air supply.

"Shut. Up," he said.

It bothered me immensely that he'd said that so calmly. He should've been hyper, sweating profusely, and ready to pass out.

You know, like I was.

"Let her go, Eldridge," Dutch said. Maybe not quite as calmly as Stanton, but close.

I tried to find him in the sea of people, but my vision kept darkening at the edges and it was tough to focus on individual details. Well, other than all those gun muzzles.

"Eldridge," came another voice—it sounded like Nikki. "Seriously, you've got no move here. You either let her go and leave in handcuffs, or you don't and you leave in a body bag."

Morbidly I wondered if the order for body bags would be for a party of one or two. Lifting my index finger, I croaked, "I have a suggestion."

"I told you to shut up," he hissed into my ear.

"Yeah, but maybe you'll want to hear me out."

There was a pause; then he whispered, "What?"

I pulled on his arm a little and took a strangled breath. "Dave and Gwen aren't at your house, are they?"

Stanton didn't say anything.

I continued. "You're in a position to make a deal. You can offer their lives for taking the death penalty off the table, and getting yourself secured to a better prison than some maximum security shithole somewhere out in the desert."

Again Stanton was silent, so I added, "Guys like you don't do well in maximum. But I know of a place in Virginia that's got some nice white-collar criminals that you might get along with."

I could feel Stanton take a deep breath against my back. He was considering it. "I'd want the opportunity for parole," he said.

Nobody said a word.

That's cuz nobody was ready to make *that* deal.

Still, Dutch said, "Sure, Eldridge. We'll see what we can do."

Stanton still didn't move a muscle to release me. I was afraid we hadn't been very convincing. And then he surprised me. "McKenzie and his wife are at Barbara Schultz's house, locked in her panic room."

I remembered the elderly woman we'd interviewed several days earlier. She'd been going on vacation. Her house was currently vacant. It was the perfect hiding spot.

I closed my eyes in relief, but it was short-lived. A second after he'd spoken, the barrel of Eldridge's gun lifted from my temple. "Tell my mother I loved her," he said.

And then I heard several shouts of *"NO!"* followed by a bang so loud it felt like a blow to the head.

A second later I was falling. . . .

*   *   *

"You look like shit," Dave said to me from the gurney next to mine.

"Back atcha," I said, grinning in spite of the massive headache.

"And you're covered in blood," he added.

"Back atcha," I repeated.

"Yeah, but all this is mine. You?"

"Mostly Eldridge's," I said. "Mostly."

"How's the head?"

"Still hard enough to take a crack against a conference table and have the table come out the loser."

Dave chuckled. I think it was one of the most wonderful sounds I'd ever heard. "Yeah, well, my hip can take a bullet pretty good too."

"So I see. You nervous about the surgery?"

"Nah," he said. "My old lady says it ain't no big deal."

"You mean, *Gwen?*"

Dave chuckled again. "Had you guessing about her name for a few years, didn't I?"

"Yeah," I said. "And I still don't understand why."

He gave a small shrug. "With that radar of yours, you can be a little smug, sometimes," he said. "Stuff we can't wait to tell you, you already know, and the stuff we don't want you to know, you know. This was just something to tease you with to let you know that maybe you don't know *everything.*"

It was my turn to laugh. "Touché," I told him. "Still, it was a lucky thing Gwen was there to get you through the infection."

"Yeah, it was touch and go there for a while. Lucky we found a good stash of meds at Mrs. Schultz's. Her safe room was decked out good enough to survive a zombie apocalypse. Too bad Eldridge smashed the landline she had in there. I tried to fix the phone a couple of times, but he smashed it beyond repair."

"Lucky us that her house is where Eldridge had you parked, Dave. Anywhere else and you might not be here."

He nodded. "He had me parked at his house for almost two days, but when the infection and fever set in, he moved me to Mrs. Schultz's, and thank the good Lord for that. And for the fact that he brought me Gwen. If he hadn't, I don't think I'd be here either. I know he was thinking he could use her against me once he got back into the Roswells' place, but I was running a really good fever by then, and Gwen helped me fake the delirium. Eldridge might've thought I was faking, but he was willing to wait a couple of days to haul us both over there and make me give it up. Anyway, he wanted access to Andy's safe more than he was willing to kill us at least. Gwen kept promising to get me well enough to tell him where the hidden safe was, and I kept 'relapsing.'" Dave had used air quotes on that last word.

"I think you've been 'relapsing' as long as I've known you," I said, returning the air quotes. And then I asked the questions I knew I needed to, but would be hard for Dave. "Can you tell me what happened?"

Dave sighed, and it was such a troubled sound. "I was headed to Mrs. Schultz's house when a truck came right up on my bumper and punched my tail. It spun me around pretty good, and I knocked my head really hard. I blacked out, I think, for a few seconds. The next thing I know, there's a gun in my face, and two guys are pulling me out of the truck. I thought I was being carjacked, but that was only the start of it."

My mind filled with the images of what that must've been like from Dave's perspective. It had to have been terrifying.

"So, they tie me up and throw me in the back of my own truck," he said next. "That gave me a good rattle to the noggin too. I think I had a concussion going, because so much of the rest of it is a little fuzzy. I remember we stopped a couple of times and I tried to call for help, but they'd put a gag in my mouth and I was strapped to the truck bed with rope. I couldn't sit up or yell. And then we stopped one last time and I heard the guy who'd pulled me out of the truck say, 'We'll wait here for the signal and take out the maid, but I get some time with the lady of the house,' and I knew that I was in deep shit.'"

I wanted so badly to reach out and give Dave a reassuring squeeze on his arm, but I held back. His voice was quavering a bit as he recounted the tale, and I didn't want to do anything that might make him feel uncomfortable, or more emotional. So I simply listened.

"So," he said, after clearing his throat. "I hear everyone get out of the truck and move off a ways, and nothing happens for a minute or two until the gunshot."

"Mario," I whispered.

"Who?" Dave asked. He'd heard me.

"Mario Tremblee. He was the Roswells' gardener. He was killed by Stanton Eldridge moments before the two guys who carjacked you stormed the front door."

Dave was quiet for a moment, probably taking that in. Then he continued. "Not long after that, I heard screams. They were faint, but I heard them. And then there were two more muffled gunshots."

"That was Rosa Torrez. She'd worked for the Roswells for three years," I said sadly. I'd learned that Rosa was a grandmother of three. I wasn't up to sharing that with Dave quite yet.

"I think I saw her near the stairs," Dave said. "She was still breathing when I passed her, and I wanted so bad to help her."

Dave's voice hitched and I averted my eyes, allowing him a semi-private moment to collect himself. A few moments later he could speak again. "Anyway, the whole time I was in the bed of that truck, I kept hoping someone would hear and send the police, but the shots were pretty faint and I doubted the neighbors heard anything. Nothing happened for a long time, but then someone came to the bed of the truck and untied the straps. I sat up and there was one of the guys who'd carjacked me, but with him was a different guy. He puts a gun to my forehead and says to come with him. So I do."

Dave paused for another moment, and again he had to clear his throat. I couldn't imagine how terrified he must've been.

"I was really dizzy from getting clocked in the head so much, but the two guys dragged me inside the house and up the stairs. Mr. Roswell's there, but his wife wasn't. Anyway, Andy looks pale as a ghost and terrified. I felt so bad, because he was standing right next to the safe in the room and it's locked tight. I kept wondering why he didn't just open it. Anyway, I was having a hard time making sense of it all, but then the guy who'd ordered me out of the truck says, 'Open the safe, McKenzie.'"

I bit my lip. *What a terrible choice to have to make*, I thought. My poor, dear friend.

Dave's voice cracked as he said, "I didn't know why he thought I'd know Andy's safe code. Maybe he thought if I installed it, I must know how to get into it, and I didn't have a chance to tell him to go to hell because from somewhere in the house we heard Mrs. Roswell start screaming. And then we heard . . ."

Dave paused again, and I knew exactly what he'd heard and it killed me that he'd been there for Robin's rape. "We heard Mrs. Roswell being violated," Dave said, his voice shaking with emotion. "At that moment, I think I lost my mind a little. I tried to shove my way past the goon holding me to help her and the next thing I know I've been shot."

I winced.

"I went down to the floor, and I'm screaming. It hurt like nothing I'd ever felt before, but then I hear Andy tell the guy that he'll open the door as long as they promise not to kill me and to bring Robin back to him. So he puts in the code, it opens, and I'm still rolling around on the floor, waiting to get shot again. I look up and I see that the safe is empty except for this weird-looking flash drive, which he hands to Eldridge.

"Mrs. Roswell comes back into the room then and they put the two of them together up against the wall while Eldridge plugs in the flash drive to a laptop. He looks at the screen and says, 'Okay, boys, have your target practice,' and right before the two goons start shooting, Andy shouts, 'Dave! Don't tell him about the other safe!'

"Eldridge tried to stop the two guys from shooting, but he was a second too late. They open fire and spray Andy and Robin with bullets."

I was staring at Dave's face while he spoke, my heart breaking for him because no amount of therapy was ever going to erase the horror of that moment. This time I didn't hold back. I reached out and grabbed hold of his hand, squeezing tightly and crying myself, for him, and for the Roswells.

It was a long time before he could speak again.

"Once the dust settles," he said, his voice barely above a whisper, "Eldridge starts typing on the computer all frantic like, and then he points a gun in my face and yells, 'Tell me where the other safe is!' but I blacked out right at that moment and sort of came to as they were hauling me out of there. I think they were worried they'd made too much noise, which is a good thing, because if we'd stayed there, Eldridge would've killed me for sure and torn apart that room, looking for the other safe.

"I came to a little bit as they were dragging me down the stairs, and they dropped me at one point outside. That was a hell all by itself. The next couple hours were a big blur. Mostly all I remember is the pain. I hurt all over. It was bad."

"But you were alive," I said, giving his hand another squeeze.

"Yeah. On borrowed time, though. Eldridge was furious, going on about how Andy had tricked him, and he wanted the money that was supposed to have been in the safe with the flash drive. I knew Andy kept a load of cash in that place—he'd told me he needed two safes big enough to hold a couple of million."

"Talk to me about that extra safe," I said. "Why'd Andy have the extra one hidden behind the mirror?"

Dave sighed sadly. "That'd been Andy's idea, and the crazy thing is that in the beginning, I'd tried to talk him out of it. I'd told him the best place to put any wall safe was inside the panic room, but he said he had a gut feeling about the extra one hidden behind the mirror. I guess knowing you made me stop trying to talk him out of it. You've taught me to trust any gut feelings, so I built him his hidden wall safe behind the mirror. It was never on any of the blueprints for the panic room; it's something I did for him as a spec order on the side. It took me a weekend, and I only charged him for materials and a little bit of the labor. He was a really nice guy and tipped me a grand for the job anyway."

"Do you want to know what you were protecting?" I asked him.

"Besides my own hide?"

I offered him a gentle smile. He knew he'd been protecting something vitally important. Something Andy was willing to die for. I was fairly certain Dave had considered that first, and his own hide second, in withholding the location of the hidden safe. "You were protecting an electronic key. One that could pick almost any cyber lock. In the wrong hands it could've been a catastrophe for our national security, and Eldridge wasn't the kind of man who would've cared about protecting our national security if it meant he could make enough money to buy a chain of islands."

Dave's eyes went wide. "Whoa."

"Yep," I told him. "You're a hero, Dave."

He blushed and turned his face toward the ceiling. I withdrew my hand and let him have a moment of quiet. He seemed to need it.

"How're we doing?" we heard.

I turned my head to look behind me and instantly regretted it. "I'm ready to get the hell outta here," I confessed.

Gwen stroked the hair on the side of my head without the enormous bump. "You're not going anywhere until the results of your MRI come back, Abby."

"I'm fine."

"Oh, yeah? How about you sit up and tell me that?"

I made a halfhearted effort to lift my torso off the gurney and gave up when the world started doing its Tilt-A-Whirl impression. "On second thought, maybe I could hang here a little longer."

"Is she giving you sass?" I heard Candice ask.

"She is," Gwen replied. "But it's refreshing given the model patient I've had to care for over the past couple of days." Gwen's voice practically dripped with sarcasm.

"Hey, I was good!" Dave protested.

"Locked in a room with Dave McKenzie for days on end," I said with a smirk. "I can't *imagine* the horror."

"Shut it, Cooper," Dave said, but I could hear the mirth in his voice.

"Has she seen the doctor yet?" Dutch's demanding voice called down the hallway. "Why hasn't she seen the doctor yet? Somebody find a doctor for my wife!" That last part sort of drifted off down the hallway, and I knew he was back on his mission to find me a doctor, STAT!

Gwen rolled her eyes, and winked at me. "He's been like that since you were wheeled in."

"If only he cared more." We all laughed.

Candice came to my head then and said, "I have a nurse coming soon to help you wash some of that off, Sundance."

"Thank you." I felt my eyes well. Being in such close proximity to someone committing suicide isn't an easy thing to handle emotionally, in case you're wondering. I was trying like hell to push the trauma of the experience out of my mind, but I'd probably have to see someone about it. Eventually.

"Do you feel like eating anything?" she asked next.

I nodded. I was starving.

"Steamed veggies over quinoa?"

I gave her a look that said, "Get real."

"Mixed greens with grilled chicken?"

I rolled my eyes.

"Zucchini noodles with pan-seared salmon?"

"Candice?"

"Yeah?"

"For once, could you think like *my* stomach?"

Candice tapped her lips thoughtfully. Finally, she said, "Nachos?"

"Now you're talking," I said, settling back on the gurney to close my eyes. "And maybe add a side of chili-cheese fries while you're at it."

Next to me, Dave said, "Hey, Candice, can you make that an order for two?"

"For an old friend like you, Dave?" Candice said. "There's not a lot we *wouldn't* do."

Truer words were never spoken.